W9-CBF-595

Three Years to Play

Also by Colin MacInnes

To the Victors the Spoils
June in Her Spring
England, Half English
All Day Saturday
Sweet Saturday Night
Westward to Laughter

The London Novels
City of Spades
Absolute Beginners
Mr Love and Justice

Colin MacInnes

Three Years to Play

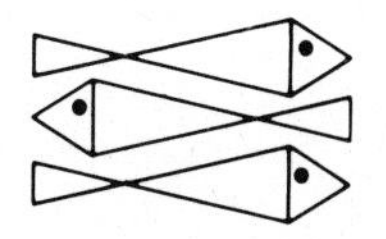

Farrar, Straus & Giroux
New York

Library of Congress catalog card number: 71-125157
SBN 374.2.7681.1

Printed in the United States of America
First American edition, 1970

For
Reg Davis-Poynter

Contents

The Plot

I

IT IS an ill-fortune to be born ill-favoured, that stout limbs and a fair wit scarce redeem. My mother, that was an Essex harlot, who waited coaches on the road to Colchester through Epping, would hide me from her visitors, lest they think an egg so horrid came from a hen whose feathers they found fair. 'Come aside, sir! Meet pretty Jane!' cried she, as she ran beside the coach, and spied there were no women in it. 'Spare some guineas from those French whores you covet, gentle masters, taste a fine English fruit before you put to sea!' And then, seeing me running after, with my lump limbs and snout and tatters, she would cry, 'Out scamp, out elf, out hobgoblin, away to the forest whence thou came', and hurl stones at me, though still running eager beside the coach, or single horses, and calling her wares out to the travellers bound for France.

It was my mother's genius in debauchery to have hit on the hut in Epping forest for her commerce. It was set beneath a hillock, in a leafy glade, and the virtue of the hill was that the coaches from London to the coast must slow their horses just beside her hut, to start their further climb. As for the glade, it was, in summer, perfection for any revelling; and part of her enticement was that as she sold wine, and was a rare plain cook, she could propose it to the coachmen as a sweet spot for the first real country meal the gentlemen could eat outside of London; beside which, she sold oats to feed the horses, and there was a brook for water. And once she persuaded the travellers into one sort of a meal, she could oft coax them to another.

Indeed, half of my mother's talent in her calling, was her real good nature: she was truly a jolly soul, and forward, as is most needful in her profession. How oft have I seen her empty out a coach onto the sward, not because of her great beauty – for this was not beyond the ordinary – but by her plump vigour of a country girl, that seemed to infect the jaded Londoners into a folly. In truth, many could not believe she was a bawd, and expected some angry forester to come raging into the hut to cry shame on them for his wife's, or his daughter's, honour.

How she became whore, is how most girls in the country do: he comes, he lies, she too, he comes again, then goes: and so did I, and her disgrace, remain. I know not how it is in Cathay, but in England what ensues is that the spoiled maid must marry who will take her, or else carry her infant and her shame to the nearest town. My mother was, to this social and divine rule, something exceptional. She had offers of wedlock from sundry droop-arsed old men, and refused them all; and, since she swore she hated cities (though she had ne'er seen one), vowed she would never leave the country. These two determinations brought her into Epping.

How this came about was that, stool-drenched and beat out of her village (with her father, the priest, and the ill-knackered elders she had despised, wielding the fastest switches), she ran into the forest trailing me, and there, like a maiden in a fable, she was taken in by an old woodcutter. My mother, in telling me of him, sighed and spoke kindly; but though his death preceded my memory of him, I know he gave no joy to her, but only refuge. The hut where he lived, and she and I, he had himself built out of logs, through which the wind whistled in winter; but in summer, hares came prettily, nibbling at her cooking scraps. And when he died, and they carried off his corpse and would her too, to be put upon the parish, she so screamed and bellowed and clung to the log cottage like one bereft of reason, that they perforce left her; and when they came back, with constables, to take her away by force, she fled into the woods with me; or, when they came yet again, and caught and pulled her into Epping, she scaped and ran back to the forest divers times: till they said all now left to them, in charity, was to cast her in prison as a notorious lewd woman.

At this moment fate, which had been unkind to my mother, smiled suddenly in the odd person of Martin. He was a schoolmaster in Epping, some said a priest long unfrocked, and he was as learned as he was besotten; and though he had been cast out of so many academies that e'en he could not tell their count, they took him back into their schools for three grave reasons: his Latin was so sweet, even the clergy marvelled at it; he would take any wage they offered, if they also offered sack; and e'en to the most judicious masters, he seemed so manifest a clown that they must feel how the boys, with Martin to mock at, would have no space left for mocking them.

How Martin met my mother is a romance, which she was fond of telling to her customers, if they asked in the hut who in God's name the old fellow was. The last time they dragged her into Epping for imprisonment as a bawd, an orderly procession of constables sweating, my mother yelling, and pelting multitudes surrounding all, were moving southward down the high street, when they met with a ragged file of Martin, followed by his straggling bobtails, moving north. At the sight of my mother's sorrows, Martin, who was in such condition as to scarce stand (this, you may be sure, was mimicked by the scholarly sprites behind him), ran over, fell upon his knees, and offered in a loud voice to make an honest woman of my mother: which was not at first understood, because his proposition was in Latin. When he repeated it in the vulgar tongue, the townsfolk were so uproariously enraptured with the prospect of this union, that they carried Martin and my mother, in despite the constables, to the justices and clergy. These were not pleased, and bade him make his offer again sober which, to the astonishment of all, not least my mother, he did, inside the town jail. Some citizens objected this would make a scandal out of matrimony, and Epping; but others thought it well a bawd should be made proper, and the schoolmaster got rid of, in one stroke. So she became Martin's bride; and that is how, in Epping, if a stranger asked where a harlot could be had, they would make reply, 'Sir, we are too honest a place for venery; but outside the parish bounds, there in the forest, you may seek out Mistress Martin.'

My mother was grateful to Martin and, I think, fond of him as of a farmyard pet, but not much otherwise; and I remember the yellings when, before he was taught better by some beatings (I mean, of him by her), he sought to climb into his marriage bed. Yet she found him useful to her otherwise, for Martin, though too tottering and liquid a thing to fight a child, miscouraged robbers, for even a witness can do this; and besides, he had a sword a customer had forgot, and amazingly, knew its use from early manhood, the which he also taught me later. He could as well, when my mother took her visitor behind the curtain, perform those little services which, for a bawd, are done usually by an older woman: as fresh drapes, warmed water, and brushing clothes cast from naked limbs. As to the gold my mother earned, which was but little since, as I say, she was not beautiful, Martin took care of this; and, by agreement with her, carried it from time to time into Epping, where some man of confidence kept watch on it for them. Who this might be, I could not discover, though I followed Martin many times to spy; but once out of the forest, where the ground was cleared of trees, he e'er detected me, and waited patiently till I slunk off. So when we were robbed, which in such a place as Epping forest we must be, especially in summer when rogues wander in vast quantity, they found little for all their ransacking and threats, and had to console themselves with my mother's favours: which I have even known her, such was her sly address, to make them pay for.

It is to my step-father, as I must call him, that I owe my writing of these lines, and indeed much else that saved me from total ignorance; for with but one pupil left, myself, he expended all his skills upon me. I know nothing of universities, though I was later to meet great poets; yet in all faith I believe that had not Martin been the lost sot he was, he would have been worthy of the best of their academicks. For as a teacher, he worked miracles, and his art consisted in this wise. Though he knew all, and you nothing, he would contrive, I know scarce how, to make it seem that you were teaching him. As:

Martin: Now, boy, what is history?

I: Faith, Martin, I know not and care less.

Martin: Sure, yet thou dost know. For tell me: what befell thee yesterday?

I: (telling him, in an eager spirit) . . . and so 'twas, Martin, in all troth.

Martin: No lies in this troth?

I: Nay! I lie? Never!

Martin: No embroideries upon thy tale?

I: What's this 'embroideries'?

Martin: Later, boy. I mean thy tale is what befell, as true as thou canst tell it?

I: Except also that I wet me at the fright of't. (I had seen a horned deer, sudden).

Martin: Then with that damp embroidery, hast thou told me history.

It was also he who gave me my name, Aubrey. It will scarce be believed, but my mother had bestowed upon me none! To her, I was child, boy, brute, knave, addlepate, or any word that sprung into her fancy. But Martin said this would not do, and I must own a name, and he chose Aubrey, saying it was a fit one for a boy of good breeding such as I.

As to who was my father, if any great revelation be expected, as that I am sprung from the loins of an earl, or even bishop, that tumbled my mother in her innocence, I must bring deception; for, if my mother be believed, e'en she could not tell me for sure. When I asked her this, grown older, she said, 'In troth, lad, I know not; for when I was a maid, I would lie with any comely boy, and in our village, these were many.'

'And so made, ceased to be maid.'

'Well, girl then. But by the saints, I know not which sporting fathered thee.'

'But mother, thou must sure know, by calling to memory the phases of the moon, which several of this multitude it might be?'

At this she pondered, putting a finger to her round chin, and said, 'All I can tell thee, boy, with any surety, is that 'twas no artificer nor tradesman, as 'tmight were it in winter: but a country lad, for we were haymaking, and I carried thee till June.'

2

One day, when I was just fourteen, and my mother caught me at some nasty practices, she slapped my arse and, calling my stepfather, said, 'Martin, unless the boy will be priest, thou shouldst carry him in to the fair at Epping, to visit the tent there, that thou knowest well enough: for thither thou hiest thyself each year, e'en if pretending to go to see the actors in the Moralities.'

Martin eyed me, mightily surprised, and said, 'Jane, how *tempus fugit*, to be sure! And to think when I first knew young Aubrey, his little hand clutched at mine, for he could scarce stagger.'

'Well, his little paw clutches elsewhere now, and I want none of it in any son of mine. So hale him away and corrupt him, but do not tell me of any particulars: for I dote on the boy, and would tear out the eyes of his temptress, did I know her.'

So Martin and I set off along the track to Epping, through the forest, and he who was habitually so free with his tongue and easy with me, chattering away as if we were two boys together, had fallen silent; and he kept glancing at me as if he saw me today, for the first time, as some different kind of creature. At length, when we were emerging from the forest, and in sight of Epping, he stayed, sat upon a log, and said to me, 'Boy, tell me prithee: knowest thou what haps behind that mother's curtain? I mean when she is visited?'

Now, this was a question hard for me to answer: for the truth was, at that age, I knew all and nothing. That my mother went inside to roll with strangers, aye; for though I was oft sent out, the hut had but one room; and besides, like all boys I was a peeper into crevices. And the converse my mother held with Martin, the stranger once departed, was very free, if not in precise particulars; and seeing the quantity of coin, I knew she gave them more than fowls and wine. And yet she had a sort of modesty in my presence; and, as I grew older, had begun to show a kind of shame.

But as to what happ'd when she was hid, I knew not. For in those days, I scarce saw a child of mine own age, so had no lewd boys, as most lads do, to instruct me, or tell fables. Indeed, save for the rare forays into Epping, I saw none save Martin and my mother (that is, beside our custom); and though I had spoke with boys in the streets there – and more oft, fought them – I had ne'er in my young life spoke with any maid: unless 'twere to shout after her some obscenity. Yet as all men do, and women, and e'en babes, I knew myself, and how my body was inclined. So was I like Columbo ere his voyage: that knew, o'er the Atlantick, there was land, yet had not trod it.

So to Martin I made reply that no, I knew not what did my mother, nor they with her; but sith the men shed their breeches (or most did), and that I doubted she used the water he carried in to wash her face with, I supposed she and they conjoined in some near manner.

To this he replied the forenoon would teach me what this was, an I so wished; but that he had three gems of wisdom to impart, anent commerce with a woman, ere I embarked on this, or sought to.

The first, said he, was that I must not get, nor give, a sickness; of whose particulars he unfolded so dire a picture as to near send me coursing back inside the hut. As to how I might tell if any woman were infect (whate'er she averred), he believed that a fair, if not sure, sign, lay in the health of her under linen: if this were sweet-scented and neat, the danger was the less; if foul and malodorous, I must beware.

The next caution was, I should not get a misplaced child by any woman. If, he said, she was one of address, this would be her care; but if not, he would give to me certain counsels, though none of these was sure. Mostly, said he, if I liked the girl well, and wished her no ill, I should remember, before lying with her, what might ensue to her, if not to me. The man, he adjoined, that fathered me, had no such consideration for my mother; though when he remarked on this, I must reflect that had my unknown father been so considerate, I should not be listening to Martin now.

At last he came to what he said was the crux, indeed very hub of the matter, namely, should I lie with any woman ever, outside of wedlock? The Church said no: but thereto I owed no duty, since it had ne'er baptised me. By the State also, fornication was forbid: but this law was so ill-enforced and mocked, that my only care should be to avoid offence to any censorious that might also possess some power. As for Nature, he did not doubt her promptings had already told me she knew naught of morals. Thus was I, as all men, subject to three imperatives, each one in a state of civil strife: of duty, law, and instinct, among which I must best pick mine own way, which was not easy. But he would offer, he said, one general precept whene'er I was in any doubt.

'Ere thou e'er lie with woman, Aubrey,' said he (and solemnly), 'ask thyself first this: "Suppose we have issue of this joyous instant, would I be proud of my child, cherish it, do it honour?" If thy reply be aye, then will thine instinct be to love, that is a noble one; if it be nay, then 'twere no more than lust, which, if forgivable, is base.'

Albeit I was much struck (beside confused) by Martin's discourse, I was also then, though but a boy, a deft article; and so I asked Martin whether, in counselling me thus, he were obedient to his own principles. At this his wrinkled face waxed wan, and he sighed and rose, saying, 'No, boy, I am not; yet these are conclusions mine own follies taught me; which I offer that thou profit by mine errors, and so peradventure escape many of thine own.' 'Twere kind indeed of Martin so to tell me: yet have I since discovered no man learns save by his faults; and that when our elders tell us theirs, purposing to instruct and help us, they are but confessing, and had better say all this to a priest.

So now Martin took my hand, and we set off down the hill to Epping: the preceptor, repenting yet wanting vigour, and the student, eager for sin, and with the powers, if not knowledge, to achieve it. And when we had wide sight of the town, and the fair spread out in the fields around it, Martin paused, baulking my impetuosity, and turned to philosophise once more:

'The fair thou shalt see,' said he, 'is but a speck or trickle of the great fairs in substantial places: of which the finest are, to be sure, round about London, to wit the Goose feast of Stratford Bow, or St Bartholomew's in Smithfield, or at Southwark, Uxbridge, Brainford or nearby.'

'Are these places, then, in London?'

'In or about it, boy; for Epping, thou must know, that seems to thee a monster, is but, as cities go, a mouse.'

'Larger than Epping, Martin, there cannot be,' quoth I, for mine eye now ranged upon it round its whole horizon.

'Ho!' cried he, laughing. 'Multiply, as I have taught thee, by one hundred, and the two thousand of Epping will become the two hundred thousand that are in London: that is, if we are to add to the walled city with its seven gates, the supplementaries that have ensconced themselves, like warts upon a bloated nose, on both sides of the river; and this, I may tell thee, much to the displeasure of authority, that finds London already far too vast for control of the plagues and disorders that perpetually afflict it.'

'And what is a plague?' quoth I, seizing on this one word amid his deluge of improbabilities.

''Tis when a flux, or pustule, infects great multitudes that fall like flies unshriven of their sins. Six years since, and yet again in those ensuing, though Epping was then happily spared, and thou wert too young, lad (being I think but eight), to remember the stricken hordes that fled fearfully from

London . . . aye, in '92 and thereafter, thousands were struck down in the great city: by the hand of God, according to the Puritans; though those of more wisdom and less sanctity believed 'twas because so many thousands camped in hovels set upon foul drains.'

'Why, then, do folk live in such peril, when there are pretty places like our own?'

'Because, boy, e'er since mankind left Eden, they have eschewed nature's paradise to build human hells. All nations have succumbed to this disease, and most men too: as did I in my youth and, I doubt not, wilt thou also.'

'Then dost thou think, Martin, I shall visit this place London?' said I in a great wonder.

'I am assured of it, Aubrey, and I shall tell thee why. Item, thou hast no resource in the country: I mean property, which is what chiefly binds men to the land. Item, thou art not bereft of wit nor, thanks to my tutelage, some scant knowledge, for the display of which thou wilt find little profit here. And item, thou art a vile lad, if not yet of unadulterated evil; and this being so, the city will beckon thee as does Jerusalem the devoutest pilgrims.'

With this, as if my tempter to the life of corruption he foretold for me, Martin drew out of his coat small coins, and bade me put them in my breeches: which were in troth the first gold I e'er handled in my life; though I knew well enough, from seeing my mother's eagerness to filch coin from her gallants, that these were what men covert most, and part with most reluctantly.

At Epping, Martin, stricken by a scruple for my spiritual instruction, ere he abetted by carnal dissolution, led me off to see the players: where but a small multitude were gathered, most seeking the greater violence of bear baitings, the sweat of Morisco dancing, the vomitings of ale-houses, or the great tents of ambulating stews, wherein were assembled bawds travelled down from London. Past all these delights he resolutely led me, in spite my eyes popping out like snails'; and discoursed to closed ears upon the varied beauties of the theatre.

'Thy dear mother Jane,' he said to me, 'twitted me upon my supposed liking for Moralities: which clear betrayed her scant knowledge in these matters, for all she e'er saw, in the remote village where she was so ill-reared, were antique theatricals, now much fallen out of favour: as Mysteries, of the nativity and passion of Our Lord; or Miracles, anent saints; or her beloved Moralities, that depict man's temptations out of virtue in a more general manner. But Popish performances of this kidney belong to the days of the old faith: and since this is discontinued in our land – or most so, in spite the sighs of recusants – they have yielded, on village stages, to the Interludes: which are, in truth, little more than roisterings and jests, having as heroes lewd persons such as harlots, cutpurses, coseners, pilferers, and all manner of ill-found fellows.'

'And this is allowed, Martin, here in Epping, where they pursued my mother to imprison her?'

'Aye, but 'tis mere portrayal, not reality; and beside, in a fair, greater laxity is permitted. Sure, the Puritans, that rule our town, are sore mispleased; yet with thrice one hundred days for blasting their fellow citizens with hell-fire, on these short three of festival, they may bite their lips and hold their peace.'

What amazed me most about the Interlude, when we stood packed beneath the platform where it was unfolded to us gaping loons, is matter to make city dwellers that have seen a hundred better plays, smile at my rustic ignorance. And this was, the very conceit that men could act: I mean, clap on a paper crown, and cry, 'Hear me, good people! For I am

King!'; or that the gawping multitude should believe this, as e'en I did. Yet mayhap my infant amaze at this artifice of the actors had in it a part of wisdom: for truly, 'tis a cause for wonder that rational, well-grounded men, who know full well the players are but as themselves – indeed, oft varlets of far lesser import – have yet this magic to delude the good sense of the audience into belief that they are kings, queens, potent warriors or gorgeous courtesans: and that solid burghers, that would peer close lest the coin tendered at a huckster's stall might be a clipped one, will natheless break out, when at a play, into tears, shrieks, laughter, huzzahs, and other strange extravagance.

But though I was bedazzled by the rantings and tumbles of the actors (which were of a sort that would be hissed and pelted at any place less doltish than was Epping), Martin grew vexed at their incompetence; and spoke out so loud against them that the bewitched rustics cried shame upon him, and pushed us off, he shouting, as they bundled him, 'Aye, he that knows not the Theatre, beside Holywell Priory, nor the Curtain in Shoreditch, knows naught of acting!' To which they rejoined, with the eternal riposte of peasants, 'If thou love London so dear, then carry thy old bones thither!'

So now as a mother that drags her son to his first school, or a father his to be pressed into the navy, Martin led me to the distant corner, set apart, where stood the garish tent pitched for the strumpets; and ere reaching it, he seized my hand, saying, 'I shall no further with thee, lad, for as with all temples, that of love must be approached alone;' and patting me upon my back, he hied him off toward the ale-booths.

Outside the tent, that was guarded by two constables (more flushed and merry than was habitual), and also some bullies that were officers to the tent (and seemingly in good intelligence with the constables), there stood a file of Epping men, and from the villages about it, that wore three sorts of faces. The most were young bachelors, sturdy fellows besotted with foul wine, swearing dreadful oaths of the wonders they would perform upon the harlots. Then stood some elder men, kept hid and peering out discreetly, as if honest husbands that had fled their wives upon some pretext. And last, were some pinch-nosed, blue-skinned weasels, shanks draped with black, that had the name Puritan printed on their faces, as if double-eyed by Satan's brand.

Though come so eager to this throng, I halted now, in spite the promptings of a jocund bully that was crying the virtues of the women yet invisible. For in troth, a great trembling and faint-heartedness had o'ercome my hot resolve; and I was learning how privy conceits of lust may alter when pushed to a real issue, and this when many strangers are about, and all is mightily strange. Till perceiving a lad who looked in a like condition to mine own, that is, of the same age and irresolution, I boarded him and made bold proposal that with such a press about us, we should repair to a wine tent till it waned less thick and eager.

The boy first heard my words with that glance of haughty ignorance which, in country parts, is proper to any youth first spoke to by another, and he a stranger; but then, relenting somewhat – mayhap that he craved, as I, for an ally that would lend strength to his terror – he condescended to come with me; and said that his name was Peter, from a village called Harden on the further side of Epping by the London road, where he had care of sheep.

In the matter of bad wines I was, thanks to my mother's apt tuition, an authority more learned than young Peter; so I got two pots for us, and began parley with him. What first spurred my curiosity of Peter, once I heard his voice, was its still pure treble: unlike mine own, which had begin to cackle strangely, as do boys' when not just their voices alter. Also, while I could boast a sort of downy stubble, sprouting in clumps as on an ill-kempt meadow, his skin was as a girl's, though rougher.

Yet this Peter, in spite his nice appearance, spake with such vehemence of the lasses he had tumbled in the fields of Harden, that I must believe, whate'er his tumbling had been, it lacked not will nor vigour. And when he asked me had my metal been so proven, I was vexed at myself for blushing; which I covered up by relating many prodigies of great ladies I had ravished in the backs of coaches travelling through the forest. In brief, it would be apparent to any of the meanest comprehension, that we were two novices, summoning up the will to cease to be so.

At length, after much fortifying with further flagons, we staggered back to the great tent, where we were instantly seized on by the bullies, hustled within, and delivered over to an elderly female, that was seated heavily behind a table o'er which her enormous dugs were spread like pumpkins: who ordered us, through a toothless mouth crowned by a bristling beard, to empty out our pockets instantly, and show what gold we had. Our little pleased her as little; but, biting our coins first, she cried out, 'These for the pensioners!', and we were flung into two separate booths, of the size and scent of privies, with canvas walls through which all could be heard: seen also, indeed, by any so inclined, for the cloth had great gaps and tatters.

My Venus was a large comfortable body, that looked less lusty than fatigued; though to kindle my fires by her allurements, she dandled a great dug about the odoured air, like a bell-ringer sounding matins. She wore but a shift, the less, mayhap, to entice her lovers by lascivious glimpses, than for the ease and rapidity of her performance. When she perceived me tardy, she gave me a great lewd smile, snatched hold my hand and clapt it to her breast, and, with her other, before I could as much as fondle her, deftly plucked off my breeches in a trice.

When I stood naked before her, covering my rising hopes with lumpish hands, she cried out, 'Lord, but thou art an ill-made fellow! Faith, I swear 'twas a boar that sired thee!' Then, tearing aside my modest fingers, she said, 'Well, there at least stands promise – come!' and opening herself up like a hippopotame's jaws, she lugged me atop her in a sweaty stumble.

At this I fell to with such a vigour, and a rapture, that she cried out, 'Nay, not so hasty, lad, thou needst not consume me utterly!' at which I clipt her the harder, like a goat clinging to a mountain top, till she yelled out, 'Double time for this one, Mother Frowsty!' and sought to heave me off, crying she was suffocate, and need not be murdered for her pains. And when I persisted, wanting more than was my due, she threatened me with the bullies who, she said, would geld me an I did not latch her; so, not liking this thought, because liking what I did, I stumbled off her in a sweaty pant.

'Lad,' said she, taking a deep draught from a beaker, 'thou art so young, so violent, and so ill-schooled in thy endeavour, that it would ne'er surprise me were this rumbling thy first.'

''Tis true, lady,' said I, hauling up my drawers, 'save for the happening of the roe deer.'

'And what might that be?' quoth she, sharply.

'Why, 'tis that I live in a forest nearby, where the deer are quite tame to those that know them. And one spring day . . .'

She leapt up, causing her cot to tremble, and cried out, 'Boy! Thou hast not lain, then, with a beast?'

'Nay, not lain, sure, yet since thou ask, I fondled it.'

'Loathsome child!' cried she, enraged, albeit with, I

thought, a part of admiration; for she did not cast me out, but gazed upon me with that curiosity which townsfolk reserve for the nastiness of rustic neighbours.

'I hope I give no offence, ma'am,' said I humbly.

At this she laughed with a fat cackle. 'Well,' said she, 'thou hast in thy favour frank speech and an honest lust, e'en though thy form be horrid.' She drank again, and handed me the jug. 'Yet may thy features wax more fair with time, as thy skill also, an thou but be instructed.'

'And who shall instruct me, madam? For here in Epping, the town is all ruled by Puritans.'

'I doubt it not,' said she, 'for 'tis a nasty place, and I am heartily sick of it already. We sigh for London, all of us labouring here, and shall speed back blithely when thy pinchbeck fair is ended. Aye,' said she, quaffing again, 'my poor body is all bruises from the louts that have o'errun me like so many nags rolling on a meadow.'

'Doll Pretty!' came a great cry through the canvas wall.

'Ah, boy, my mistress hath others for me, and thou must away. God speed thee, lad, wax comelier if thou canst, and learn to love beasts with two feet, beside four. And shouldst thou e'er venture into London, and have a guinea in thy breeches, why! ask any honest caitiff in Bishopsgate where Doll Pretty lies a-waiting, and I shall take thy guinea, and thou thy pleasure, like two old comrades-in-arms, fighting a fresh battle.'

With this, she gave me a great slap upon my rump, and I stepped out to torrents of cursings from Dame Frowsty, for that I had so o'erlingered. I found Peter attending me without, and we hastened to a pot-house, where no two young men in England could have vaunted their amorous valour as did we to each other till night fell, and I staggered home.

3

The plague did not visit Epping that autumn, but the small-pox did; and mayhap it was one of those gentlemen from the coaches that brought death into our hut for my mother, and a face scarred like a stone to me. Only old Martin, nature deeming him blasted enough already, was spared any hurt. A church burial was refused my mother; but a sect called Barrowists, when they heard of it, said prayers beside her grave which was in a clearing of the forest; though the words they said of her were so unkind, that I think it was more to rebuke priests, than to succour my mother's soul, that they gave her Christian burial.

I mourned my mother honestly, with no false tears; for there was not alone the shock all those young may feel at such a loss – as of sensing they are defenceless, and thus pitying themselves more than lamenting the departed – but there was also that my mother was less a parent to me, than a sort of friend: for we would oft converse together like two boys, one being older. Nor did my mother e'er beat me, save sudden in wild anger, which was as soon forgot; and she so packed my limbs with meat, and wine beside, that I was as stout as hideous. Moralists may say, and will, that she taught me, not least by the example of her life, many an ill lesson: but one I am thankful to her for, was to be frank: for sith she ne'er made pretence to be other than she was, I got this habit from her; not knowing then how precious 'tis to a man's wisdom, if not to his ease of motion in the world: where to be candid is to make many enemies, and wherein do you but hold a modest opinion of your virtue, you may earn the contempt of the unthinking.

Martin was honest with me about her little gold that was stored up in Epping. He said that by the law of England, he being lawful husband to her, 'twas all his; but that knowing she loved me well, as he did too, I should have one fifth. This figure he explained to me as follows. For him, two parts for that he was wed to her; one part to sustain our hut; one further part, because he was now old; and all the rest for me. And troth, e'en I, though quite ignorant of money, could understand he would need more than I. For my mother gone, how could old Martin live?

The answer he found to this perplexity, induced my departure from the forest, and our separation. When Martin had wed my mother, though his impulsion first came from wine rather than charity, there was surely some splendour in so mad a gift from one poor creature to another. But truth was, that being pander to my mother for so many years, Martin had grown fond of this existence; and one day I came into the hut from hunting coneys in the forest, to find a fresh slut there, that Martin had scooped up from the highway; and who, said he, would now be 'my new mother'. This woman being brutish and ill-disposed, beside not yet twice my age, I saw that this trinity would soon erupt in warfare; so I asked Martin for my fifth, and said I would set out – using the pretty phrase of boys in every century – 'to seek my fortune'. He did not attempt much to dissuade me, being already firm fixed under the slut's thumb; whom, to subdue also (or as a farewell gift), I hauled onto my mother's bed, while Martin was away fetching the gold, to initiate her, as 'twere, into the commerce of the hut.

As may be supposed, my intent was Sir Richard Whittington's: that is, to set off, though without a cat, for London. Though ere deciding on this, I suffered many vacillations. For one thought I had, seeing the coaches passing on their way to France, was to elect myself post-boy, if I might, and travel with one; France seeming to be some promised land, if so many gentlefolk hied them thither. There was also a timidity, which will make Londoners smile (though not, I think, country boys), to confront this Babylon of which I had heard such fables. So what I at last determined, was that I would take the Epping road over to Harden, and seek out my friend Peter, ask his counsel, and find some labour on a farm there, before I decided whither I might carry myself further.

So after a farewell at my mother's grave, where I scattered marigolds, and embracing old Martin that wept buckets, and an ill leer at the slut (that was still abed), I set off southerly to Epping and beyond. Do I close mine eyes and ponder on't, I can catch still the wonder that assailed my heart when I ventured onto the highroad out of that little kingdom whence I had ne'er stepped in fourteen years. I say not a word gainst riches: for I love them well, and by God's grace and charity have since won some, if not in ways that He would bless. Yet I believe he who takes coach, or e'en rides horse on his first journey, forfeits a rapture that besets a young traveller on foot, howsoe'er hard his journey. It was a chill morn, but with a late sun, and the countryside all golden; and I sang to the birds those country songs – all roundelays of copulations – that were my mother's part of my instruction, to match Martin's arithmetick and Latin.

This sprightliness, as all else, could not last forever; for after some miles and hours, a traveller yearns for company, and I had seen none, save for some horsemen that had galloped by in a great cloud. Yet if I craved some society, I was determined to be prudent in its choice. In heart, I was not a mistrustful lad – indeed, I think otherwise, for like all those born sturdy, I was open; yet I knew that if highways carry pilgrims, they also entice rogues. Against any such I was armed by my youth and tatters, that made me a poor prize to any ill disposed; and also by a poignard, forged in Italy, that I had filched from a fornicator in the hut, leaving him only with the scabbard. As for my small store of gold, this I had secreted by wrapping it tight in a cloth beneath my drawers; being sure if any sought to finger for it, I would swift be wary of their intent. This made sitting, or the relief of nature, something troublesome; but as all bankers know, well to guard gold, costs pains.

Bye and bye I fell in with two fellows, that I espied from afar off, they seated upon a bank, so that I could take choice of walking by them on the further side. They said naught but a mumble to my 'Good-morrow' as I passed by them, though they eyed me close; and when I had gone on some distance, I could hear their footsteps coming after. I looked all around, to see if there were any farm where I could go upon some pretext, but the countryside was bare, which was doubtless why they chose their resting-place. So knowing that to be fearful is to lose the battle ere 'tis fought, I decided to imitate their tactic, and sat down by the road to eat at a loaf and sausage that the slut had with an ill grace made ready.

As they approached, eyeing me still and muttering together, I perceived they were of unequal age, one of mayhap five summers more than I, the other an older fellow: with about them, in spite their ill attire, a sort of swagger and bragadaccio. This time they hailed me, and the elder cried out, 'Well, lad, wilt thou not bid us share thy breakfast with thee?'

To this I made no reply, save for a deceitful smile, and tendered them some bread and sausage which they seized upon, and gnawed.

'And hast thou no wine also, boy?' the elder said.

At this I held out both my hands, shewing them I had

nothing (though feeling the dagger cold upon my breast, and the gold tucked under mine arse), and bestowed on them a doltish, zany grin such as is deemed meet in countryfolk by those that know them not.

'He hath money to buy it, though,' quoth the younger, frowning mightily.

'Does my comrade speak true, lad?' said the older, with that authority of thieves for the possessions of another.

Thanks to the lessons of old Martin, I could speak fair English; but I knew better my mother's village talk which, truth to tell, to him who knows it not might be some Aetheopian. In these tones I replied to them, with a forlorn gape; and said I had hoped, on seeing their honours, that they might have a drop to grant me.

'Nay lad, not so,' said the elder, sighing, and doubtless supposing I was too poor a sot for aught save sausage, though his companion still eyed me evilly. 'For thou seest before thee, boy, two men that deserve well of their country, but are cast aside by it, ungratefully, to starve on the Queen's highway.'

'God bless Her Majesty!' cried I, pulling like a milkmaid on my forelock.

At this the older fellow smiled, gave me some sort of a salute, and said, 'Aye, lad, thou seest before thee two of my Lord of Essex's poor veterans.'

Now, the history of our times was not Martin's dearest love, for that he preferred greatly to impart to me those of Greece and Rome (which I e'er confused); yet knew I that, though my Lord of Essex flitted half o'er the globe on the Queen's business, his wars with France had been some years over, and were now suspended. So that if these two warriors had been cast aside, as they pretended, they were veterans not so much of wars, as sturdy beggary.

'An' who be my Lord of Essex?' said I to the older fellow. 'Be he our King?'

He laughed at this, with a few foul teeth, and cried, 'Nay, lad, though rorty Robert would fain lie with our Sovereign Lady, did she but ope up her stiff old legs to him.'

At this I gaped, mine eyes popping at such intelligence, and was pleased to see I was winning the old soldier's favour; but not the younger's, for he was still peering at me, examining my dress for any hopeful bulges, and sitting e'er closer to me. Till laying a hand upon my shoulder, more in a grip than friendship, he said, 'And where art thou to, boy, and whence from?'

'Why sir,' said I, 'I must to the lazar-house; for my poor mother dying of the small-pox, and I still infected, I am ordered thither by the constables.'

At this he unhanded me as though I were afire, and gazed at his arm as if 'twould shrivel instantly, and these two warriors backed fast away, holding their bellies too as if they would vomit up their sausage. I made as if to run after them, crying, 'Kind sirs, do not forsake me!' but they looked not back.

After a while of going on I reached a ford, and went down for water, hoping also I might find there some countryman; for I was beginning to wonder had I not o'ershot Harden, or did it mayhap lie hid from the highway on one side or t'other. There I perceived no man, but a horse browsing; yet knew there must be a man near, for it was saddled, and the bridle lashed round its foot to prevent straying. And sure enough, not far away, I saw, deep in a copse, a fellow lying sleeping, well appareled, with a saddle-bag beneath his head, and a sword lying on the grass nearby his hand. Not liking this, I backed away, but the horse whinnied as if in warning, and the fellow started up, grasping the blade: but seeing only a bumpkin, he fell back easy, though still holding to his steel.

'Art thou from Epping, lad?' he said.

'Aye, master.'

'And in Epping, there is no special stir?'

'Stir?' said I.

'Aye – stir: as there might be some alarum, or a pursuit afoot.'

'I saw some horsemen travelling fast.'

'To London?'

'Thither, sir.'

He nodded, felt in his purse, and held out a coin, but not giving it.

'Boy,' said he. 'Hast thou e'er seen me?'

'Ne'er in my life, sir,' said I.

'Thou art a sharp lad: here, hold fast to this. And if thou betrayest me, may it buy thee a trollop with the pox. Farewell.'

I waded across, and climbed up to the road on the further side, where I was clubbed and, lying in the dust half stunned, felt the coin torn from my hand, then a great shaking of my frame. But I had the wit to lie as though half dead, and after a few kicks, the warriors (for it was they) stumbled down towards the ford, and when I heard them splashing in it, I sat up carefully, and rubbing at my head, watched them.

They had spied the horse and, holding cudgels, beat noisily about the bushes – which made me think they were no soldiers, for do not these proceed by caution? Then there was a cry, and the older was spiked through with a sword from out the leaves and, if he was in truth a veteran, was now one of life, not armies. The younger sprang into the bushes, and dragged out the stranger of the horse: who, not able to pluck his sword from out the corpse, must wrestle with his attacker, that being lustier, dragged him to the stream and pressed his head beneath the water.

At this I sprung up, in spite my cracked head, and plucking out my poignard, and clutching a great stone, I ran into the stream, and hurled it at the soldier. It did but hit his back, yet this made him swing about, whereat the man drowning pulled upon his leg and he fell in the current also. By now I had come up and, leaping on him with all my weight, I held him fast; at which the stranger, half rising, and using me as hammer, forced my body down on his attacker's, till the weight of two made the third man drown.

Thereafter was a great panting of us twain, then the stranger (still sitting in the stream) put out his hand, and said, 'Beauty thanks thee, and begs thy better acquaintance.'

'Sir?' said I, gasping.

''Tis my name,' said he, 'or what they in St Helen's call me: not, as thou canst see, because I am, but am not. And what may thy name be, lad: is it Christopher, that succours travellers?'

'Nay, Master Beauty, I am called Aubrey.'

'Well, Aubrey, thou and I must bury two corpses without priest; or else hang on the gallows ourselves, with no priest neither.'

So we lugged the warriors into the bushes, he plucking out his sword and wiping it on the grass, and stamping out any blood; and then Beauty caught his horse (that had watched all this traffic of humankind still browsing), and said to me, 'Aubrey, I must away; and since thou hast shared one murder with me, I may tell thee I have another on my conscience, beside these two poor fellows.'

At this, pardee, I looked alarmed, knowing there is no gratitude in evil-doers; and that, if I had helped him, 'twas more by instinct, and fear of the two soldiers for myself, than that I trusted him.

'Nay, turn not away from me,' said he, smiling, 'for I wish thee no ill, so thou swearest silence. Farewell, then, Aubrey; and shouldst thou e'er come to St Helen's, in Bishopsgate, thou hast helpmate in Beauty that all know there, in especial the constables.'

With this he sprung on his horse, I still standing watchful, for I had lost my poignard in the stream; and seeing he meant no harm to me, I cried after him. 'Good Master Beauty, those villains filched my coin!'

'The labourer is worthy of his hire!' cried he, and flinging me a handfull, forded the stream and trotted up the bank, and off.

I tarried a while, hunting out the coins with scant success, for his lavishness had scattered them around; and for my dagger, which by good fortune I recovered, like Excalibur; and after washing my split head, I made off fast, and when I reached a lane to the eastward, turned away down it; for if the corpses were uncovered, I wished not to be seen upon the highway.

Upon this track, I met with divers villagers, to all of whom I asked the way to Harden: to which some said 'twas near, and others that 'twas far; and there was yet another party of these pilots who declared that 'twas in Somerset, or Scotland, or the Great Cathay. I have oft wondered on this incapacity of countryfolk to know their birthplace; and surmise it is in part they know not what you say, in part that they have privy names for villages (so that Harden might be Squire Somebody's), and in further part their deep mistrust of foreigners (*id est*, any born four miles off), that makes them cleave the secrets of these muddy hovels to their sweaty bosoms. But now Fortune, that had spurned me, turned her rays upon me;

for in an orchard, where they were gathering apples, I spied Peter.

He greeted me, and brought me up among his comrades, with much boasting of my being a ravisher of harlots in country fairs as perilous as he; while they all stared at me, with that huge-eyed glare that I swear peasants learn from their close contemplation of the animals they tend. Peter said, when I unfolded my purpose to him privily, that I had come at a good time if I aspired to bide a while in Harden; for in this season of fruit-gathering, many spare hands were needed, and he could forward me to the farmers as an honest lad. 'And for sport,' said he, 'I mean the pursuit of cherries, and not apples, there are many maids ripe to pluck from, and the fields are not yet chill nor damp.'

4

He who knows only the country at harvest time, knows it ill: for then, though the labour be as for Hercules, and wages scarce furnish ale, there is a sort of merry bluster, sith so many free hands are hired; and beside, the weather is still wanton. But when all is gathered in, and the itinerants wander off to whence they came, and frost forms, the first snow feathers, and the nights consume the days, then doth the country reveal itself the tyranny it truly is. The labourers, scarce needed, shiver and grow humble—they that had so roistered in the prime! And the masters, worse misers, I vow, than any I met in cities, shut tight their warm doors, and only sally out to scold or to deny.

I alone was kept among the transients of the harvest; for being so young, I could be paid in groats; and because of the foulness of my duties, which none else coveted, save a great oaf named William, that needed a disciple, or assistant: and this was tending goats: that are evil animals, well fitted for Satan to inhabit when he visits us on earth. Yet these goats, though horrid by sound, scent and habit, were less brutish than honest William: who, I verily believe, had more of a beast in him than they. He was a great, crass, lumbering fellow, though swift when he so willed, with a zany glare that masked a pin-wit guile; cruel as most country fellows are, but more by default of sense than disposition. His drooling lips could not wrap themselves around my name, for he called me 'Orb'; though in the matter of sceptres, I must allow that he was king, not I; and he took great joy to flourish his pride in this about, and e'en tried to woo me with't, mid the goat-dung, till I perforce turned my poignard on him (I speak not now in any metaphor), and advised him the nannies would make fitter pasture.

As for young Peter's chief companion, this was a bewitched boy called Simon – 'Simple Simon', as you may suppose, to those of us that remembered childhood. But if I say 'companion', that was not truly so, since this affection commands fair measure, each to each. No, 'twas rather that this Simon followed Peter cow-eyed about, hanging upon his words, and pestering him with his love beyond endurance. Friendship, they say, like love, is oft made of opposites; but for such an antiphony to soar, the singers must carol the same air, e'en if in counterpoint. But while Peter was a forward, eager lad, dark, fierce, quick-tempered and nimble, poor Simon was a vacant moony loon, gazing for stars in puddles.

We all lived in a kind of hut, or country tenement, with some dozen others (I, as far estranged from William as courtesy twixt goat-herds may permit), rising, eating, quarrelling and sleeping in an eternal circle of monotony. The saga, or Methuselah of this rural household, was one Colin: an antique shepherd much given to sententious interference, and precepts well matched to the reign of good king Hal. But he served some purpose for the settling of arguments, since each fighting cock could flush his comb upon him; and also for borrowing groats from, for we played dice with passion, having naught else to do.

In this art Peter instructed me, for I knew naught of't; and after pledge of direst secrecy, he imparted to me certain knavish practices which, to the skilful, may aid fortune, as 'twere, by peeping behind the cloth that binds her eyes. And in return for this privy wisdom, I taught him to read and write a little; which none of the lads at Harden knew aught of – not e'en ancient Colin – affecting, like all ignorant of what they sigh for, a great contempt of learning culled from books.

As for the book with which I taught young Peter, this was no Bible, nor Book of Common Prayer, but an excellent brief volume, that I bought of a peddlar in Harden village after much haggling, which was Master Robert Greene's *Notable Discovery of Cosnage*, together with *The Second Part of Conny-Catching*: which I may recommend to all rural lads visiting cities, as I would Master Dante's devout compendium for those venturing into Hell. For herein are plainly writ all the dexterities of conny-catching and cross-biting whereby the innocent are deprived both of that pleasing virtue, and their gold. Peter, already a deft student of dice, was enraptured by Master Greene's devious wisdoms concerning cosening at play with cards; in which the setter, verser and the barnacle are all allies to the downfall of the conny. And as for venery, we read deep into the skills of cross-biting, whereby the harlot and her pander fraud voluptuaries that have more gold than prudence. We spent long hours mastering other talents – or, since this was as yet but principle, studying them diligently: to wit, the arts of the nip and foist, that are noblemen among cutpurses; the priggar that entices horses from underneath their riders;

the courber, that steals from the street, by a hook, or curb, through windows, in his practice of the lifting law; and the black art of picking locks.

Indeed, as well as his initiation into these splendid mysteries, I might say Peter owed to Master Greene that I could teach him to read or write at all. True, I was a patient pedagogue, having studied this art from Martin; yet had not Peter been so bewitched by the texts I laid before him for his instruction, I doubt he would have learned so quick. Which makes me wonder if, in schools, 'twere not better, for the swift enlightenment of the spry youth of our kingdom, that Master Greene were appointed chief professor of the realm, and his books put before the lads as sacred texts.

It was perchance the inspirations of Master Greene, and the freezing horrors of our labour, and also the wild ambition of two earnest fools in their fifteenth years, that impelled Peter and me upon the great adventure of running off to London to see what connys we could catch ourselves: not divining, in our wilful folly, that a text is no rival to experience, and we were more like to be caught than catchers. But more, the whole wild dream of London, this Rome, this El Dorado of our inventions, lured us thither like young Jasons ravishing the Golden Fleece. And yet we paused: for youth is as timorous as it is bold, rash and fearful by alternates. And what at last forced us out of Harden into the great world were but little incidents: yet such, as those who have studied lives of heroes shall well know, can oft be the less determining the greater.

The Gabriel that expelled me from the chill Eden of Harden, was honest William; who, in his last and most resolute assault upon my virtue (in the goat-pen), got poignarded for his pains inside the gut; and ran lamenting to the farmer, as the Angel might to the Almighty, had our First Father declined his invitation from the Garden. The perplexities of Peter were less dramatick, yet as troublesome; for Simple Simon, who sang at church in the choir there on the sabbath, transferred his worship from things holy to the person of young Peter by appearing, in the barn, still decked out in his surplice, and inviting Peter publickly to lift it, and spy what lay there, for 'twas all his to use. It was not the pestering of this that troubled Peter, but fear lest the village gossips might hale him before the bishop's court, there to be gelded. For in a village, the accuser, if he be false and shameless, hath a horrid power to vex an honest man.

And so, in the New Year of our Lord, 1599, we set off on foot, chosing a saint's day for our venture, when all would be besotted. We made swift progress into Chigwell, and there slackened; for the pilgrimage now thronged so thickly, and we thought to be lost among so many of all states and sexes that were coming in to London, to seek their fortunes there.

5

When we enter into the world, it should seem a wonder to us; though mostly we greet it by screwing up our eyne, and letting out a scream – the first of many till the last fine rattle of mortality. So if we may speak of births that are true rapture and revelation, I can think of none more so than a country lad's first sight of a great city. For a week, Peter and I drifted about London like Sir Francis in his circumnavigation: scarce sleeping, eating, e'en speaking our amaze: spellbound, hallucinate and rapt.

From I know not where – mayhap some history or chapbook – I had stuffed into my pate the conceit that a great city was but a small one writ large: that is, I thought that here it would be country, and then there, behind walls like a great castle, an urban island in a rural sea; for that London should straggle so, endlessly interminable, I was not forewarned. Then, I supposed all citizens would be oppulent and sedate: I had no concept of such a stew and riot of accents, dresses, races, ages, noises and stenches as we found. Crowning all, in my vision, was a palace set upon a hill; and it took us days to discover that the Queen lived far beyond the City and, beside, was away then upon a progress into Hampshire.

But 'twas not the Queen I knew in London, nor my Lord of Burghley neither, but, as may be remembered, Doll Pretty, the harlot of Epping fair, and Beauty, chief cutpurse of the highway: who both had told me that by Bishopsgate, without the City walls, they might be met; though whether they could in troth be found there and, if so, would cleave us to their breasts (or whether, indeed, 'twere wise to nestle near such bosoms), gave Peter and me pause. But after our first days of wandering, we felt the need, like migrant birds, to find some nesting-place; and also for counsel as to how we might best apply our talents – to wit, our ignorance of all save goat-dung and chapped udders – to city husbandry. Another discomfort was that we lodged nowhere, save under bridges, and in carts at markets. This was in part because we were jealous of our small store of coin, and also that our perambulations carried us far and wide; and further, that we feared to offer ourselves at any inn, both for the reason that these seemed too glorious for such as we, as that we were still wary of all authority, being but lads, and without any credit in the city.

Most countrymen that come to London settle by the outskirts where they first aboard it: often forever, though some few beloved of fortune may later penetrate its heart. So Bishopsgate and Shoreditch were good places for us to rest in, being the first that we had seen; and with many Essex voices that seemed friendlier to us. Also more suited to our purse and prospects. For whereas the City, within the gates, is prosperous and splendid, outside it is a shambles, like a cow-pen beside a manor. True, there are old villages not far from London, that are neat and healthy; but betwixt the great Cow and her surrounding kine, there is a hodge-podge and higgledy-piggledy of tenements, where lodge what the Londoners call *inmates*; and against these the citizens, my Lord Mayor, and e'en the great Parliament itself, are resolutely hostile: calling constantly that they must be torn down and ploughed under, for the City is jealous and fearful of the riot and squalor of these Moorish encampments. But fast as they are rooted up, like bindweed they re-plant themselves; and like bottle-flys, the inmates come winging back. For the owners of these desart lands make guineas out the groats for hiring; and as for the inmates, howe'er oft they may be flung into a Bridewell, pressed to the navy, or driven out of honest parishes by the constables to their very borders, they return like drunk dicers to the gaming-table, and risk another throw.

Now, when it came to finding the robber Beauty, who had promised me such favours in return for mine, I was o'ercome by modesty: for as Peter said to me, 'Marry, lad, wilst accost honest citizens of London, saying, "Good sir, can you uncover for me a notorious thief and murderer I am seeking?"' So we thought it better to begin asking for Doll Pretty among the females, chosing those whose forward manner and lewd dress proclaimed they were sisters to her calling. But here we had no good fortune neither: for first Peter, mistaking his target grievously, stepped up to a goodame who, when she heard him, cried out for all to hear she was no harlot, but a tripe-wife, and would have him in the stocks for so defaming her.

Whilst I, sidling up beside another, was right in my judgement of her commerce, but wrong in thinking she might help me; for all the knowledge she would impart was her levy for a 'scamper' which, I discovered, was London talk for a quick clip in an alley, without she remove her skirts.

Discouraged, we turned into an inn that was called the *Hangman of Ongar* which, by its good Essex name, we hoped was friendly, and there ordered ales. After more than one of these, we were accosted by a fellow whose mien won so little trust from us, and he well conscious of it, that by a kind of paradox, we could scarce mistrust him. He greeted us with that formula the city vulture has e'er used to the plump bumpkin: 'Marry, honest country lads!' cried he, 'as I may know by your fair limbs and open faces. And how like you London, prithee?'

'We like the city well, but not all of its citizens,' quoth Peter, with a marked glare.

'And our ale: does it find favour with your gullets? For being, as I perceive, Kentish men, you surely hopp'ed before you ran, with a swift step like young cockerels a-malting.'

'Aye,' thought I, 'if this be London wit, and if he cannot tell Kent from Essex . . .' But what I perceived was, the fellow sought offer of some ale; so in spite Peter's frowns (for I thought this rook might be of some service to us), I bade him take seat and swill.

'You may call me Gropenut,' said the fellow, 'for that is how I am known about St Helen's. The name my father, and the priest, gave me, is quite otherwise; but about this parish you will find few, I may tell you, that remember their own baptisms, or would wish to.'

'So one called Beauty would be born otherwise?' said I.

At this he stared at me, and glanced around, and whispered, 'Sure, but you lads are not employed privily by the constables?'

'Nay, nay,' said I, 'but I met this Beauty, some months back, upon the Epping road.'

'Then,' said he, 'thou wert that young St George that saved Beauty from the dragons.'

'Aye,' said I.

'Brave boy: he will wish thy further acquaintance, now thou art come to London. And mayhap, also, find employment for thee; and thy friend also, be he well disposed.'

'I am that to all, that are to me,' quoth Peter.

'Well said,' cried Gropenut. 'And now, to prove my love for you two lads, and the friendship I share with you for honest Beauty, I shall perforce restore this trinket to thee.'

At this to my entire amaze, he handed me the purse which, as I have already told, I had kept tied fast betwixt my limbs in the most privy of hiding-places. Peter leapt up, and seized on an ale jug to assault the fellow, who stayed quiet, smiling. And I, calmed as much by wonder as by delight of holding to my purse, held back Peter and, all my anger become curiosity, asked Gropenut how he had performed this miracle.

'Thou shouldst consider my name,' he said, 'which, in troth, is not of my own choice, but bestowed on me by those that admire my mystery. I am of a truth, lads, a foist: and having from boyhood, almost, discovered that prudent men like thee hide one treasure nearest to another, I have skilled myself in purloinments from that warm and secret region.' And seeing my mouth gaping at all this, he said further, 'I think, lad, thou hast not yet oped up thy purse to count in it.'

I did this, and found it full of pebbles; wherat Gropenut smiled again, and handed me my coins, counting them out one by one, yet holding the last one in his fingers. 'This I take leave to keep,' he said, 'both for the dignity of my calling, and to offer you young fellows ale.'

After we had drunk healths, and Peter still with a mighty

suspicion and reluctance, I asked Gropenut whether, besides foists and highway robbers, he knew any kind harlots and, in especial, one Doll Pretty.

'Why, better than the back of my own hand!' he cried, holding this up and letting slip from it onto the table, again to my astonishment, the poignard kept hid close to my breast that he had also ravished. 'Doll Pretty is one of the Genoa Doge's women as, indeed, Beauty is chief among his men.'

When I asked who this Italian was, he laughed, and said this Doge was as much Englishman as I, but so named about St Helen's because of his magnificence. 'East of the City,' Gropenut said to me, 'the Genoa Doge is King, as thou shalt find; and I counsel thee, lad, to learn this well, for do not imagine my Lord Mayor is chieftain outside his narrow walls. Indeed, the Genoa Doge hath but one peer to his supremacy, which is his elder brother, that is the Venice Doge. These twain, verily, are like the Cecils: for as the one family rules the kingdom, so does the other Bishopsgate.'

'Then I must think sir, if Beauty and Doll Pretty are their servitors, theirs is a kingdom that my Lord Burghley would fain see conquered and destroyed.'

Gropenut looked sly, and spoke in level tones. 'I shall tell thee something, boy. The dynasties of villainy outlive those of virtue.' He rose, and said, 'But come! The two Doges, thou wilt understand, are persons of too rich a consequence for me e'er to approach them. But Doll Pretty I know well, and shall carry thee to her, and thy friend, if she be standing at her post. But first, may I counsel thee to withdraw and secrete thy gold again – the which, I know not how (and here he handed it to me) has found its way once more from thy doublet to my fingers.'

It was a new feeling, and a happier, to stride through London in the company of a citizen. True, we lost that company ever and anon, when Gropenut darted off to try a foisting. But at length we came into Shoreditch, anent which I should warn all country boys that dream of magnificences in London; for though there are some well-suited houses there, it is most like a parson's metaphor of hell: that is, foul, dank, noisome and unwelcoming. Yet here it is that many country gallants come, seeking the girls' paid favours; and what blinds their senses, in that ancient oblivion of lust and liquor, is that sin seeks squalor.

Doll Pretty lived inside a tenement which, by its scent, was one vast privy. She dwelt on the first floor (favourite of harlots, Gropenut told us, for speedier traffic betwixt wantons, yet security from the street) and, as she oped unto his knock, gazed upon Peter and me lasciviously, believing us suppliants for her favours. I was not in truth saddened that she knew me not, for how can a harlot remember one among so many, and that a green lad at a country fair? And indeed, when Gropenut recalled me to her memory, despite a fair gap-toothed smile, as if I were her lost Adonis come again, I doubt she had notion who I might be. Yet she was courtly to us, and bade us enter; for a harlot, unless abed, sees ever in a young man a possibility, if not presently, then for tomorrow.

'Faith!' cried she, 'aye, yes, Epping! Marry come up, those country gymnastickals! I swear I was black and blue months after, though not, God-a-mercy, poxed or child begotten.'

'Then am I not yet father, ma'am,' said I.

'Nay, but persevere, lad!' cried she. 'For I am not the only layer of eggs in London, though I may cackle best! And thou, lad,' she said, turning to Peter. 'Sure, but the tales thy comrade told thee of his saddling must make thee wish to prove if I ride fair as he declares.'

I believe Peter, who was a rash and eager lad, would have put her to the test instanter, had not Gropenut begun a whispering with the lady, and much nodding too, which led her to cry out at last, 'Aye, aye, they are well suited for't, and I shall step outside to fetch in Beauty, who may expound all to them more fully than can I; for in the matter of procurement, he is chief counsellor to the Genoa Doge.'

So saying, with smiles and curtsies to us like a countess, she hobbled off, her great arse wobbling like a whale's, leaving Peter and me in a mystification which Gropenut would not alleviate. So we filched some of Doll Pretty's sack, and waited patiently.

Anon she returned, and with her Beauty: who, in comparison with the blood and dust of our last encounter, was now decked out like a painted courtier. He greeted me fondly, though with that love rogues have, which is composed not of affection, but of interest; yet this I shall say for the villains I have known (as I may, I believe, of that villain which I near became), that if they are treacherous in their fondness, neither are they hypocrites: I mean, they make no pretence to love you more than your value to them; yet, while you preserve their credit, their affections are true enough.

Beauty toasted us, and swore he believed Peter was as gallant a lad as I; and he declared (as were he His Worship the Lord Mayor) that we were both welcome to the City. And then, growing grave, like a clergyman expounding a theology, he thus embarked upon his proposal for our corruption:

'I doubt not, lads,' said he, 'that you know well that in London, as indeed elsewhere in the world, to live, a man must be endowed with pelf. Now, to come by money, there are but three ways, and no others: to inherit it, which is not for such as we; to work honestly for't, which is but slavery without its name; and then, to procure it in some manner from those that have won it the two other ways.'

To this we said nothing, and if country boys are oft mocked

by citizens for their silences, the rural habit of sustaining a long gaping pause proves useful when some dubious offer is put before them.

'Your silence, lads, suggests to me agreement; or, if not yet that, a desire to hear more. Let me, then, speak to you of harlotry. In this city, whores are numberless as cobbles; yet, as cobbles do – though slower, in their case – the bawds grow, with time, too well-trodden, and are cast aside. But while every man is born a fornicator, unless he be gelded for Master Champernoun's castrate choir, not every woman is born – or made, as 'twere – a harlot. Ergo, the old cobbles must be replaced constantly by new.'

We were still silent, and Beauty, first quizzing us intently, offered more of Doll Pretty's sack, and then proceeded:

'Now, just as the great replenisher of cobbles for the city are the quarries of the country, so do the rural parishes provide the novices for our bordellos. The reasons for this will be evident to lads of your understanding. Item: the country hath more females than the city; item: the city virgins are better advised and, being born here, feel not the lure of our grandiloquence; and item, our lechers like apple-cheeks and dugs like melons.'

All this with a great grin for his evil wit that pleased us less than he supposed, for we were, pardee, country boys, and they our sisters; or if not consanguinious, we felt we should have the use of them, not Londoners. But he continued:

'It will thus be as evident that the rural maidens must be entrapped into this honourable calling. True, many need no trapping: they cast themselves upon our shores like stranded seals. But others need some allurement, and 'tis here, I vow, that you twain could be of service to the Genoa Doge, and to your pockets.'

There was a pause, which Peter broke to say, 'You wish us, sir, to turn pander for your fraternity.'

At this Beauty shed all his glow and darted at Peter an ill look, which I sought to cover over with some jesting. For in two matters, I thought Peter to be mistook, one small, one greater: the small, that it was scarce prudent to defy a cut-throat in a brothel; the greater, that I guessed Peter would accept the offer; and there is this about corruption, that it must be defied or embraced entirely, else is there no reward to virtue or to vice.

'Aye, pander!' said Beauty with a steel glint I liked not. 'For consider: you are well fitted for't. You have but to return some six or so miles outside the City, and join the procession that proceeds here daily. Among it you will surely find some doltish virgins that will trust your country voice and manner. But bring them hither, and you will be rewarded.' Here he paused, frowned, and looking mightily impatient, as if the Lord Chief Justice with six trials pending, he concluded:

'You may, lads, decline this fair offer if you wish; and leave this place presently, and none will harm you. But . . . and this, mark well, is a big but. If you refuse, and yet wish to engage in any occupation that the justices might not love you for, then you must hie yourselves off to Southwark or elsewhere, I mean south of the river or beyond the territories that are ruled by the two Doges: I mean my master Genoa, or his brother Venice. Think: London is large; but remember, so are their powers about the East.'

These three honest subjects of the Doges gazed on us, and I glanced at Peter, nudging him, whereat he cast down his eyes, leaving the oratory to me. 'We are your faithful servants, Beauty,' I said.

'Nay,' said he, 'henceforth the Genoa Doge's. Take this: 'tis for the journey. You have a week, huntsmen, to bring in the plump does, when better fortune shall await you.'

With this pretty bombast he stalked off, seen away from her abode by Pretty. Gropenut clapped us on our backs, and handed me, yet again, the poignard. 'Bear this close,' said he, 'and all good fair fortune.'

I took Peter by the hand, and in the other, carried the knife for greater security of it, and of ourselves.

6

Peter and I decided we would ply our commerce as panders on the south side of the river, and for this we had divers reasons. The secret one, which we scarce confessed each to the other, was that must we entice innocents into the grasp of the Genoa Doge, we preferred they should be Surrey lasses, or from Sussex, rather than our own. We wished also to cross London Bridge whither, in our earlier peregrinations, we had not yet sallied; and visit the church of St Mary Overy nearby, of which we had heard such fair reports, all telling us the cathedral of St Paul was but a chapel set beside it. I had also a memory of Martin's lessons to me, for he doted on the tales of Master Chaucer, and I wished to see whence the pilgrims had set forth, and say a prayer there to the Wyfe of Bath; beside all which, we had heard much of the stews that, in their looseness, were said e'en to surpass those we had visited about St Helen's.

We did not set foot upon the Bridge, for we were accosted on the river banks, nearby the conqueror's Tower (whereat we shivered), by the watermen, that almost shovelled us into their boats, and told us – which was true enough – that to encompass the full beauties of the Bridge, it suffices not to cross by it, but rather see its splendours from the river. Nor did we regret our choice, and the small expense of coin, for this other reason; that from the water-level alone 'tis possible to intermix, as 'twere sparrows among gulls, with the great craft of all qualities that sail up from the oceans to the City: furled emissaries of a hundred realms, that came into London from the great world beyond. We saw some Spanish vessels that had been took: which reminded us of infant memories, for though I was but four years at the time, none in England that could then see or hear might scape the frenzy of the Armada, and its rupture.

Landed by the south (and after dispute and much rude speech anent the wages of our transit), we wandered among the stews; though, being morning, and the harlots all snoring in empty beds, we saw little but some voluptuaries creeping home: than which sight, I trow, there is none sadder; for the promise of last evening's lusts are all turned into dust and shadows. We spied the Bear Garden, and determined to return there; and loitered not beside Clink prison, determing the opposite. We saw also divers theatres, all asleep now, for their players and public were fled till early summer: to wit the *Swan*, the *Rose*, and a new theatre nearby to it, of which we could not find the name, that was a-building. Peter said sure, but we must come there also in our time; but I, having ill memories of the Interlude at Epping fair, said that Peter might see plays if he so wished, but I would prefer the real play of the baiting and the brothels.

And so we set off southerly, not hastening, for in truth we were mispleased about our mission. I do not think this was that it hurt our consciences o'ermuch; but rather that, if a lad be bold in accosting a lass met by true hazard, this does not mean that, as an older man, he is adroit at it by calculation. We were, in troth, roisterers, but not yet rakes; and this made us ill equipped for our endeavours.

Some five miles out, where the City fell away, and we

had glimpses again of cows and hens and such familiars, we tumbled upon an inn that had tables set outside to greet the spring; and though, as ever with our English spring, whate'er poets may aver, 'twas chill, we sat there, both for the spectacle of dame Nature at her annual cosenage, as for the better opportunity of spying any larks that might be lured inside our snare. And we had not been there long till Fortune, that is rightly named a jade, and e'er favours villainy among novices, bestowed upon us, coming up the highway, a brace of maidens of about our age, and unaccompanied, and seeming lost and full of wonder.

At the sight of them Peter, who was a more forward lad than I (or mayhap less anxious as to consequence), sprung up with a great flourish, as if he were landlord or the ostler, and bade them prithee to be seated so that they might refresh themselves: all this with such an earnestness and courtesy of address as to calm the fears even of a nun. So after that simpering and dallying which is common to females ere they do what they intend, they laid down their fair arses on the bench, and took to observing us, seeking whether we meant them ill, or otherwise.

Now, hard experience has taught me that, if you are cozening a man or a woman, 'tis best to weave a simple tale, howe'er false the garment; and that, indeed, whenever you must lie, let your false lie as close to true, as may be possible. But Peter did not adhere to this wise principle: for he set out to bedazzle these two maidens with a tale such as would puzzle a priest giving confession to a witch.

We were, said Peter, two brothers (he and I resembling each other like fish and fowl) that were of gentle birth in Surrey. Our father, which was a lord, had married recent, after our dear mother's death (here Peter heaved a sigh), a widow evilly disposed to us, that had a son of her own by a first marriage; and so skilfully had this wicked female played upon our poor father's feelings (so that her son might be made heir instead of us), that he had cast us out, till we, despairing of the world and all its vanities, had set out from home upon our way to Oxtown, to study to become clergy there.

The younger, whose name was Lucy, was much affected by this sorry story; but the elder, that was named Jenny, asked Peter where Oxtown might be found. 'Why,' said Peter, ''tis a great seat of learning, nearby Catbridge, that is its rival in these matters.' And from which part, asked Jenny further, of Surrey did we come? 'Why,' quoth Peter, 'we are Portsmouth men, for our father, beside a nobleman, is ship's chandler there.'

At this Mistress Jenny smiled and nodded, and asked us to excuse them for a while, but that she and young Lucy must carry themselves inside the inn for some privy female purpose; and when Jenny came forth from thence without her companion, she came over and said to Peter, 'Varlet, if thou wish to lie with woman, thou shouldst ask my Lord thy father for a guinea and seek out a harlot, leaving honest maids in peace.'

Peter sprung up at this, and defied that she dare impute such an ill intent to him. To all this she listened calmly, then said, 'What is more, fellow, if to conny-catch thou must pretend thou art from Surrey, I rebuke not thy foul geography; but prithee at least use a true Surrey speech to a girl that is born and bred there.'

At this, to calm her, and seeing we had sustained, as soldiers say, a reverse in our initial action by the dexterity of this Amazon, I asked Jenny to be seated, and said we were honest Essex lads, that loved teasing pretty lasses, and meant no more harm than that. 'So bring out thy companion once again,' cried I, 'and let us drink to both fair counties, and your fairer faces.' 'Lucy,' Jenny made answer, 'shall stay inside the inn, where I have begged the landlord to keep watch on her, until I see the fair side of your two arses on the highway.'

I did not share Peter's vexation at this rejoinder, and must admire Jenny's spirit, for she was a roaring girl, beside comely; and though she seemed but young, I was so struck by her deft address, that I began to wonder if she was herself, like Lucy, a true country lass, or peradventure one wiser in the ways of London than she pretended.

'Come now, Jenny,' cried I, 'do not be triggered with us, for we mean thee no evil, and beg but to gaze on all the fresh flush of beauty for a while;' and with this I essayed a hand upon her arm, which earned me a sharp slap. But a lad learns he need ne'er fear a girl's slapping: for only silence and departure are the true signs of their ill-favour.

But Peter, in a huff, rose up and would have no more of us, I guessed part by vanity, and part because he had cast eager eyes on Lucy, and would cast more, e'en if neath the chill gaze of the landlord. So I, putting a seemly gravity on my pocked face, said softly, 'Jenny, thy name is dearest to me in the world, for 'twas that also of my mother.'

She made as if to laugh at this boy's habitual of comparing a girl's virtues to his mother's, when all he seeks is to woo her from those same virtues; but when she saw that I spoke true (at least, of Jane being my mother's name), she asked how my mother did, and who was my father.

'In truth, Jenny' said I, 'all I am sure he did was lie with her, for who he was, I know not; as to what she was, why! hers was an honest commerce in its way, at least men say 'tis the oldest.'

'Well then,' cried she, 'we are well met; for I belong to that same sisterhood as did thy mother.'

'Jenny, I can scarce believe it!' cried I, seizing on her hand, which this time she did not deny me. 'But if this be so, why art thou wandering on the Surrey road, or dost thou seek country commerce?'

To this, with a brazen coyness, she revealed she was come out of London to the Surrey road on the same ill errand as ourselves; and that Lucy was the first fish she had landed. 'And let me tell thee,' said she, 'in this angling, a wise girl that plays innocent hath defter rod than any boy; for the damsels yield confidence easier to another.'

'But sure,' said I, 'thou art not bawd to all these fledglings for thine own circumstance alone?'

'Why no,' said she. 'I am procuress of these lasses to the Venice Doge.'

At this I told her we were but two faces of the same coin, for I was servant to Doge Genoa. 'And hast thou then served him long?' said she. 'For though of the Venice band, I know many of his brother's, yet not thy fresh face, pardee!' And so we exchanged secrets; or rather, I must entice them from her, since those with greater knowledge know its greater value.

Well, 'twas thus, said Jenny. The Venice Doge was elder, as I knew, and when the brothers' empire of villainy was first established in East London (at approximate the time of the Armada), the Genoa Doge was but a stripling, obedient to his brother in all evil. But now, such was their prosperity, and the augmenting vanities of Venice, and envies of Genoa, that he, though maintaining forms of deference to his senior, was gathering all the wickeder followers to his person. 'Indeed,' said she, 'thou hast done well to enlist in the Genoa camp, for therein, I am certain, lies the future.'

'Then why, Jenny, hast thou stayed faithful to he of Venice that is declining?'

Here she heaved a sigh, and flicked her lashes, and let a sad smile wander o'er her face, which all assured me she would next speak of love. 'I have told thee, lad,' she said at last, 'I was a bawd; but what I told thee not, is that I cared little for the life, and wished for better. And he who has helped me to a smoother path is one of Venice's most faithful courtiers, that is called Sad Jack.'

'And what so saddens him, my sweet, since he hath thee?'

'Ah, that he hath me not, for one; for he is much older than we twain, and wearied of luxury, though in his youth 'tis said he enjoyed many. But now he most loves fond converse, and I can hear him patiently.'

'And how stands he to the Doge of Venice?'

'Both well and ill; for he is not much used upon the Doge's business, but is to him as 'twere confessor, like my Lord of Canterbury to our Sovereign.'

'Thou are not wed to him, Jenny?'

'Nay, nay; yet while he calls me rarely to his room – and then most that I may hear soliloquies – he is jealous of any who cast eyes upon me with that look thou wearest now; so an we meet again in Bishopsgate, be wary.'

At this there stepped out to us from the inn, and not to Jenny's pleasure, my friend Peter that had his arm about the waist of Lucy; and she gazing up at his scarce bearded face, as if 'twere Apollo's, and she Daphne.

'Oh, Mistress Jenny!' cried she, holding Peter by his sweaty paw, 'he has told me such fair tales of London, and so sweetly!'

'Aye, I warrant,' quoth Jenny.

'Let us away then thither!' cried she, looking first up the London road with rapture, then back toward Surrey safety with disgust, her eyes ending planted on the fair face of Peter, which wore a noble glower to mask its lewdness.

'Trip away, children!' said Jenny, pointing up the London road, 'and we shall follow close after, fear not!'

Off they went interclasped, and I said to Jenny, 'Thou wilt not let Peter steal away the fruits of all thy labour?'

She smiled and said, 'Once o'er London Bridge, his pate shall be well cracked by one of the Venice bullies. But sith she is so happy in his company, I may use him to carry her so far without dispute.'

'Thou art a hard lass, sweet Jenny.'

''Tis a hard trade, as thou wilt learn. For know also this: thou shouldst not, nor Peter, come hither south of the river on this business, but stay northward, in Middlesex or Essex. For hereabout is territory of the Southwark barons.'

'Yet hast thou come here also, on Venice's affairs.'

'Aye, but I am a Surrey lass, and beside a woman, and so less marked. But did those of Southwark spy thee and know who sent thee hither, thou wouldst surely suffer. For the Doges, that rule north of Thames, are as nothing here.'

She rose, and we set forward. 'Aye,' said she, 'and find fledglings of thine own, lest Beauty punish thee for idleness.'

'But Jenny,' said I. 'Suppose Peter clings fast to his Lucy, or essays to?'

'Then, lad,' said she, 'he must sever allegiance from Genoa, and come to us of Venice; and mayhap may we make him pander to the damsel.'

'I had not thought,' said I, 'to find base affairs so patterned on those highest of the State.'

'Well, what is a State but a great stew?' quoth Jenny.

7

And so it befell: that Peter, who had been chief recusant to these fraternities, such was his passion for young Lucy, entered the service of Doge Venice. Of Lucy, he enjoyed free favours and, I believe, her affections; but for these he must bring many to her from the thoroughfares, for whom her favours were not free at all. But I stayed unstitched to such entanglements: not, as those wanting charity may suppose, that my features were so foul no bawd would entertain me as her pander in Genoa's court; nor yet, that I was more virtuous than my friend. It was rather that I craved my freedom, which I do not believe a pander hath, in spite his luxury; and also that I was much bewitched by Jenny, whom I saw when I was able, though not oftentimes, for that the courts of Venice and Genoa, though still close allied, were oft on the verge of a disruption.

I became, rather, in the Genoan palaces (that were a village of brothels, ale-houses, dicing and bowling-rooms, and places of illicit accommodation all about St Helen's), a sort of base Mercury: that lad who in any household, and e'en one worthy, is called on for tasks for which all others are too proud; and by these mean services, learned much of London, and the high politics of Genoa's realm. Of this, there has already been presented Beauty, that was a courtier less puissant, I discovered, than he had insinuated to our country candour, for he was but one of several rogues that hung about Genoa's skirts; Doll Pretty, too, who belonged to a multitude of bawds protected and bullied by the Court; and honest Gropenut, the witty foist, and court jester whose japes none found as merry as did he.

As for the Doge himself, Genoa, I scarce more than glimpsed him; for in that manner of the great of being e'er absent from the mean sources of their grandeur, he came little to St Helen's or, rather, to those parts of it that most sustained him. He was short, swart and colheric, dressed like an alder–man; and indeed, many of his familiars, which he brought sometimes to game or tumble, were sage city gentlemen, and e'en noblemen from the West. Where'er he proceeded, surrounded by much bowing and curtseying from his tribe of flunkeys, he was followed like a shadow by a young monster known as Breakbone Charles, that had been a wrestler ere he lost an ear and half his nose; and this great boasting varlet was chief protector of the sacred body of the Doge.

Beside Pretty, for whom I had some fondness, my chief friend in this ill assembly became the Doge's son, a lad that was named Cecil: this, so he told me, in honour of those upstart clerks that now ruled England from beneath the Queen's farthingale. For the Genoa Doge was a worshipper of the powerful, and hoped his son might grow to be as great a man as hunchback Bob: and to this end, now Cecil was waxing out of boyhood, had set him to study at the Inns of Court. Cecil had but one defect that made friendship difficult with a man, which was that he scarce was one; for in his green age, he doted only on his own sex, and after my ill encounter with the goat-herd William in the dung-pits of Harden, I wanted no more of this. Yet here, I soon found, I was in little danger; for all Cecil's affections were laid at the feet (or elsewhere, I doubt not) of his cousin Robin, that was son to the rival Doge of Venice; a lad I had not seen yet, though Jenny told me, when I enquired of him, that he was indeed a sweet and gentle fellow, much loved by many more – and more honestly – than he was by Cecil.

'Aye, Aubrey,' Cecil said to me, sighing, 'I know that country lads know little of these loves, which are peculiar to the grace and elegance of cities. Yet just as thou feelst tenderly to Jenny, and lie dreaming of her, so do I of my fair cousin Robin.'

'I hope I shall lie other than dreaming with her ere long.'

'Then as thou shalt feel then, that is, enraptured, so do I when Robin is beside me. But alas! Such is the coldness of our fathers now, they do not care for us to gambol as we used to when both boys.'

'Mayhap 'tis the complexion of the gambolling that misplease them.'

'Not so: for city men, e'en greatest of whoremongers, have an understanding of these sweet affections.'

Of a truth, though I had no fondness for Cecil's inclination, I did for him; and joined not in the mockeries of such stalwart gallants as Master Beauty, that would sell their horns gladly for a guinea. For Cecil was of a fond, frank disposition, that must come to him from his mother, for the Genoa Doge had none of it; and though he was an idle, dreamy fellow, who did naught for his father's business but waste what money he could plead on books and ruffs and other fancies, he was kind and generous, ne'er speaking harsh when he could so without danger. Puritans will say that, beside his vice, he was a parasite; which is all true, save that I have come to think the idle oft harm less than many puffed up with zeal.

My chief task became what is called *touchman*, and this – and greatly to my credit – in our fairest brothel. As those who frequent such places of infamy will know (having mostly discovered it to their cost), the chief purpose is to extract for a least part of honest service, a greatest of the coney's gold; and to achieve this high purpose, besides the bawds, and bullies like Breakbone Charles, and masters of the Vincent's Law of cheating like Master Beauty, or plain sellers of watered sack, potato brandy, or French wines made of dandelions, there is an intermediate (that was I, the touchman) whose business it is to steer the coney in and out of the harlot's bed, and void his pocket, with despatch. The scientists of stews, that know their ropes as doth a mariner his cordage, have no need of any touchman, being brisk and practised about their affairs; but others are coy, besotten, laggard or disputatious, and on these the touchman must seek to work his wiles. For this he does not so much need strength (there being other functionaries for violence), nor beauteous charms, but a plausible swift wit, and a fair temper. And since, at a trial, I was found apt in this deceitful art, I was employed at it; and by these means, grew to know many that came to us, and all their foibles.

Among these, was one Master Bowes, called Bully Noll by us of the establishment that knew his manners, who came always in company of a servant, Moses, that he treated as a serf. Not, truth to say, that I had great sympathy for this old man, that was a dodderer and chatterbox, much loving discourse of those fair old days by which senility renders itself tedious to youth, as I doubt not I shall to my young grandsons. This Moses came ever first, alone, to spy out the climate of the brothel, before reporting backward to his master, Bully Noll, that all would be found fitted to his liking. I wondered at this excess of scruple, until some told me that this Bowes, being a recusant, feared not cutpurses nor constables, but the Star Chamber; and true, at this time, when privy priests of the old faith (and in especial, Jesuits) were being much sought out and kindled, he had cause for fear; and even we: for had not the Parliament declared that any harbouring of recusants should be fined, and fined heartily again?

Bully Noll was a gentleman: that is, one who, having money, and what he called a name, believed himself to be one; of which the chief proof consists in manifesting to sweaty others, that they are not. Now, it was not unusual for such to visit brothels, despite the ease that fortune gave them to debauch servants, or e'en these girls' mistresses; for I think they liked our filthy coarseness, as does a glutton mussels after lampreys. Yet usually, these gentlemanly rakes were young, being of the Court, the universities, or the Inns of lawyers;

whereas Noll Bowes was an elder man, whose curiosity and passion might have slackened with the disabling years. But he came oft to us; and I surmised this was because of some secrecy anent the persecution of his faith, that made him wary of any society more fair than ours.

While this Noll was about his carnal business, and old Moses dabbling in the sack we offered him, as part recompense for his master's largesse, he would snatch at my sleeve and, if I scaped him not upon some courtly pretext, sing an endless lament to me about the vanished virtues of our realm.

'Ah, boy,' quoth he, 'thou mayest speak to me about my Lord of Essex (which I had not), but pray tell me, what is that popinjay beside good Robert Dudley, that the Queen loved better and found worthier? Indeed,' said the old gabbler, oiling himself with sack, 'my dear late master, father to young Noll, that is Sir Ronald, was follower to Leicester in the Netherlands, and there perished: leaving, alas, the rule of his household to that upstart ravelling upstairs.'

'Guard thy tongue, ancient, or Bully Noll will pluck it out thy aged chaps.'

'The old fear not,' cried he. 'For when the grave beckons at our age, 'tis not fearful, but a refuge. Thank thee, fair lad, for this sweet Rhenish. Now, thou art a fair youth, so prithee tell me: art thou a younger, or an elder son to thy dear mother?'

'Like our first parent, Adam, my creation was unique.'

'Then are thou both elder and younger, and thus a composite of vice and virtue. For hast thou not marked, boy, how the elder son is ever Satan's child, and the younger, that of all the saints?'

'Bully Noll, then, is the elder?'

'In troth. There is a second son to Sir Ronald, Jack, that is away fighting now in Ireland; but the darling of the nestlings is young Allan, that his elder, Noll, treats as a scullion, though this but makes his virtues shine the brighter.'

'And this Allan comes not whoremongering with his brother?'

'May the Saints preserve him from it! Nay, the lad is a staunch Puritan, and chaste as any lily.'

'Then, grandfather, being what I am, my love must be for Bully Noll.'

'To thy shame, then. But here comes my master, who, being sated of one passion, will, I doubt not, soon gratify another. Bring some more wine, lad, but not for him this cat piss with which thou hast so kindly replenished mine ancient gut.'

I must have some parley with Bully Noll concerning coins, for he was one of those habituals that, by courtesy of the stew, we did not tax before they snuggled with the girls, but made posterior settlement as twixt gentlemen. But when this was done, Noll Bowes, first dismissing old Moses to look to the horses tethered in the yard, drew me down upon a chair, saying he wished converse with me; and opened up with words that e'er herald the asking of a favour:

'Thou art, Aubrey, a discreet lad, and sensible, for I have oft observed thee nearly. Now, tell me, boy, prithee: in what faith are thou baptised?'

'Why, in none, sir.'

'None. Art thou then pagan?'

'So I must suppose, sir. For my only baptism was by the waters cast upon me by the midwife that, so my mother told me, attended me at my coming.'

At this intelligence he frowned and bit his lip, then said, 'Thou art not, then, an enemy to the old faith?'

'Why, no, sir, to none: begging only they invite me not to the rack presently, nor to eternal fire hereafter.'

'Yet for thee a promise, lad, is still a sacred thing: I mean, if thou sayest, "Noll Bowes, I swear I shall," then thou wouldst do it?'

'That would depend on what, sir.'

'Aye.' He gazed about the ale-house portion of the brothel, where he was happy in that best protector of secrecy, which is a din. Then he leaned forward:

'Before I unfold my purpose to thee, boy, I ask first a conditional small promise: which is if thou sayest nay to what I beg, then thou forget also that I have asked it.'

'Why, sure, sir,' said I, growing curious, and scenting gold.

'Know, then, lad, that I am what is called, by their enemies, a Papist: that is, what I and mine would call a Christian, and the only kind.' I nodded sagely, as if this were a revelation to me. 'Well, boy,' quoth he, 'thou must know that we of the true faith in England, are presently a flock bereft of shepherds. Yet loving and fearing for us as they do, some saintly spirits come among us from the holier parts of Europe, but are also oft entrapped and made martyrs as was brave Campion of blessed memory.' Here he crossed himself swiftly, in a motion as if harnessing his doublet, then stared at me awhile, as if enquiring of me.

'Say on, sir, in safety,' I said to him.

'Well, boy, in brief, a priest is coming over, and we need help to bring him in.'

I looked at him. 'For that, sir,' I said, 'the penalty of capture is a burning.'

'True, lad: the fire.'

'Sir: why pagan Aubrey? Are there no bold followers of Rome?'

For a while he stared angry at me, then, seeing this would not be to his purpose, he answered thus: 'If thou knewest the tally of the martyrs, Aubrey, thou wouldst not ask this of me.

No: why I come to thee is, first, because we are all watched close, and thou not, at least in such a business; and next, e'en for a holy traffic like bringing this saint in, we must have recourse to those less holy.'

'Sir,' said I, pleased that I could speak pertly to him, 'they who frequent brothels should perchance not reproach others for their scant sanctity.'

He looked hard at me again, then sighed, put on a grim smile, and said, 'Aye, lad, aye . . . but what sayest thou to my intent?'

'Why, this: that you have spoke to me of saintliess and peril; but not of what would most incline me to your purposes.'

'Ten gold pieces, Aubrey, and a vow that if thou reveal aught, e'en if put to torture, I may slay thee.'

Any man, unless himself a Papist, that were asked to do what Bowes now did of me, should tender an instant nay; or, if an aye conditional, ask for at least an hundred pieces, and ship to France soon after. But I was young, not knowing yet what real danger and pain are; and besides, my brief life had but one guiding principle, and this offer of Bully Noll's, if I accepted it, would forward me in my prime intent.

In the hut where I was reared by my mother and by Martin, I had learned, by the whole shape of our three lives, one absolute reality: there were the few rich that could buy even bodies, and the many poor with only toil and flesh to offer in return. And my young heart was possessed by a furious desire to step out from among this multitude of victims, and in with that small body of the elect which rule others by their gold. Besides, my good mother, with her example, had imparted two further precepts: which were enjoy thyself, certes, but ensure that others pay for it; and if thou must thyself spend, for each groat gone, hold two.

Now it needed not a large experience, but only my own

good sense, to tell me that in the company of cozenage to which I now belonged, for every Doge Genoa that grew prosperous, a hundred that served him dies poor as they began; and that to rise up from the ranks among the generals, the chief promotion in a rogue's life was the first. Within Genoa's empire, I could scarce hope to soar, howe'er apt I was, from among the humbler levies; and as for trying my own hand at any villainy, like a conquistador seeking a new country, I knew London had few Americas, and many a Cortez bolder far than I. Therefore, though I liked not Bully Noll (nor trusted him overmuch), and knew none would help me if I failed at the high treason he offered me (for such it was), this first clear summons from Dame Fortune was too imperative for me to dare ignore it. So I said I was his man, and would hear more.

At this he called a glass for me, and took on an imperious familiarity that those who, one moment pleading humbly, adopt when they suppose that they have won you; which did not trouble me, because I thought I might be the winner in this transaction.

'Hearken, Aubrey,' said he. 'Thou must to my house to speak of this, and I shall send old Moses soon to fetch thee, on pretext of some venery, when I shall unfold more of this business and more privily. But a word of caution here. My younger brother, Allan, is traitor to his father's faith, and must know none of this. So when thou comest, act, pray, the simpleton, and answer any curious question with a gawp.'

'Thus, sir?' said I.

'Od's life! Thou wouldst deceive Master Walsingham's direst spies!'

'Pray that I do so, sir,' said I.

8

The Venice Doge, which might seem strange, lived where once monks did. For when King Henry fiddled with our faith, for reasons related to the altar, the sceptre, and the marriage bed, he fell on many church possessions and devoured them, oft spewing them up again, for ready gold, to courtiers and others of more substance. Of these plundered estates ecclesiastical, there were several east of London, just outside the walls: which, earlier in our century, were counted worthy to house the greatest. But London, like the sun, moves ever westward; and when, Elizabeth succeeding to her father (with two swift, sad intermissions), new palaces appeared along the Thames, the older places eastwards lost their glory, and fell into contempt; the more so as the fields about them vanished under crawling tenements to house the city superfluity, as I have related. So, from I know not what lordling, or his steward, the Venice Doge bought for himself, with the profit of vicious crime, a chauntrey nearby Spitalfields, and there held court.

Like his young brother Genoa, that dwelt inside the City walls, he of Venice received not many of the rogues that were his subjects, inside his palace; but only a few of trust that bore to him gold, and parchments tallying his infernal revenues. His lord high treasurer was one Amos, a false courtly fellow, apt at the mysteries of reckoning. The Doge's familiar was Sad Jack, that cherished Jenny; and there also dwelt with him his son Robin, for whom this young gallant's cousin Cecil, son to Genoa, sighed in vain.

I could ne'er have set my coarse feet into mighty Genoa's house, I being the least among his servitors; but at Venice's chauntrey I was admitted, in part because the slave of another is not deemed so ignoble as one's own, but more because Jenny held high favour there with Sad Jack, and he, in turn, with Venice; so that I was allowed in by the porter at the postern door. The purport of my visits was to see if I could bewitch Sad Jack into a blindness, and creep into Jenny's bed. For I had decided to wed Jenny.

Pray do not mock at my presumption! True, I was but approaching my sixteenth year, was born ill-favoured and made more; and possessed as treasure nothing but good health and a fair wit. But I had soon decided that no man could advance far in the business of harlotry, without a woman to instruct and guide him. Besides, I believe that if men are apter at gaining money, women are more so at holding fast to it. If I asked my conscience if I loved Jenny, it must give the true answer I did not; though I admired her certainly, and, more certain still, yearned to lie with her, and that not for but one night. Why I admired her chiefly was in her good sense to see that harlotry is a fine commerce, but an ill pursuit; so that, if she must lie with men she cherished not, she preferred one, Sad Jack, to multitudes, e'en if she must be civil to him, which she need ne'er to a passing, careless many. As for my prospect of prising her loose from Jack, my plan was to steal from him first her fidelity, and then her person; and proceeding by that principle of all country boys seeking to catch wives, I knew the first step was to get her abed, and the next, fast with child.

Lovelorn Cecil, hearing privily of my visit, had given me a note that I must seek to pass to Robin; so I made this my excuse when I begged from the porter leave to enter. This porter was a tall lank fellow by name Herman, that had been formerly a player in the theatres, and could bespatter you with verses like a fountain, did you indulge him. The which

I did: for to be the familiar of a porter is to be one also of his house.

As he swung ope the postern to me, Herman spake thus:

> Welcome to thee, fair Aubrey. On what errand
> Dost thou, stealing from neath Genoa's eaves,
> Come hither privily to the Rialto?
> Seekest thou Jenny who, unclasping Jack,
> Is e'en in the privy, for mine ears
> And nose inform me that she sits there presently?

'Aye, Herman,' said I. 'And I bring tidings to Robin from his Cecil.'

'An ill, pocked Cupid. Go thy ways to the tilting yard, where Robin exercises with a sword that is not the dart Cecil cherishes. As for Jenny, I shall tell her thou art here in due season.'

It was part of the Venice Doge's grandiloquence that he wished Robin to be a gentleman; of which, in England, one of the proofs is that instead of taking life with a dagger, as is the vulgar habit, it must be snatched more prettily with a sword; so that young Robin took lessons from one of my Lord of Leicester's veterans who, being a soldier and not a fop, instructed Robin not only in the elegancies of swordmanship, but in the foul tricks whereby a man may slay; it being his principle that no man should draw sword unless to kill, and that honour is no substitute for life. These two were playing in the yard; and the soldier used no button to his sword, but made Robin rehearse with a naked blade, so that he was oft pinked, and grew to be swift and wary. I stood watching for a while, with admiration; though reflecting that once inside its distance, a sword is useless, and a dagger a more faithful weapon, albeit base.

'Robin,' quoth the soldier, wiping away sweat, 'I had thy life four times.'

'Whereof I see as many proofs as my pierced doublet. May my four lives spared, earn thee as many.'

'Marry, I shall have need of them, lad, for I grow fat and heavy-footed. Prithee, say to thy father I have earned my fee, and let me deplete the hour I owe thee by the time to cozen Herman for a draught.'

'Go thy ways, then, Corporal. And know I love thee for the precious skill thou has imparted.'

'None more so, so long as men hang swords about their bellies.'

Robin turned smiling to me, but frowned when I handed him Cecil's letter. He was a tall red-haired youth, as fair as I am ugly; yet what I cherished in young Robin, and indeed all did, was that he seemed born beautiful yet bereft of vanity. This I believe rare: for while many that are comely hide their knowledge of it, to spike the jealousies of those less well-favoured, like Arab steeds they cannot mask their content at being blessed by nature. But Robin was or prince among dissimulators or, as I believe, thought little of his graces.

'Ah, poor Cecil!' cried he, folding the letter, and tucking it away. 'Why is it, Aubrey, that those to whom we wish to give, want ever more? For Cecil has my friendship, that I withhold from many, and in despite of both our fathers. Yet this suffices him not, he must needs my love.'

'He is of our age, Robin, and yet not of it: for he is still swaddled in boyhood, while thou and I, though but pimpled fledglings yet, grow crests and spurs.'

'Who in London would believe that a lad, like Cecil, whose father can order fifty skirts lifted to win his favours, sighs vainly for his cousin's?'

'When thou hast understood all of this world, Robin, I

prithee expound it to me; for in truth, why this one cherishes this, and the other that, perpetually amazes me.'

'As I am amazed too by thy lust for Jenny. Oh, fear not: for though I see, I keep silence, save to thee. Blush not, rustic! for it maketh thy pocks glow like fireflies. Away with thee, rather, to the buttery, where thou wilt find Mistress Jenny exercising her tyranny over my father's scullions.'

Which was indeed so; for Jenny, in despite her youth, had become, as consort to the Venice Doge's chief counsellor (I mean Sad Jack), housekeeper of his palace; there being, as also with Genoa, no female Doge – indeed, who Robin's mother was (or Cecil's) was of those questions that most of both kingdoms deemed it wiser not to ask; for both Doges seeking to rise up in the world, neither would lay proud claim to a harlot as mother for their heirs apparent.

But one glimpse of the buttery sufficed to show that Jenny was mistress there not merely by court favour, but by her art of management; for she was one of those woman, rare as a fair March day, that can achieve authority over her kind without caterwauling or scolding; and this, beside her limbs like ripe pears, was what I cherished in her. Also, that she cooked like an angel, or as it may be imagined heaven's Servitors can do. And I have e'er believed that she who cooks well, lies well; and if ill, ill (which, if it be so, makes a swain's telling his comrades that he 'marries her to get a good cook' not so foolish as it may seem).

Jenny greeted me fondly, but with that condescension women e'er practise when a man appears in their particular domain – as kitchen, nursery, or, if a harlot, bedroom. I tried stealing a kiss; but won only a swift slap about my bum. Yet if Jenny was determined to repel me, she should remember that I am my mother's son; so that if nature had endowed me with all masculine artifices, daily example had taught me those of women also. Nor did she yet realise that in choosing to board her in the buttery, instead of waiting till she could receive me in her privy chamber, I had, like a good general, marked my strategy. For here I make bold to impart some precepts in the great art of seduction, which all men must study, or remain else bachelors or cuckolds (this last meaning that the woman hath first been the seducer).

The unskilled suppose that, for the seduction of a maid who simulates reluctance, the fairest battlefield is a bedroom and the most favourable company none, except for two. This is indeed so after final victory but, for the preliminary skirmishes, a more public place, with many present, is more apt. The reason is that all women descended from our mother Eve, love to show others they are cherished, yet suppose that these others protect their virtues from any assault. This makes them both boastful and imprudent, conditions favourable to the seducer, which he would not find in the solitude of a bedroom, should he e'er entice her thither.

Now, beside this buttery there was a small dairy for the churning. In the making of butter, there arises a nice moment when one hand turns the wheel, while the other pours the cream: a product so luscious, and costly in London, that no housewife that respects her art would dare lose a drop. My intent was, while chattering sweetly to Jenny anent high affairs of Venice and Genoa, to snatch up her skirts, and seize her in a posture so familiar that none of the wenches outside in the buttery would e'er believe, if she should call out, that she had not consented to it freely. And this I did, holding the door fast with mine arse.

Now, ardour feeds upon resistance; and what unmanned me was that Jenny, while I grasped and fumbled, continued with her pouring and her twirling, as though but a child were about her skirts. At which, vexed, I bit her neck, whereat she downed jug, let wheel, and breaking free, turned round and took my hands.

'Aubrey,' quoth she, 'I shall not lie with thee unless we wed.'

'Jenny, I wish no other!'

'Aye, Aubrey, I doubt not. But to wed, thou art still too young, besides being a pauper.'

'I am soon fifteen, and any priest would take me for near twenty.'

'When thou art sixteen, then, if thou alterest not, nor I. And I must have consent, also.'

'For whose care I save thine?'

'But I care: Sad Jack must give me to thee, freely, at the altar!'

'An he say nay?'

She shook her head. 'Then I also.'

'Thou lovest him not, Jenny!'

'Nay; but I must be given by him.'

I kissed her, and she too. 'Let us to him, then,' said I. 'Pray heaven he does not stab, nor poison me.'

'Thou hast no patience, Aubrey.'

'I, yes, but this is eager,' said I, drawing her hand down.

'Fie!'

'Let us seek him out, Jenny, and pray his sadness increases not our own.'

Sad Jack was tending mulberry trees in the garden orchard, for he had learned from Cathay how to make silken hose. In truth, I could not understand why Sad Jack was so named, for he looked it not, being substantial; and as for his converse, though it was mined with ironies, I ne'er found it melancholy.

'How now, pander, thou walkest with my bawd?' said he. 'Shun his society, Jenny, or he shall have thee in Genoa's stews and grow rich of all thy foul increment.'

'Nay, Jack, the lad is honest to me, if to none other: for today he has spoken no bawdry, but of wedlock.'

'Twixt thee and he?'

'So says he.'

Sad Jack gazed on us and shook his head. 'Ill-matched,' said he. 'A nuptial twixt pock and pox.'

'By thy leave, Jack! An I were so afflicted, wert thou also.'

'True, Jenny. And of what, beside his allurements, does this spotted unripe fig make offer to thee?'

'Of his name.'

'He hath none.'

'Well, Jack, then, wedlock. And that, though thou call me after every bird and flower, and even star, is a word thou hast e'er withheld from me.'

'Marry, and rightly. For I should be mocked for espousal with a strumpet, as thou for wedding with a dotage.'

'Then be our kind ancient, Jack, and deliver me to Aubrey in due time at the altar. For if men love swearing oaths, women love it the more, be there but witnesses.'

'Aye. But why, prithee, should I yield up my treasure to this pilferer, and he, besides, of the Genoa faction?'

'First, to win him to Venice, and his talents: for in the novitiate of villainy, none is more apt than Aubrey. And then, Jack, to give to me what thou canst not, and he will: which is to be made an honest woman.'

'That, sweet, thou canst ne'er be. But no matter: these are deep questions, that must be deeply pondered. Also submitted, in due form and time, to the opinion of the Doge, for we are of his household: where, my dear Jenny, thou surely wishest to remain, and not be cast back into the stews with thy beloved.'

'Thou shalt speak to him, Jack: thou hast his ear.'

'But not his powers: look, where he walks stately, sniffing among his herbs. Pray, children, he be not at the rue.'

For in his herb garden, Doge Venice had appeared, arms behind back, brooding, like a hen on eggs, about his treasures. He was taller than his brother of Genoa, and more sombre; and seemed more an abbot than chief pander of St Helen's and the parishes adjacent. He glanced towards us, and we all bowed, at which he raised a finger, and passed on.

'Go thou, Aubrey,' said Jack, 'fall upon thy thick knees, and petition him, for that is the privilege of varlets before their monarch.'

'Not I, Master Jack, go thou!'

'Nay, Jack, do thou speak with him: that is, if thy heart inclines thee to our favour.'

Sad Jack placed a hand on each of our two shoulders, and said, 'I shall consult my better judgement, and acquaint you twain with its decisions. Meanwhile, depart peacefully about your several loose occupations.'

So we went back to the buttery, where Jenny drew sack, and chased out the girls to set some order in the house. 'So we shall win thee to Venice,' said she, smiling, 'as we have thy comrade Peter.'

'He loves Lucy still?'

'That thou must ask him, for men speak no truth to women in these matters, as thou must know. But Lucy sure dotes upon him; and for his bright eyes, and I wot not what else, would lie with sixty every hour to win his smiles by yielding him their base coinage.'

I took her hands. 'Jenny,' said I, 'with thou and I, it ne'er shall be so: for mock me not, but I shall become Doge too in my good time, and shall sustain thee honestly.'

'Shall I then name thee Pisa? For Venice and Genoa are bespoke.'

'Aye: and let my tower lean heavy.'

'Come, then.'

'To the dairy once again?'

'We did not end the churning, Aubrey; do thou pour the cream, and I shall twirl the wheel to make a pat.'

9

There is no Londoner feels himself more so than a country boy six months in the city; and Peter and I, that but yesterday were gaping at each town midden, as if 'twere the Holy Grail, sauntered about now like those born to the land of Cockayne, and with a special contempt in our dilated noses for any rustic lout newly arrived, to stare as we had. For such corruptors are big cities that they can transform an honest peasant into city trash within few moons; whereas a lifetime will not make a true countryman out of a boy that is city born.

We could not often meet, to exchange our Londoner's fresh gossip, for beside he was Venetian and I Genoan, our duties to these republicks held us fast there. Yet in the early morn, we could foregather: I because then all slept within the stews, whose morning is at noon; and Peter on pretext of setting forth to find custom among the markets of the West for Lucy. To cross the City had this further use to us, that prying eyes which knew us were far fewer; beside which, we both cherished secretly the magnificences of Whitehall and Charing Cross, and though half alarmed by them, sauntered about like little lordlings, decked in a cheap finery we thought noble, and which to the judicious must have marked us for the pert pimps we were.

To cross the City from the east to west there was, to lads of our age, one hazard: that could be escaped only by taking boat up the river, or walking outside the walls through Moor

Fields and then by the orchards to the north; and this was the prentices. I know the Queen rules England, and my Lord Mayor the City, but in truth, within its bounds, the real tyrants are these diligent savages. By law, they are bound to their masters' obedience like Sir Walter's blackamoors to his, and within their workshops, they may indeed be serfs; but when they swarm forth loosed together, they are venomous as bees, and none, not e'en the constables nor the Queen's horse themselves, can withstand their onslaughts. And on those of their own age that are not also prentices, they impose an especial terror, for they harbour towards us an absolute animosity. In this they are like soldiers, that divide the world into fellow warriors (whom they kill or love), and then all the rest, that are but contemptible zeros to them. This contempt, we that were not prentices did not fear so greatly, though we misliked it; but for prentices it sufficeth not to sneer, unless this be coupled with a bastinado, to teach humility to all not privy to their exalted servitude. So that, if e'er we heard their rallying cry, 'Prentice!' we became country boys again, and made off like hares.

But this day, being early, we saw none: or if some, those dutiful, peering jealously from work benches at our freedom; their envy the sourer, doubtless, because they knew this was a morning for a hanging.

'Who are the victims, Peter?' I asked, for it was he who had heard of this spectacle from the plackets of his stew.

'Some say Papists, others Puritans; be it either which, they are fanaticks, impatient to meet their Maker.'

'The Queen has a fine impartiality in their despatch. Mayhap, being near to paradise herself, she craves company of her loyal subjects.'

'Hush, no treason, Aubrey, or we shall see thee also disembowelled.'

'Not I, ever: for there is no faith I shall suffer from save that in gentle Aubrey.'

'Yet that thou art like to, and I also, should the justices e'er uncase our practice with the drabs.'

'Use not that sour word of sweet Lucy. She still cherishes thee as fondly?'

'Aye, Aubrey, but I begin to wonder. This commerce with her seemed so sweet, as did at first its jointure. But now I grow jealous of those mercenary hands that dabble in her pool.'

'Yet eager for their toll.'

'Aye. Thou, Aubrey, hast more wisdom, or better craft and fortune, I know not which. For Jenny rides free for thee to ride, and thy wages proceed from thine own dishonest toil.'

'Do thou then likewise, Peter.'

'I am born idle, Aubrey, beside rash.'

'Cease then the vice that pricks thee harder.'

'Thou art a moralist, Aubrey, and shouldst, I vow, be riding to Smithfield in a cart beside the Jesuits and Barrowists. And yet it is not thou only, nor mine own heart, that tell me this; for I am also preached at by Master Robin.'

'The heir to great Doge Venice deigns speak with thee?'

'Oh, he is not proud, as thou well knowest. And because I pass swords with him, for his practice (of which art I know naught, and am but his foil), we hold converse upon the mighty world and its great affairs – or, in troth, he does, for I tally but one syllable to his hundred.'

'And what counsels he?'

'That I should become a soldier! "This life, lad," says he, "is not thine. Thy rustic innocence is apt for bloodshed, and not whoredom."'

'So betrays he the interests of his father.'

'Scarce, Aubrey! For vain fools such as we are thick as

chestnuts in the forest of St Helen's, all ripe for the shaking of any rogue that's master of our wills and greed.'

'Peace, Peter! Thou layest weight on thy wits too dense for them to bear.'

'Yet Robin speaks fairly to me, for he has no advantage to his counsel, and thus wishes me well, for which I cherish him.'

'And he thee?'

'I? I am but one stone to step on in his father's court. A face, no more.'

We had come into Smithfield, that must surely be hallowed to man, and beloved of angels, since so many, in so many reigns, have died here for their several faiths. Yet may I not be damned for thinking that to perish for virtue, if such it be, is less rational than to perish for a vice, if this cannot be scaped. A martyr to holiness has my wonder, but not admiration; for how can we tell, from all the warring preachers in the kingdom now, what word is holy? And who would be martyr to a doubt? But for a victim of men's justice, I must feel pity; for there we know what rules are broke (e'en if we mislike the men who devised them for their profit), and deny them ourselves as often as we dare.

This was a sad hanging: for there is about the shuffling off of Papists a sort of ecstasy and venom in the devouter parts of the populace, that induces a heroic rapture among the beholders. But today we had but Puritans: not, I mean, those of the ornate tincture that command all our lives in the City and who, if they do not kiss the skirts of my Lord Archbishop as raptly as he might desire of them, take care to avoid any prescriptions by the Council. No: these poor Puritans were of some disputatious fragment of no such account and, indeed, of a species as much misliked and harried by my Lord Mayor as by Master Cecil. Which proveth to me this: if thou wilt found a sect, be sure 'tis one well endowed, so that it may prosper thee not only in the world hereafter, but of now.

So to witness their departure from the world that they despised, and which despised them, into the glory eternal of their inventions, we were but some hundred; and many from the markets, casting a swift disdainful eye at the preparations beside the gallows, would not even leave their stalls; while the sellers of sweetmeats and confections did scant trade. There were four fellows in the cart: and if they were not martyrs to their faith, they surely appeared so to their fortunes, for they were ill-kempt and ravaged, besides tattered. Master hangman was late, so that they must stand bound in the cart, praying and intoning anthems in a cracked treble; the crowd scarce thinking them worthy of the rotted fruit that they had gathered up. Only once did that Lord of Executions, which is the mob, manifest ill pleasure; and that was when one of the fellows, seeing he had an audience not likely to stalk out on his sermon, presumed to address them on their own ill condition, and the bliss that awaited him. But none likes to hear vengeance denounced by any victim, and the fellow's mouth was soon stopped with stones.

My lord hangman, when he strode up at last, was brisk about his business: for this was no execution of State, wherein his mystery can be more prettily propounded; and indeed, by his doltish appearance, I would take him for some apprentice in the craft, as yet unworthy of its loftier presentations. For he showed neither ceremony nor zeal; and as if they were spring lambs, strung them up, disembowelled, and, when he cut out the heart and privies, scarce let the multitude observe these organs (that should be held on high like trophies), but cast them away into a basket, wiping his hands upon his greasy jerkin for better purchase on the next. All died without lamentation; and indeed, they were despatched so fast there was scarce time for any, and the crowd soon dispersed itself to livelier occupations.

I felt a hand upon my sleeve, and this caused me to start, not only that the spectacle gave me such an ache, but also by that guilt which is the perpetual companion of a pander. But I need not fear, for it was old Moses, servant to Bully Noll the whoremonger. But since I knew Noll to be a Papist, I wondered at the ancient's attendance here.

'How now, good Master Moses,' said I, with that readiness to speak first which is ever the instinct of the guilty, e'en though innocence aboard him.

'Good Aubrey,' said he, 'I crave you spare a moment for my master.'

'Has Bully Noll come hither,' said I, 'to gloat papistically at the despatch of heretics?'

'Hush, nay!' said he, ''tis my true master, his young brother Allan, that is here, and he to weep, not gloat, at their departure. Now come, speak a word with him, I prithee.'

Now this I was not apt to do, for Bully Noll, his brother, who I knew misliked him, was the patron of our stew; and besides, with Noll cozening me to succour his privy Papists, I had no mind to embark on an acquaintance with this weeper for disembodied Puritans.

But the old fellow seized me by the arm, with that claw grip of the senile, and Peter trailing after, we came to a lusty fellow standing melancholy in a gateway; who by his resemblance of a fresh egg to an addled, I saw to be Allan, brother to Bully Noll.

'God bless us, Master Allan, sir,' quoth old Moses, fawning on his master like a leveret, 'and this is the honest lad I spake of, Aubrey, that could perchance further thy fair intent to those thou deemest God's elect.'

Young Allan heaved a sigh, and gave me a woeful gaze,

which I trusted more for its frankness than its fair understanding. Yet there was this about him that won from me an instant part of cordiality. I know not why it is, but if a man be born guileful yet good-hearted (such as I credit myself to be), when he encounters any that is clear a born innocent, he assumes towards him a sort of protectiveness, like a goose for a lost gosling.

'Master your dismay, sir,' said I to him, 'and tell me how I can be of service to you.'

'Aubrey,' quoth he, clasping my two hands, and brushing aside a tear, 'I am no coward before any man, yet the shuffling off of these poor saints unmans me quite.'

Well, thought I, if these snivelling wretches be saints, I shall burn no more candles; yet I said, 'We live, sir, in times of dire tribulation: for I wot not e'en God Almighty knoweth in which of so many diverse manners we are enjoined to worship Him, truth lies.'

'E'en so, Aubrey, e'en so,' quoth he.

Here ancient Moses, that was peering about like a cat scenting at hounds (though doubtless 'twas spies and talebearers he feared, of which there were e'er many cocking their sharp ears at executions), said to young Alan, 'Sir, such matters should be whispered privily: do thou, I beg, carry Aubrey to our house, for any converse on such occult religious matters.'

To this I agreed, but first paring away Peter, for I did not wish my friend to paddle in these deep waters. So we three remainder set off across the City towards Blackfriars, where lay the mansion of Sir Ronald Bowes. And on the way, though Allan hugged his moody silence (for which I was content), Moses, that was, as the old and children ever are, a chatterbox, took on himself to demonstrate the buildings to me; and in particular, the theatre near the river.

'Aye,' said he, pausing to rub his ancient back while Master Allan strode glumly on, ''twas rebuilt there three years since by one Burbage, to replace the older that stood here, as I well remember. This Burbage is a crafty fellow for, beside the erection of theatres, he acts also in them, like a landlord that both builds his inn and sells the ale. 'Twas he that set up our first playhouse, called the Theatre by Shoreditch, some quarter century past; but now I hear this is pulled down, and the timber carried across the river yonder for a new theatre on Bankside whose name I know not.'

'By the Bear Gardens and stews, and the prison called the Clink,' said I, proud of remembering these chief points of beauty that I saw on my visit with Peter into Southwark.

'Aye, but there are also prettier things: as the Paris gardens, and beside this new playhouse of Master Burbage, there are the *Rose*, some twelve years standing and, to the westward, the new *Swan*. 'Tis indeed a conglomerate of allurements for those that love such things; but say not so, I prithee, to Master Allan, who would burn every theatre as the church doth heretics.'

'But the theatre here stands not open to the skies as do those I chanced to see upon Bankside.'

'Why, nay, lad, in Blackfriars 'tis otherwise: for here the theatre is enclosed, both for performance when the clemency is not such for plays outdoors, and also that the gentler kind of person may proceed there; for here we are not far removed from Whitehall, whence few of the proper sort would venture across to Bankside, I may assure thee. Beside which, the acting here is of a different stamp: namely, for the most part all by boys, from infants scarce unswaddled to lads of thirteen or thereabouts.'

'That play grave men beside women? That must be a pretty piping out of false beards and farthingales.'

'E'en so; and 'tis not to the taste of all. For most prefer the open theatres wherein men play men and, for the women's parts, lads near enough to be man, save that their voices are as yet uncracked.'

'Of what age, Moses?'

'Thine, Aubrey, which I guess to be some fifteen summers. Some younger, though but little, since their statures must not be too mean to act as ladies; and some older, though few lads' voices, as thou knowest, stay sibilant beyond seventeen, if even.'

This discourse was arrested by an impatient cry from Allan, that waited on us beside his father's door; so we hastened forwarder, and were let into a small mansion, somewhat decayed, that I ween was of an earlier age than our monarch's reign, if not her father's; with inside, a pretty court and garden, where Allan took me; and for a while I could scarce hearken to him, such was my surprise and pleasure at this piece of country caught up in London: a great joy indeed, which those who ne'er penetrate from noisy streets beyond the fortresses of houses, would e'er guess at.

'Moses hath told me,' Allan said, 'that thou, Aubrey, art an honest lad, in spite thy calling; and that, indeed, because of this ill trade of thine, thou must be apt, deft and resolute by application as by nature. Hearken, then. These gifts, given thee by God, thou hast in most part employed for evil; and I would ask thee now if, for thy soul's salvation, thou wouldst not also use them to further the Lord's work rather.'

'As how, sir?' said I.

'As so, Aubrey. Thou knowest I belong to a sect of saints called Barrowists, which are as persecuted for their inclination to the extremities of Reform, as are the Papists for their withstanding of it. For thus it is: our good Queen, and our nation's Church, are like a man crossing a river from Error to

Redemption that gets stuck fast in the middle; so that while he has scaped the one, he has not attained yet to the other, and lies stranded in an empty nowhere, pining for both shores, but daring not to sail on to either.'

'In sooth, sir,' said I, 'is this not called compromise?'

'There can be none with Satan!' Allan cried. 'No, nor e'en less so, with the Lord! The choice is absolute, and our realm has chosen neither desart nor pasture, but lieth in the voided ditch between.'

'And how, sir,' said I, 'can I help you pluck it out?'

'By helping me put these about,' said he, removing from his jerkin a bound book, and handing it to me as if 'twere a bar of gold.

I glanced at its pages, and soon devined it to be that which might cause any man to lament he had learned letters: namely, a canting, dissenting tract so replete with hell-fire and damnation as to shrivel up its very leaves. I handed it back reverently, and said, 'How so, good Master Allan?'

'Hearken, lad,' said he, in a great whisper, though none could hear us but the rose bushes and thrushes. 'From our brethren overseas, and especially in its holier parts as the Netherlands and those of the Switzers, or in France, e'en, since the Nantes Edict of yesteryear, come vessels manned by saints of our persuasion bearing sacred volumes of this nature that none dares print in England now for fear of losing his ears, if not his life. These are brought privily to me in bundles, upon the Thames; and unknown to my brother Noll (that is, as thou must know, a horrid Papist), I secrete them in the house here, till I can unloose them among the faithful in this city. But alas! My proclivities are known and watched, and I cannot move, bearing them about the town, as freely as I would wish. But thee, lad, none would suspect of this; for beside that thou art young, no spy would conceive a friend to the saints in any of thy calling.'

'And whither would you have me carry them?' said I.

'To houses in the city marked by sanctity, as were those of the Israelites in Egypt that the wrath of the Lord should not fall upon them.'

Marry come up! thought I. What lunatick brothers have I not fallen among? For the one, Noll, will have me succour Papists, and the other, Allan, Puritans; yet for the faith of neither do I care a fig. Still, Bully Noll had offered gold. So: 'And what, sir,' said I, 'would be my reward for this?'

At this he looked sad. 'Aubrey,' quoth he, 'of the world's goods I have none, for my brother Noll rules all my dear father's substance.' But now he brightened, and his eyes gleamed with a frantick glare. 'Yet think,' cried he, 'of thy immense reward in Paradise!'

You may wonder, knowing the little rogue I was, why I did not bid Allan a pert adieu, and betake myself to Bishopsgate among my kind. But why I did not, was that I liked this fond fantastick fool, and trusted if not his guile, his heart; while reason told me that if I was to embark on plots with Noll, whom I mistrusted, his brother would be a friendly spy inside the Bully's camp, though Allan would not know I used him so.

'Sir,' said I at last, 'you ask much for little – nay, I mean little in this world which, being a poor lad unblessed like you with sanctity, I must consider. I prithee, therefore, let me think more of this, and take good counsel, before I promise aught to you.'

'But let thy counsel be discreet in such a matter.'

'Have no fear: I shall say naught to Noll, as you may suppose, nor to any in the camp of Genoa, where your brother is no stranger. But I have friends in the other camp of

Venice, that I trust with my very life, and would acquaint of this.'

'As the lad Peter, that was with thee?'

'Nay, wiser far.'

'Older, then?'

'Better: a woman.'

At this he started, and mumbled into an anxiety, for the sweet word of 'woman' seemed to conjure up in him a deep mistrust (that I have oft found in Puritans though, in sooth, they be horny fellows, within the sanctity of the marriage bed); and I doubt not he would have cast off the thought of me as helper had not, at this instant, a servant run up – not old Moses, but a far younger fellow, that cried out, 'Sweet master, take care, your brother cometh!'

'How, Daniel?' cried Allan. 'Is he within already?'

'Nay, not yet so, but old Moses hath espied him in the street, and sent me to you with a warning.'

At this Allan looked much disturbed, with that guilt writ on his face which can be seen plain only on those of the candid, and starting up and grasping me, he stuffed me behind a yew hedge, bidding me kneel and make no sound; himself then walking whistling, with his guilt-of-innocence writ plain for any of discernment to observe.

'How now, oaf!' cried Noll, bustling in, and gazing on Allan with the fierce reproof of those that, wishing to uncover sin in another, find none. 'What business art thou at, or else which idleness?'

'Why, brother, at those of living neath thy yoke: which finds all my business idle, and all my idleness, thy business.'

'Malapert!' cried Noll. 'Thy business is to do honour to our house!'

'Do thou instruct me, then, not by precept, but fair practice.'

'"Tis thy obedience should instruct thee, for I am thy elder.'

'Our father, that was both our elders, ne'er taught us obedience was servility.'

'Go to! 'Tis I shall speak now in his name, for I am become he, thy master.'

'That I served willingly, for he wished no son of his to be a slave.'

'Go thy ways! Let silence be thy mete reply to just rebuke!'

Whereat Noll strode into the house, and Allan, pulling me from the hedge, hustled and harried me to a small postern in the garden wall. 'Do thou think, then, of these things, Aubrey,' said he, pushing me without into a backwards lane.

'Aye, marry!' said I, tumbling into a great heap of ordures that was thrown there.

10

At my attic room in Doge Genoa's stew, I was sometimes wakened up out of my dull slumbers by an evil trick of Gropenut's, who had no business to rouse me, or come up. And this was, that the lewd cozener would steal up upon my sleep, lift the counterpane, and run a sly hand up my leg into my belly, and there tweak me. At which, I would leap up indignant (as he expected), and cry, 'Out, catamite! Go carry thy scurvy paw into thine arse, where it is more habitual!'

'Nay, but, sweet Aubrey! Confess that, in thy loins, thou sweatest for my favours, as Master Cecil doth for thine!'

'Out, whoreson!' I would cry, shuffling up, and seizing on an ale flask. 'Out, or I crack this empty vessel on thine own!'

As 'tis with all jesters, Gropenut knew never when the folly had outstayed its welcome. And yet I confess I was pleased by these visits of Genoa's clown, for the fellow beliked me, and gave oft, if not good counsel, good intelligence of all the high gossip of Genoa's court.

On this morn of which I speak, he came more seemly, and told me there was one without that desired converse with me, but who would not enter into Genoan territory to unfold himself. 'Then must it be one from Venice,' said I, casting swift on my clothes, for I hoped for a message from my Jenny.

'Aye, sage, 'tis Herman, doorman to Venice, that awaits thee. And sith thou hast dubbed me catamite upon occasion, and most unjustly, I must ask what commerce thou couldst wish with one that is notorious for his vices above any in the parish of St Helen's.'

'If he comes privily, Gropenut, as thou sayest, 'tis not to divulge his matter to an addlepate prattler such as thou. Avaunt, then, coney-catcher, do thou go seek out thy prey, and leave me to speak honestly to honest men.'

'Honest!' quoth Gropenut with a great leer, and gesture of perfect obscenity. 'Do thou not stretch down to pluck a coin up from the ground, is my only council; else shall Master Herman rob thee of thy scant virtue.'

I found Herman awaiting me far enough from the stew door to be deemed by any Genoan in a neutral territory, and he beckoned me to follow him without first letting out a word. And this, I confess, I was pleased enough to do: for the peahen style of Herman's dressing, and his mincing prance as he picked a dainty path among the offal of the alley, were such as to draw all eyes, and hardly fewer jests: the which, I will say, he disdained with a perfect serenity or, for aught I know, welcomed.

He drew me into an ale-house, greeted me with the courtesy that was his wont (as 'twere, my Lord of Essex to one just dubbed knight), and handed me a letter plucked from his bosom. ' 'Tis not for thee, lad, as thou mightest hope,' said he, 'nor from thy besotted Jenny. Nay, 'tis a love song of a different tune, being from Robin to his Cecil, which he desires thee to convey privily to thy master's sighing son. Albeit 'twill not ease his suspirations: for sith I have steamed it ope for closer perusal (a holding to the light not sufficing, for 'tis folded, I wiss, into an octavo), I find our Robin beseeches thy Cecil to master his vain ardours; and though he promises honest friendship of true cousins, he denies the fond hopes that languishing Cecil hath of his more ardent favours.'

'Then may thou, Herman, hope to step into the breach from which gallant Robin withholds his fire.'

'Into the breeches, rather! But nay, in troth, Aubrey: for a downy duck like Cecil I confess I sigh not. Now, were it Robin, or e'en, in an extremity, the pock-marked lout Aubrey . . .'

'Sigh in vain, Herman. For in all troth, in any extremity I would seek out my mother's nanny-goat ere thee!'

'Being country born as thou art, I doubt it not. Three generations will not suffice to wipe the dung off all thy foul rustic progeny, and embellish them with some dim tincture of a courtly urban grace.'

'Why, Herman! Art thou then thyself of a London parentage since the time of the first Tudors?'

Here Herman gave me a coy smile, and crafty, and pushing up his face (that was painted, albeit discreetly) close into mine, he whispered, 'I shall reveal to thee, Aubrey, what none other knows – save, I wean, every gossip in St Helen's. And that is, I am a Kentish lad, and country-born like thee.'

At this I confess I was surprised, for Herman had all the gloss of a great city corruption, or so it had seemed to my ill-tutored eyes. 'How came it then,' I said to him, 'that thou art today the very paragon of the perfect city popinjay?'

He quaffed a sip, with his eyes rolling in the air, as if consulting both his memory and my own understanding, then said, 'I am in troth the very creation of my beloved Kit.'

'Herman, thou speakest to me in riddles.'

'Aye.' He paused a long moment, then continued, 'Thou knowest, Aubrey, that I was once an actor – that is, a boy actor in the theatre?'

'Who knows it not?'

'True – it is not for want of my boasting in the matter. Well, now – perpend. He who first won my country favours when I came to London as a lad, and he who then launched me like a meteorite upon the stage, until I became, for a brief while, the cynosure of lordlings as of groundlings, was this same Kit: or Christopher, that departed this poor world, which wept for him, but six years since, almost to the day.'

'But who is this Kit, or Christopher?'

Herman sighed, as if at a child that asks why the sky is blue, and then intoned, while gazing with sealed eyes and in a rapture, 'Who ever loved that loved not at first sight?'

'Why, none,' said I.

'Thou findst it apt?'

'Aye, marry: so felt I when I first clapt eyes on Jenny.'

'Thou! Jenny! Aye . . . Well, puddinghead, the words were first writ, and emprinted this last year, of another couple, illustrious also, named Hero and Leander. And he who writ them was this same Christopher, also called (as is well known to all that are literate save thee), Marlowe.'

'I know not this name.'

'Poor Kit, how would he groan did he but know he was unknown to Aubrey!'

'Beshrew me, Herman, but thou must be patient with me,

prithee. Be a kind nurse to mine ignorance, and swaddle my scant learning.'

Here Herman eyed me gravely, and declared; 'Christopher Marlowe was the richest ornament of our language that was, is, or e'er shall be.'

'And he wrote plays . . .?'

'Aye, marry he did: and I acted in 'em.'

'As a boy actor.'

'Boy, stripling, juvenile – have it as thou wilt.'

'Why ceased thou so to do?'

'Because of two deaths, Aubrey: one of sweet Kit, that was my patron (besides being my lover and, I may add, though thou believe me not, my brother also), and then because my stones fell, my beard sprouted, and my exquisite piping treble expired into a basso.'

'With which thou couldst no longer play at women.'

'E'en so.'

I pondered. 'But why not, become a man, act one?'

He shook his head sadly. 'So mightst thou think, Aubrey, but so doth it fall out never. For consider. A boy of thine age, or little less, or little more, is forced up by skill and husbandry of the actors that instruct him, into the portrayal of some heroine; but when his voice cracks, and he is fitted for this no longer, he is once more an unripe thing for the grander parts of hero: he cannot, I mean, be princess in January, and king in June. Besides which, the grown actors covet the heroic parts themselves, and permit boys to play heroine less by the profundity of their art, than by the peculiarity of their voices.'

'Then Herman,' said I, thinking upon this. 'The life of a boy actor is a short one.'

'Shorter, Aubrey, than a maid's. For she has scarce emerged from girlhood, than she is deflowered, and a maid no longer. So was it with us. From boy zeros, we soared giddily into infinities: cherished, applauded, and admired. From this pinnacle we tumbled back, upon a trick of nature, into a nothingness and oblivion from which there is no leaping back.'

'How long, then, Herman, this brief glory?'

'At most, child, three years: aye, though we knew it not, we had but three years to play.'

It was so much the habit of Herman to say e'en 'Good morrow' with a vast complexity of gesture, expression, and intonation, that for the most I discounted the exaggerations of his excess. But now I could see he was not playing tragedy, but feeling it; and indeed, the fellow wept, and not actor's tears. So believing the best sympathy is silence, I called for more ale, and embarked upon a false quarrel with a neighbour anent joggling upon mine arm, or some such folly. From this I was recalled by Herman, who was now blowing his long nose with a cambric, yet smiling, like the sun on an April day.

'Pardon me, fair Aubrey of the bepocked and lurid countenance,' said he, 'for playing on my heartstrings in thy presence, which I know renders me more tedious than is habitual.'

'Play on, Herman,' said I. 'Thou art my friend.'

'Aye, marry, I believe it: if a friend be he who supports his comrade's burden uncomplainingly. But no matter: do thou say on, if thou hast further matter in thee for my interrogation; and have no fear now to dismay me.'

'Then my thanks, Herman, and I would ask thee this: in a company of actors, how many?'

'Of all species? In round numbers, thirty: of which shareholders (that is, joint partners in all theatrical effects such as dress, instruments, plays, and theatre itself if there be any), rather less than half; then some dozen junior actors, not yet fledged partners; then the boys – let us say three to five, accordingly. Thus, if the play be about Amazons, there would be more; if about monks, fewer.'

'I may speak again of Master Marlowe?'

'Speak on.'

'Beside him, who else has written plays?'

Here Herman threw up his hands, as if I had asked how many clusters in the firmament. 'First, lad,' said he, 'I would say that there is none *beside* Marlowe, who was verily one sun among the planets; but others would tell thee this is an ill-judged affection of mine own, so I may pluck out some others among legions for thy sage consideration.' He paused. 'Though God wot,' he said, ''tis like telling thee which high road out of London: for this depends on whither thou wouldst journey; and likewise, which poets writ the seemliest, is in truth a matter for the inclination of thine own heart and mind.

'Howsoever, like Paris twixt his Goddesses, we must choose; and sith he should cast the apple upon one of three several ladies, let us, for the sake of sweet simplicity, pluck also three out of the multitude. Well, there is Marlowe, as I have said; and of whom no man can speak more fittingly than he did, in lines that are imperishable. Then there is Jonson, baptised Benjamin, but called Ben, that is much sprung into favour these last years; and indeed, sprung out of it, at least in the estimation of the Council; for but two years since, when he wrote, with another, a satire named *The Isle of Dogs* (that was performed over at the *Swan*), he was clapt with his players into the Marshalsea.

'Of our third deity deserving of the golden apple, I speak more in justice than by love: for while many cherish him, and some exceedingly, I find him tedious and inept; and he is called Shakespeare, baptised William. True, he has writ poems also, on themes amorous and tragic, that want not melody, though of a tinkling kind, or else o'er sonorous, like the two extreme pipes of a church organ. But as for his plays, these are either histories, of incomparable tedium (with I know not how many legions of interminably prattling noblemen), or else comedies of the lighter sort, pretty enough for an idle afternoon, but lacking substance, and besides filled with complexities of speech and action, so that few may scarce know who is who, or which word what. Three small triumphs I must allow him, though. He wrote a pretty piece about two lovers of thine age, although Italian, called Romeo, as 'twere Aubrey, and Juliet, his Jenny. This lacks not fire, and has in't one excellent writ part, that of an old nurse, which I would fain have played, and indeed sought to, but he would have none of me. He wrote also a pastoral-nocturnal anent divers Greek fairies, that hath also pretty passages in it, and a stout clown's part, Bottom, that actors love, because it can e'er command cacklings from the more besotted portion of the groundlings. (In this also I hoped to play the part of Queen – I mean of Athens, not of the fairies; but was cast out at the first reading, when they said I wanted in regality). And then it must be allowed that out of all the porridge-pot miasma of those unendurable historical things aforesaid, there did emerge Falstaff, of whom e'en thou hast surely heard; and for this creation its creator is greatly praised. Yet I think wrongly; for by the invention of Sir John, there is no art, only copying of nature; sith thou hast but to look around St Helen's – and indeed, inside this very pot-house – to see a thousand of such noisy, tedious fellows.'

'And what manner of men are they, those who write plays? I mean of what station, region, understanding?'

'Aubrey,' said he, nuzzling into his ale, 'thou shouldst be chief inquisitor of the Star Chamber, appointed to unlock secrets from reluctant breasts. Put then upon thy rack, I would say this. Most writers of plays proceed from the universities: as from Oxford, Peele, Lyly, Lodge; or Cambridge, mighty Marlowe, Nashe and Greene.'

'This Greene is called Robert?'

'The same.'

'I have read his book of coney-catching, Herman.'

'Oh, and thou canst read, Aubrey! But read rather his plays; for in the catching of coneys, he has but little to instruct thee.'

'Yet I would fain speak with him, being my preceptor.'

'Then must thou in paradise, for he is shuffled off some eight years since in a sad sloven fashion, namely an ale-house argument, such as thou hast discreetly undertaken with thy fair neighbour here.'

'And thy two other chief writers, Herman, besides Marlowe: they are also learned men?'

'Jonson assuredly, who beside being a writer and an actor (though in this last, o'er bombastick for my inclination), is also a deep scholar. The other, no: for this Shakespeare is a rustic fellow, out of Worcestershire or some such rural desart, who lacks learning; and indeed, poor Robert, ere his death, reproached him for this, and rightly. For there is about his lines a sort of pert country flavour, pretty in its way, but lacking substance and, above all, gravity.'

At this, looking grave himself, Herman arose, and first fidgeting with his clothing and his hair (that I suspected to be a wig), bestowed upon me a smile of multiple bedazzlement, touched my shoulder saying, 'Forget not Robin's letter, child,' and then made off, sailing between the tables like the royal barge, that is admired by all.

II

Cecil came by but rarely to his father's stews, both by inclination (I mean the lack of it), and because the Genoa Doge, as I have said, wished to hoist Master Cecil out of the world of his own infamy; in which Doge Genoa differed but little from lordlings of our age, whose burnished arms would scarce bear any scraping, lest the tarnish underneath stand clear revealed. I must therefore carry Robin's letter to him at Genoa's mansion in the City, before the nightly rumpus in St Helen's claimed my duty.

Doge Genoa dwelt in the very heart, or fortress, of that most discreet and worthy portion of the City, fast by Aldgate, and within the walls. Here are not found, indeed, the greater palaces of commerce round Guildhall, but houses whose very modesty is a sort of ostentation; since all know well that, if some are richer than the householders here, few are, and far more are poorer. 'Tis also a part where dwell many foreign-born, perhaps because of its nearness to the river, who crouch about London's skirts, hoping she will drop guineas; nor are the Londoners offended by their presence, for there is a confraternity of merchants that confounds all realms and language: their sweet secret tongue being that of gold, which they speak one to another by swift clinkings.

To see Doge Genoa's house – trim, solid and fine-flavoured – you would ne'er suppose its riches proceeded from trulls and drabs, but from harvests of the most sober sort; nor think its owner to be other than some citizen that would be alderman one day. True, if you plucked at the bell, as I did, you might stand amazed that a householder so worthy had a doorman of such peculiarity; for this was

Breakbone Charles, chief custodian of Doge Genoa's person.

'How now, whoreson!' cried this fellow. 'Hast thou come to try a fall with me?'

'Breakbone,' said I, 'I know thou couldst crack every bone in my poor body, as a farmer chews larks' wings. Forbear, therefore!' I cried, for the lout had enfolded me in a wrestler's grip that near snapped my ribs.

'Thou art well punished, Aubrey,' said he, releasing me to the rubbing of my chest, 'for thou knowest the Doge beliketh it not that any of his servitors approach his house.'

'I bring tidings for Cecil, Breakbone.'

'A letter? Yield it to me.'

'Nay!' cried I, backing the distance needed to start a run. 'Either thou summon him hither, as is thy duty, or I carry it away, and he, not receiving it, will know whose intermeddling he must blame.'

Perceiving he would not catch me if he ran, and fearing to leave his duty at the door, this Hercules shook his great ham at me, and slammed inside. I waited, and soon out stepped Cecil.

''Tis from Robin?' said he.

'Even.'

'Hold it yet, and I shall walk with thee, for I wish none to spy it in the house.'

When we had turned three corners, Cecil plucked the letter from my hand, and stood reading it all unaware of jostlers, as if alone upon the moon; then sighed, folded it, and laid it to his breast. Till spying me, as if I was now entered into his world, he said, 'Thou sawest him?'

'Aye, Cecil: we played swords.'

'Would he would pierce me too, and not only my heart.'

I answered naught to this; but saying the hour was

forward, and I must to St Helen's, I was starting off, when he said, 'Aubrey, I would walk further with thee.'

'Come, then, amble!' And we set off.

After a silence, and wishing both to quell plaints and answer curiosity, I said to him, 'Pray tell me, Cecil: how can it be that thy father, the Genoa Doge, can bestride worlds so opposite without a tumble?'

'Well mayest thou wonder, as I have, indeed. But to all questions there is some sort of answer, and I may offer thee these three. The first is gold: which, in suffisance, will buy anything, or most; and power and protection, certainly. Next, my father, though a rough and hard man, hath spirit, besides courage. And last – and this I surmise more than truly know – he is himself in process of an alchemy that has transformed many rogues into men of honour: to wit, he is slow sinking his affairs in Bishopsgate, and fast swelling those he hath here in the City. So take warning, Aubrey; for I prophesy that within five years, if not before, St Helens will be for him a memory, and yet another honest merchant will be born.'

'And his fair son, a knight, or courtier.'

'Then shalt thou be my page,' quoth he, smiling at last. 'But nay, 'tis as I say: and there is other matter. Besides that my father craves safety, which is wise, and honour, which for him is folly, he has further reason to abandon Bishopsgate. Thou knowest, Aubrey, that within the City, which is governed if not entirely by Puritans, at least by the most decorous of Anglicans, there must be no rejoicing: I mean in public, for what happens oft behind these frowning walls, is another story. Thus is it that all playhouses must lie without; and as for entertainment of a more vicious sort, which is my father's skill, the more so.

'Now, to the compass there are but four points. So standing in the City, if we look westward, there is the Court, government and cathedrals: ill-fitted places for my father's commerce, though I doubt not the nobility have their panders, as the people have my father. To the north is mostly country: orchards, dairies, farms, with fair harvest for milk and turnips, but an ill one from vices. East, therefore, among tenements and hovels, my father, and my uncle Venice, built their empires as young men, and prospered greatly.

'But now' (here he gripped my arm and swung me round), 'we turn south, and gaze across the river. Aubrey, thou art not yet here a year, yet hast thou not noticed how the south bank grows and flourishes into a riot of places for public entertainment?'

'Why, even.'

'Aye. In my father's commerce, the south rises, the east declines. Were he young today, I doubt not thither he would hie him. But besides he tires of this business and, as I say, seeks others, there are already firm established in the south empires as potent, if not more so, as his own. To conquer St Helen's, he won many scars, on both his skin and soul. Though not yet old for life's battles, he wants none of this one.'

'And his brother Venice?'

Here Cecil glanced at me, looking cautiously, as did ever a Genoa man when questioned upon Venice, or aboutways. 'I may say this to thee,' quoth he at last. 'The quarrel twixt my father and mine uncle, which I lament as, indeed, does my cousin Robin – for we recall the days when these brothers were true brothers – is due to a principle that may be called historical: namely, that when kingdoms rise, they form alliances; but when they decline, they fight. In short, not to speak disrespectfully, 'tis a case of two curs snapping o'er a meatless bone. When St Helen's flourished, there was no argument, or little; now that it crumbles, there are a million, yet with but one real cause.'

'And thine uncle Venice? How shall he trim his sails to this ill wind?'

'By sailing to a magic island of his own invention: I mean, while my father sets out on fresh voyages, my uncle will sink into the comfort of his plundered monastery. Or would do, for here's the rub. Two men of sense would say, "Come, let us divide peaceably what remains, and part upon our several ways." But because of this curse of Cain, they battle, being brothers.' He stopped, for we were nearing Bishopsgate. 'Cousins,' he said, 'are wiser and speak sweeter. Robin and I could settle this difference in an afternoon.'

'Thou wilt not, Cecil, step in a while and drink thy father's wine? For surely, a prince should visit his kingdom sometimes.'

'A Doge, Aubrey, is elective, not hereditary. Yet I will go with thee, and remind myself whence came my fair doublet and my fat fees to the Inns of Court.'

'Do thou: for 'tis too early yet for any roisterers to molest thy person or thy conscience.'

So we stepped in, where everyone was preparing, in a tired ill humour, for the later plucking of the gulls. Cecil was greeted fairly, yet with some part of contempt, for they liked him that he was not as his father, and despised him for the same reason. And his tale of these brothers quarrelling brought to my mind those other sons of Adam, Allan and Bully Noll.

'Pray tell me,' said I to him, when we were served and seated. 'In matters of religion, we live in times when all men must walk warily, like a cat upon a cord inside a kennel. My own simple is in silence or, if speech, agreement with the last that preaches at me. Now, in this matter of thy father and thine uncle, how stand they in their obediences, professed or actual?'

'They twain? Why, their great faith is Mammon, and their high priests, themselves. But if thou speakest of what tinctures they assume as being necessary for the advancement of their purses, if not salvations, I would say that, in the great arc that extends from Papacy to Puritanism, they stand poised somewhere in the middle, or wobble rather: both faithful followers of whatever doctrine the Queen presently decrees, yet my father inclining slightly down the puritanical slope, and my uncle towards the papal. In brief, they are Anglicans of the Low and High denominations.'

'And he, Cecil, who has slipped right down into either extremity: I mean to Rome or Zion. He must be a great saint or a great fool?'

'Or a creature of habit, Aubrey; Papists in particular, who cannot change faiths like coats, or will not. Or else, mayhap, one of obstinacy: for men will die rather than admit to error, not of doctrine, but of opinion.'

'Whatever the cause, the danger is no less.'

'Aye, marry: for we live in an age where martyrs are made easy.'

There are those that can enter anywhere without that their presence, however high their state, be much marked; and others that stir up a great surge and eddy, like a galleon in a pool; and such a one was Bully Noll who came in now, spied me, and lumbered over scattering turmoil and confusion. He gazed haughtily on Cecil, as though to say, 'How darest thou exist, numbskull?' and sat heavily beside me without apology for his intrusion, or explanation; preserving a fierce silence, as though to tell Cecil he should be off from society so illustrious.

But Cecil, in despite his maidishness, was a cucumber cool creature, beside being his father's son, and he said courteously to Bully Noll, 'Good even, sir: is there aught that I may have them bring to you?'

'Aye, sir,' said Noll. 'Some fellow that will carry you away.'

'For that, God hath given me two legs,' said he. 'But they are weary yet, and until they have recovered their full vigour, I shall continue, by your leave, to plant my arse where it already nestles cosily.'

As is ever the way with bullies, that advance too quick and then retreat too far, honest Noll now illumined his ill features with a slapt-on smile, and cried, 'Marry, my pardon of you, young sir: but I would hold converse privily with Aubrey.'

'Then shall I yield him up to you,' said Cecil, 'when you have honoured me with a toast to his good fortune.' And without waiting for a reply from Noll, he called over the potman for a bottle.

A peculiarity of catamites (as I might call Cecil, though more by his youth, than inner inclination) is that the iller a man treat them, the greater their affection: at least if, besides insolent, the fellow be also lusty, howe'er ill-favoured; and I could perceive a waxing blink of admiration behind Cecil's lashes for this nasty Noll.

'Thou comest oft hither?' he now asked the Bully coyly.

'Do thou ask Aubrey that!' cried Noll, with a great horse's laugh. 'And he will tell thee the gold I squander here keeps that wastrel son to Genoa in his dainty linens.'

'Thou knowest his son Cecil?' Cecil said.

'Aye marry, no: but when I do so, I shall offer him a tumble if he but persuade his father to make me freeman of his divers stews.'

'Stews? Who speaks of stews? For these are palaces!' cried a harsh voice, and we rose to see great Doge Genoa had stole up on us. 'And what makest thou here, son? For thou knowest thou art forbid.'

''Twas that I chanced on Aubrey.'

'Chance not on pot-boys, rather chance thee without and hie thee home. And thou, varlet, to thy work, which is not to idle with my custom.'

'Well, he was invited to us,' quoth Bully Noll.

'Thou art here to invite harlots, Noll, not knaves. Thou hast, I vow, all thy old father's insolence: that stayed in my stews as though he were mine host.'

'If you liked not my father, old Sir Ronald, then you liked well his guineas.'

'Better than thine, for they fell freer. Come, Cecil, away!'

Noll filled his glass, and glowered after them. 'And that is indeed Genoa's son?' said he.

'Aye, even.'

Bully looked half abashed, then let out another of his donkey brays. 'Marry come up!' cried he. 'An he were willing, I would have sealed the bargain in an upstairs room.'

'An he were willing,' said I. 'But Noll, time presses on, I am soon to duty, and I doubt you have wished to see me for the glance of my fair eyes.'

'Nay, even so,' said he, lowering his voice and hoisting his shoulders over the table till he could spit more conveniently into mine ear. 'Thou rememberest thy promise, Aubrey?'

'Anent the priest? Aye; and I remember thine anent the gold.'

'Fear not; and tonight I need thy service.'

'In the small hours, then; for I do not play here, Noll, like thee, but earn my keep.'

'That I shall order with Master Beauty, and for gold he will release thee, and Doll Pretty.'

'To what end?'

'Thou must, Aubrey, to Wapping, by the river; and there meet one that awaits thee, in an inn named the *Twin*

Hemispheres, to wit a mariner, called Lucifer, who hath tidings for me anent (speaking soft) a man of God coming in upon this tide.'

'And how shall I know this mariner?'

'He is a blackamoor.'

'I have not yet seen one.'

'Nay? Then shalt thou this night; and fear not, he will not eat thee.'

'Doll he may – or some other. Why must she come also?'

'That thy converse with Lucifer should stir up no prying of the spies: who, seeing thee and she, will suppose some carnal commerce is toward.'

'Thou hast planned well, Noll.'

'Besides I am no fool, this is most needful; for the enterprise, I do not hide from thee, is perilous. Now, hearken. If Lucifer hath for thee but tidings, bring them to me at Blackfriars, and I shall reward thee; if, further, he hath with him this very Man' (he stopped and stared at me), 'do thou also bring him, and I shall reward thee double.'

'Aye. Noll, an I be caught at this (or he), thou goest free, and I, mayhap, hang.'

'Aubrey, an thou bring me not him, nor tidings, then I keep my gold. Thou art yet free: choose.'

'And Doll?'

'Yield her to Lucifer, an she cry not out at his swart skin; if she so cry, bastinade her rump and despatch her to Beauty in St Helen's. But in whichever fall, let her not know what is toward.'

I thought for a long while: of Noll whom I mistrusted for his spirit, and his brother Allan for his wit; also of the gold; but most of my unblemished neck. Then thought I too of Jenny, and my hopes to marry her, and set up with her in some commerce of sufficient honesty.

'Noll,' said I, 'I will do what thou requirest of me. But understand me well' (and here I looked hard at him). 'I am young, poor, and unprotected; but I am no nothing. God willing, or the Devil, I shall not fail thee; but be warned if thou shouldst fail me, in any fair particular, and I survive it, I am well instructed in the use of daggers.' And I drew out the hilt from my breast beneath his nose.

He frowned mightily, then threw me a toothed smile and said. 'Aye, Aubrey. Do thou fetch Doll.'

If women were e'er soldiers, they would ne'er fight a battle – unless, that is, the rival commander would put forward the engagement till they were full accoutred. For do a man but say to a woman, 'Light of my life, let we step out a pace,' and she must embark upon a great flurry of disrobing and regarmenting and adornment of her countenance. I swear it was near an hour before Doll Pretty stood at the stew door, with a look as to say, 'Now marry, Aubrey, why dost thou linger? Let us away!' So with this great lump of concupiscence upon mine arm, I set off at last from Bishopsgate towards the river.

Doll Pretty, like a girl freed from school, was all a-chatter. 'Now tell me, prithee, Aubrey,' said she, 'thinkest thou the world will come soon to an end?'

'Why, assuredly, upon the Judgement Day.'

'Nay, nay: I mean in some six months or more, when the old year leaps into 1600.'

'This should end everything?'

'So say many and, in particular, the witches.'

'Why! They have witches here in London? I thought 'twas our country privilege.'

'Not so, Aubrey – though a man, pardee, might suppose as much. But know that we women – and, in especial, those given to my calling – must of necessity oft frequent certain goodwives that have science to restrain fertility: without whose cares, indeed, we poor drabs would be perpetual nursemaids. Well, of these worthy dames, I tell you, many are adepts in peculiar sorceries.'

'Let them beware the hangman and his faggots.'

'Aye, marry; but with us their mystery is sacredly secure.'

'And these shrews foretell an apocalypse on New Year's Day? Well, Pretty: hear rather the magician Aubrey; who can tell thee of a surety that on the last day of December it will hail, and on the first of January, snow, let the New Year carry any cypher the priest pleases.'

'Aye, but the witches say . . .'

'A pest upon them, Doll! Let them corrupt thy fair belly as they wish, but if they disjoin thy slender wits, why! they should be clapt into Bedlam, and thee also, which is in troth convenient to our stew.'

'Heaven preserve them! For we bawds would be but hens dropping eggs continually without them. Which brings me to our journey, child, of which Beauty gave me no particular, save that I must meet a seaman, that cannot stray far from his ship and so come to us. What manner of man is he, or knowst thou not?'

'Aye marry, I do: he is a blackamoor.'

'Jesus have mercy!' cried Doll Pretty, standing fast in the street like Lot's wife turned into salt.

'Come now, Doll,' said I, tugging at her, and kissing her melon cheek. 'Thou that hast sustained valiantly every hot oaf in Epping willst not fear the dark arms of Africa.'

'But a blackamoor!' cried she.

'Well, Pretty,' said I laughing, 'I doubt not when he sees thee, and thy great mountainous sweet person, his terror will exceed thine own.'

'Terror?' cried she. 'Who speaks of terror? I would have thee know, Aubrey, I have lain with Breakbone Charles, the wrestler; and she who can survive his elephant embraces need fear none.'

'Well spoken, Pretty, like the honest English harlot that thou art! And bethink thee further: do the fellow displease thee, thou hast but to say him nay, and I shall defend thee with my dagger if he molest thee. Yet remember: be thou coy, so will Beauty's purse.'

'Aye,' said Doll Pretty. 'Let us tarry here no further.'

The Romans, 'tis said, built London because they met a river; and up its waters since, have sailed ships innumerable. So that this city, that seems so much a place set on dry land, is more truthfully a great harbour. Yet to know this, you must leave behind London Bridge, and the great frowning Tower (that I ne'er passed, nor any Londoner, I wot, without a shudder), and proceed into the port, that is a different world. For here mariners are kings; and just as the citizen feels all arsy-varsy in the country, so must he in this acreage of mast and cordage. And indeed, unless he be armed or, better, in good company, he must take care, especially by night. For the streets become decks; and beside the rampaging of the sailors, there is the press-gang to be considered. Yet with Doll Pretty, I feared little; for I vow she could fell an ox, and had a further precious art of ruling the quarrelsome and besotted with a skill any man might envy.

We found the *Twin Hemispheres* in the Highway, that is chief thoroughfare of this watery realm; and if Rome be full of churches, I swear Wapping outdoes it in its quantity of inns. We entered, and found this was a sedater place than the generality, with older mariners of substance, many being captains, intent more on nautical affairs than those habitual to sailors, which are grog and wenches. Doll Pretty, who sniffed this faster even than did I, assumed instantly (she who could out-bawl the town crier, and fling her skirts over the rooftops) a decorous mien, and matronly; and laid her great arse upon a bench like an abbess in a pew for her devotions.

We called for brandy (Noll being host at our festivities), and I asked the potman were Lucifer, the blackamoor, expected. Aye presently, said he; and there (pointing) was his chair habitual. So we quaffed and waited; Doll Pretty glancing round about, although discreetly, with that apt eye by which a bawd can e'er unbreech all men and see how it lies with them, or otherwise.

I, meanwhile, was pawed at by an old ringed mariner that asked me, did I wish to buy a parakeet; to which I made answer that Doll sufficed me, which earned me a cackle and the offer of some wine. 'Aye marry,' he said, pouring me a glass. 'I can hood my bird at night, but for woman there is no cover that brings silence.'

'Except man,' said I.

'Beshrew me, e'en so they gabble,' cried this ancient. 'Which is thy ship?'

'None, sir: I come here to meet one of your fraternity.'

'Well, here's to thee, landsman! For i' faith, though 'tis true no man be man that be not sailor, yet do you keep the ports warm for us, and your wives ready.'

'Aye, and gladly. Whence come you to this harbour?'

'Out of Ireland whither, like so many, I have conveyed the armies of my Lord of Essex: whom I know well, for I served with him in the Island voyage, two years since, to the Azores. On a ship called *Garland*, my Lord Southampton commanding, who is now also massacring Papists as Captain to Earl Essex.'

'Fair commanders, ancient, and fair ships?'

'As to the *Garland*, 'twas no bed of roses, I assure thee; and my Lords of Essex and Southampton, though gallant warriors, were but soldiers, in truth, bedecked in colours of the sea. For none was a sailor like the greatest that commanded me, which was Ralegh, on the Guyana voyage: whom e'en a landsman must know to be the rarest navigator since Drake.'

'In Guyana, saw you blackamoors?'

'Aye, a-plenty; and Caribe Indians to boot. With the first, I have sailed in ships often, and they are cunning seamen, and hot-blooded in a quarrel.'

As he spoke, Doll Pretty was pulling at my arm, and turning, I saw him who must be Lucifer: a great gaunt fellow in a swashbuckling attire, yet with a steady mien, that gazed about the room from large dark eyes. I rose and, approaching him, said, 'Art thou Lucifer? For I am Aubrey, sent hither by Master Noll.'

The blackamoor surveyed me from his great height, as a wolf gazing on a coney, then placed each hand upon my shoulders, with a grip locking like a thumb-screw, and said, 'Boy, I belike thy face, for it remindeth me of the pitted cocoa-nut.'

'My thanks, Lucifer,' said I, disengaging my poor limbs from his embrace. 'And wilt thou honour me, and my fair friend Doll Pretty there, with thy company to void a flagon?'

'Aye readily,' said the blackamoor, peering at Pretty like a fox on a Christmas goose; where she sat simpering, flashing her lashes like a watchman's lanthorn.

At the table, with the grandiloquence of a Don, he seized on the Doll's plump paw and raised it to his monstrous lips, there to bestow a hot wet kiss upon it, with a smack like a muskatoon; and heaving his huge bulk into a chair beside her, he released not her hand, but clutched at the other, which he laid upon his oaken thigh, nuzzling her neck the while. 'Thou hast a scent,' said he at last, 'as sweet as the four warm winds of Africa.'

Doll Pretty, who was unused to courtesies of this specie,

but rather to 'Unfrock, trull, and that speedily,' beamed mightily at his words and, taking up his huge ham hand, planted upon its interior, or pinker side, a lingering buss, saying to him, 'This comes with mine heart, good Master blackamoor.'

And now, though I called for wine, and essayed, time without number, to insinuate my poor person into their amorous converse, these twain might have been Eve and Adam solitary in Eden, for aught they recked of the *Twin Hemispheres* and its company. Till at last, determined to cut down to the pith of our purpose here, I plucked at the blackamoor's great arm (that was by now become, like Ralegh, an explorer of realms unknown), and cried, 'Good Master Lucifer: the Doll yearneth for thee, as I can see; and I believe thy fine feeling is reciprocal. May we not, therefore, step aboard thy barque, where such sweet purposes may be consummated more conveniently?'

At this they both glared at me, like a bride and groom whose wedding is disturbed by some varlet crying out her belly was made swollen not by him, but him, then shook themselves, like mastiffs after a delicious quarrel, and smiling, rose to their feet, with arms still laced about each other as a bundle of magician's snakes. 'Aye, boy!' cried out the blackamoor, in tones that made several start up, and reach for the pommels of their swords. 'Aye, I shall escort you thither, thou to quaff rum, and I nectar' (gazing on Pretty's burning chops).

'Lead on, then Lucifer,' said I.

In the street, though Pretty hath the weight of a malt vat, he near lifted her along, so that her feet dangled across the cobbles. And after many a twist and turn, as if in a very maze (and he stopping at each corner to lather Doll with a lingering and noisesome buss), we smelt salt, and came into a pool, or dock, where lay several small vessels, lit dim by lanthorns. Onto one of these we clambered by a plank, he lifting Pretty up like a sack of swedes, her huge thighs naked to the moon. Then stumbling into a small room, or cabin, on the after deck, he laid her down, uncorked a bottle with his teeth, handed it to me, and began once more to slobber with his darling.

But Aubrey, mindful of his duty (and his gold), and fearing the ship might circumnavigate the globe ere Lucifer and Doll desisted, grew fierce now and, tugging at the blackamoor, I cried, 'Good Lucifer, forbear a while: but grant me one moment for my task, for thou hast till dawn for thine!' Whereat, complaining mightily, and with a fond glowering at Doll, he seized my hand, led me to a dark trap cut in the deck beside his cabin, and crying, 'Down the ladder with thee, lad!' made off to his more pressing business.

With a prayer to St Aubrey (if there be one), I clambered cat-like down into the gloom, hearing naught but the soft slap of Thames upon the outer hull. Till after what seemed a vast descent for so small a vessel, my foot slithered onto planks, and I peered about me, one hand still upon the ladder, and the other on my knife.

'*Soyez le bienvenu*,' said a sepulchral voice.

Marry come up! thought I. I have been sent to garner in not just a priest, but a Frenchman to boot, that are our enemies, or were but recently. But here my prayer to St Aubrey was answered or, more truly, 'twas St Martin that rescued me, for my old schoolmaster and step-father had grounded me in fair Latin, and with this I was able to make some explanation with the Voice, whose face and form I knew not yet; and I conveyed to him that which a priest would well understand, to wit that our first steps must be upward, out of this hold onto the deck, where we might determine matters further and more comfortably.

Upon the deck, in the pale light of the cloudy moon scudding over Wapping, I had further reason for dismay, which was that this priest (whom I could descry to be young, mayhap but ten years my senior) was decked out in all the panoply of priesthood! A pest on conspirators! thought I. Have they no wit to disguise this man of God in habillements more profane? Well, honest Aubrey shall not stroll through the streets on the arm of one whose dress would summon about our ears every spy and constable in London!

So telling him to wait a while, I tiptoed to Lucifer's abode (whence grunts and caterwaulings were from this distance audible), and peeping in, perceived, as I hoped, the blackamoor's garments scattered on the floor. Insinuating a hand deftly in, I seized on these unobserved, and carried them back to the reverend gentleman: whom I had great labour in persuading (my Latin stumbling like a lame horse) into substituting for his own: which, when he did, I bundled up, wrapped round a marlin spike, and dropt into the Thames.

Having now upon my hands and conscience a priest, a Frenchman, and one whose breeches dangled to his ankles, I decided a wherry would be our safest conveyance to Blackfriars. So closeting the priest inside an alley, and conjuring him, upon threat of excommunication, not to budge an inch, I set off for a neighbour dock, and there found some watermen, to whom I unfolded a sorry tale: which was that my master, a gentleman from Blackfriars, had visited a bawdy-house, there lost his garments, and been forced to buy others that were ill-matched; besides which misfortunes, he was so loaded up with spirit as to be near senseless. They laughed at this, and said 'twould be double fare, for beside that the hour was late, my master would surely vomit all over their neat vessel.

I returned then to Father *Français*, and warning him, in periods worthy of Master Cicero, that if he oped his mouth to say but one word, I would slit his holy gullet and leap overboard, I half carried him to the wherry, where we flung him down into the bilge, and so set off upstream. Had it not been for the sharp prick of my anxieties, I must have delighted in this voyage. For I had ne'er seen London, from the Thames, by night; and the moon kindly casting aside her cloak of clouds, the whole city lay about us as we rowed gently on, only our oars spoiling the huge silence.

At the wharf nearest to Blackfriars, I paid the men well, and thanked them, and we hoisted our bedraggled passenger up onto the planking. As they made ready to depart, the priest, to my horror, began to rain blessings on their heads by holy signs utterly forbid within our realm, and cried out, '*Soyez remerciés, mes enfants!*' But I clapt my hand over his anointing lips, seized on his arms, and with a wave of good cheer to the vanishing watermen, bundled him along some alleys to the postern in the backwards of Bowes mansion, and there rang.

A wait interminable brought Daniel, armed at all points, and calling for the watch to repel robbers. I swore violent oaths at him, and told him to fetch Noll before I climbed over the wall to slice his nose; who soon came, admitted us and, at the sight of the priest (the postern now being closed again), fell on his knees, bussed at his hand, and began gabbling prayers and incantations. But I was eager for bed, gold, and safety; and breaking rudely in upon their holy offices, though putting my soul to peril, doubtless, I seized upon Noll and shook him into some sort of sanity; whereat, emerging as a sleeper from a dream, he said, 'Aye, my thanks to thee, Aubrey: bless him, I prithee, Father!' But this was by no means to my purpose, and I cried, 'The gold, Noll, the gold! And remember thy sacred promise before the man of God!' Which recollecting (though reluctantly, so it beseemed me), he unfastened his wallet, gave to me what was promised, then fell back upon his knees. But I, thrusting the gold close to my breast beside my dagger, made Daniel let me out into the lane, and so set off to Bishopsgate: the gold jingling softly, and I thinking of Jenny, whose hair is of the same rare hue.

12

I had reflected on my commerce with the brothers Bowes, Allan and Noll, and come to this conclusion: that I could not serve both, for beside that, with time, the one would learn what I did for t'other, two brittle eggs of conspiracy sat ill packed in the one tight basket. Following inclination, I should have served Allan; but Noll had asked first, and also paid.

So like a broker laying off his petty merchandise, I decided to give Allan's work to Peter; and sought him out, therefore, at Lucy's stew with Venice, where I found them at table, and in a state almost matrimonial, that is, bickering like ducks; and on seeing me, they poured on my head a very torrent of recriminations, the one anent the other, and when I cried mercy, united to abuse me.

'Lucy, my love, and Peter my companion, have pity on poor Aubrey,' I beseeched them. 'For see: he hungers while you twain have eaten.'

At this they waxed repentant, and buried me in meat and ale, continuing their prattling battle with less ardour; which gave me occasion to observe them, and notice that Lucy grew wan with her ill trade, and was fast aging; and Peter was marked by that discontent which falls on panders that are without wine, or resignation.

'Gossip Lucy,' I said at last, 'I must confer on matters of

high state with my lord thy spouse, whom I trust thou wilt graciously yield up to me a while.'

At this she pouted, as do ever women when a man seeks to distrain their man, and with many a 'hasten home soon,' and 'tumble in no mischief,' she at last released him to me.

'Ah, women!' sighed Peter in the street – as men have said, I doubt not, e'er since Adam bemoaned Eve to Abel. 'Thou lovest Jenny, as I know well; but wait, Aubrey, till thou sharest with her not just thy heart, but bed, board and privy.'

'Thou shouldst be monk, Peter.'

'Not I: I should be Moor, and have some score packed privily in my zenana.'

I steered him towards Blackfriars and, as we walked, unfolded Allan's hope to him, of peppering the realm with Calvinistic texts; saying there would be small reward in it, yet also, I deemed, small danger; and telling him too (in part) why I forswore the mission.

'Aye, but,' said Peter, 'suppose I must hide these papers Allan gives me to sew among his faithful? At Lucy's I dare not, for beside she is a blabbermouth, for whom a secret is a thing too precious to be kept hid, but must adorn her mouth like a jewel sparkling on her breast, the seneschal of Venice, Amos, keeps constant watch on all his master's people; and comes peering and prodding at us without warning in all hours.'

'Luxury, Peter, hath not dulled thy wits.'

'Bethink thee! Sharpened, rather; for my luxury, Aubrey, is the provider's; and like the cook at a banquet, mine is toil, and only the glutton's, ease. But hearken now: would Jenny secrete the volumes for me? For I would have many a fair pretext to visit Doge Venice's domain.'

'Perchance, though I like not to stir Jenny into this sour

pudding. Yet methinks now I see a light. Robin, as thou knowest, is disciple to the sword, e'er seeking fresh prophets for instruction. And Allan, so Moses tells me, when not praying, likewise; his high hope being to serve the Swedes in some slaughter of Popish innocents. How sayest thou if I bring Allan with thee to meet Robin? For if Doge Venice's prince learns to love him, while they hack at each other's gut, would not Allan presently have pretext to bring bundles for Robin to secrete, and thou later carry to blue-nosed dissenters?'

'We can but unfold it to them for an aye or nay. Where lives Master Puritan in his earthly condition?'

'We stand before his door. Do thou await me, Peter.'

After some parley with old Moses, and assurance that Noll was locked up with his Jesuit (secreted, Moses whispered, in a gap betwixt two stairs), Allan appeared, whom I persuaded of the neatness of our plan. And indeed, his eye lighting at the mention of a sword, he fetched his, and we set off across the City; Allan all courtesy to young Peter (whom I presented as the devoutest smuggler in the realm), and his face only clouding when we passed a church, at which he would frown, mutter imprecations and fetch a great curve into the highway, so that his feet might not step on soil ruled by bishops.

At length we reached Doge Venice's chauntrey where, leaving the other two to kick their heels into better acquaintance, I first sought out Jenny; to whom I was admitted by Sad Jack, for Herman, he said, was gone by his master's leave to see a play.

'And what, boy, beside Jenny's skirts,' said Jack, 'brings thee plotting hither? For I perceive two secretive fellows loitering, that I believe are thy companions.'

'Thou seest, like the owl, excessively,' said I.

'Aye, but this bird is deemed wise by rural sages, such as thee.'

'Well, true, Jack, I have troubles; but not to o'erbrim thy topped cup of gloom, I shall not uncork them.'

'Troubles?' said he. 'Well, let me tell thee I am acquainted with them – at least their essence, if not particularity. For all troubles of mankind, Aubrey, are of three species. First, health, or lack of it; next riches, or their absence, to which I would add talent, that makes riches; and then love, or lust more usually.'

'The three segments of thy philosophy have not squared my circle, Jack. For my trouble, which I bear for another, concerns matters spiritual.'

'As of religion?'

'Even so.'

Sad Jack flung up his hands. 'To encompass these, reason and good sense are powerless,' cried he. 'Tell thy friend (who I doubt not is the moodier of the twain without) that all laws deduced painfully by mankind from centuries, are vain things beside one utterance of any believing he hears the voice of God. Prophets, Aubrey, make their own laws, and disdain nature's; which is why they are sanctified or burned.'

'Then am I in no peril of either.'

'Nay: for thee the stocks, belike, or galleys – not the martyr's flames. Go seek out Jenny, then, whose own fires, if my nose belie me not, are wrapped around a succulence of cherry pies.'

I kissed Jenny and, eating my pie (whose stones, tallied, said she loved me), told her of Allan and our intent: which she liked not, and I liked her for not liking, for my wife must be prudent in all things save adoration; yet when I showed her Noll's gold, and gave it into her safe keeping, she relented, and said I must do as I thought best: which is how a woman should answer a man ever; with this understanding, that if he fail he is to blame, and if succeed, give thanks for her good counsel.

'And Robin,' quoth I, nibbling another tart, on which Jenny had spooned cream. 'Is he at his slicing and stabbing?'

'Nay, reading, pardee, at plays. For I declare Herman hath infected him with this mummer's madness, so that his nose is e'er in a book, and his sword rusting.'

'Marry, thou shouldst not forejudge. Hast e'er seen a play?'

'But once: at the *Curtain*, by Holywell, when I was child; of which I recall naught but slumber and puking.'

'I must carry thee, Jenny, across the river, there to see one.'

'Not I, Aubrey: for all say 'tis but an assembly of snatch-pockets and sots, with pimpled gallants lifting petticoats in the sweaty press.'

'I will to Robin, then: loose not thy heart till I return, nor thy girdle neither.'

Robin greeted me and asked news of Cecil, laying aside his book, which I took up. 'This is a play?' said I.

'Nay, neither: 'tis a poem of perpetual duration, writ by one Spenser, Edmund, that died this very year.'

'But the book is well thumbed.'

'By Herman, doubtless; for see, 'tis printed some ten years since.'

'And who is this Queen Mab?'

'Our own dread sovereign, says Herman; though to my treasonable mind, she is no more fairy than is she virgin.'

'The poem pleases thee?'

'Well, Aubrey, he speaks much about a river; and as 'tis with these, that have cataracts and whirlpools to excite the senses, and also ponds and backwaters to calm them, so is it with Master Spenser: to him sometimes the heart hearkens; but oftentimes, the eyelids droop.'

Sitting beside Robin, I unfolded my thoughts to him of Allan, disguising naught, for I would rather save Robin an hour's fret, than serve Allan a twelvemonth. He hearkened in his father's pensive style, then said, 'I see no impediment. What we shall do, is lay these pages of holy disputation in the garden hut beside the nether wall. Then, if any officer or spy discover them, we may aver they were stuffed o'er the wall by some devout meddler unknown to us.'

'I may bring on Allan, then?'

'Aye, with his sword, and Peter.'

Jenny had carried out more tarts, with an infusion of citrons, and we sat in the garden neath the warm sun like four councillors. Allan who, like all Puritans I have encountered, worshipped argument, and could ne'er leave a pebble on the ground without plucking it up to turn it over, had seized on Robin's book, glared at it, sniffed like a bull scenting a dry cow, and flung it down, beruffling its pages.

'You like not poems, sir?' quoth Robin.

'There is but one: the Bible,' Allan said, as a doctor ordering physick.

'Aye,' said I, ''tis a pretty poem enow: what with Solomon and Sheba, and Susannah's wanton Elders, and slim Jonathan dallying with David . . .'

'Fie, fie!' cried Allan. 'I speak of the parts heavenly, not profane.'

'Why, sir!' cried Robin. 'In the Bible, say you, there be profanities?'

'Nay, nay, cried Allan, waxing apoplectick. 'My meaning was . . . well, come, sir!' cried he (a smile breaking through his frowns). 'Let us engage with arms, rather than lips!' And plucking out his sword, he beckoned Robin to the tilting place, where they engaged with a great flash and flurry.

'He fights well,' said Peter, 'for a youth matched to a man.'

'So, Peter, must we ever with our elders, lest they squeeze us with their supposed sagacity.'

'And he wields a pretty foil, with his fair limbs – ah, touched!' he cried, as Robin pierced a point.

'"Fair limbs", Peter,' quoth I. 'And what is this, prithee? Hast thou so swift forgotten Lucy when thy lascivious eyes embrace young Master Red-breast?'

'Mock me not, Aubrey; for thou knowest well how, in Epping, simpering Simon sighed for me in vain. Nay, 'tis somewhat other. Thou, Aubrey, as I, art country bred; but thanks to old Martin, thy preceptor, thou art no addlepate. And thus it is, that when I encounter one of mine own age, as Robin, that hath learning, then feel I woefully diminished.'

'Learn then, good Peter! For thou hast a ripe brain that lacks but the dung of knowledge.'

'Learn beside Lucy, sayest thou? Pore over books while she screams out for bed, wine, cards, and bed again?'

'Leave her then, Peter.'

'Lucy?'

'Aye. She is not, let me tell thee, like Elizabeth our Queen, the one only of her species in all London.'

'Wouldst thou leave Jenny?'

'Never.'

'Why?'

'I love Jenny, Peter.'

'And I Lucy.'

'Then let me blush into a silence. Save, Peter, to say this, the forthrightness whereof, thy friendship will forgive me. There are flowers that, though buds, wax fruitfully and blossom; others that soon wither and decay.'

I was glad the swordsmen stumbled sweaty now in search of citron, for I could see Peter liked not what I said; and that I had, indeed, hovered on that extreme verge of candour that may endanger friendship, though sustain and bind it also. Allan was the victor, yet but nearly; and by the inward smile hovering on Robin's face, I wondered if the lad had not, mayhap, conceded hits less to honour Allan's sword, than to assuage his vanity.

'Robin!' cried Allan, slapping our host upon his heaving back. 'For thy swift skill in arms, I shall forgive thee thy ill taste in letters.'

'Absolve me absolutely, then, by admission that thou thyself, Allan, hast cast glowering eyes upon these same texts I cherish. For besides thou art a gentleman, and well instructed, thy fair nature would not condemn aught writ unseen.'

Casting his eyes about, as though the sharp snout of Master Calvin might protrude o'er the garden wall, Allan lowered his voice, and told us, 'Marry, yes; and of all the plays I read e'er, I admired most those of Master Thomas Kyd and, in especial, his *Spanish Tragedy*.'

'Anent the Armada?'

'Peace, scholar Aubrey!' Robin cried. 'Nay, 'tis a drama whose dark hues Allan cherishes because it reeks with fierce odours of damnation.'

Allan smiled, then frowned again. 'Read, then, Robin,' said he, 'if thou must squander hours worthy of better service to thy Creator. But at least, I prithee, escape the double profanity of witnessing them in the theatre.'

'Well, I have not yet.'

'Nor I.'

'Not I, neither.'

'Heaven be praised!' cried Allan, throwing up his hands like a divine summoning the elect from hell-fire. 'Why! Even my Lord Mayor that, though he call himself Protestant, is to my thinking half Papist and half pagan, hath sought to forbid them utterly. For 'tis well founded that, besides the obscenity of the performance of the painted players, they are the very bee-hive to every roguish and lewd knave in London.' (At which Peter and I traded glances, our determination to see these plays waxing stronger).

In the heat of this argument (on a matter of which none of us knew aught), we had not perceived the presence, as if wafted in from nowhere like a spectre, of the Venice Doge: before whom we all rose, Robin presenting us. To Allan, first thus honoured, Venice said, 'Bowes, Bowes . . . was not thy father good Sir Ronald?'

'Aye, sir: the same.'

'A right noble gentleman,' quoth Venice, 'that I knew well ere thou wert breeched, and loved.'

Neither the breeches nor that the chief pander of East London knew his father, pleased Master Allan; who but bowed gravely, saying, 'Sir, I, too, loved and honoured him.'

'I doubt not,' said Venice. Then casting a languid eye at Peter, on whom he bestowed a nod (as from a monarch to a scullion), he turned to me, listening to his son, and said, 'Ah, of my brother's company. And how doth Genoa?'

'Fittingly, sir, for a man that is a fair master, and of a family which all who serve, cherish.'

He smiled; and I dare swear I feared more the sun of Venice than the gusts and storms habitual to Genoa; for this was a stateliness that masked malice.

'And my sweet nephew Cecil?'

'Even so, sir.'

'Aye. Thou hast played swords, Robin?'

'With this gentleman, that hath ere little vanquished me.'

'Yet nearly, sir!' cried Allan. 'For I swear did thy son Robin hold my stature, he would, not I, be laurelled.'

'And thy books, Robin?'

'Sir, to this gentleman I am further much the debtor; for he has imparted to me sage counsel concerning plays.'

'Be thanked, sir; for he who serveth my son, shall I serve. And thy cyphers, Robin?'

Here Robin's crest fell, and his father, after a silence, said, 'Mark these also, son. For unless thou turn priest or soldier, thou must be master in calculation.' He gazed slowly round at us, as if inviting a denial. 'Gentlemen, I must, by your leave, leave you. The garden commands my presence for, as I totter into my decrepitude, my feet carry me into constant communion with things natural.' With which fair false words, the Venice Doge bowed low, raked us with a glance, and wandered off among the trees where once monks walked, chanting litanies.

Like courtiers when the monarch has passed by, we were all now for departure. So leaving my friends to their various farewells from Robin, I ran to steal a last kiss from Jenny; who, mayhap jealous of my absence, wanted more, so that I must carry her to the buttery, and there dally; and when I came out, more prostrate than had been the swordsmen, I found Peter and Allan impatient for me in the street. So with apologies anent helping Jenny with a custard that needed stirring, we set off for St Helen's.

But around a corner, I was seized on by one of the bears out of the Southwark pits, and enfolded by crushing arms and claws: belonging, when I could catch a glimpse through sweaty hairs, not to Bruin, but Breakbone, Genoa's guardian. Who, as he squeezed and battered me, cried out, 'Learn thy lesson, traitor! That no pander to Genoa may steal treacherously into Venice's abode!'

Then came, I wot, a miracle, or near so; which was that mighty Breakbone, that must weigh near a ton, flew up, as a lark, into the sky, circled a summersault as a tumbler, and landed on his broad back with crack like cannon; and over him stood Allan, that, when the ruffian sought to rise, plucked at his hair and banged his pate down on the cobbles, where he lay still.

'Allan,' quoth I, rubbing my sore limbs, 'if thou battlest with Apollyon likewise, then is mankind saved, and not I only.'

13

He who transferreth his allegiance, must look for ill favour from both realms; for that which he hath left, swears vengeance; and to this which accepts him, he is suspect; and each believes him still serving the other.

This I discovered when I joined Venice from Genoa. After Breakbone's attack, I wanted no more of my old masters, for I could not believe the lout would assail me, that had served Genoa well, without cognizance of my Lord Chancellor Beauty or, even, the Genoa Doge himself. But when I asked Jenny if she could insinuate me into Venice's favour, there arose a great hum-ing and ha-ing with a buzz of 'ifs' and 'buts'. True, Jenny loved me; true also, Robin liked me; truer, Herman eyed me fondly. Sad Jack was no enemy, nor even Amos, Venice's chief minister. But the Doge was wary: for I had served his brother, and so bore Cain's mark.

What persuaded old Venice, was deft Robin. Besides drumming into my pate Latin, Martin had run figures through my head until 'twas a very rosary. London had further schooled me how to apply these skills, for in the stews, I juggled constantly with coin. (From Gropenut, too, I had learned how two and two make six.) Robin, appraised of this, and wanting aptitude himself in cyphers, had asked his father could I not be two useful things: pot-boy in the kitchen, and prod mathematical to him. At length Venice consented;

though it was understood that, like a novice in a monastery, I but served probation.

But this was well enough; for if Venice frowned, Jenny smiled; and I found that, unlike Peter, the nearer to my darling, the more I cherished and esteemed her. Taking my hand one day, when the kitchen was voided of the wenches, she said, 'Aubrey, dost thou wish thy son to be a bastard?'

'Marry, sweet, an thou wed me, then thou takest one.'

'Aye, but our son . . . '

And when my dull wit seized her meaning, I enfolded her as Breakbone Charles had me, and smothered her in busses. 'When, Jenny, when?' cried I.

'Have a care, puddinghead, or never!' cried she, prizing me from her belly. 'Come next spring.'

'Then, Jenny, we must wed instantly.'

'Sit, Master Impatience, pray, and hearken.' Then she took my hands again and, pressing them to her bosom, said, 'Sweet Aubrey, God wot why, for indeed thou art an ill-favoured saucy fellow, but in troth I love thee, and would be thy wife, and mother to thy children.'

'Then, Jenny,' cried I, 'we . . .'

'Peace, peace – perpend. Thou hast seen, Aubrey, how life is in London; and in especial, the ill life of our sick trade.'

'Aye, marry, but . . .'

She bit my hand, and cried, 'Silence! Now, Aubrey. If we wed, we must wed decently. Look not so droll at me: I do not ask that thou turn pardoner, but that thou seek out, I aiding thee, some trade which, if not the most honest in the world, should leave thee, and me, and ours, sleeping sure at night.'

'Aye, Jenny.'

'Think well on this. For I tell thee, Aubrey. If to wed is to raise one more slut into the stews, then I would wish no child.'

'Jenny, thou wouldst not to the witches . . .'

'I said, think well; and better, an thou lovest me, and him' (patting her belly).

'Jenny,' said I, rising, 'what wit I have is thine. Also what little wealth, for all I have yet got, is in thy keeping. That this sufficeth not, I know; and I shall strive further, and deal ever faithfully with thee, do thou but promise to preserve our child, and thy love for me ever.' To this she made no answer, but smiled on me, and led me into the dim buttery.

While later I was unfolding to woeful Robin high mysteries geometrical, Herman approached, bowed low to us with pert ceremony, and said there stood without a greybeard that wished word with ambrosial Aubrey. So I begged leave of Robin, and went out to find Moses tottering at the door.

'Oh, gentle master, thou must come instantly!' cried he.

'Now marry, Moses, I have foisted Allan's troubles, by his leave, on my friend Peter, whom thou shouldst acquaint of this whatever, rather than me.'

'Nay, sir: 'tis Noll that seeks thee!'

'Then let him seek otherwise!' cried I. 'For beside that I must work here, I want no more pledging my gullet for a priest's person.'

'Softly, good Aubrey! He bid me give thee this ('twas gold), and say he awaits thee presently.'

Well, gold alters cases, or most; so I said I would come when I might, poured the coin into Jenny's bosom, and returned to Master Robin and Archimedes.

Robin, prying from me that I was bidden to Blackfriars, gave me leave to go, if I would carry an epistle to his Allan. So this bargain sealed, and the letter, I set out westward.

Now mayhap that I was suspect to Doge Venice made me cautious, and moreover, there is ever the watch that sinners set for their own kind; yet I grew certain that the foxy fellow

I had thrice noticed (at first idly) on the further of the highway, had some ill purpose to me. 'Well,' thought I, 'who shall live, shall see,' and I entered an ale-house, and there anchored myself, waiting.

Bye and bye, in came Reynard, who gazed at each face save mine, then, as if seeing sudden his brother from the Americas, cried, 'Why! Art thou not Aubrey, that hath brought me oftimes to my trull?'

Well, perchance had I, for many came to the stew, though few knew my name there; but I smiled heartily, and said, 'Why, marry, aye! Thou art that customer which had the pox from Sarah, and came lamenting to us after on thy misfortune.'

'Nay, not I!' said Fox indignantly. 'I had no plaint gainst thy bawds, nor against thee, that took me to them.'

To this, still smiling, I said nothing, for I have oft observed with those that you mistrust, each word is a coin wasted.

'I may sit down beside thee, friend?' quoth Reynard.

'Make thine arse free,' said I, kicking aside a chair.

The fellow ordered ale, fretted his palms, and leaning to me, said, 'Ill tidings out of Ireland.'

'So?'

'Aye; my Lord Essex, they say, hath held commerce with Popish traitors, and the Queen is mightily displeased.'

'God save her!' said I, drinking.

'Amen. For though virgin, she is in some sense our mother.'

'May we show duty, therefore.'

'Aye; yet there are some that lament her virginity, and swear Essex should be our sovereign.'

'As she wills, so be it.'

'And declare further that, do she not yield to him, he, for the common good, should enforce her obedience to him.'

'To what end?'

'Marry, a throne needs heirs. And since the death of Marie of Scotland, twelve years since, we have none that are not disputed.'

'Methinks Marie's fate should damp ambition.'

'And thou hast lamented it?'

'Fellow, when the Scots queen died, I could scarce stagger.'

'Yet now thou art man, dost thou not cleave to my Lord Essex's hopes rather?'

I drained my jar, and slammed it on his hand and held it hard. 'Varlet,' said I, 'I know not why, but thou hast followed me, boarded me, and sought to provoke me into treasonable discourse.' Now I screwed the pewter, pressing still. 'Seek other chickens, Fox! And remember, as he must, that provoked hounds have teeth.'

I rose, but he darted to my arm while I, with that free, clutched my dagger, holding it hid but poised.

'Aubrey,' said he, with an evil glance, 'put up thy knife, and be not arrow neither to another's Bowes. Consult well thy Stars; and mark they blink not in a Chamber thou hadst best ne'er enter.' Saying this, he plucked his sleeve out of my hand, and vanished.

I followed to the street, but slower; for who is this? was what sore perplexed me. If some privy cheat, seeking to cozen me for his silence, or even a fief of Doge Genoa's, I reeked it not overmuch; yet should he be a spy put on me by the Council, then I trembled.

I descended, and took counsel of myself beside the river, throwing base coins for the naked boys to garner. The State, I knew, mislikes villainy, but will support much of a lesser nature; but when majesty sniffs treason, the lips of tolerance are curled back by fangs. My promise to Noll was nothing;

for this was none sworn to a true friend. Only my hope of gold for Jenny might raise me above my fears.

Well, let Fate in the form of Master Straw-head there decide for me, thought I, and I called the boy over, showed him a larger coin, and threw it far: in he plunged, swam under like an otter, then shot up with a great grin holding high his arm. I waved to him, and thought, 'Boy, I trust thou art an honest Mercury.'

So I walked up the river to Blackfriars; which reaching, I circled cautiously like a sentry, till I entered the alley behind Noll and Allan's house. Past this I walked, not stopping, then, seeing none, came back and rang. Out instantly popped Daniel, as if lurking gainst my arrival, and bustled me inside the house, and up a stair, and to a library, where Noll was pacing like a weary lion.

'How now!' cried he. 'Must thou loiter in each pot-house when I summon thee?'

'Noll,' said I, 'in one such pot-house, I was waylaid by a spy.'

At this he paled, seizing me (as if I were Reynard), so I could scarce tell my tale coherently.

'And thou toldst naught? Nothing betrayed?' cried he.

'Thy wit should tell thee, Noll, that were I traitor, the constables, not thou, would be my audience.'

'But he had knowledge, sayest thou . . .'

'Aye, but expressed in riddles; making his scant store seem much.'

'Aye, aye . . . spies dangle secrets as an angler doth small bait . . . Did they know all – or less than all – they would be here, and we in irons.'

'This does not follow of necessity.'

'Unclasp thy whole thought to me!'

'Noll, 'tis possible they know enough to nail thee; but also that thou art their bait, which may hook for them others that they know not.'

'Others? Others? Who spake to thee of others?'

'None, save my native wit. For sure, if thou art secret Papist, others are, friends belike of thine, unknown yet to them.'

He stared at me, plucked up a flagon, poured twice, and handed me a glass. 'Aubrey,' said he, 'thou art farseeing for a boy; and seeing so far, I doubt to trust thee.'

'Why, Noll!' cried I. 'Thou seekest a dolt to serve thee in this business? Understand me well! I share not thy faith, but a love of mine own life, surely; also, to deal openly with thee, of thy gold. Ask thyself this, therefore: what cause have I to harm thee, and have I not served thee well ere now?'

'Aye, true, Aubrey,' said he, relenting, 'but if thou wert ta'en and put to torture . . .'

'Enough, Noll!' cried I. 'Put to torture, who can be sure of silence? But if thou hast doubts of me, do thou pluck out of hiding some honest Papist that thou trustest, rather than ask me, whom thou accusest of betrayal!'

Noll had never Allan's smile (I mean one proceeding from the heart, not teeth), but now he looked tender at me, took my hand, and said, 'Well, Aubrey, pagan or heretic though thou art, I trust thee.'

'Then do so, Noll, till my deeds warrant other thoughts in that nest of suspicions which is thy brain.'

He said naught to this but, pacing again, and glancing outward to the river, turned suddenly and stood, and said to me,

'Aubrey, ere little, like the Merlin thou art, thou hast spoke of "others" in this business. Of these now I must tell thee, for our intent tonight is to convey the priest thou knowest, privily to these same "others".'

I said naught.

'Knowest thou who is my Lord of Southampton?'

'He is a nobleman, a soldier, that fights in Ireland against Papists, and hath sailed neath my Lord of Essex to the Azores.'

'Naught else?'

'Nothing.'

'Well, true he fights Papists presently; yet is he one.'

'In the Queen's service?'

'Aye, as are many of her most gallant servants. Forget not, Aubrey, that my Lord Howard, that commanded against the Armada, was of the true faith also.'

'And 'tis to my Lord Southampton we must carry thy French friend?'

'Aye.'

'But not, sure, to Ireland . . .'

'Nay, nay; he is come to England on pretext of business for his commander, my Lord Essex, and now waits a mile from us in Essex House.'

'And what the purpose that his pretext masks?'

'A true marriage, with consecration that no priest of the Queen's church can e'er bestow.'

'And why this haste? Is the lady, perchance, with child?'

Noll glared at me like a thundercloud, and cried, 'How knowest thou this?'

'Peace, Noll! I know it not, but used my wit; for of hasty and secret wedlock, and howsoe'er exalted, there is ever but one cause.'

He frowned mightily, then said, 'Well, 'tis so. The lady that bears his fruit is near her time. This explains haste. As for secrecy, besides that my Lord desires holy wedlock, not the mummery of Protestants which, in God's eyes, but createth bastards, there are affairs of State to be considered.'

'Affairs of State,' said I gravely, curious, and hoping he would continue.

'Aye, and not those for the ears of a St Helen's pander. Yet I shall tell thee this much, that thou understand the peril that commands my gold and thy courage. The lady waited till last year upon the Queen; and the Queen hath not been petitioned, as she ought, for her approval.'

'Marry come up!' said I.

'Aye, may the Blessed Virgin, to protect us!'

We were both still a while.

'But Noll,' said I. 'My Lord of Southampton, as thou sayest, is a Papist.'

'Is a true Christian: of a father and mother both properly baptised.'

'Then hath he no privy priest, that he must cumber thee with this perilous enterprise?'

'Aubrey,' quoth he, 'in the days of the first Christians, when they were persecued by the Romans, 'twas a first duty of these scant saints, before God and their consecrated brethren in the faith, to aid, succour, and protect one and another. So is it now with us. Our priests, even they that minister to the most powerful who cling devoutly to the true religion, are harried, tortured, put to cruel death. So must we bring in more: who, serving God before any terrestial monarch, fear not, and come to garner souls against all danger. Such a one is he whom thou hast brought hither' (now Noll glanced upward at the ceiling), 'that I intended not for this particular purpose, but for our wolfed flock in the City. Then cometh yestereve, from Essex House, a privy message that they have no priest, and seek one that shall come speedily to his holy office there.'

'Well, Noll,' I said, 'I am idolator of naught save wit and courage, yet those who have these, I shall serve faithfully.'

14

This time, no boat carried Reverend France, but a modest coach, into which stepped he (dressed as a serving man), I, and Daniel, but not Noll; who, in spite his love of priests, came not: saying both lie and truth, which was that he feared not for himself, but for all his house, should he be taken in Father France's company. Well, I could not complain of this; for had Noll braved the business, there was no need of Aubrey, nor rewarding him. My duty, said Noll, was to deliver His Reverence at the great House, there wait patiently, then bring him back to Bowes mansion, and my gold.

The priest, that had learned some little English in his between-stairs closet, and who espied I was his companion from the docks, pressed my hand, and said, '*Benedicite*, my son,' to which, save a slight bow, I made no reply, being determined to grant no pretext for his bursting once more into his own tongue. The coachman, that seemed to be well instructed, took, like a good Christian, no broad and easy path, but carried us on a pilgrimage about half London: he, and the lackey up behind, watching doubtless for any that might be watching us. Till at length, we rumbled to the nether door of a huge house, and were fast admitted through its lofty wall.

Then across a great stoned court, with fellows standing cloaked and I guessed armed, and in by a small picket to the kitchen regions; where, amid flunkeys ceremonially attired, and haughty too, that fell on their knees at the sight of Monsignor France, a steward, or chamberlain, or I know not what, bedecked like a peacock with six arses, after being also blessed by France, led him away to the nobility and his holy business, followed in due order by a flight of flunkeys;

leaving Daniel and me, staring at each other's noses, in a great room like a chapel.

'So far, so well, Daniel,' said I.

'Aye, lad; yet till I sleep in my bed in Bowes mansion, shall my heart not beat happy.'

'Thou servest strange masters, Daniel.'

'Which master is not, tell me? Yet in troth, servants have genealogies, as do the families to whom they minister. My father was servant to Sir Ronald, and his to his.'

'And old Moses?'

'Marry! His forebears held stirrup to the first Bowes at the conquest! Tell me, Aubrey: bethink thee my Lord of Essex would permit we rest our bums on his hard benches?'

'Fear not, Daniel, take thine ease! But 'tis of my belly I think rather. In this vast palace, can there not be refreshment for two honest varlets that put their lives in peril for their Lordships?'

'Do thou follow thy nose and seek: for here is much fine ware to eat and drink on, but not of.'

So pulling ope a door, I peeped: and found a great hall, of pillars and cloth hangings, yet no sign of man nor meat: but from the floor above, came sounds of far voices, so that I must suppose lords, lady, priest and serving men were all attendant at the ceremonies there.

Well, thought I, here lies grandeur but not sustenance, so let us try other doors, for 'tis writ seek and thou shalt find, knock, and it shall be opened unto thee; so I oped (without knocking) the first door, and there saw, seated behind a table reading, a bald man: that looked up at me and said, 'And who art thou?'

'Aubrey.'

'And who is Aubrey?'

'Sir,' said I, 'I pray you pardon, I am a serving lad about

my master's business, that must wait with my companion in the nether hall (pointing), where we lack any entertainment.'

'As wine?' said he, pulling a flagon from a table, and pouring me a glass.

'God prosper you, sir,' I said, drinking. 'And my Lord Southampton also,' raising my glass toward the ceiling.

'Well, 'tis his wine,' said the gentleman, that watched me with his doe eyes, smiling. 'Yet again, Aubrey?'

'Sir,' said I, 'I have my comrade, Daniel, that thirsts: may I not carry him a glass and so return?'

'Aye, marry: carry him the bottle, for I have another.'

Which I did, tiptoeing across the hall, still empty, to succour Daniel: who asked me what this fellow was, that shunned the wedding, yet drank the bridegroom's wine.

'Daniel, thou art as wise as I: belike a secretary, or scrivener, for he was reading, and had pens; and perchance a Protestant, misliking Roman practice.'

'But all are Romish here, for we saw all kneel.'

'Well, I know not, till perchance he tell me, or let it slip.'

'An ancient?'

'Nay, of half man's span, as near as I can guess.'

'Go cozen him, then, and bring more wine; for a Romish nuptial, let me tell thee, outlasts a banquet.'

When I returned, the fellow was once more reading; and as he put down the book to greet me, I asked him if I could see it: at which he was surprised, and said, 'Thou art lettered, Aubrey?'

'Aye, sir; I write a fair hand, and am a swift reader, for I was well grounded by a learned scholar.'

'Then share we but one of thy two gifts,' said he, 'for though I read swift, I write ill.'

'These are Chronicles, I see, writ by one Holinshed, anent

our history.' And this spark of vanity was to prove I knew letters, for I thought he misbelieved me.

'Aye, I read them first some twelve years since, and have found much profit in them.'

'You are belike a scholar, sir?'

'Nay, I labour not in libraries, but in the theatre.'

'As what?'

The fellow, that had a soft insinuating voice, though bell-toned and precise, said, 'Why, at many tasks: for I am partner with others in a company, my Lord Chamberlain's.'

'That is now at the *Swan*?'

'Aye, but we build a new theatre presently, where, God willing, we shall work this year coming.'

'Marry, aye, "God willing": for some believe next year to be doomsday.'

'Thou also?'

'Not I! For I am promised three score years and ten, and shall have but garnered sixteen by that time.'

'Well spoken, Aubrey! And what is thy trade, or art thou ever servingman?'

'Why, no . . . In troth, sir, since you have nurtured my curiosity, I must in honour yours, and tell you I am a pander.'

This seemed not to surprise the gentleman, nor provoke frowns nor smiles (as was habitual with strangers when I told it), and he said, 'In what quarter?'

'By Bishopsgate.'

'I know it well: for when I first came to London, I lived by Shoreditch, and then, some three years since, shifted to St Helen's.'

'But now no longer?'

'No, I have crossed the river, like mighty Julius, to Bankside.'

'May your triumphs be as his, sir. Nearby the *Swan*?'

'Aye, twixt this and our new theatre, by the river.'

He had poured me another glass and, raising it, I said, 'To its good fortune, sir, and yours: how shall it be called?'

'The *Globe*.'

'Then may the whole world enter it,' said I.

'Amen, Aubrey, and much thanks.'

'I may be seated, sir?'

'Prithee.'

'And may persist in the impertinence of my inquisition?'

'Do thou chose the questions, Aubrey, and I the answers.'

'A fair compact. Then, sir, you are not native here, but country born?'

'In sight and scent of country, yet in a town.'

'As where?'

'Warwickshire; and thou in Essex.'

'How knew you that, sir?'

'By the exquisite, nay, dulcet manipulations of thy vocables.'

'You mean my speech?'

'Aye: have I guessed well?'

'Truly! I first saw light among the leaves of Epping forest.'

'Wert thou there nurtured, peradventure, by a hart?'

'Nay, sir, by a harlot, that was my mother.'

'Thou jestest, Aubrey?'

'No jest! And so I tumbled, shuttlecock of fortune, into my present ill occupation.'

'Which pleaseth thee?'

'It did, and doth not: it served, but serves no longer.'

'Why, Aubrey? Wilt thou turn honest?'

'No, sir, I would wed Jenny.'

'And who is Jenny?'

'My Juliet.'

At this he stared at me, and said, 'Thou hast seen this play?'

'No, nor read it neither; but I know Juliet is the perfect heroine of our age, and I would be her Romeo.'

'And Jenny, or Juliet, will wed no pander.'

'That, sir, is the rub; I am enforced into honesty not by virtue, but by love.'

'Well,' said he, laughing, 'mayhap honesty will engender virtue, as love does honesty. And who was thy father, Aubrey?'

'Sir, without blasphemy, I am consequence of a conception which, if it be not immaculate, is an equal mystery. I know not my father. And you yours?'

'Aye, my father was a glover.'

'Then have you learned early, sir, to put your hand into apt places.'

'Aubrey, an thou turn malapert, I shall lay it across thine Essex ears.'

'Forbear, sir! For be my ears stopped, my mouth must sing louder, that I may hear mine own dulcet manipulations.'

'Thou art a saucy rogue, Aubrey.'

'True, sir: yet if a man have but his wit, then must he live by that little which he hath.'

'Aye, marry! And thou that so lovest speech, hast ne'er seen a play?'

'In London, no, sir, but in Epping, yes, inside a goose fair.'

'And it pleased thee, or mispleased?'

'Neither. For I was then a young gander unfamiliar with its kind, that yearned to be with bawds, not see actors treading them.'

'Aye, at Bankside, are we and the bawds also rivals for the public favour. Yet now thou hast attained to the ripe maturity of St Helen's stews, thou wouldst not wish to see plays also?'

'Aye, sure, and shall I, when I can coax Jenny thither.'

'Then if Jenny can curtsey, which I doubt not, and Aubrey can bow, which I doubt, thou hast but to circle the *Globe*, when it is full created, ask at the gate for one Master John Heminges, that is my co-mate in our enterprise, and he will waft thee and thine into the theatre without payment of a farthing.'

'Marry, I thank you, sir, and for her also. And who may I say sent me to Master Heminges?'

'My name, Aubrey, is William.'

''Tis an honest name.'

'So thought my father when he gave it to me.'

'I may pronounce it when I address you?'

'Roll it round thy long tongue, Aubrey, an it please thee.'

'Yet my exquisite vocables would fain make my "yous" "thous", and of William, if thou wilt, Will.'

'Speak to me, as to any, as thy heart commands, and thy wit and prudence counsel.'

At this the door oped, I turned, and there stood a lady, young yet not so, and swart. She looked at Will, at me, and pointing, said, '*Qui est-ce?*'

'*Rien*,' said he. '*C'est fait?*'

'*Bientôt*.'

'*Bien*.'

'*Bien!*' cried she, harsh.

'*Vas maintenant*,' said he, and she went: of all which I made neither head nor tail.

There was a silence, Will looking at me, yet beyond. Then he said, 'Doth thy learning embrace French, Aubrey?'

'But bashfully, like a shy virgin's. This lady spoke it?'

'Aye . . .'

'As does the priest.'

'Thou hast brought him hither?'

'Aye, and from Wapping, from a ship, at peril of my skin.'

'Then art thou in some sort Cupid, Aubrey; for without him, my Lord could ne'er wed.'

'Thou knowest my Lord of Southampton, Will?'

'Near nine long years.'

'And met him how?'

'Aubrey! Whether thy nose or tongue be longer, know I not. Have a care, lest the one be slit, and the other cut.'

I could see I had angered him, and looked bashful, casting down my eyes; and indeed, I had no wish to hurt his humour; but was prod on by that goad of curiosity which has e'er been my bane and my salvation. So I said naught, and when I looked up, Will's anger seemed abated, though he had risen.

'Thou knowest the stews, Aubrey,' said he, 'and I may tell thee they share with the theatre one particularity: that in both, persons of the most divers sorts, that never would cross shadows otherwise, do there.'

'And there met thou my Lord.'

'There met I him, learned to know and love him, and am bidden to this feast to honour him. Bidden, boy, yet absent: for lords are like planets, that are encircled by pale moons which shine with their reflected light; and, set forever in their orbit, spin powerless to creep close or depart.'

'"Depart", Will,' said I, rising also. 'So must I, lest my master seek me, or Daniel be sunk into a stupor.'

'Farewell, lad. I go home till the leaves fall burnished; then back to London, where I may hope to see thy volcanic countenance, shouldst thou erupt beneath the heavens of the *Globe*.'

'Expect me, breathing smoke and fire.'

'Aye, and a great deluge of larva from thy lips, I doubt not.' He took my hand. 'And hearken to Juliet,' said he, 'for she speaks wisely to her Romeo.'

'That I should leave the stews?'

'Aye: cast thine eye around at thy companions, and say, "Do I stay, I shall become them".'

'Heaven forfend! And that done, Will, I shall bid thee to our wedding.'

'The christening, rather, of thy firstborn: for weddings make me weep.'

'Then must thou come sooner, for the one is like to precede the other, in country style.'

'Jenny is with child?'

'Aye, a son, so her heart tells her, or her belly.'

'A son, thou sayest . . .'

'Aye . . . Thou hast one such?'

'Had, and these three years, have not.'

'I had no wish, Will . . .'

'Go thy ways, Aubrey, lest thy lips languish from excess, leaving no strength to clip Jenny's.'

'But hers can revive mine.'

'Aye, I warrant. God be with thee.'

So I left him there, and was stepping across the great hall bemused, when I stood frozen and amazed in fear: for the doors of the gallery had opened, and a company stood, lit by flares: and before them, holding his bride's hand, a young man that, though older than he, conjured up Robin to me; for his hair fell gold red, and his face and form shone with the same hard grace. They descended; and my wits flying home from exile, I fled into the nether room, where waited Daniel.

I quieted his rebukes and plaints anent my absence, and quaffed the remainder of his wine, which multiplied his rages. But into us was quick shuffled Master priest, and the coachman and attendant flunkey, with orders to be off instantly, away with you, begone!

So we hastened out across the court, and through the wall, where in the lane guards stood watching by the coach, who said all stood well, none lurked – a woeful prophecy! For round but six corners, we were assailed by muffled minions that leapt onto the coach and nags like hounds closing for the kill. The coachman lashed forward, the coach tilted, and the doors wrenched ope, Daniel and I fought each side, the priest cowering. I fell out on my assailant with a smack, dagger already free, and stabbed, stabbed: he groaned, I caught his hair, and crying, 'Die, Reynard!' stabbed again.

The coach was vanished amid shouts dying. I stood, flung my dagger o'er a wall, and walked quick softly: round a turn into the arms of constables, that seized me, crying, 'Why, knave, art thou daubed red?'

15

It was said by my comrades at the stews that, just as no soldier be one until battle, so is no bawd nor pander such that hath scaped prisons. Well now, in the Clink, I had won my battle honours: though as is doubtless with soldiers too, the merit was hard bought by the discomforts. For I was beaten to fresh bleeding by the officers, flung into a boat's bilge with other wretches, and locked in a chill cage where I now lay, sorrowful and smarting, awaiting dawn.

Yet my brain, though battered, had been puzzling my best path from this predicament. Certes, I must ne'er avow, unless twisted by tortures, that I knew aught of privy priests; but in equal, I knew it useless to plead innocence. So hungering, I cooked up a tale to feed my spirits.

Ere light, some dozen of us fellows were brought severally before examiners. My turn came late, which gave me hope they deemed me of no account; yet seeing three when I was ushered in, muttering and scanning parchments, my heart faltered.

'Who art thou?'

'William, sir,' said I in thickest Essex.

'Thy trade?'

'Goat-herd.'

'That tends goats in London?'

'Nay, sir: I am come up here to seek my fortune.'

'And hast found it, rogue, for it shall be the gallows.'

'Why, sir?' cried I, falling into a great rustic tremble, my knees clacking and my hands clasped. 'How have I offended?'

Now spoke another, not hectoring, but snake-douce, 'Thou art no William, thou art Aubrey.'

'Born William, sir, and so baptised as a true Christian.'

'Thou art, moreover, servant to Noll Bowes.'

'Nay, sir, my master is called Colin, as honest a greybeard as I a youth.'

'And hast, yesternight, carried privily to a House I name not yet, and treasonably, a priest.'

'A priest, sir? I? I spit upon priests, your worship, and the Pope, even.'

'And further, hast slain one of the Council's officers, cruelly, by stabbing.'

'Sir, what is this! I, honest William? That is known in all Epping for his humble obedience to the Queen's laws?'

Now spake the third: 'We squander time; let him be beaten.'

At this I was carried away, struggling and trumpeting my virtue, by two Goliaths that flung me in a cage, and whipped me till I yelled and bellowed, but still crying innocence. Then they dragged me, half living, into a cell where I lay weeping and bleeding among several that watched, saying naught either. Save that one said, 'And so hath Genoa vengeance of thy treachery,' and this was Gropenut.

Well, in an inferno any friendly face is welcome, and I

struggled up, he aiding me, and nursed my wounds, and drank water that they had. 'Poor lad,' said Gropenut, 'how art thou come hither, and what secret have they sought to wring from thee?'

'Marry, Gropenut, I am for groaning more than speech, do thou tell me what makes us companions in misfortune.'

Here he heaved a sigh, and said, 'Ever and anon, Aubrey, as thou wilt discover do thou live thy full span, the State, like a great monster, or Leviathan, heaves up its bulk to crush rogues, vagrants, vagabonds, idle beggars, forgers, false dicers and the like. This done, the Leviathan subsideth, till its next rising: which is called a Purge.'

'Of which thou art victim presently.'

'Aye, marry. The Queen (may she prosper!) prods My Lord Treasurer; he, the Council; it, the Lord Mayors and Chief Justices; they, lesser magistrates; these same, constables and watchmen. Propelled by this profusion of legality, watch and ward are kept, Bridewell and the Clink refurbished for fresh tenancy, and a multitude of defenceless knaves, as I, are netted from their harmless and habitual avocations, and salted like boned herrings into dungeons.'

'And what fate awaits them?'

''Tis at a throw of his worship's dice: bodily labour, mayhap, as beating of hemp, scouring town ditches, abating shelves of the Thames; or, for fish female, making of flax, spinning coarse cloth or, for those favoured, laundering the fouler privy garments of the gaolers.'

'May thy dice fall even, Gropenut!'

'Amen. Yet I tremble; for I am indicted on an affair of false dice, under impulsion of Groom Porter to Her Majesty, and I shun branding.'

'For but dicing, false or fair? That were an excess of purgation!'

'So say I; yet I fear for my forehead, that it carry not an *F* forever, or my cheeks be scarified therewith and powdered in bright hues, be the executioner a man of malice.'

'Lord have mercy, Gropenut! But why falleth presently this thunderbolt?'

'The realm, Aubrey, is disturbed: from Ireland come rumbles of my Lord Essex's aptitude to treason, France still cries murder for the death of Marie, Spain glowers vengefully, the Scots, that blow e'er hot and cold, breathe hot now, coveting the old Queen's crown for the bow-legged Presbyterian that rules them. These menaces from without stir those within: Papists plot, Puritans pray purgatory, the mighty dream a resurrection to the War of Roses, and the poor suffer.'

'First ever, be the times unripe.'

'E'en so; I tell thee, Aubrey, be a State in turmoil, the chief victims are the needy; and of these, the first chosen, honest cozeners as we. So hearken, and be warned by Gropenut, thy old comrade in knavery: do thou escape this charge against thee, flee also London for a while.'

'I cannot, for I have Jenny.'

'Aye, and shouldst thou stay, Jenny hath a fine corse to weep over.'

'Yet will the Venice Doge protect me, and thee, Genoa.'

'Thinkest thou so? Then art thou greener than a maypole. For I tell thee: were the times habitual, they would lift not their least finger in thy succour; and in the present eruptions, even these high paladins must themselves think of flight.'

'Gropenut, thou art Job's comforter indeed.'

'So let me be, more fully; for I have poured lamentations in thine ear anent mine own miseries, yet not heard thine.'

I unfolded my affair to him (omitting some particulars that touched my pledged faith too nearly), to which he listened like a justice, that has ripe understanding of the laws and their evasion.

'Well,' said he, 'if thou canst bear further beatings bravely, my opinion is, they will indict thee on some trivial matter.'

'How so?'

'Use thy wit, lad. Thine examiner flung questions at thee that seemed deadly javelins, but which are, I wean, but needles. Aye, patience, hear me! All that he knows concerning thee, he knows not, but guesses; for spies have told him this, not witnesses: Did any see that at the coach, to know thee?'

'None save Master Fox.'

'Who may tell what tales he wishes to the devil. But had there been witnesses, to pin the guilt upon thee fast, then would they have confronted thee with these, and driven the pins deep.'

'So can they but beat me to confession.'

'So say I: what saith thy poor aching body, I know not.'

And so it proved; for daily I was lashed, daily examined, and e'en thrown nose to nose with fellows that had attacked the coach, and swore they knew me; but my cries of denial sprung so true from my cut lips, that I could see, in spite their wrath, they doubted. Well, said they at last, they would prove it out of my own lips or another's ere I scaped them; but meanwhile, I was held upon a count of vagrancy.

If Justice be blind to one thing, it is surely Time; for weeks passed, and nor Gropenut nor I were hailed before any magistrates; and so we diced, gossiped, quarrelled with each other and our fellows, waiting none patiently, yet waiting ever.

'Gropenut,' said I one day, 'dost thou know aught of theatres?'

'Aye, marry, much; for there is no apter place to my calling than their cockpits, the crowd being close packed, besides rapt.'

'Then what is the company of my Lord Chamberlain?'

'One of many, yet of few: that is, there are but two presently, but born out of others, like a jelly-fish, that propagates itself by self-division.'

'And of these two presently, which other?'

'My Lord Admiral's.'

'And of Chamberlain and Admiral, which greater?'

'If greatness be age, my Lord Admiral's, that took his livery some twelve years since, or more . . . aye, 'tis more, fourteen. But if it be prosperity and fame, why! my Lord Chamberlain's, though it were formed but five years since.'

'That plays now at the *Swan*?'

'That does, aye, yet did not, nor will not. For when the Council contracted the profusion of Companies into these two, they rivalled each other at the *Rose*. Yet when their new theatre is full built, my Lord Chamberlain's men will hie them thither.'

'To the *Globe*.'

'Aye, that is as yet all posts, mud and ladders.'

'And what other companies of this earlier profusion?'

'Well, in my younger days, there was the Queen's, and her would-be King's, my Lord of Leicester's; that died when he did, sharing their common tears with our liege's pearly weepings. Then, if we must speak of Companies, though I would say nurseries, there are the child players, as those of St Paul's or of the Chapel, that are now but recently dispersed; but of these I know less, for the theatres wherein these infants warbled were enclosed, with admission denied to the sweaty vulgar.'

'And when winter comes, how fare the Companies?'

'As we all do, ill. In summer, when citizens are abroad, the theatres are filled daily; but in winter, they must to smaller closed theatres that are ill-lit and chill, as at Blackfriars; or perform, if so commanded, in houses of noblemen, or the Queen's palaces, even.'

'So theirs is a hard trade, Gropenut.'

'Actors'? Aye, it is; and much like ours, it beseemeth me. For as with us, many aspire to riches, yet few attain them; yet as with us also, if a man have talent, and naught else, still may he hope to rise, and to win fame. And where else, I ask thee, can a man do this that hath neither birth, riches, nor learning to assist him?'

Into this pleasant converse there now plunged my familiar, the assistant executioner, that seized me by an ear to lug me to my daily beating. And shouting curses at me, and bestowing kicks, he hauled me to the cell wherein these ceremonies are enacted, that held also the foul tools of his calling. Yet when the door clanged to, he unhitched my ear and said, 'Fellow, thou hast kept silence here, save for thy howlings.'

'Master, I can tell thee naught that is not in my heart.'

'Nor in thy will, neither, for I know well when a prisoner cries all, or part, or nothing. Hearken to me, then. If thou canst keep silence under the lash, canst thou also without fear of it?'

'Sir, I hold discretion to be part of virtue.'

'Marry, thou shouldst be courtier. Well, to business (lowering his bull's bellow). I am to carry thee to the Chief Gaoler, before whom thou wilt stand humbly, and in perfect silence. Upon thy tangled pate, he will pour maledictions to which, if thou answerest but one syllable, beware! Then shall he dismiss thee.'

'Dismiss me whither?'

'Come!' cried he, grasping my arm again, and once more lavishing kicks and bellows.

He carried me through vaults and tunnels, and up winding wet steps, to an oaken door, on which he knocked gently till, after six knocks and pauses, a muffled voice cried, 'Enter!'

Within, seated behind a table, was a huge fellow, blotched and empurpled, save for two bright eyes; that was quaffing wine and, with his free hand, scratching at a forest of hairs upon his breast. 'Go!' he shouted at the executioner, gazed at me long, and saying nothing.

Then he leaned forward, and said, 'Aubrey, thou art a scurvy rogue.'

'Aye, sir,' said I.

'Silence!' cried he. 'Hearken to me, piss pot. That thou art pander, know I well. That thou art traitor, mayhap also.' Now he rose. 'And that, if I e'er see thy sly pocked face again, I shall with these two hands (raising them) throttle all breath from thy foul poxy body! Now, begone!'

I stared, oped my mouth, shut it when he raised both fists, then turned and ran swift through the door, that was not locked. I stumbled along corridors towards more light, and down a stair, and through a small door, and out into a lane and sunlight, and the arms of Jenny.

16

A man should not weep in the arms of his beloved, which I have done but twice, ever; but now, for an instant, Jenny was boy and I girl, for she seized on me, took me in her arms, and half carried me round corners into an ale-house; where she sat waiting till I recovered my lost senses, which was soon: for I enfolded her so violently that she must cry shame! and declare I would provoke a scandal.

At length, when I had drunk a flask, and eaten, and begun

the next, she said, 'And guess, Aubrey, who is thy saviour.'

'Why, thou, angel!'

'Nay – thou: or the gold thou hast earned, rather, and entrusted to me; which now lies, alas, tinkling in the breeches of the Chief Gaoler.'

'Whom thou hast bribed for my delivery!'

'E'en so, and we are now poor again.'

'Rich, Jenny! For I have thee.'

'Aye, and I Aubrey: yet (stroking her belly) must we think also of Master Not-yet.'

'Well, I have gold due to me from Noll, an he deny me not.'

'Aye, and thou must seek more, do thou wish to hear church bells ringing at our wedding, not our funeral.'

'Cast me not back into dejection with that word, Jenny! For now I am free, I am soldier to thee, and our young son.'

She smiled, but turned grave again. 'I doubt not thy valour, Aubrey, nor thy faith,' said she. 'Yet are the times unripe for our prosperity, as I must tell thee; for much Thames water hath flown neath London Bridge since thy departure.'

'Well, let me fill but one more glass to nourish courage, and thy sweet lips telling, I can bear tidings howsoever ill.'

'Hearken, then. In St Helen's, there have been two upheavals, one touching us but generally, the other nearly, and with danger. As to the first, there is much murmuring of rebellions, treachery to the Queen, disorders in the State: which has the effect, besides others, that all shun debauchery, fearing spies within the stews, or poking behind their backs within their houses while they dally with us. The justices and officers have waxed sudden swift, harsh, and pitiless, not just to us poor wretches, but to all.'

'Aye, marry; I heard some of this within the Clink.'

'Yet this thou hast heard not yet, I trow. Twixt Venice and Genoa, the fight now waxeth fiercer: since each trembles, and their commerce wanes. Yet Genoa, that is more foreseeing, or more fortunate, in this civil war of the defeated, is the victor.'

'How so? For if Genoa be more villain, Venice hath apter brains.'

'Because in a war, civil or other, the antagonists need allies; which Genoa hath, but Venice, few or none. For thou knowest well how Genoa, masking the ill sources of his fortune, has ever consorted, in the City, with persons of power and substance that now protect him, at least in part; while Venice, that has, as 'twere, retired from the bustle of Bishopsgate (save to glean gold from it), has neglected his alliances, and now stands alone.'

'And what ensues?'

'That bawds, panders, bullies and the like that once served Venice, now flee, like Wapping rats, into Genoa's stews, so that the fortunes of Venice are much fallen off. Beside which Genoa, that is as arrant and treacherous a knave as e'er wore poxy breeches, hath, Venice suspects, cozened the justices, and set spies and constables to gnaw like terriers at his brother's heels.'

'And what sayeth Venice?'

'Well, he is of a humour philosophical, as thou knowest; but from what I have wormed out of Robin and Sad Jack, his intent is, like a ghost, to vanish for a while.'

'Whither?'

'I know not: belike to the country, out of London.'

'Yet, as a ghost also, to return and haunt St Helen's?'

'Marry, I can but hazard he will lie hid, waiting, and watch the times.'

'And thou and I in all this confusion, Jenny?'

She held my hands and said, 'Aubrey, thou must also away a while.'

'Wherefore?'

She nodded towards the Clink. 'Thou art bribed out, boy, not freed by justices; and a score of spies know thy fair face which, pardee, once seen, ne'er forgot.'

'Then must thou with me, Jenny.'

Still holding my hands, which she pressed, she said to me, 'Nay, Aubrey: nay, but hearken! For three sound causes, we must separate a while. First, that thou art safer far alone, till such time as any hue and cry diminish, for sure! that corrupt Gaoler will cry that thou art scaped (and cut the ears off some poor turnkey for't), and thou wilt be ferreted till their ardour is abated; and if thou art encumbered by a great pregnant bitch, thou art more palpable. Next, I am many months gone now; and Master Nobody will not thank his loving mother should she trundle him along highways, and, at night, carry him in barns or under bushes. Then, there is Venice, to whom I owe some duty; and who, do the sun shine again upon his fortunes, clouded now, may have power once more to serve us, do we but serve him in adversity.'

'Jenny, my love, thou art too wise to be a woman.'

'And thou too passionate for thy good.'

'Well, that thou shalt see, I promise thee, this very day; for 'tis not only my heart that bursts on seeing thee.'

'I doubt it not: and 'tis fit, for our son should be fed by his father, ere he leap out and snatch his mother's dug.'

'And Jenny: if I go a spate, thou wilt be true to me?'

'As thou to me, Aubrey.'

'And where wilt thou tarry? And how live?'

'Why, still at the monastery of Venice. For if he flee it, and his fellows, I shall remain as housekeeper, or watchdog; and if justices, or Genoa, or whichever usurper might be, should take possession of it, well, they will need a cook.'

'And more, which is what I fear.'

'Trust me, Aubrey, and to providence. For I shall be sustained by my love of thee and our son, my claws, and Lucy.'

'Lucy will stay also? And what of Peter?'

'Peter, with less speed than thine but equal surety, has encumbered Lucy's belly as thou this.'

'Pardee! A monastery turned nursery! And Peter will go or stay?'

'Go, if does Robin, that he cherishes.'

'O'er cherishes: Lucy will poke out his eyes.'

'In truth, Aubrey, though she still cleaves to him, the more so as she hopes her child be not a bastard, they are much fallen asunder; and their flame that burned bright, flickers.'

'While ours waxeth.'

'Amen and forever, Aubrey.'

We walked out into Paris Gardens, holding hands, and past the *Swan*, that made me think of Will, and the new *Globe* that his company were building; and as this lay in the direction of our journey into Southwark, and so over London Bridge, we sought it out, though Jenny was reluctant, and begged me to make haste.

There, like a half-cooked pie, it stood beside the river: with builders swarming on it yet, as is ever their custom, indulging in more ribaldry than labour. We circled it, and it seemed to be some sort of an octagon, and I traced thirty steps or thereabouts to each side. Across, altogether, it was near a hundred paces; and in height, twixt thirty and forty, the less rather than the more. Peeping within, we saw what must be the cockpit, for the groundlings: near sixty paces broad.

Perceiving a grave fellow, that stood arguing with the workmen, when he had desisted (shaking his head and muttering), I approached him and, bowing, said, 'Good sir, saving your presence, may you not be master John Heminges, that is controller of this fair enterprise?'

'Aye,' said he, 'and who art thou?'

'Why, sir, I am Aubrey, and this is Jenny.'

'May heaven prosper thee, Aubrey, and thee also, Jenny (bowing to her low), yet as you may perceive both, I am much occupied, and moreover, perplexed as to the cause wherefore I am honoured by your fair address and goodly company. Unless, mayhap (his face now brightening), you have witnessed my performace on stages more solid than this (pointing within the *Globe*).'

'Why, no, sir,' said I, 'we have not that honour yet, though shall do, surely. Nay, Master Heminges, if I venture to board you, and wish you, as I do, all fair health and prosperity, 'tis because of the kindness to me of Master William, that I know a little, and who said to me if I approached the *Globe*, why! I should approach you also.'

'Oh, so thou art friend to Will, Aubrey.'

'But acquaintance yet, sir, though I hope to be his friend.'

'Well, thou couldst find none better. And the approach to me he counselled thee was, I doubt not, to permit thee to watch actors labour to thy profit, without detriment to thy purse.'

At this I blushed, and said, 'Sir, I am a poor lad, fresh out of the Clink.'

Whereat he laughed, laid a hand upon my shoulder, and said, 'Well, Aubrey, we must find thee better entertainment: and sure, when this theatre come to be one, which, at the present progress of these honest toilers, will be Doomsday, then art thou right welcome, and Jenny also, to one free entry, but (poking my breast and frowning) one only. For consider: if what we give thee for naught delight thee, then should thy joy, free bestowed, transform itself, on a next visit, into a fair proof of gratitude, which is gold.'

'Why, that I promise you, sir: do I venture a second fling, the wager shall be mine.'

'Well spoken. And now thou art half inside the *Globe*, I mean by promises, wilt thou not see it half completed also?'

'Why marry, sir, gladly!' said I, though Jenny plucked at my sleeve and frowned.

'Well first,' said Master Heminges, waving his hand about the muddy marsh whereon we stood, 'you will observe we have selected, with that practicality which was e'er in the character of actors, the most moist site on Bankside; so that our *Globe* must stand on piles, as do (saving thy presence, Jenny) those of many bums, both male and female.'

'And why, sir, chose you not better?'

'Because of the old adage, of first come, first served. For see! The *Swan*, *Rose* and Bear Garden, not to speak of stews, inns and houses of ill-fame generally, have all forestalled us. So must we to the marshes: yet, if it be true earth itself swims in some sort of a vapour, it is but apt the *Globe* rest also on the waters.'

We were now, clambering over bricks, straw and poles, within the cockpit. Master Heminges gazed around forlornly, then with a sudden laugh, seized my arm and said, 'Aubrey, art thou dowered with invention?'

'As fits my nature, sir, I hope.'

'Then dream! For out of this conglomeration of confusions, thou must picture the *Globe* fair spinning on its poles. Thither, behind us, is the entrance gate: narrow, as that to paradise, lest honest lads like thee creep in for nothing. Before us, within three sides of this curiously squared circle, lies our realm, the actors': with stage and, above it, Lord's room, or balcony, whence we hurl truths at a loud and indifferent multitude. About us, already rising, is the gallery, that will reach (do it not tumble by the scamped labour of these scurvy artisans) three stories high; wherein shall sit persons of greater consequence, if no more understanding, than the groundlings'. Surmounting all, will be first the *heavens*, or canopy that covereth the actors, next a flag, hoisted to announce performance (and lowered bedraggled should ill fate send rain), and then, most magnificent of all, the symbol, emblem, trophy of our theatre, to wit an image of Hercules, bearing up the globe.'

'We must away!' Jenny whispered.

I silenced her with a hard slap upon her rump, and said, 'A very splendour, sir! A grandiloquence indeed!'

'Aye,' said Master Heminges, 'though locked yet in the dark womb of futurity. But no matter: on mankind are enjoined faith, hope and charity; and though actors have, mayhap, but little of the last, they are richly endowed by its two sisters.'

'Well, sir, I am beholden to you indeed, and Jenny also' (pinching her rump again to force a smile). 'Yet now you will pray pardon us, and let us join to our thanks, adieus; for my Jenny, as you may perceive, is big with child, and tires easily.'

'Marry, indeed: we must not let thought of our creation banish all that of hers. Give thee good den, madam' (kissing her hand which she snatched away and, his back turned, licked off the kiss), 'and to thee, Aubrey, better acquaintance, avoidance of the Clink, and a prompt, steady patronage of our endeavours.'

'Aye, truly, sir,' said I; and bowing to him, helped Jenny out through the rubble into the marsh, and so back begrimed onto the highway.

'Aubrey,' said she, 'an thou set foot in that theatre, or

indeed any place neighbour to the Clink, then art thou mad, and shall I turn nun.'

'Then shall I be violator of convents,' said I, seeking to soothe her passion.

'Actors!' quoth she. 'They are bawds as we, yet we are honest in't, and they but panders to lewd ignorants, pert prentices, sly inky students from the Inns, poxed Court gallants and, if any noblemen, then or catiffs or catamites, or both conjoined.'

'Well, Jenny,' said I, 'mayhap Master Heminges would agree with thee: yet such as they are, they love plays.'

'Aye; an I keep not close watch on thee, thou wilt catch their infection.'

So I kissed her over London Bridge, and fondled her into Bishopsgate, till, nearing Venice's abode, I assumed a more cautious and decorous mein. None seemed about outside, nor aught untoward, and so we entered.

None would we find until, looking into the garden, we saw a council, or parliament, proceeding; with at the head of the rustic table Venice, Sad Jack and Amos flanking him, Robin adjoining, and Herman hovering like an attendant sprite. Perceiving us, they halted their deliberations, and Venice said, 'Come hither, Jenny, and thou also Aubrey, you may both be seated.'

Well, then they embarked on a digestion of all the pros and contraries of flight, or to stay, or to depart yet not depart, each speaking otherwise, with projects and plans irreconcilable. Till at a pause, one more of doubt than of decision, I said to Venice, 'May I pray speak, good sir?'

'Speak, Aubrey.'

'Sir, I have heard, and Jenny here has told me, that you have thoughts of a sojourn in the country; yet in a place that shall be discreet, and also not far from London, should you wish for swift tidings from it, or to return as fast. Now, as you may know, I am Essex born, from nearby Epping, and there in the forest, dwells the most honest man in England, my step-father Martin, that loves me, and is of ripe years and understanding. Moreover, when I say "in the forest", I mean verily; for his hut is embowered quite, and thus well hid; yet hath four walls and fires, as shall be needful, winter approaching; and yet again, though planted well within the forest, 'tis not too far from Epping for intelligence of the outer world.

'Now, sir: if you should wish it, I know Martin would receive and succour you, and yours, and this without question; and as to reward, ask none other than your love, though should you deem fit to enfold this with a purse, I do not think he would deny you.'

At this they all stared at me, and Sad Jack said, 'Marry, the lad should be ambassador.'

'And thanked,' quoth Robin.

Then Amos to Venice: 'Sir, 'tis very well, 'tis very pretty; but beside we know little of this lad (save that he served your brother), we know less of this hermit Martin, that dwells in hid bowered huts, and will serve strangers for love only.'

'Aubrey,' said Herman, piping up behind us so sudden that all turned, 'beside being an honest youth, and candid to his friends if not to others, has oft told me of this Martin, and of Epping, without motive or purpose to deceive me; and I believe the boy means us well.'

All eyes fixed now upon Venice who, turning to Jenny, said, 'Aubrey speaks true, lass?'

'Aye,' said she.

He nodded, and we were dismissed from their parley to the kitchen; where we found Peter had come in, glowering, and Lucy, weeping. For they had been flung out of their attic by

Genoa's men, to whom all other bawds and panders of the house had now gone over. 'And what shall become of us?' cried Lucy.

'That thou shalt wipe thy snout upon this cloth,' quoth Jenny, 'drink this ale, eat this pie, and then bestir thyself to help me in my work, and so earn the bed I shall prepare for thee and Peter.'

'Peter,' said I, taking him apart, 'drink this, and let me toast thy son-to-be with mine.'

'Aye, but not wife-to-be as thine,' said he, with an ill glance at Lucy.

'That is thy choice, on which I shall say naught save, by thy leave, this. A bastard belongeth to his mother, not his father; and so long as . . .'

'And so should it, and it shall.'

'Have patience, Peter. And, as I say, so long as the babe remain babe, or child, or boy, the father rests oftentimes content to be so by nature, not by law. But as babe waxes to child, so does child to man; and one day Peter, when thou art older, and mayhap enfeebled in comparison, a young man issued from thy loins may call thee to account for his ill rearing.'

Peter grunted at this, and said no more; and I half regretted my sage counsel, for who, advising a friend honestly, yet contrary to his inclination, has not earned sulks and frowns? So to turn his thoughts, and thus his wrath elsewhere, I said, 'And what of Allan, and his texts, tracts, and holiness typographical?'

'Marry, they are in Fleet ditch.'

'How so?'

'How thus, that I went where he directed, upon a wherry, to a ship that was manned from stem to stern with Dutch dissenters; who gave me a great bundle of their holy writ which, after some sacreligious gins, I tumbled into the wherry, thinking to bring them in beneath the Tower, and thence carry them into the safety of our stew. But in spite the blessings which the Hollanders had called down on my head, the Puritan saints failed me; for one curious waterman in the wherry, that had peeped inside the bundle privily (these rogues being practised pilferers), drew out a tract and swore, though I doubt he could read, that it was heretical, and hence treasonable; an did I not give him gold, he would disembark me not beneath the Tower, but in it. Ensued, as thou hast supposed, an argument: fair speech first, then foul, then blows, then flash of knives. Well, they were three, I one, besides being at fault should they betray me, so catching up the bundle, I flung it in the river where Fleet meets it; and there, by God's mercy, so weighted was it with His word, it sank instantly, to their vast vexation.'

'Alas! then no gold from Allan, Peter.'

He smiled. 'Allan is no usurer, like Noll: he pays for intent, not fulfilment. See, Aubrey!' and he showed me coins.

'Guard it then well, Peter, for in such times it is e'en more precious.'

Now came to us Robin, loaded up with news, which, seated at the kitchen table, he unburdened. 'It is decided thus,' said he. 'Tomorrow, my father and Sad Jack in the coach, and Amos with followers that stay trusty upon horseback, will set forth for Epping, and there lodge. Thereafter, will Amos seek out thy Martin, Aubrey, and bring him to my father, that they may judge of each other, and this business.'

'And I, Robin? Must I not go with them to show where Martin dwells, and speak with him in thy father's favour?'

'So would I think best, and so said my father. But Amos

that is, and has long been, his chiefest counsellor, and, as Jenny will tell thee, as confiding as a cut cat, mistrusts thy plan and, to be open with thee, will have none of it until . . .'

'Marry come up!' cried I. 'Then can my Lord thy father carry his woes elsewhere, do he disdain me, and mislike my friends!'

'Peace, Aubrey!' cried Jenny. 'And speak not so to Robin, to whom thou art debtor for a thousand bounties.'

'Nor sever my discourse in its spate, prithee, till it at least be ended!'

'Speak, then, Robin, though touching mine honour . . .'

'Aubrey, I vow thou art a very Spaniard! Now hearken, I prithee; and blame not my father, who loves thee not yet as I do, nor as Jenny, and knows that if Amos is o'er jealous and mistrustful, his purpose is my father's safety. So, to resume. Amos would spy out the land alone, like a good soldier if wary, before my father venture beyond Epping. And bethink thee this, Aubrey, which may loose one of thy frowns, if not their whole corrugation. If aught evil befall, I mean in Epping, then canst thou ne'er be blamed; for none there will know we are come thither by thy counsel.'

'And how shall Master Amos discover Martin?'

'Why, thou shalt instruct him.'

'Marry, no! Lather his chops, rather. Let him, like the good spy and soldier thou accountest him, pry out Martin by his own long nose.'

'Aubrey!'

'Peace, woman!'

'Children!' cried Herman, in a voice *castrato.*

'Then wilt thou not,' said Robin, in the silence that ensued, 'tell me where dwells Martin, and so I, Amos?'

'Thee will I tell anything, e'en why I love a jade like Jenny.'

' 'Tis that she loves thee, Aubrey, and so supports thy passions.'

'Well, let me bear blame; though in troth, Robin, beside I like not what I have said I mislike in Amos's intent, it beseemeth me thy father, by his choice, falls into double error.'

'Construe me this.'

'He would hie him to Epping secretly, where I have offered, and he half rejected, perfect privacy. Yet before he be content that his refuge be one indeed, he must lodge in Epping, where each pot-house gossip must know that he is come there.'

'This he has foreseen, Aubrey. For he will spread about he lodges but one night, being bound for France; then either move on beside thy Martin or, if not so, elsewhere in some further region.'

'Well, I wish him fair judgement and good fortune. And what of we remainder: I, Jenny, and Peter and his Lucy that have tumbled hither? Does he wish none of us no further?'

'By no means. The day after his departure, a caravan of valiant youth, to wit I, thou, Peter and Herman here, will embark in the baggage-cart, bound also for Epping; where we shall learn either from Martin, or at the inn, where my father and his followers have disposed themselves. Jenny, by her wish, remains; and Lucy, if I read aright her eyes, would bear her company, if Peter say not nay.'

'Why no, an they have some protection; for we have seen how thy uncle's bullies respect thy father's houses.'

'That neither is forgot. Two ancients in my father's service, both veterans of the Flanders wars, will bide here, and their swords. If this suffice not, and their own resource, to Jenny or to Lucy, they must now say so, and shall come with us.'

'This is spoke of already with thy father,' Jenny said, 'and I shall remain.'

'As to me,' quoth Lucy, 'if I must flee ever, 'twill not be to Essex, that I know not, but to Surrey, where I am not forgot.'

'Nor mayhap remembered,' said Peter sourly. 'Yet thee, Robin, shall I serve as thou desire.'

'Then knows each one where he stands, or she,' said Robin, rising. 'Do thou come with me, Aubrey, for as our chief practitioner in arts rural, thou shalt drive the cart, and I would have thee cast thy blacksmith's eye upon it, and the nags also.'

In the hall without, he chided me for my suspicions not of Amos, which he forgave, but of his own fair intent toward me; and I took his hand, kissed it, and asked him pardon. In the midst of which marriage of true minds there was a bang on the front door, three paces from us, whereat Robin seized his sword, and I plucked out the kitchen knife that was the first thing I had sought out when I returned, for I felt naked without my dagger.

Robin swung the door open, and there stood Cecil.

'Lord have mercy, coz,' cried Robin. 'What dost thou here?'

'Let me enter, sweet Robin!' cried he and, without bidding, hastened within. 'I must speak with thee, cousin, and that instantly!' he cried, clutching at Robin's doublet.

'Speak then, but not here, do thou come into my privy chamber. Nay, glide not away, Aubrey, for I have need of thee, I mean anent our business in the stables.'

I got a glare at this from Cecil, but held my peace, and we proceeded in silent procession up the stairs. The door scarce closed, Cecil burst into a flood of protestations, watered, from time to time, with showers of tears.

'Robin, my heart,' quoth he, 'thou knowest I love thee, and, so loving, cannot love my father for the evils that he brings upon thee and thy father's house. And this I have made bold to tell him, braving his wrath which, as thou knowest well, quick surges, and sinks slow. And to him I have said this, and sworn it on my life: that if he force thy father, that is his own brother, into exile, I can do naught, whate'er my heart and conscience tell me; but that if he force thee, Robin, out of all fortune, and of London, then am I no son of his, and he may take all his high hopes of making of me a gentleman, and so bringing credit to his name and house, and stuff them up his arse, and fart them out on all the aldermen and merchants he consorts with.'

'Thou spake thus to thy father, Cecil?'

'Aye, marry, those very words! But this is not all – hear further. My father has this day, for the first time of his life, understood that his son, I, whom he had deemed a watery pliant thing, is obstinate as he, and wilful. And indeed, as I screamed at him (rousing all Bishopsgate, pardee), and he bellowed back, he paused after a while, then said, "Zounds, I had not thought my blood ran in thy veins!" "Marry, and my mother's too," cried I, "that was most roaring strumpet of St Helen's!" "Aye, so was she," said he. "Well, then," said I, "do thou not . . ." '

'Calm thyself, Cecil, I prithee, and shriek not at me as at mine uncle; rather, tell me the issue peaceably, and with less speed.'

'Robin, this is the bargain struck twixt him and me. Do he defraud thy father, and harass him out of London, then must he take son if he will lose brother.'

'Cecil, I stay perplexed: what does this mean?'

'It means that my father, Genoa, has sworn solemnly, and before witness of Beauty and the six chief bawds that rule his houses (each of whom, on my insistence, was summoned in), that thou, Robin his nephew, stand in his eye and fortune, as equal in all substance whatsoe'er to me, his son Cecil.'

'But cousin, none and naught could make me more brother to thee than I am already.'

'In heart, Robin, mayest thou so be, as I, sure, to thee, and more than brother! But this consanguinity and love are not gifts Genoa can bestow. What I have sucked out of him is other: 'tis that thou art henceforth, beside my cousin, my equal heir to all he has and shall have.'

'And he swore this?'

'Before witnesses, as I say, and tomorrow he shall before a notary; else do I shift myself, and that instantly, across the river to Bankside, and enter the service of his rivals there, to whom I shall unfold, as pledge of my casting him off utterly, all secrets known to me of his dominions.'

'And what said he to that?'

'That an I did it, he would kill me: or, being my father, have me killed.'

'And thou thereto, what?'

' "Father," said I, "thou hast a choice: and think not I misunderstand it, or its consequence to the final issue. And thy choice lies thus: thou must slay me, for which thou wilt be cursed and mistrusted by even the basest monsters of thy calling, or thou must take Robin, my cousin, into thy house, inside the City, as thy son." '

'Into thy house, Cecil?'

'Aye; and he has promised.'

Robin sank onto a couch, as if faint and struck half dumb, and Cecil beside him, weeping, and grasping for his hands. And when I glimpsed Robin's eyes wet also, I thought, 'Enough of this waterfall of cousinly lamentations, I must away.' But Robin, raising a hand from Cecil's, said, 'Stay, Aubrey, a while;' and then, after stroking his cousin's shoulder gently, said, 'Cecil, thou hast my heart, but this I cannot.'

'No, cousin?'

'No. Now, I have heard thee, and all these words that bear witness to thy love, so hear me also, and with gentle patience.'

'Aye, but Robin . . .'

'With patience, cousin. That love I bear thee, and have ever, and e'er shall, lives its own life so long as I mine, and thou thine, and naught but our deaths can sunder it: not even hatreds of those twain that have engendered us. But as to living with thy father, or taking a groat from out his fortune, that I will not, no, Cecil, never.'

'Because thou lovest him not?'

'Because I love my father.'

'And not me.'

'Cousin! What love would that be to thee to do what my heart tells me truly that I must not?'

'Cousin! It would be love to me to do what my heart tells me that thou shouldst.'

' "Shouldst" is not kind, cousin.'

'Nor thy refusal, when I tender half my inheritance and all my life.'

'Cecil, I tell thee, nay.'

'Robin, an thou leave London, my father shall need no cuthroat to slay me, for I shall myself do it.'

Marry! thought I: this is a scene for the *Globe* theatre, were it not that, ere now, the groundlings would be strolling homeward, or, if still present, seeing sunset illumine Master Hercules! So I put further thought to word, and said, 'Masters, you make heavy weather out of fair breezes.'

At this they both stared at me as if I had sung roundelays in church.

'Hearken, good cousins, sons, nephews, brothers! Robin will leave London. Cecil will slit his own gullet should he do so. Then why, pardee, should not Cecil sheathe his poignard, and leave London also?'

'Leave it with Robin?'

'That Cecil should come with us?'

'Aye, marry, and why not?'

They gazed at me, then at each other, and then laughed, yet so close to their weeping, that I felt I must harry them further into sense.

'Now, consider,' said I. 'I know little of thy two fathers and, to be open, would not know more, for it is their sons, not they, I cherish. Yet should you do this, that is, flee together to the country, here is the prophecy of Aubrey the famed fortune teller of Essex. Thy father, Cecil, Genoa, will burst into a violent passion, and swear he will slay thee, Robin, his brother Venice, and I know not who else, yet do none of these; and on reflection, perceive that if he has lost a son, he is freed also from a contract that he hated; nor will he believe, I ween, that this son be other than a Prodigal, that will one day return to him (as I foresee also – but no matter). Thy father, Robin, Venice, will raise up his brows to the summit of his pate, then lower them into a fearful frown, and yet say nothing; for he, on reflection, will equally perceive that Cecil can do him no harm, and that his brother Genoa, author of his misfortunes, will be vexed as a sow that litters a rat in error. Is this not so?'

'Well, yes,' said Robin.

'In an approximate,' said Cecil.

'Then one last word from the sorcerer Aubrey, who is, in sooth, weary, beside neglecting his angel below stairs. Do thou, Robin, unfold to Cecil all he should know anent our journey; and do thou, Cecil, descend from the heights of thy fierce passion, and consider such matters mundane as boxes, cords, harnesses, and whether the nags have five legs, or are ill shod. Do you twain but this, and tomorrow I am your servant for all packing, saddling, cursing, or whatsoever. Until then, gentle cousins, adieu.'

With which I slipped out and down the stairs panting with fatigue and, to tell all the truth, lechery. In the kitchen, Jenny was tapping that foot, and folding those buxom arms, in the style familiar to all who have made women wait beyond expectation.

'Thou hast been long away!' said she, glaring.

'Aye, marry,' said I, catching her up, 'let us to bed.'

17

I was waked by birds carolling ere dawn; and hearing wheels, and neighing, peeped out to see the coach rumbling through the nether gate, circled by horsemen, in the first dim light; which made me wonder if Doge Venice, its chief occupant, knew aught of the cuckoo, Cecil, that had come into his emptied nest.

Soon others were bestirred: and there began a bustling and rumble, as all embarked on preparations for our own voyage on the morrow. As is habitual in a turbulence, all became generals, and none would be common soldier: orders were shouted from attic floor to stable, countermanded in buttery and pantry, executed ill, obeyed nowhere. Yet at length, to the astonishment of all, there was no more to do; and we sat to eat fare magicked up by Jenny, Lucy hindering.

Robin, prod on by Cecil, that wished to drink toasts to our

departure (and also, I ween, drown his own terror that Genoa might erupt and carry him away), had sallied to plunder Venice's cellar, the which I doubt he would, had the Doge been in his customary seat. So we drank heavy; and Herman, rising on his swaying shanks, spake thus:

'My masters, and gentlemen all! Odysseus, so Homer saith, that was greatest traveller of antiquity, did ever, with his gallant henchmen, ere their perilous transfer from one isle of enchantment to the next, partake of copious libations. As he and they, so we. Yet hearken further! If we must speak of Greeks (that none did, nor wished, save Herman), that are, with the Jews, the mother and father of all learning – the one, that is the Jews, in topicks sanctified, the other, Greeks, in matters secular – then must we allow that Homer, though first father (or, as 'twere, Adam scholastical) of all these, should bow his grey head, and close reverently his blind eyes, before his scriptural descendants, which are, in chief, Aeschylus, Sophocles and Euripides: to wit, all writers and concocters of plays. Aye; and as Homer did, and must, so ought we also. By which I mean that of all those who, since centuries remotest, put pen to paper (or, for aught I know, reed to papyrus, or e'en blazoned stone with chisel), the most illustrious by far, are those whose arts were consecrated to the theatre. Therefore perpend. Surveying, as I do now, an assembly of fair youths all dight with wit and scholarship indescribable, that is, Robin our gentle host, his coz blushing Cecil, gallant Peter, and bepocked meddlesome Aubrey (though he meddle not where he might, pardee), I grieve natheless to bear witness that not one of these – nay, not a one save I – has e'er entered into a theatre, nor heard a play.'

'We hear one now,' said Robin.

'Flatter me not, youth, 'tis but a rehearsal. Hear, therefore, and mark me well. This very afternoon, over at the

Swan, situate on Bankside, will be performed, before an audience that wants but our company to please the actors, a play: to see which (though it be, to my thinking, as ill-married and languorous a confection as was e'er writ) I would empress you all, and that with extreme urgency. For on the morrow, we must withdraw from all haunts habitual to fame and felicity, that is, London, to I know not what bog, ditch or midden dear to the soul of Aubrey, that was weaned there; to endure which, we should fortify our spirits (as I do now mine with these – your healths!) with one peep, or glimpse ultimate, of the true palace of this city, which is the *Swan*.'

'But what is this play?' saith Robin.

'One apt to thee, thy father, and the occasion: 'tis *The Merchant of Venice*.'

'Now hearken to me, and well!' cried Jenny, raising her voice and person. 'Do thou go, Herman, into what rat-hole pleaseth thee, but alone! Or at least not with my Aubrey, that has but yesterday scaped the Clink, and lost all our gold with it, and shall stay fast here, as I live, till he be safe away!'

'As for me, Herman,' said Cecil, ''tis the Merchant of Genoa that enlivens my apprehension, and I would stay hid to scape his minions.'

'Aubrey!' cried Herman. 'Hast thou not more fettle, or art thou so hen-pecked already by this jade that, if thou take not heed, she will assuredly en-cuckold thee?'

'Well, I would dearly love to see a play,' said I, braving the artillery mounted in Jenny's eyes.

'And brave Peter, art thou founded on rock, or shifting sand?'

'Well, I stand even.'

'Thou, Robin, that art, in this enterprise, our Odysseus?'

'Well,' said he, 'let us crush wine without, inside the

garden; for I perceive that in this kitchen there is a Cyclops, that will prohibit all straying from her cave.'

My Jenny, that wanted not art to cozen men into obedience to her will, lacked yet (though she has well learned it since) one stratagem apt to the armoury of womankind. And this is, if the man say, 'I will,' reply not, 'So shalt thou never;' but rather smile, hold thy peace a while, and then, when their wilfulness is lulled, deftly extract submission. This is so, in especial, when a body of men must be so tricked: for they will instantly withdraw, murmuring, 'What! Are we to be ruled by petticoats?' and stoking each other's fires of rebellion, do that which the woman had wisdom to detest, but not force utterly to forbid. In brief, we sneaked through the postern gate, our sails set for the *Swan*.

On Bankside, it seethed; and it was not the disturbance of my mind, nor in the Venice and Genoa factions, that made me see others as I was, for the noise and bustle had a hard sharpness not habitual. Prentices had declared holiday, and were out in numbers; the Sheriff's men abounded, and the Knight Marshal's; and as for the populace, they were rebellious all – men jostling, women shrill. Is it the turmoil of the times, thought I, or fear of fast approaching Domesday?

We had scarce struggled in, when the play began. For a while, I could hear little, so restless were the groundlings, so far the actors (for we were stuck fast near the Gate). The audience was much as Jenny had denounced it: about us a press of prentices and varlets, fledgling lawyers who disputed louder than the players, gallants that gazed everywhere save on the stage, and, in the galleries, persons of sober sort that fluttered cambrics to their nostrils in disdain of us and even, seemingly, the actors. Set apart, surrounded by servitors, were noblemen like cardinals; and a few younger had even intruded onto chairs set beside the stage.

As to the play, I own I could make of it neither head nor tail: or rather, it was like a dream: in which flashes of sense, and witless phantasy, are alternate. In chief, it concerned one Bassanio, that loves a maid I would rather salute than bed with, that is named Portia; and loves also an elder man, Antonio, that hath contracted a debt to one Shylock, an Israelite. Three scenes alone stayed planted in my remembrance: the first by its tediousness, the next, its scant probability, and the third, its sorrow.

The first was a sort of duel, or country guessing game, twixt three gallants (one swart as Lucifer) as to which of three caskets, aptly pricked, will win them their lady (and belike the caskets also). Now, e'en an Essex lad of twelve, and a simpleton at that, could have plucked out the winner: both because he is hero, and that an offer of base metal is e'er more credible than one of gilt; beside which, he would guess that, if three actors must pluck out a casket, the last must be the winner, else there could not be three speeches made.

The next was a trial scene, anent the bargain twixt the Venetian and the Israelite, that provoked from the young lawyers round about me, exceeding merriment: for the judge was none other than the same heroine, Portia – that is, a woman! Marry! thought I – this can scarce be. For were I haled before the justices, and found it was a damsel that must pass judgement on me, I would leap out the dock and offer her violation, rather than suffer such indignity.

Well, now, as to Shylock, that is a Jew. Each time he stepped on, he was greeted by the groundlings with such braying laughter, and shouts of foul abuse, that I could scarce hear what he (or the actor) said. Yet when, at the end, he is betrayed by his daughter, whom he loveth dearly as his gold (or equally, yet loveth), there fell somewhat of a hush at his wild lamentations. Which made me suppose the intent of the writer was, that this man be not comical, but much abused. Truly, I know not: for I have ne'er met a Jew (who are but scant, I ween, in London, and in any event, frequent not brothels), so am no judge if this Israelite were as they are, or his persecution by his debtors, apt.

What I most lacked in witnessing this spectable, was its proof of love: I mean between man and woman, for Herman had told me this is chief topick in the theatre, yet here it wanted sadly. For Portia is more nun than jade, or schoolmistress, rather; and as to Bassanio, I warrant our lustiest strumpets would have none of him, even for gold. Well, thought I, I must see *Romeo and Juliet* instead; which carried my mind to Jenny, and the scoldings that awaited me.

'Sir, is this not thy poignard?' said a voice, as we struggled out. 'Or, to be more precise, utensil culinary?'

'Gropenut!' cried I. 'Whence hast thou sprung, like Mephistopheles?'

'From hell to paradise!' said he. 'For besides thy carver, I have plucked more down from this *Swan*'s belly that I did e'er in any theatre.'

'Aye, but how art thou freed?'

'By modesty,' said he. 'That is, by learning not only from those ripe in years, but from a green fruit, to wit, thee. For when thou camest not back into our cell, I meditated much, then pried out of our honest turnkey (by promises like those of Signor Antonio) the manner of thy evasion. Then sought I, and achieved after much blustering, and beating, a word in the eager ear of my Lord Chief Gaoler, thy deliverer: who, when I persuaded him, sent a fellow into St Helen's to fetch Beauty, bearing ransom; and so am I now poorer in riches, but richer in that richest, which is freedom.'

'Then must thou drink with me to thy deliverance, and meet my friends, can I but find them in the press.'

We foregathered without, and hied us to an ale-house, that was so close packed we must carry our ale into a neighbour garden, and there quaff it on the sward. And instantly, as 'tis after a funeral, a dispute arose on the virtue of what was now expired.

'Aye, but Antonio lacked all resource,' said Cecil. 'For all he need do, is hire some fellow to fling Shylock into a canal.'

'Or slit his gizzard,' said Peter, 'as he would the Venetian's breast.'

'As to that,' said Gropenut, 'did the Jew have any science, he could both have carved the flesh and spared the blood.'

'How so, for they are wed like man and wife?' said Robin.

'As thus. He must, in a fire, heat a sharp blade to red heat. Next, procure, and place adjacent, scales for neat measurement. Now, as any skilled cook will tell thee, meat, howsoever raw, if cut by a hot knife, will bleed not a single drop; the fire congealing the blood instantly. So had but Shylock to carve neatly into Antonio, slice by slice kept thin, and weigh each upon his scales till the exact measure was precisely rendered.'

'I marvel,' said Herman, 'at such a commentary. For is butchery the whole matter of this play? True, it is ill-writ, o'er long, and what little art and grace it have, all pillaged. Yet in some scenes . . .'

'Pillaged how?' said I.

'Well, it is writ by Shakespeare, that is chief thief theatrical from loftier men.'

'As who?'

'Why, as from Marlowe, principally.'

'Thy Marlowe ever!'

'Aye, ever my Marlowe! Speak what thou knowest, Aubrey; till then, hold thy peace! Christopher wrote, five years since, *The Jew of Malta*: which is to this, as Apollo's countenance to thine.'

'Aye, well, say on!'

'Shylock is stolen from Barabas, Marlowe's Jew: that hath a passionate eloquence, and profundity of soul, this scribbler can ne'er encompass.'

'And why these plays anent Israelites?'

'Because, as any less ignorant than thou would know, one Dr Lopez, a Jew and Portugoose, that was privy physician to our sovereign, sought to empoison her, at the behest of Spain; or so it was put forth, and, in any event, he hanged for it.'

'Thy Marlowe I give thee; but how canst thou know this Shakespeare thought of any Jew of Portugal?'

'Didst thou but mark the text, rather than ogle Whitehall strumpets in the galleries, thou wouldst have found thine answer. For gainst Shylock, 'tis clear said,

> for thy desires
> Are wolvish, bloody, starved and ravenous.

Well, "wolvish" pertains to wolf; in Spanish, wolf is *lopez*; ergo, Shylock is he.'

'Then is this Shakespeare but a borrower, like Antonio?'

'Will? He is the magpie of every rival's yard – I say no more than what is known to all.'

'"Will", sayest thou?'

'Aye, Will, or William: Master Shakescene.'

'He is country born, hast thou not told me?'

'Aye, from Warwickshire, or thereabout.'

'Thou hast said Worcestershire.'

'They are all one.'

'How looks he?'

'Looks? Well, had he acted in his own morality today, thou wouldst have seen better than I can tell thee.'

'Why, he acts also?'

'Aye, and ill as he writes, were't possible. Why he stayed off today, I know not. It cannot be modesty, for this he knows not; more like he tires of his own creation, for 'tis an old thing, that I saw first three years since.'

'Aye, aye, Herman; yet tell me, prithee, more of his face and form than of his failings.'

'His face? Why, he is bald-pated (by excess of lechery, 'tis averred), hath doe eyes, pretty enough, and the beard of a boy that fingers the first sprouting round his lips. As to his stature, he is nor tall, nor short, but, as in his art, middlewise. His voice, when he speaks, which is not oft (for he listeneth, rather, to replenish his scant stock of conceits), is soft, yet even: melodious, some might say, though not I, for he hath clung to the imperfections of his rural nurture.'

'But this must be my Will!' cried I.

'Thy Will?'

'Aye, William, that I thought scrivener.'

'Aubrey,' said Herman, rising, 'be thy will what it may, mine own is to absent myself herefrom, while I have life and breath: for mark how the crowd surges and presses in.'

We all rose then, but as we were moving out, one plucked at my sleeve, and it was Daniel, servant to Noll; and he drew me aside and said, 'My master commanded me, should I see thee ever, to give thee this.'

'Gramercy, Daniel. I am but one day freed, and in sore need of it.'

'Aye, so heard I; and sallied into Bishopsgate, to Genoa's stews, where I won naught but frowns and buffets.'

'True, I am ill reputed there, and long dismissed. But how fared you all that night? I had thought to come asking, and for my gold also, but feared capture were I seen beside thy house.'

'Thou wert well counselled: Bowes mansion lies in siege, and Noll trembles at each knock.'

'Aye, but what found they when the coach was halted?'

'Nothing, because it was not. The coachman whipped his nags, and cantered forward, lashing at the fellows, as did the outrider too, with I plying my dagger, as I glimpsed thou didst with thine.'

'And then?'

'We scaped them, for by Mary's grace, they had not thought of horses; and we carried the poor priest, that pissed a very puddle in his vestments, to another safe house, true to the old faith, of which thou wilt not ask me for the name.'

'And so found some ease.'

'Yet unease, for we live but by our rosaries, and *Hail Marys* rise from Blackfriars in a stream to heaven.'

'And Allan, meanwhile?'

'Is fled.'

'Mercy on us! Are Puritans to be exiled also?'

'Nay, nay – 'tis otherwise: his brother, Noll, my master, has expelled him.'

'On what ground?'

'That loving him not, and he hating the old faith so extremely, Allan might betray Noll to the justices.'

'That would Allan never.'

'No, not by treachery, I think either; yet by folly or fault of prudence, possibly.'

'And he is gone whither?'

'None knows, save for old Moses, that is gone with him.'

'Well, God save them.'

'And thee, Aubrey, and us all.'

I ran to recapture my comrades, which was like breasting water, for the streets vomited out people, struggling and running into Southwark. And there, near St Mary Overy, there were brisk barks of 'Prentice, prentice!' and from all quarters swarmed these lads, bearing cudgels and crying, 'To the Marshalsea!'

'What is't?' said I to a fellow that was grinding knives, and seemed placid in this din.

'Give me work, and I shall tell thee,' quoth he.

So I handed him my kitchen knife which, having spat on it, he rubbed upon his trundle wheel, sparks flying off.

'It is,' said he, nodding towards the scurriers, 'the consequence of this morning's folly.'

'Of whom?'

'Of several. Perpend. My Lord Chamberlain issues a warrant to his Knight Marshal, to distrain a feltmaker's servant, for supposed robbery, that labours in Blackfriars, but dwelleth here. So comes Sir Knight upon a horse, his retainers following on foot, armed at all points like ambulatory castles.

'But, friend (turning the blade over, and quenching sparks with supplement of spit), if thou knewest Southwark as I do, then wouldst thou know equally the King Marshal's men are loved hereabouts, e'en by those of good repute and substance, as is the Devil by holy friars: for these officers of the law are violent, foul-tongued, ruthless fellows, that will batter ten doors down where one suffices, and e'en these ten ill chosen for their purpose.

'Yet at length they lay hands upon the feltmaker's lad, beat him, and cast him inside the Marshalsea. Of this, tidings swift flow o'er the river, to Blackfriars, where this fellow is well loved by felting prentices: who, on pretext of coming southward to the play, gather about the Bear Pit, and now sally forth, as thou hast perceived, to rescue their closed comrade. Two groats, sir: half price, if thou hast another.'

'I carry but one weapon.'

'Two, I dare hope. Best thanks.'

'But they can ne'er succeed against a prison and armed officers?'

'Nay? Well, I know not – do thou go see! But ponder on this. These are not only prentices; but conjoined with them, in occasional alliance, are divers veterans of the wars, of which thou hast sure seen many wandering the streets, crying shame on the commanders that have filched their meagre wages, and left them unpaid, though oft wracked by honourable wounds, for years now. The prentices are hot and rash; the soldiers cold and skilled; 'tis a perilous combination, and I would not be this moment in the trembling boots of the Knight Marshal's men.'

I pushed my way down towards the Marshalsea, but soon the press that held me before, was doubled by another surging on me from behind; for with great cries of, 'Make way! Yield passage to my Lord Mayor and Sheriff!', some horsemen came over from the City, and kicked their way to a halt nearby. Whereat the Lord Mayor, pausing to place spectacles (which roused a great gust of ribaldry among the multitude, one fellow crying, 'God save my Lady Mayoress when thou fumblest for her!'), read out a proclamation, of which none heard the words, though their purport was clear to all. Thereupon, the more prudent sort dispersed, albeit unwillingly; and the cavalcade spread out, drawing daggers, swords and bastinados, and seized on several fellows so much at random, that I backed like a badger into an alley; from which, after a while, turned weasel now, I slunk back up towards the river; passing once more the knife-sharpener, that winked at me and cried, 'Thou art well saved, lad, from whipping or the pillory? Guard well thy weapons, each and several.'

So I hastened over the Bridge, and began to think now of a new peril that awaited me, which was my Lady Marshal Jenny, who would sure be not pleased to hear my tale undiluted; so, as I walked, I improved upon it in my mind, which was to say what had detained me, was my converse with Daniel.

Well, at Venice's abode all was in order, and each one had safe returned; Gropenut having hooked himself like a burr onto all doublets. In the kitchen they were at wine again, roaring at Gropenut's jests, and scarce noticing the ill glowers of the girls. I had scarce set foot inside the door when Jenny, ignoring their cries of greeting, hauled me inside the buttery, and there cuffed me; so I her, harder; so she again. Whereat Herman poked his nose around the door, and tried to feed her wine, saying, 'The quality of mercy is not strained, It droppeth as the gentle rain from heaven;' but she bundled him out, and cried, 'Aubrey, thou wilt break my heart one day.'

'But not with this,' said I, handing her Noll's gold.

'Aye, marry no,' said she, growing swift calmer.

The Play

I

ALL JOURNEYS I have read in legends, and e'en those heard related, and myself experienced, start well, continue ill, and end up neither; and so it was with us. By breakfast, for we had risen soon spite our debaucheries, we came into Stratford, Bow: I driving with Herman beside, Robin twixt Cecil and Peter on the nether seat, and Gropenut perched up on the baggage: for though we had tried to turn him off, plying him with early ale, he swore God had chosen him guardian to Cecil, since they were both Genoans, although traitors now.

Ere dawn, when I had waked her to say adieu, Jenny had tried to share with me Noll's gold; but I said no, we were provisioned for the journey and, at Epping, if there were not Robin's father, there would be Martin; besides that I was no boy now, and could live as e'er might be; while she had herself to consider, that carried our child. So she took from her neck a locket, shaped as a heart, and that I knew she treasured (for though she had told me much, she ne'er told me who gave it to her, nor why, nor did I ask), and hung it about my neck, and said, 'Aubrey, this is mine, that shall travel with thee ever,' then kissed me, and swung over on her side, leaving me her rump to speak to, and no further voice to hear.

'Aye, Stratford!' said Herman, gazing as if a prince upon a privy. 'Atte-Bow, forsooth, not atte-Avon, where shaketh thy friend Will his spear.'

'Mar not the morning with thy low envy, Herman.'

'Marry! The yokel, sniffing the country air, and swelled by the superiority of handling horses, waxes ironical.'

'Nay, hungry; let us pause here to swell man and horse.'

It was still warm enough to eat out doors, though needing a fire, on which we heaped orange leaves, aromatically. All seemed at ease save Robin, that was pensive; and I guessed it was that his father's downfall touched him more nearly than he allowed; and perhaps that, must he travel with all men and no maid for company, he would have wished Allan there, rather than pert Peter, or cloying Cecil.

'And now we approach thy realm,' quoth Gropenut to me, 'where shall we travel next, and where lie this night?'

'Why, we may lodge at Snaresbrook and, with ardour, good fortune, and our mare not foaling, push on to Epping on the morrow.'

'I like not that, pardee!'

'Not what?'

'Why, the straight ford to which we have come, is well enough, e'en though it smack already of an excessive rusticity for my palate. But as to the snare's brook, I like that less: we must look to our arms and accoutrements, for I would be no hooked fish.'

'What vexes thee, Gropenut, about the country,' Peter said, 'is that there be less fish there to hook for thy cozening.'

'Oh, I fear not that: for unless rustics be bereft of pokes, and walk naked as the Red Indians, I doubt not my hand will be kept busy.'

'Poking inside their pokes,' quoth Herman.

'Aye, marry, and elsewhere, I trow, be they not celibates.'

'Is it true, Aubrey,' said Cecil, 'that country folk are more virtuous than we?'

'Peter and I are thine answer, Cecil. Nay, I would dub rustics identical in substance, and different in form: in principal, because in a village, secrecy is forbid by close proximity of few.'

'Yet hast thou haywains and byres where none can observe but beasts; while in the city, are but houses, with as many spies as windows.'

'Do thou lie in a byre, Robin, e'en innocently, and I promise thee beasts will know of it, and not with four legs, neither; for it is the going and coming that are e'er noted in the country, unlike towns.'

'Provided his coming be not espied,' said Gropenut, 'Robin may bide easy in his byre.'

So soon we swung northerly, and continued; the rest falling into slumber, while Herman, beside me, prattled on.

'I doubt not, Aubrey,' said he, 'that the sight of thy native haunts induces in thee something of the joy of the caged bird that is set free?'

'Well, yes, and I avow it. I love London, aye; but this also, and fondly.'

'Then wilt thou understand it when I tell thee this: that yesterday, when we came into the *Swan*, I trembled like a girl at her first ball. For such was my rapture in the theatre, when I laboured there, that I can ne'er return without a pleasing pain.'

''Tis sad thy pleasure was so soon cut off.'

'As said the Moor to the eunuch – aye, marry, yes. But no matter: mayhap, Aubrey, one day, by God's good grace, or the Muses', I shall step onto that stage again.'

'To be man actor – I mean of men?'

'Aye: though there is a lustre in playing of women's parts that e'en Alleyn might envy. For believe me – and here speak I not by puffed vanity – though the boy actors be few, they can make or mar a Company's repute.'

'And who is Alleyn?'

'Who is Alleyn! 'Tis as though thou saidst, "Who is Drake, or Essex, or Ralegh"!'

'Well – who?'

'Edward or Ned Alleyn is, beyond question any, and by acclaim universal e'en of his direst rivals, the supreme tragic actor of our age.'

'Thou hast played with him?'

'Aye, and unforgettably. An actor's first duty, Aubrey, among impositions that are legion, is his simplest also; which is not to forget the words put in his mouth. Yet I swear to thee, that though I was firm in memory, and precise in certitude of what I spoke, when Ned did, I have been near struck dumb.'

''Twas in Marlowe's plays that thou hast heard him?'

'Aye: for he was principal in all; and beside acting in 'em, captained the whole company, and managed its business to boot. For Kit, thou must know, though haloed with genius, was ne'er actor; so that one of these must teach his thought to the remainder players, as did Alleyn.'

'Yet Will hath no need of such, being himself actor beside writer.'

'Thou and thy Will! Yet this is true enough: he is as a pregnant midwife, that can both make flesh and deliver it.'

'And who is his chief tragic player?'

'Burbage: one of a great tribe, of which the ancestor is James, that was with Leicester's men, and has built theatres beside acting in them; and of whose multitudinous progeny, Richard is chief actor to Will Shakespeare, beside being his friend.'

'In the company of my Lord Chamberlain.'

'Marry, I have an apt pupil here! Aye, that thou sawest yesterday, all spitting from the Rialto. Beside Burbage, there are John Heminges . . .'

'Who I know also!'

'Peace, pupil, not o'er apt, prithee. Heminges, I say, that, like Alleyn to Marlowe, is manager for Will; then Augustine Phillips, Thomas Pope, William Sly, George Bryan that all (save for Burbage) came to the Chamberlain from Strange's company.'

'Who is this Strange?'

'Ferdinando, Earl of Derby, that died some five years since, bewitched, they say, which were indeed passing strange.'

'And what of those comical?'

'Will Kemp would I place highest, as do also the groundlings; who, if they err oft in their assay of tragic acting, are sound on comic. He it was that played Bottom, and the part sat well on him.'

'No other?'

'Many: as Robert Armin, who, I have heard, shall take Kemp's place with my Lord Chamberlain, that leaveth it; for actors, though faithful, are also fickle; and fly from one Company to another as fame, fortune, or fury summon them. Thus once was Kemp with Leicester's Men; and Heminges, that thou sayest thou knowest, who is with my Lord Chamberlain now, and was with Ferdinando Strange, as I have related, was ere this in the Queen's Company. Yet marvel not at these permutations, nor censure the actors for them neither; for beside that the Companies rise and fall, as do their patrons, by advancement or disgrace and death, 'tis apt that an actor gain enrichment by experience of fresh fellows.'

'And who else among those comic?'

'Why, Richard Tarleton is much esteemed, though I prefer Kemp, albeit he is broader; then John Sinckler, that delights in playing schoolmasters, but delights not them.'

'And what of the boy actors that play women?'

'Aye, what of them? For since my day, they are much

fallen off. Nay, smile not thy smile of ignorant superiority; for I tell thee that, as all good actors do, or most, I esteem my comrades honestly. Thou hast heard me praise, Aubrey, and lavishly; then let me blame also if I see fit.'

'Blame then, or praise.'

'Well, there is Master Goffe, Robert or Bob, whom thou hast ogled yesterday; and that I nor blame nor praise, for he is a half-baked egg.'

'Who played what?'

'Portia.'

'That was a boy?'

'Aye, and with substance secreted neath his skirts.'

'Truly, Herman?'

'Marry, do thou unfrock him, Aubrey, and see: he will not deny thee, that I may promise certainly.'

'Why! I could well swear him maid.'

'Made is he, and nightly, but not by maids. Hadst thou but seen him playing Juliet, thou wouldst have leapt up on the stage and ravished him.'

'Mercy on us! And the groundlings know this?'

'Why, yes, in their minds, but not in their inventions. For oft, when I journeyed to the theatre in the days of my vanished fame, lewd fellows would cry out to me in the streets, "Shame on thee, Herman, thou hermaphrodite! Cast off thy breeches, boy, and don thy skirts, and I shall buss thee!" Yet, when I acted 'fore them, these same fellows would stare silently agape, till their wives nudged them into normality.'

'And as to Will, Herman: Master Shakespeare that thou lovest not: how does he act? And temper, I prithee, thy spleen with justice, as thou hast promised me.'

'I will. First to be said, is that he acts small parts, yet well chosen; which, in his own plays, he may ensure himself by writing them. Now, as to why he does this, my spleen saith he cannot act the greater, wanting art; or that, being shareholder of the Company, he may, after doffing his costume, his small part spoke, dart round in dress ordinary to the gate, and there, like a fishwife at a Billingsgate sunrise, count up the money of his customers.'

'And what saith thy justice?'

'That sith he directs his plays – I mean disposes the actors, and corrects their faults of speech, if he find any – he may not with ease be constantly upon the stage, acting a chief part. Though spleen rising once more, I may say Alleyn could do this, if Will cannot.'

'Thou hast seen him oft act?'

'Enough to judge fairly, yet not enough to yawn. I saw him yesteryear, in a play Ben Jonson gave to my Lord Chamberlain, called *Every Man in his Humour*: in which his companion actors were those I have recounted for thee mostly, with John Duke and Christopher Beeston, additionally. Also Henry Condell, that is companion to John Heminges, and each what I may call the graver sort of player. Not dull nor pedantic – nay, in no sort – but I mean beside being fine actors, scholars.'

'And thou, Herman, wert of the graver sort of player?'

'Mock me not, Aubrey! The answer leave I to thine own lewd divination.'

'Then tell me, Herman, and be not offended at my question. If Will writes plays that fill up theatres, and is sustained by actors on whom thou thyself bestowest praise, why withhold thou any from this Shakespeare?'

'Thou art guileful, Aubrey, beside curious. Well, I shall try to answer thee fairly. In petty, that he liketh not my acting, and hath said so; not to my face, but my behind. In chief, that I hold of the theatre, in mine honest judgement – and such as its true worth may be – a concept otherwise than his.

For to me, it is either learned and solemn, or is nothing; or, to revise myself, a small thing, little. Thus comedy is, true, comical; and for this loved by the many, if not by those of any discernment. But tragedy is the peak, the summit: hard, if not impossible, of full attainment; and in this great art, he is not great.'

'He has not writ tragedies?'

'He has essayed them: as *Titus Andronicus*, which is such a torrent of blood and hacked off limbs that the stage must be washed after the performance. Or *Richard III*, that hath the Crookback in it, certainly; yet is so mired in the fallow of mud historical, as to be too dense a thing for my ploughing. Beside these, of tragedy he has writ nothing, or near nothing.'

'Yet he may improve, Herman; for he is not old, and may write great tragedies.'

'He is a half-spent thirty-five, if I mistake not. Marlowe, that reached the summits whereof I speak, was lost to us ere he was thirty.'

'Yet, as thou lovest Marlowe, or did, so is Will also loved, seemingly.'

'Aye, so is he – and by thee, Aubrey, whom his mere name has I know not how bewitched.'

'And by thy brethren also, Herman – I mean other actors.'

'True, by many; and by writers too, pardee. For this I will say of him, though I love him not: he is not jealous; no, not e'en of talent, where he discern it. Thus, many I knew spoke well of him, and this I allow freely; and younger writers, as John Marston, or Thomas Dekker, that are spurned by Ben Jonson's rising sun, are warmed by his. Well, let them be warned! For if he has plucked the kernel from riper plums, he may presently from the first fruits of these fledglings.'

By now the concourse on the road had thinned, and of those travelling, we were of the fewer moving outward, against that more coming in to London, which is the Great Moloch, swallowing a multitute it spews not out. Perceiving our passengers were still snoring (the day waxing warmer, although autumnal), Herman and I decided we would not pause for noon refreshment, but press on; though halting, at a brook, to water horses and serve nature.

As we stood there, skimming pebbles across the stream for a wager (I pledging one buss – no more – gainst a bawdy song from Herman), we heard horses approaching; and at length, in a flurry of hooved dust, there appeared before us a Cornet, and two of the Queen's troopers, of which the first climbed off his horse and, coming to us, cried, 'Fellows, we need this cart!'

'And we,' said I, raising my voice to rouse Robin and the rest.

'And thou shalt have it, do not fear, for we need it not long nor shall we harm it.'

'Need it for what?' said Robin, descending the cart with all our comrades, so that we stood six face to face with three.

'Thou art master here, fellow?' saith the Cornet.

'Aye, and no "fellow" to thee, soldier.'

'Give thee pardon, young sir,' saith the Cornet, with salute sarcastical to Robin. 'For if I command thee, 'tis that I am commanded by my Captain.'

'To pillage her honest subjects in the Queen's name?'

'By no means, good sir: have patience, for it stands thus. In Snaresbrook, we have learned, are robbers, highway marauders, that will set forth ere long for London, and upon this road; and there we would halt and capture 'em.'

'Then God speed you; but why our cart?'

'Because, sir, not wishing to offer up our young lives by the seizure of such scant fellows, we would, rather than assail direct, lay ambush for them; and so we need a cart to block the highway.'

'And why ours?'

'Sir, a poor soldier has but to ask any citizen that he protects, or night or day, for the least service in this duty, and this citizen e'er answers, as do you, "Why me?"'

'You will not spoil it? For see! it carries all my father's goods.'

'Well, to be open with you, this chest, or that pillow, may be nest to a bullet ere an hour. But you and your followers shall stay aside unharmed and, indeed, protected; for we shall be guardians to you; and had you not encountered us, 'twould be the robbers, not ourselves, that had your cart, and not with asking, as I do courteously now.'

'Follow them, then, Aubrey!' said Robin. 'Lads, do we climb again aboard.'

So off we set, in manner martial: in the van two troopers, and behind, escorting us, the Cornet; until we reached a bent cleft cut through a hillock for the road, that the military had selected for their foray. Here were more soldiers; and a Captain of such dignity and magnificence that he disdained our greeting, and ordered the Cornet to dispose 'those supernumaries' on the hilltop, out of danger, if not sight.

'Marry!' cried Gropenut, ''tis better than a play; and I who have oft dreamed of trailing musket for Her Majesty, may relish now my lack.'

'Provided the thieves lack any glimpse of us,' said Peter.

'Fear not; for we are, as generals, disposed far, yet not too far: convenient for command, yet distant from disaster.'

'Aye, Herman,' said I. 'Yet I like not the convenience at which they have disposed our nags; for though unharnessed, they are bridled up too near.'

'Beside which,' said Robin, 'if they swing round our cart further, they will surely snap a shaft.'

'Peace! Lie low! Here come their adversaries!' cried Cecil, that had climbed up, gainst orders, in a tree.

Thus began, on the 10th day of October, in the year of Our Lord, 1599, the great Battle of Snaresbrook Gap: a high feat of arms that emblazoneth on the escutcheon of I know not which regiment of clumsy rogues, glory imperishable. For the thieves, that possessed the good sense to send one of their number forward the main body, who, with sagacity outshining that of the defenders, had thought, spying a bending cleft, to ride first up the hillock and reconnoitre, were warned instantly by his cry of, 'Scatter!' which they tarried not to do; leaving the gallant defenders to defend nothing.

This perceiving, the ingenious Captain, that had marshalled his men in formidable array behind our cart, cried out, 'God's blood! Forward, and entrap the villains!' But the cliffs enclosing them being too steep for their horses, they must first hoist aside our cart, that they had ere little disposed so prudently to prevent passage; to effect which with the celerity and dash that are a prime rule of all military manoeuvre, they must cast it violently into the ditch, breaking two wheels and an axle; and having accomplished this, they galloped off in hot pursuit of their enemy, that was by now nearing the edge of Hertfordshire, if not further; while to complete the rout of all save their dread adversary, they had so ill hitched our nags to a rotted elm that, affrighted by the clamour, they had wrenched free and headed severally off, the bay to Suffolk (where he was doubtless foaled), and the chestnut back to London.

In vain did we, for a full hour, try to right the cart; vainer our search for any farmer that might lend a horse to haul us out, or let us borrow it to carry us to Snaresbrook. A further perplexity was that, on reckoning our joint fortune, it was ill-balanced; for if on the broke cart we had food and wine beside furniture, we had, to the surprise of all, no gold.

Yet why surprise? For I have oftentimes observed, that when a band of comrades sallies forth, each supposes the others rich till, upon any urgency, all find none is. Thus, I had but Jenny's locket; Peter was penniless, robbed of all plenty by Genoa's bullies; Cecil had fled in such passion from his father's house as to forget prudence; Herman, beside a thick volume of plays, had naught; Gropenut, that we knew rich by the plucking of *Swan* feathers had, with more generosity than foresight, bought a cask of ale for us in Stratford; while Robin, in whom our highest hopes resided, had had it enjoined on him by Amos and his father to carry no gold, that might tempt robbers, sith he would need none until Epping.

What now, then? Abandon our possessions, and proceed? Stand guard on them, and stay stuck fast? Divide in parties, one to stay, one go? Or wait, braving approach of night, till some Samaritan appeared along the way to succour us?

We chose first the last and, as it proved, worst. I know not how it was in Israel, where seemingly Samaritans abounded, but in England, if you be shipwrecked on a highway, one of three things ensues: that none come – though the road, ere then, were bustling; that some do, survey you as if ringing leper's bells, and scurry forward without halting; or that a loon witless and fantastickal appears from nowhere, possessing nor sense, nor (more to the purpose) horse, nor knowledge of where one may be got, that cries, in tones fit for the Book of Revelation, 'Why! Your cart be ditched, masters, and be broke!'

Father Sun decided us at last, for he was departing to the Americas, the shadows lengthening. What we would do, said Robin, was walk fast to Snaresbrook, that could not be far, leaving the cart to the protection of the dark. There, on security of our chattels, we would hire a horse and blacksmith's lad, and bring it in; and since, in desperate doubt, any issue seems more sage than none, we set off briskly, bearing what wine we could.

Our march, which fortune decreed, should be downhill mostly, was enlivened by libation, as by a rivalry twixt Gropenut and Herman as to which could sing songs bawdier. In this trial of wit and lewdness, Herman emerged victor: not that his ballads were fouler (for that were scarce possible), but because Gropenut's were of that sort which require embellishment of gesture, that the night forbade. Anon, we could hear churchbells; at which, less through reverence than thanks, our choristers desisted; and so we came into Snaresbrook.

I should have warned my comrades that in country places, man patterns his habits on animals', not least in their hours of rest and rising; so that all our hammering on the blacksmith's door earned us naught but a surly, 'Tomorrow!' Well, if he would not serve us in his forge, we could at least make free of his nether barn where, among a profusion of rusted things mechanical, we cracked the remainder bottles.

'Tis a fatality of drinking wine, that 'tis better to have none, than to have much and then, still being awake and merry, discover the bottles are quite voided, and no means to replenish them. In such a condition, men may wax quarrelsome, e'en desperate; and I was meditating a pledge of my locket with an innkeeper against better fortune on the morrow, when Peter said, 'That I had Lucy with us now, for she could swift earn the price of many a flagon!'

'She is misprized,' saith Cecil pertly, 'if this be the sole reason of thy need.'

'Well, I have another.'

'Peradventure,' quoth Gropenut, 'could I seek out some

old crone – for sure, every village hath its witch – and offer to serve her, exchanging the sorcery of my flesh for hers of some base metal, astrologically transposed into gold coin.'

'Thou knowest not our rustic witches,' said I to him. 'For there is not one that hath given aught to any, save ill counsel or the colic from her brews.'

'Beside which,' said Robin, 'witches ride broomsticks, not coney-catchers such as thee.'

'Or goats,' said Peter, 'which is somewhat similar.'

At this there was a silence, broke only by a sad belch from Gropenut, till Herman rose suddenly and said, 'There is naught for it, comrades, but in the general interest, I must go market mine arse.'

'Here in Snaresbrook?' cried I. 'And in this night and chill?'

'Marry, unless the choristers be about their practices . . .' quoth Peter.

'Have no fear!' cried Herman, 'and await in patient trust the replenishment of thy bowels by rich Bordeaux or Burgundian. For I am a fellow of infinite resource and, by moonlight, passing comely.'

With this he vanished, and we fell into a doze, with only a horse's snort, and a far owl, to disturb our drowsy dreaming; till we were awoke by a great clank of flasks, and in staggered Herman, bearing a full chest.

'Herman!' cried Gropenut, easing the corks out with a horseshoe nail, 'thou art a subtile fellow; and from this day, I forswear all mockery of catamites! Thy health, gallant Ganymede, and yours gentlemen!'

'Yet how,' said Robin, 'didst thou encompass this? For though I am thy junior, and the assault of maids be simpler, I do not believe I could have yet cozened a kiss, and not this treasure, certainly!'

'You will all have observed,' said Herman, 'that the soldiery infest this fair locality.'

'Aye, marry, do they!'

'This gave me hopes, which swelled into certainties when I heard the distant clamour of their carousals, that those we encountered might have comrades here; for troops, as you must know, have e'er headquarters, besides hind.'

'Which thou hast discovered.'

'Uncovered, rather. Now, soldiers, 'tis true, have not the particular aptitudes of sailors; who, in matters of boarding, mounting stern cannon, scraping bottoms and the like, are without equal. Yet are the military also versed in assault, pillage, discharge of guns, binding of captives and such arts; so to them I addressed myself, on pretext of complaint about our cart.'

'To their officers, mayhap?'

'Nay, for I am a modest fellow, and sober withal; and besides, with them I would have drummer-boys for rivals. So I made plaint rather to the Quartermaster who, as those that have studied armies all know well, is a very fount of military gossip and corruption.'

'And what said he?'

''Tis not what he said, but did; of which the crushed fruit, to wit that of the grape, is now coursing down your several gullets. And since, ere I returned to you, mine own hath been copiously filled by the kind master of my nether quarter, I will ask pardon for leaving you a while to discharge, into our host the blacksmith's glowing forge, their sizzling effects; and so wish you fair vomiting, snores multiple, and dreams honester than mine own.'

2

I was woke early by Robin, that drew me out into the yard, where it was still dark, and said, 'Hearken, Aubrey: we must back to the cart ere light, else will it be pillaged, if it be not already. Yet why I have summoned thee apart, is this. To resurrect our comrades from the stupor will cost hours: let us then wake but one, mayhap Peter, and he bring up the others when he may.'

'Aye, and we must wake the blacksmith, also.'

'Or his journeyman: who, if I mistake not, may be yonder,' and he pointed to a dim hut. 'For coming out this morning, I was pissing on its planks, when I heard snores.'

'Let us rouse him, then: for we may persuade him easier than his master, do we start soon, before his hours.'

'So thought I; also that thou, being native here, shouldst parley with him.'

'And offer what? For he will not budge an inch for our fair faces only, if I know Essexmen.'

'Or any! Well, I have thought on this: and I believe, though my father box my ears for't, we must make sacrifice of some part of our cargo.'

'Let me then try my skill at cozenage.'

'Twas an ill start to our enterprise, for the fellow sprung out clasping a great hammer, and crying murder; but I soothed him with broadest Epping, a flask of wine, and promise of fair fortune. At length, when cupidity had driven out fear, he heard us fairly; and said he would take his master's worst horse, least cart, and some tools, and see what he could do; but that whether he succeed or no, he must be rewarded.

So first telling Peter, we set off; and reached the cleft

quicker than we came down, dawn breaking withal. Naught was thieved from the cart, save Gropenut's cask, which was a fair hostage to our good fortune.

Master Journeyman, who examined all nearly (goods as much as breakages), pondered deep; and after scratching, sucking, and darting glances at Robin's city dress, emerged from his meditation with a proposal that did honour to the greed of Essex clowns. 'Twas this. If he spoke fairly to the blacksmith, he doubted not his master would exchange his raddled cob, and creaking dray, that we had now come up in, for our whole cart: which, he assured us, 'twould be a sore undertaking to make whole – if, indeed, it were not past all resurrection. As for himself, all he begged was our great bed, for he was getting married.

A bargain, alas for us, depends as much on circumstance as essence; and the more I argued gently with the fellow, the deeper he dug in his turd-clotted toes, till at length (as I expected) he made motion to mount his dray and go, lest his master beat him for tarrying about another's business; and as for us, said he, we could stay here if we wished or, if we would ride with him, give him but a chair. At this I turned to Robin in mute enquiry, he nodded as silently and sad, and I told the fellow we agreed his bargain, if his master did; and that he was a roynish rogue, who I hope was made cuckold in our bed.

Our troth pledged to this ambassador, we must now seek confirmation from his monarch: who, when he heard terms of the treaty from the journeyman, flung up his great hams in horror, and swore his cut cob had begot half the thoroughbreds of Snaresbrook; and that his dray, which creaked like an old floor, beside having lost planks and crooked wheels, was not one of those London wagons, that are ill-confected, and ours broke withal.

To this Robin replied, who was now waxed hotter than the forge, that our cart had cost his father twelve pounds to his sure knowledge, that the blacksmith's dray might fetch, with good fortune, as many shillings in a bankrupt's auction, and that he knew not how it was with the Essex craft, but any London prentice could mend our cart's few faults in an afternoon.

'Do thou go mend them, then!' cried the blacksmith, hammering a white-hot shoe and showering us in sparks, 'Do thou go haul thy wreckage to London, and thy tail also!'

This rummage brought on our four comrades, that stood about Robin and me, glowering. And Herman, raising his voice above the soughing of the huge bellows that the journeyman was plying with a great grin on his sweaty freckles, cried, 'Aye, Robin, 'tis as the Quartermaster told me yestereve: that he has ne'er seen nags worse shod in England, and his Captain has mind to carry custom from this fellow to the new forge on the Epping road. I shall away to him, and make report; and ask him, moreover, to lend horses to heave out thy cart.'

At this all fell silent, and the bellows too; and I asked the blacksmith to step aside, and favour me by brief converse. 'Friend, said I, 'I marvel at the ignorance of these Londoners, and grieve for their arrogant ingratitude for your kind favour to them. Yet do me this bounty, prithee: ride with me only up to their cart, which is not far off, and of a surety you will see 'tis a fair bargain. Moreover, our young master Robin, whose dress and jewelled sword you have sure marked, is son to a man of substance that I serve, and who is now lodged in Epping; whence, since he lacks not gratitude, he will surely send some reward to any that have dealt fairly with his son.'

'Well, yes,' said he at last, 'do thy master have on his cart a chest, for my wife lacks one for linen, and I am no carpenter.'

So gathering up Peter and the journeyman, and the wife summoned in to guard the forge (whence she chased all my remainder comrades), I set off with the blacksmith once more with cob and dray to the ill-fated cleft: where all was as before, save that now the chairs had vanished. The blacksmith eyed the cart forlornly, and the chest covetously, and entered into fierce dispute with his journeyman when he learned of his lien upon the bed. At last we heaved all save bed and chest from broke cart to cracked dray, and leaving the journeyman on watch, returned to Snaresbrook; the blacksmith lamenting his ill fortune, and railing on me, an Essex lad, for imposing four Londoners upon his kindness. And so, reaching the forge, all climbed into the dray with half our furniture; and like wrecked sailors in a leaky tub, we departed Snaresbrook, bestowing on it a choir of maledictions.

Of our journey that afternoon, nightmares still trouble my sleep when I have eat pork or swilled excessively. For beside I now knew we would ne'er reach Epping by night, both because of its distance and our snail-paced cob, it came down to rain on us in autumn torrents, hurled by a mounting gale. Nor were our spirits aught uplifted by the ribaldry of yokels at the sad spectacle we afforded; and 'en less that, having swallowed all of Herman's wine, we were bereft of inner sustenance. In this adversity, two were stalwart, and three not (for I say naught of myself): Peter, that was reared hard, crouched silent, but uncomplaining; and Herman whistled merrily to the winds, till all asked him to desist; but Cecil and Gropenut were all plaints, and e'en Robin: which makes me believe what I e'er have and shall, which is the virtue of rural tutelage.

We slept that night, as easy as fish on land, under a moist haystack; and I, rising at dawn, soaked and shivering as a cat fished from a river, discovered that our cob, mayhap by antiquity, or by a broken heart for leaving Snaresbrook, had yielded up its ghost to the gods equine. So rousing Peter, who I thought the only one that could sustain this misfortune without slitting his own gullet, I said, 'Come! There is a light yonder, let us see if all we Essex men are surly as the blacksmith.'

It was a cottage and, dawn breaking, they were already milking. I bade good-morrow to the farmer, and told him of our condition; at which he said naught save to call out to his wife that she must give us hot milk and cakes, and let us dry our clothing; the which she did, with no questions save would we like some cold pie also.

At length came in the farmer, with his pails, and thanking him, I said we had four comrades out under his haystack, who were as we had been ere he had succoured us; and peeling off my locket, begged him to take it, would he but favour them as he had us.

He answered he wanted naught of lockets (at which I thought his wife looked sad), but that if we would yield him up the cob's corse, he could replenish his pocket by calling in the knacker; and he told his wife to heaten up her pie, and more milk, and make ready for four guests further.

The dismay of our fellows when we waked them, was equalled by their amaze at the promise of a breakfast; of which they partook as ravenously as had we, the farmer eyeing us calmly yet cautiously withal (and I noticed his hand was near a tilted axe). And when the pie, and a fellow of it, were both gobbled up, Robin said, 'Sir, you are indeed welcome to the cob, but this will not requite your bounty: and so I beg you, make free with our dray as well; for we must swift to Epping, and without the cob, it hath no service to us.'

'Nor, in troth, hath the furniture,' said Cecil, 'unless we must, like snails, carry it on our backs.'

At this word of 'furniture', the eyes of the goodwife lit up like one that seeth the Grail, and she and the farmer walked with us up the hill; and though I could see the farmer thought little of the dray, his wife was in raptures at the couch and tables. 'This you must never do!' cried she, wringing her chopt hands with glee. And Robin, that is not so young as to know not when a woman's 'nay' be her 'aye', cried, 'By no means, madam! 'Tis all freely yours.'

The farmer, who was clear pleased with this (though, as is the country style, he sought to hide it), said, 'Well, wife, we must requite them also.' 'Aye, husband!' cried she. 'So come you with me, lads, you shall not lack sustenance for your journey.' And carrying us back to the cottage, she loaded into two sacks a ham, some loaves, an excess of apples, and six flasks of dandelion wine of her own confection.

As if to show us she was indeed now smiling, the jade Fortune brought out the sun: which, though watery, was warm; and bidding adieu to the farmer and his dame, that sent a lad with us to show us a short cut (of which I was wary, knowing these), we set off for Harden: for thither I had persuaded Robin we should first go, before discovery, he of his father, and I of Martin, further away in Epping.

As landmarks familiar came into view, Peter grew restive, as a horse scenting its stable; till, when he saw from afar the hutments of his birth, he broke into a run, halloahing. For he had spied, tending his scraggy sheep, old Colin; and when we all came up, the shepherd, peering at us with rheumy eyes, let out a shrill cracked cry, and fell on Peter's neck, mewling and slobbering; and when he perceived me, flung his lank arms about me, and cried, with a gusty expulsion of ill breath, that he thanked God he had lived to see lads as honest as we alive, and come back to Harden.

He led us then down into the hut to eat, exclaiming ever to

our comrades (whose names he had not asked, nor what they were) that he could not believe it, 'twas past all credence, how could it be, did he dream or no, and so on without spate, his stream of senilities interspersed with many a 'Lord have mercy!' and 'Come thy ways, my masters, tarry not I prithee,' plucking at six sleeves, and herding us into the hut as though we were his flock.

There, while we ate, he rang on the great bell, that serves to announce births, deaths, fires or other mishaps, the arrival of soldiers or itinerant harlots, the coronation of monarchs or a hanging; and this brought in from the fields the labourers, all agog, of which Simon, at sight of Peter, swooned, and William, at that of me, grunted with a great lecherous grin, and enfolded me with arms caked in goat dung.

When this turmoil was appeased, I consulted with Robin as to what now; and made proposal to him that, as I knew the way, and 'twould not be easy to borrow more than one nag, I should ride over to my step-father Martin in the forest, and find if Doge Venice lodged there, or where else; and so bring over his father's coach to carry him and the others forward.

And when this was agreed, old Colin, that had been intruding his chopt ears betwixt us, beside fussing like a hen-wife over all, cried out to Robin, 'Master, our Aubrey will surely not return ere nightfall, so you and yours must lodge here; and for this, I offer you hospitality of my sheepcote; where you may rest your heads upon the ewes, that are as warm pillows.'

'Yet beware the rams!' said Gropenut, eyeing William's ogling of my person.

'Aye,' quoth Herman, 'and the ewes also,' and he pointed at Peter and Simon, that were flashing jealous eyes at Robin.

'Ancient!' quoth Gropenut, seizing on Colin's tattered gown. 'Thou that hast endured four score winters here, pray tell me: why should a man that be not bereft of reason, wallow in country mires when he could grace cities?'

'Why, I was born here,' quoth Colin.

'And I in an Edgware ditch, but did not there remain.'

'Why, man must eat; and we, as the ewes their lambs, must nourish cities, beside ourselves.'

'Yet wouldst thou not rather, in the commerce twixt mankind, be recipient than donor?'

'Why, no, sir: for if I may moral on thy conceit, a donor, though he give unto him that hath not, is yet wise enough to save that better which he hath; and so, when we send kine to market to embellish city bellies, they are the leaner, and the sleek stay for our masters' pots.'

'Then are country folk cozeners, that tender tough flesh for the fair goods we furnish from the towns.'

'Why, that may be, sir. Yet tell me, prithee: what hast thou, beside the goodness of thy fair presence, tendered to us now for the tough meats we set before thee?'

This silenced Gropenut, and won plaudits from the yokels, who delight above any in the putting down of city vanities. William, that had gone to hitch the nag, poked in his blotched face to summon me, and crying, 'Have with thee, goatherd!' I bade farewell to all, and promised tidings on the morrow; and being hoisted by William on the nag (whose service in this, beside lewd fingering of my thigh, I needed not), I cantered off into the forest.

There is, at the thought of a return, a joy; but this may surprise into a sorrow. For how does man know that he has aged? Well, if his teeth drop out, sure, or his hair, or he be not in most things able; but also when he perceives what he once knew, and finds it changed: and, reflecting, sees 'tis not its alteration, but his own. For the forest, though beautiful and golden presently, seemed smaller, or less wreathed by mystery; and when I came up to Martin's hut (or my mother's, and mine own), I marvelled this cabin that had seemed so vast had, in a bare year, so shrunk.

A call brought out Martin that, being old, had altered not; and from him came none of the ecstasies of aged Colin, but a clasp, a sigh, and a whisper of, 'Aye, Aubrey! Little Aubrey that is waxed into this!' And he took me by the arm inside where, the old odours assailing me (that are chief remembrancers of childhood), I wept in the wine he proffered.

'Well,' said I at last, 'and where is thy slut, Martin?'

'Marry, I sold her.'

'Why! Art thou turned slaver?'

'Nay, innkeeper: for thus it was. Of this woman, I soon grew weary; for beside that, as thou knowest, I am past age or taste for lechery, she lacked what thy dear mother had abundantly, which is good cheer and wit. So once, when some troops lay here, and a sergeant fell enamoured of her person (and she of his), I accepted his offer of a gold chain (plundered, I doubt not) for her more dubious worth.'

'And how innkeeper?'

'Because a brothel needeth women, and an inn, but wine; and lacking the one, I procured the other with thy mother's gift, and hung out my sign: so am I now landlord of the *Forest Hart*. This is the taproom; and in the woods without, yet near, I have builded some huts for those, like thy friends, that wish to linger as my guests.'

'So they are come?'

'Aye, and haughtily. In vain have I said that if the *Hart* be too humble for their company, Epping hath eight good inns. But no: they must both despise and tarry.'

'Well, I shall seek them out, and pray them mend manners to my step-father that taught me all.'

'Not "all", Aubrey, if thou hast friends like these: for if my lord Venice be haughtier than the Doge whose name he borrows, he is also silent; his steward, Amos, opens but his mouth in plaints; yet their familiar, that they call Sad Jack, mayhap to redress the tally, pours as many syllables of gossip into mine ear as their brief grunts of silence. And from him I learn thou hast fallen, as the scripture sayeth, among thieves.'

'Marry, Martin, I did not learn knavery in Epping?'

'Of a sort, aye, yet not of another; I mean if not honesty, to preserve withal an honest heart.'

'Fear not, that beats still for those I cherish. Let me go parley with them, for I bear tidings e'en knaves must know.'

Peter and I, when we came first to London, were sure a spectacle of rural oddity; yet do I not believe a yokel in town is such an absurdity as one city bred lost in a country exile. For upon two stumps, frowning fiercely yet folorn, sat Amos and Sad Jack: who, when they saw me, vented, ere I could ope my mouth, their venom at their displeasures on pretext of our delay.

'Well, as I warned Venice,' quoth Amos, when he heard my tale, 'thou wert apt only by incompetence, and these follies of thy journey prove it.'

'I am competent, Master Amos, to have my step-father Martin expel thee into the woods, an thou rememberest not thou art guest in Epping, and no more bully in Bishopsgate!'

'Peace, prince,' quoth Jack, 'for I perceive that, like the youngest in the fairy-tale, thou art come home to claim thy kingdom. Well, we are thy subjects, presently.'

'And where is my Lord Venice, whose thou also art?'

'Nibbling at nature, haunting harts, dallying with does – in brief, he is gone walking in the woods.'

'Well, he has not bit deep, for here comes he.'

Doge Venice heard me out with better humour: though the fate of our cart won frowns, and the name of Cecil, clouds thunderous; and after a parley apart with Amos, he said,

'Hearken, Aubrey: I have decided thus. My son and his comrades shall remain presently where they are; though this purse will procure them better entertainment. For beside I wish none of my nephew Cecil, we are too cramped for comfort in thy Martin's inn. There is this, moreover: that in ill times of turmoil, a son should not be beside his father, but apart; for thus, if danger strike at the one, it may avoid the other.'

'Then, sir,' said I, 'may I be your privy Mercury, and volley twixt either camp?'

'Do so, and I shall requite thee.'

'And how find you the forest, sir?'

'Pleasantly; nay, scowl not, Amos, nor Sad Jack, smile. For you have all observed how, in London even, I dote on gardens; and hereabout, there is none other.'

'And for the same cause, am I sorrowful as at hearing sermons.'

'Hear those from these sighing trees, then, Jack, that preach peace and no damnation. But Aubrey, art thou not hungered? Do thou take this piece to Master Martin, and say 'tis so clement yet, we would eat out doors. Come, Amos! Cast off thy cares, and ours, by carols.'

I had heard, yet not believed – for he was so testy and tart a fellow – that Amos could sing sweet and, indeed, been in his sanctified youth, a chorister; and when he embarked upon a ballad, I could see that if the sanctity had fled, its voice remained; for he was melodious, and brought Martin out faster with his dishes. Yet scarce had Amos entered on his final stanza, when with a blasting of brambles, there tumbled headlong upon the sward a youth that, rising, seized upon our provender. I had whipped out my knife, but lowered it when I saw Allan.

'Welcome, good Master Bowes,' said Venice calmly.

'Sir!' cried Amos, 'have a care, lest he may . . .'

'Peace, Amos, for he is peaceable, and I know him: he is son to old Sir Ronald, an honest lecher, client of my stews ere thou hadst breeches. An you are hungered, Master Bowes, pray eat.'

'Your pardon,' said Allan, blushing as a boy, 'and thine, Aubrey, also; but I was half starved, and being without resource . . .'

'Fall to!' quoth Sad Jack. 'Keep excuses for dessert.'

'But that I yet cannot!' Allan cried, though fingering the meats yearningly. 'For Moses, my old servitor, hath fainted before the inn, and I must secure him first.'

'Do this,' quoth Venice, 'and we shall patient for you.'

'Aye, sir!' cried Amos, once Allan was gone off, 'but if he be Bowes, he may be brother to Bully Noll, that is familiar to thy brother of Genoa.'

'An it be so,' said Venice, 'we must not blame Abel for Cain's sins; else wouldst thou charge me with my brother's.'

'He is an honest man,' said I, 'although a Puritan.'

'As who might say,' quoth Jack, 'an honest maid, though strumpet.'

Back came Allan, bearing old Moses, whose zeal with a knife and glass showed scant proof of faintness. And when his mouth was freed of feeding, Allan laid bare how he had tumbled hither.

'I am, sir, a dissenter,' said he to Venice, 'and of a strict persuasion; and in these troublous times, when faith is made felony, and holiness heresy, many saints of our sect have fled London and its courts ecclesiastical for the kinder country.

There is also that my elder brother, who is a Papist, fears equally for himself, and thus fears my presence in his house.'

'Truly,' said Jack, 'are brothers ill brethren in our acquaintance.'

'And how comes it,' said Amos, 'that you fled so ill provided?'

'Indeed, we did not; for though I had scant resource, good Moses here would share the savings of his service with me. But alas! In a village some distance back, being taken by a colic, he had unbreeched himself inside an inn where, being about his business, some varlet foraged all our fortune from his poke.'

'Was this, mayhap, in Snaresbrook?' said I.

'Aye, how knowst thou so?'

'Yet whither,' said Venice, 'was it your intent to journey ere this misfortune?'

'To Scotland,' said Allan. 'Where as you know, sir, though they be barbarians, they look kindly on dissenters.'

'And this you now may not.'

'Nay, unless we walk, and live on air.'

'Hearken!' said Venice, rising. 'Do you and your ancient enter our huts and rest; and awhiles you dream, shall we of how to forward your interests.'

'Grammercy, sir,' said Allan. 'Moses, let me serve thee.'

When they were in, Venice said to me, 'Aubrey, thou shalt carry these twain in my coach to Harden, and there leave them, then bringing the coach back on the morrow.'

'And there entertain them, sir?'

'Fairly: no more, no less. For if this be some spy set on me by my brother, Robin shall watch him; yet shall this Allan not be near me, to unravel my intent.'

'Master,' said Amos, 'the woods are vast, and have space for two graves none would uncover in a twelvemonth.'

'Amos,' quoth Venice, 'I love thy faith and boldness, less thy good sense; let it be as I say.'

'Sir,' said Sad Jack, 'may I not ride with Aubrey on both journeys? For thus, will you have more eyes and ears to serve you.'

'Aye, and less mouths a while, for I have enough of counsel. Aubrey, where are there deer in Epping?'

'If you be huntsman, sir, where'er you are not; yet they are legion, and to spy them, I would advance this counsel, though you wish no more. Walk downhill to the stream, and silently; there sit, number to ten times ten; and within as many minutes, you will see as many.'

So now I went in to Martin, and all that strangeness we had felt to clap eyes again one on the other, vanished; so that I thought almost to hear my mother come bawling into the room, as used to be. I answered a thousand of his questions, both because youth loves to prattle of itself, and that I wanted to hear my step-father's commentaries on what I had wrought, or ill-wrought.

'Well, as to stews, and pandering,' said he at last, 'thou mayest say that I have, with thy mother, lived in the one, and been the other; and so may not preach without repentance. Yet be that as may be, I do not think my life, and thine, identical: for here, Aubrey, 'twas my life, and not my commerce; yet thou in London hast made commerce of thy life.'

'And so saith Jenny; yet Jenny, who began as I, and so remains by serving Venice, would have me quit the life wherein I met her, and whereby I still presently sustain her.'

'And what else wouldst thou be, Aubrey?'

'Marry, I know not: for though apt, I am apt at nothing save at being apt. I had thought to be a soldier.'

'Mercy, no! For if thou art rebel slave to Venus, thou

couldst ne'er stomach servitude to Mars. Is there no honest commerce that beckons thine inclination?'

'Well, I have met persons in the theatre; and had a conceit I might serve these in some menial office. For playhouses, as thou must know, are not all strutting actors and brave tinsel; behind their scenes, as 'tis with stews, are merchants, and merchant habits.'

Then I told him of Master Heminges, and the new *Globe*, and, when he pressed me (for I had a strange impediment to tell of him) of my brief colloquy with Will.

'Thou hast spoke with him?'

'Aye, as I tell thee.'

'Not seen act, I mean, but privily conversed?'

'Aye, as I say.'

Martin gazed at me. 'Aubrey,' said he, 'thou hast aroused in my breast the demon envy.'

'How so?'

He made no reply, but went to his bedroom and came to me with spectacles on his nose and two torn volumes. 'These,' said he, 'have I o'er-mumbled oftener than a litany.'

They were two poems, one *Venus and Adonis*, the other, *The Rape of Lucrece*; that saw light one six years since, the other five; and were inscribed each to Henry Wriothsley, Earl of Southampton.

'I knew not,' said I, 'that he wrote verses also.'

'Well, but his plays are, beside being plays! Yet these also he writ, for the closet, not the theatre.'

'Before he wrote plays?'

'Before, yet after; some six were already writ; more, or as many, are writ since.'

'And why these, then?'

'Do thou ask him! Yet I would hazard two guesses. The one, that in those years the plague locked up the theatres, so that for actors, time hung heavy. The other, in reproof of fools that said he was mere mummer, and lacked learning.'

'He lacks it not?'

'No man does, Aubrey, that has learned.'

'And thou knowest his plays? For I have seen but one.'

'Some, not, sadly, all. For not all are printed, as his poems are; and if so, oft ill presented by piratical rogues that thieve his thought.'

'Why should he not print them, as his poems?'

'Marry, that he may act them! He and his fellows, and not others. For thou wouldst not, Aubrey, have me display my craft as innkeeper of the *Forest Hart*, by serving tapster to the landlord of the *Bear* in Epping.'

'And these poems, Martin, that are printed? Why didst thou cherish them, that knowest Greek, Latin, and all writ in England?'

'Because I do know these! Stand in a forest, Aubrey, beside its tallest trees: gaze at stout saplings, thrusting up vigorously; then, only, because the loftiest are known, canst thou perceive the promise of those rising.'

'Yet how canst thou tell this, from two poems, and some plays ill-printed?'

'Because in these poems' (here he took up and flourished them) 'is a gage that cannot be mistook! First, language: his is a new voice, that disdaineth not its root, yet blossoms into fresher flower. Then substance: his *Venus* prefigures all that is comely and loving in his soul; his *Lucrece*, what is dark and terrible in all ours.'

'Then tell me, Martin; for I am confused by scant knowledge and excessive counsel. Who, to thy mind, is chief playwright of our age?'

'Of our age, Marlowe; of all ages, Shakespeare.'

'And Jonson?'

'Well, he is chief in bombast. Nay, nay, I speak unjustly; for he hath force, eloquence and wit.'

'And this thou canst tell of Shakespeare by two poems, and some mangled plays?'

'Aubrey, I need not know thee at thirty to divine the man thou shalt be from the youth before me that bears half those years.'

'And yet he is no scholar.'

'Son, let me turn traitor to my craft, and tell thee this! To be a true scholar, is to know; a true writer, to understand. Now, knowledge impedeth not understanding, surely; yet does not the gift of one, ensure that of the other.'

'What must a writer have, then?'

'Invention, which scholars hate; and by this I do not mean mere fancy, but the aptitude to see deep, feel deeper, and reveal all with clarity and in a fair form; with passion, yet dispassion; with wit, yet mocking, never.'

'And he has all this?'

'He has more! For to the great rage of my fraternity, he also possesses learning, though not theirs.'

'How so, if he knows no university?'

'Aubrey, where learns his art a soldier? In a school?'

'Marry, no, on a battlefield.'

'There, yes, and from his comrades that have trod others. So is it, sure, with him; for thou hast but to read one page inside these volumes, to see he has studied his peers, digested their meat, then spoke out with his own voice.'

'Which peers in especial?'

'Marlowe, certainly; and this shows his greatness, for he has rivalled greatness. Spenser, as have all that read in England, from Queen to schoolboy. In style, or early style, I would prick John Lely, that wrote *Euphues and his England*; in shape dramatick, Thomas Kyd.'

'Well, I must see further of his plays, an thou holdest him in such esteem.'

'Let thine own judgement serve thee, Aubrey; yet I trow thou shalt not waste thine hours.'

And now came in Sad Jack, with Allan and old Moses well refreshed, and liking the hospitality proposed by Venice (in which I much doubted their wisdom). They entered in the coach, which Amos had made ready, and Sad Jack climbed up beside me over the horses' rumps. 'Spoil not thy master's coach,' said Amos, 'as thou hast his cart.'

'Nay, nor his soul neither, by inciting him to murder,' and I whipped up the horses ere he could reply.

We drove in silence for a while, through the lattices of last leaves, that sprinked us with their own rain, for the sky was blue. 'Thou wert better served inside, Jack,' said I.

'With a Puritan? I had liefer a damp body than damp company.'

'You love not Puritans?'

'Nor Papists neither, nor any so jealous of their salvation that they prize evasion above any performance.'

'Then thou art for this world, Jack.'

'Aye, and of it; though many will tell thee I mislike it.'

'Well, it is a large thing to mislike.'

'Aye, marry; and in truth I like it well enough, e'en though I do not, as does a mountebank, cry praises of what I cherish.'

'And how camest thou to cherish Venice, and he thee?'

'That, boy, is a question thou mayest not ask, yet I shall answer. I cleave to Venice not for what he does, but is.'

'"Does" I know partly; but this "is"?'

'Is a rogue, and knows it.'

'And this excuses all?'

'Excuses nothing; yet renders him, unlike his brother, human.'

'How camest thou to his trade?'

'By seeking to prevent it.'

'How?'

'Aubrey, thou art a curious fellow, and of a most mockable discretion.'

'Well – how? Let the horses only, beside me, be witnesses.'

'Lash them not, then, or shall I thee when thou shalt prattle. I was a spy once, in service of the sheriffs.'

'Set to seek Venice?'

'To destroy him.'

'And turned coat?'

'Had it torn off. For I was of the people of my Lord of Leicester, and when came his end, came mine.'

'And so changed his livery for Venice's. To serve him how?'

'Not, as thou thinkest, by betrayal of the sheriffs' secrets, for he knew all, or most. But by being his tuning-fork.'

'That tells him the true note of his intent? Then hast thou sung false thy tune anent Genoa.'

'Not so: I warned Venice, and he heeded me.'

'Then why fled?'

'Because he heeded me again, and his own counsel. Genoa, I tell thee, will o'erstep himself, fall further, and Venice will return a double Doge.'

'Fall further why?'

'Because Genoa has made friends of import and of substance, that will betray him when they sniff his danger; and because, though more forward and urgent than his brother, he lacks his patient guile.'

'Or his tuning-fork, and bludgeon.'

'And who is the bludgeon? Amos?'

'Aye.'

'Well, he is a fool, true, yet not a fop, like Genoa's Beauty; and he has, beside, what is as rare as precious in our ill trade – or in any honest too, pardee – which is that he is loyal.'

'To Venice alone.'

'Well, he serves him, not thee or me. Why mislikest thou Amos so?'

'Because he does me.'

'There speaks vanity, not reason. And if, Aubrey, all that worship thee not be villains, then, paragon though thou art, there may be many in the world.'

We had come out into the fields, and could see, afar, Harden spire. 'So you brought not the maids,' said Jack, 'only their corruptors.'

'Beside others, that have not yet corrupted.'

'And that will, I doubt not, corrupt one another. How was my Jenny?'

'Thine?'

'Though thou art her thief, thou canst not rob me of her affections.'

'Nor would seek to: thou art bidden to our wedding.'

'Nay, for 'twill be funeral of my hopes; yet you shall have with my benison a daubed chamber pot, in remembrance that Jack saves you chill flights out to the jakes.'

All were abroad at Harden save for Gropenut, that acted host till they returned. Old Moses helped me feed the horses, and I told him one of his ripe age, Colin, would soon entertain him.

'Hath he his teeth?' said Moses.

'Some sure, though I have but tallied his fangs by sight, not touch.'

'Then is he not ripe, but ripening, and must boil potage for his elders.'

'As elders, Moses: thinkest thou the elder to Allan, Noll, knows where he is fled?'

'He knows not, yet may know.'

'Expound me this.'

'Before we left, came privily to Noll, Genoa; and mine ears, which Noll thinks half stopped, heard half their converse. To this effect: Genoa, fearful, like all, of rumbling authority, and knowing Noll is Papist and so menaced, put in Noll's head that he should or flee himself, else yield up Allan to the constables: for any heretic is worth another.'

'And fearing this, Allan fled, as Daniel told me. But does Noll know whither?'

'Have patience: for there is, as in all things, cause and effect, occurrence and sequence, order alphabetical and mathematical . . .'

'Well, I have patience . . .'

'So: Aubrey is from Epping, and is now vanished out of London. Genoa and Noll know this, and Noll learns, moreover, from loose pantry chatter (not mine, yet mayhap Daniel's, who is also Papist), that Aubrey hath held converse with his brother Allan. Then Allan too vanishes: so may he not have followed Aubrey's footsteps?'

'And how learned Allan where these led?'

'From Lucy, at Venice's abode, whither we ran ere running further. For Allan, whose trust thou hast half won, conceived we should travel north through Essex, and if fortune led us to thee, beg counsel and some succour.'

'Then fortune obeys him better than does she me. Go thy ways, Moses, for I see him beckon thee.'

Inside the hut, where Gropenut had mulled wine, he was embarked on a dispute with Jack. Our elders, I know, e'er tell us youths that we are humorous, and lovers of hot debate.

And yet there is surely none more quarrelsome than those of middling years: and not, as with us, sharp, swift and soon forgot, but nagging like fishwives over who sells the ranker cod.

'Beshrew me, no!' cried Gropenut. 'She shall ne'er allow, nor shall her ministers, that he sit where sat seven Henrys, beside her father.'

'Her Scots cousin shall wear her crown,' said Jack, with that art of saying little, but with infallibility, that enrages disputatious prattlers.

'Rather Dauphin, Infante, or my Lord of Essex, even!'

'He never: for he shall hang ere long.'

'Art thou turned prophet, beside sage?'

'Well my sagacity I give to thee, for it is needful; yet to my prophecy I do adhere.'

'Then prove thou art prophet by relating what thou hast e'er truly foretold.'

'That today I would meet a fool.'

'Thou saidst so before thy glass?'

'Nay, before I met thee.'

'Well, 'tis said fools persisting in folly become wise; and sith thou hast claimed sagacity, thou art of long persistence in't.'

'Peace!' cried Allan. 'For here come Aubrey's friends.'

'Welcome and amen,' said I.

3

He who knows not country winter knows it little. In cities, 'tis an impediment to much; in villages, to near all save mere existence. There was, beside, a cold e'en skaters hated, and drifts that made of farms, islands. Nor might we struggle in to Epping at the thaws, for 'twas our duty to stay hid; and to strangers, hospitality waxed wary, for all feared the troubled times. Set beside all these, that our Londoners would, after a while, have rued their dear city e'en in summer. So did the season's grip render us languid, quarrelsome and distressed.

Nor did the hibernation of Harden damsels make aught easier. In the soft seasons, swains lack not lasses here in Essex, nor fields for conquest; but e'en in a more clement and happy winter, Jack Frost is a great enemy of passion: I mean not of its fires, but the means of quenching them. Epping, though not, 'tis true, a Babylon, could offer maids less fettered by the freeze; but thither, as I say, we could not.

So there arose, among us, girlish pouts. As to true catamites, the only among us all was Herman, now slave to William: whom none could accuse of acts unnatural, so much was the goatherd a child of nature, and amorous of all living things. Cecil, 'tis true, loved Robin, as half did Peter, that Simon loved; and William still gazed fondly on me when unmolested by Herman or his goats. But in truth, these were but fancies of lads that are yet half men, half boys; soon to be mocked and forgot within a woman's arms.

Another affection ripened which, though chaste (as I believe), was strong as any; and this was twixt Allan, the Puritan, and Robin, the pander's son. What drew these together, beside proximity, was the serious spirit that each had: Allan all gravity, yet Robin, in spite his gaiety, deeper in feeling than the rest. They were oft together; and Allan, that had wit surprising in a saint, wrote hymns in praise of Robin's virtue, or to encourage him thereto.

The secret of banishing our pets and frettings was discovered by the resource of Herman. Why should we not, said he, since we had naught to do, and long to wait, act in a play?

Yet when we cried out in rapturous approval, he grew grave, and issued us a warning. He was, he said, or had been, an actor: that is, one holding his art to be vocation, sacred, and commanding will and duty. Therefore, if we would have him teach us, we must yield utter obedience to him, and promise of earnest toil. He wanted, he said, no soldiers that enlist for drums and pageantry yet, at the first bullet, flee. Let us then sleep on this, think well, and declare our firm intent upon the morrow.

The bold (or rash) were in equal numbers to the cowardly (or prudent). As novices, he had Robin, Cecil, Peter, Simon and myself. As self-rejected, there were Allan, that approved not plays; Gropenut, that loved sleep better; Moses and Colin, that were too old; and William that understood not whereof he spoke.

Had we but guessed the tyrant masked by Herman's habitual gay mien, we none of us, I vow, would e'er have surrendered to such slavery. We thought 'twas a frolic, to kill time: 'twas us the slave-master near murdered! Herman, the mocker that we mocked, became the lawgiver before whom we trembled. There were oft tears, tantrums, dire threats of desertion: and to these he replied only, 'Go, then, an thou be not worthy!'

I had thought he would make us act in some play by Marlowe, for he knew these better than most do the Lord's Prayer. But when I suggested this, he cried blasphemy, and said that not one of us was worthy to utter so much as a single line. No, since we were ill actors, we should lean learn from an ill play; and he made us con *The Comedy of Errors*, writ by Will, that Martin had sent over; and which Herman called a plagarism of Plautus, that had but one virtue, it was the shortest play he wrote.

I believe that, had there been any other occupation for us,

we must all mutiny against Sergeant Herman and his drills. Yet through lack of this, and by the obstinacy of our natures, we persisted: till at length, like young riders that must take forty falls from ponies ere they master them, we won some enjoyment from our canter. Yet praise from Herman, never: but rather,

'Aubrey, thou sittest as one in direst childbirth.'

'Hast thou wet legs, Peter, that thou walkest as one on stilts?'

'Buss not as doth the woodpecker, Simon, but as a maid.'

'And thou, Cecil, master thy passion: this is no scene of bawdry.'

'Robin, there is no part writ for a statue. Be flesh, boy, not marble.'

And to all,

'I am but twelve feet off, yet can hear nothing! What would they hear of these mouse noises inside the *Swan*?'

'You are endowed with bodies, beside mouths: let both act, yet neither in excess.'

'Nay, nay, nay! And nay again! I beseech you, first ponder the meaning before utterance!'

At length, to the frenzy of the villagers of Harden (they lacking all distraction until Christmas), our play was unwrapped, in the packed and sweaty hut, for their delight. Beside the five parts that we lads played, Herman acted in all others: with this curious effect (that perplexed the less alert among the rustics), that he spoke oft to himself, and sometimes to two selves: leaping from place to place at each transformation; and beside this, fierce whispering our words to us when we forgot them. There can scarce have been, and in all England since King Alfred, a more marvellously ill performance: but we thought it majestickal, and won thunders of rural stamps and shouts at its conclusion.

After this, though Simon fell away, we four remaining pursued our studies with a mounting diligence and curiosity: not acting whole plays now (or e'en attempting to), but speaking scenes, exchanging parts, conning passages by rote endlessly. Herman's severity, though he was still a tartar, waned some little when he saw our craft waxed as much; or if not our skill, our perseverance. Nor did we defy his tyranny, for if he bludgeoned us, 'twas for his art, and not his pleasure.

Robin was, by consent so universal as to banish envy, our chief performer; and one day when we had pleased Herman (or not displeased him), he said Robin might read out some lines by Marlowe he had writ down: in which his hero declared what poetry was, and, by his own words, gave proof of this declaration. Robin, rendered speechless almost by the rare honour of at last reading from Marlowe, did this ill; and snatching away the paper, Herman bettered him:

> If all the pens that ever poets held
> Had fed the feeling of their masters' thoughts,
> And every sweetness that inspired their hearts,
> Their minds and muses on admiréd themes;
> If all the heavenly quintessence they still
> From their immortal flowers of poesy,
> Wherein as in a mirror we perceive
> The highest reaches of a human wit—
> If these had made one poem's period,
> And all combined in beauty's worthiness,
> Yet should there hover in their restless heads
> One thought, one grace, one wonder, at the least,
> Which into words no virtue can digest.

Then later, as weeks passed, our ardour cooled: as is the

case in any art man learns, when he perceives he can do it so, but only so. In any pursuit, eagerness impels at first, and also ignorance of all that must be conquered. This once understood, most rest, as we did, content with that little which they can, and seek not to master what they fear they cannot. All of us, that is, save Robin; who pursued his readings of the plays with Herman, Cecil sometimes languidly assisting.

This expense of Robin's spirit at study in plays deprived Peter sadly of his company; for Peter cherished him, and envied these stolen hours. Nor was young Peter pleased that, as he sought to cling to Robin, so wanton Simon would cling to him, whom he chided and disdained; but for this Robin rebuked Peter, saying that those that seek friendship of the one, should not despise the yearning of another.

As for puritanic Allan, he seemed less wearied of this life than we: mayhap that, being older, he was less fretful; and also that, seeking holiness, his mind had matter to divert it. True, he continued his courtship of Robin's soul by writing hymns for him, and sacred elegies; beside telling our friend that love was of the spirit, as much as flesh. These affections were pledged, in his turn, by Robin; but less, it beseemed me, of a sort spiritual than fleshy, for he coaxed Allan into sword play in the yard, as they had done in London; which exercise, if it exalted not his soul, at least warmed his body.

Yet to warm Allan's spirit, there now appeared in Harden yet another pilgrim seeking refuge, to wit a preacher who, by the extreme excess of his dissention to all doctrines save that of direct revelation from the Almighty, made Allan seem almost Pope. He was a lean, sharp, yellow monkey, ill-formed though rugged, for he came among us through snow in but a shirt. His only beauties, if fearful ones, were eyes like lamps, and a voice of passionate melody, to which even Herman hearkened in his rare silences. He lacked learning, but not certainty; charity, yet not faith; and his name was Mr Thorpe.

Mr Thorpe's doctrine was of harsh simplicity. All churches, bishops, priests and ministers, all texts, commentaries, articles and sermons, were an abomination (and in especial, our Sovereign Lady, that was the Whore of Babylon). All these should be consigned to an immediate fire, and not tarry longer for that where they would roast eternally. In their stead, stood saints: which all could be if God ordained it so, yet few were, as few Whitstable oysters nourish pearls. These rare elect (of which Mr Thorpe was one) had direct congress with heaven; and must reveal its dictates to lesser flesh, and command utter obedience.

I know naught of religions, nor ever have, nor I think shall. Yet in Master Thorpe's decree, I saw a peril. The hound which, hearing its master's horn, pursues the fox and rends it, may, because of this capture, suppose its own slobber lips blew the commanding note; and if God spoke to Mr Thorpe, might not he believe him Him?'

Had Allan not been with us, I fancy we would greet Mr Thorpe, feed him, and perceiving his mission, urge him (with kicks, if need be) to pursue it otherwise. Yet because he was, by Allan's worship of him, infused among us, we all fell uneasily, and in varying part, under his fierce dominion; all, that is, save William, who mayhap took him for another goat. So, beside miserable, we waxed sober. All acting ceased, and Gropenut mulled ale in guilty privacy of the hen-house.

By now, these buffetings of bodies by the winter, of mind by anxieties for safety, and of souls by the gospel of Saint Thorpe, had made us all fit for Bedlam: to whose vicinity, indeed, Peter and I thought of escaping privily, for beside hate of Harden, we yearned for Jenny and for Lucy. But then came two miracles: the new year, when the world ended not; and January was two days April, and all thawed.

To escape Harden, and to hear tidings of Doge Venice, Allan and Robin and myself set forth on foot into the forest. Ere we reached it, we must swim through mud: for thaw, however welcome, is a worse impediment than freeze. But once into the woods, we could sniff spring, although so far distant, and the trees yet bare.

Traversing a brook, we heard a shout; and hands to weapons, ran forward inside a copse. There stood one, holding some stags at bay, and, on the ground lay another, imprisoned by the antlers of a fierce buck.

'Heaven save us, 'tis Noll!' cried Allan.

'Save him rather, and we Daniel!' cried I, starting forward.

'Twas no long battle, for the herd soon took fright; nor was Noll much harmed, bruised chiefly, but no blood.

Had Abel saved Cain from lions (and not been slain by him instead), I doubt not some scene might follow as we saw now: first, joy all man feels that saves a man, both saved and saviour; next, swift recollection of prior hatred; then wonderment how this accident of salvation might temper ancient grudges.

As we walked through the forest towards Martin's inn, Allan and Daniel sustaining Noll, the elder brother said, 'Well, Allan, as thou must flee, so I, for the dungeons are gorged with true believers; and thus was I speeding to the sea, to France, when this mishap befel me.'

'As I earlier to Scotland. Truly, there will be naught soon in England save time-servers and trimmers.'

'Genoa is safe?' said I to Noll.

'Nay, marry, is he not! For he also is pursued, in spite his false friends the City merchants, that are swift to buy safety by denying him. And yet 'twas he, Allan, as I must confess, that first put me on to harry thee, that I might not be harassed. Aye, and more, e'en whispered I should pursue thee here, and yield thee into his hands to curry favour with the justices.'

'Brother, God hath sure sent the deer to teach us, by fear of it, fear of Him; and that brothers should so ever be, and learn their common enemy.'

'Amen,' said Noll (though I think he misliked this forgiveness which, as with counsel, is easier to bestow than suffer). 'Amen, and henceforth shalt thy wisdom, Allan, rule our house, and I, thy elder, be thy ward.'

So came we to Martin's, and before his tenant Venice; who welcomed Noll fairly, though I spied a privy smile at this spectacle of fraternal reconciliation. Sad Jack moraled (saying, would that Genoa might repent likewise), and Amos, as was his wont, frowned; for he knew Noll was client to Genoa, and liked him e'en less than he did Allan.

As to the future, Doge Venice said he liked it; for with the finer weather he had gone into Epping and there, by discreet and dignified enquiry, gleaned gossip out of travellers from London. True, they said, the purge still raged there, but abating, as is the nature of purges; for e'en in a colic, when the bowel be empty, it can not be voided more. From Ireland, the news was ill; for Essex had consorted with the rebel Tyrone, and was held now at York House, in London, under the Queen's extreme displeasure. Yet, as 'tis when a boil is lanced, relief follows on the torture. And though there was still talk of rebellion, and fear of it, the Queen's ministers now thought they had its measure.

To this relief was added another which, though few admitted it, I think ran deeper. Every New Year is a time of hope and of rejoicing, however briefly; but this one, in especial. Those who read this, of which few, if any, shall live to see the death and rebirth of centuries, may mock at the premonitions that hung over us – and e'en those of learning and sagacity – as the last day of 1599 yielded to the first of 1600. Well, they may mock; yet as January advanced, and the globe continued on its course as ever, the rejoicings, though muted, were universal.

On the morrow – for we all tarried over at Martin's inn – came yet another astonishment. For I was woke early by my step-father's pot-boy, who said there were four without that knew me, and had struggled through the night to find us; and on descending with a lamp, found these to be Cecil and Mr Thorpe, bearing with them half dead in body and spirit, Doge Genoa and his steward Beauty! I summoned them inside, ordered fire lit, wine brought, and food heated; and, as these succoured them, heard Cecil's story, when I drew him privily aside.

Genoa and Beauty, said he, fleeing also London and seeking, like repentant prodigals, some aid from betrayed Venice, had stumbled into Harden, and there fallen among my comrades. 'And father though he may be to me,' cried Cecil, 'I told him the villain that he was. And that beside being a treacherous usurper, he was like to lose not only his fortune (and that stolen from mine uncle), but his brother and his son withal.'

'And what ensued?'

'That he wept – but I know his tears: which are, like fountains, for display, not measure of repentance. But hardly had I spoke (in which, as thou wilt guess, unsavoury particulars of my father's trade stood clear revealed), when up rose also Mr Thorpe, like Moses before the Israelites (I mean when they worshipped the Gold Calf). "Tremble" cried Thorpe. "For thou art surely doomed and damned!" "Nay, pity!" cried my poor father, slobbering. "None,

none!" cried Thorpe. "Hell-fire awaits thee, an thou dost not instantly on thy knees, beseeching absolution!" '

'On which he and Beauty fell, little, I must avow, to seek forgiveness (for I know my father), but more to scape the fires not of Hell, but Thorpe; for beside their miseries of mind, they were chill, starved and weary. At length, after an hour of prayers, commitations, and admonitions, all bestowed on them by Thorpe in heaven's name, they were allowed to eat; but not before the Saint had made them swear they would to mine uncle, Venice, to ask pardon, and aid in his conversion also.'

'And so they are here,' said I.

'Aye, yet not trembling, albeit Thorpe forced them to crawl penitentially through the dark and mud. For my father, that will ne'er repent of aught, is yet a man that can change course, and forswear yesterday, if he deem it prudent. So will he, doubtless, ask pardon of his brother Venice, but for error, not for sin.'

'And he has thy pardon, Cecil?'

'Aye, marry! He that has suffered Thorpe, needs no more racking to repentance! And besides, now he seeks his brother's friendship, so may I my cousin Robin's once again.'

'Unless Noll drive Robin from thy heart!'

'Why! Is he here?'

'Nearby; and in fair uniformity to thy father and his brother's junction, Noll is reconciled to his.'

'Then must I to him instantly!'

'Patience, Cecil! It is not yet dawn. And prithee: what shall we do with Master Thorpe? For Allan, now he hath Noll, will think more, I trow, of the salvation of Bowes mansion than of his own.'

'Let him stay here a while! For my father will use him to urge clemency on mine uncle Venice.'

'Who will give credit to such a ranter?'

'Not if I know him. But Venice hath a wry wit that the pleasure of my father's shame at such an advocate, may flatter.'

And so indeed it was. For after all guests of the *Forest Hart* had risen and assembled, we endured another sermon from Master Thorpe; who succeeded at least in this, of making any that had offended (as Noll or Genoa) seem less offensive by comparison. At length, taking him apart gravely, Venice thanked him; yet said he remained disturbed by a worse sin than consanguinous quarrels, which were the horrors he had seen yestereve in Epping: a pit of iniquity so deep, indeed, that none but a saint could e'er drain it.

'And what is this?' cried Thorpe, his eyes starting like a huntsman's on report of otters.

'Why, there are harlots there, corrupting honest travellers.'

'In Epping? But 'tis a small place.'

'Yet of greater evil than any I saw, ere my regeneration, in the sinks and stews of London!'

'Harlots, you say! Strumpets! Whores!'

'All three in one!'

'I must away, and be about my Master's business!'

'Tarry not, and God speed!'

It may be noted that Cecil, a lad oft too passionate for sound sense, had yet much of his father's cynic humour, and had doubted the depth, or truth even, of Genoa's reformation. I also, of Noll's. Yet there is this that explains the reconciliation of each pair of brothers. Allan and Noll, if one hare, the other fox, were both hunted now by the Queen's harriers, and so brothers in distress. Venice and Genoa, the tiger and wolf, were pursued equally by baying packs not ecclesiastical, but criminal; beside rival animals of diverse carnivorous species. In these conditions, old treacheries and grudges were forgot: or at least, deemed of less import than an alliance to combat enemies.

Thus, in the calm ensuing on these storms, the future was debated with some confidence; that is, between the houses of Venice and Genoa, for that of Bowes, in the form of the two brothers, had gone plotting and pledging into the woods.

'Brother,' quoth Venice, 'all is far from lost, and I am sure of it; but we must, as does he that jumps a wall, fall back a little to leap higher.'

'As how, brother?' quoth Genoa.

'We must leave Bishopsgate, sell all we can there, and venture across the river into Southwark.'

'Now, heaven preserve us!' Amos cried.

'Beshrew me!' quoth Beauty, picking his large nose.

'Aye, thinkest thou so?' said Genoa.

'I do: hearken! All we need fear, is that there are kingdoms there, and kings – I mean stews that are governed by several chief panders. Who these are, we know; who we are, also; and if we determine to deal faithfully with each other, united, we shall overthrow them.'

'Yet are they well entrenched, with many followers.'

'As was Alfred when came the Saxons, Harold the Normans, and St Helen's panders when thou and I were young; yet all were o'erthrown, and new kingdoms built on theirs. Consider also this: all London, for luxury, moves westward; for lechery, to the south, where all the new theatres are, beside the bear pits, that erstwhile stood about us in St Helen's. In troth, we should have crossed over long ago, and built there our own transpontine realm.'

' 'Tis to set all at hazard!'

' 'Tis to set naught: for in Bishopsgate, we have lost, or

are losing, all. It comes to this, brother. Either we must withdraw from London utterly, and sustain self-chosen exile by that little salvaged from our enterprise; or else . . . well, think on't! I, like those two other brothers, shall go wander in the woods, leaving thee to thy counsel, and thy counsellor.'

And to me also he left mine, and mine also that was Martin; for I went in to him, to bid farewell; and also to tell him of a purpose that had possessed me at hearing of Venice's intent: that I would to Southwark too, yet not with Venice, but inside a theatre.

'Well, God be with thee, Aubrey,' Martin said, when he had heard me out. 'And I doubt not thou wilt find there, or in some other, honest employment. But how wilt thou live, and Jenny, till thou hast won a new master's favour? And shall thy Jenny accord with thee to abandon Venice?'

'As to the second, surely, for this is her wish; as to the first, I have what I earned from Noll, or its remainder, if Jenny has been thrifty.'

'And also these,' quoth Martin, who rose and fetched in the one hand, the two volumes of Will's poems, and in the other, a purse.

'Aye and nay, Martin,' cried I. 'For these I may take (the poems), but not thy further bounty; for I have not forgot how thou dealt fairly with me in thy gift from my mother's inheritance.'

'Ah, but consider!' cried he. 'This is my first offering to thee, for that was hers. For I did not earn what I gave thee then – 'twas she; but these are the fruits of mine own labours as an innkeeper.'

'Well, I shall take them, as thy gift to Jenny and our child. And this thy gift to me, of Venus and Lucretia, I shall cherish for him who gave it, and who made it.'

'Aubrey,' quoth he, 'if thou shouldst e'er see this man again, say this to him, I prithee: that he has one who loves him, though he know him not; and that our number will increase, sans surcease, in his life, and beyond death.'

The Theatre

I

OF THAT little that is Christian in me, I have most thought (and said ere now) that the injunction put upon us to faith, hope and charity, is most apt to our condition in this world; and in especial, at its chief undertaking, which is marriage. For to woo a maid, needs hope; to pledge her, faith; and to endure her, charity. For I loved Jenny as maid; yet as wife, though I loved her more, I suffered torments from her.

For this there were, I trow, four chief reasons. First, the miseries common to all wedlock, of which I shall say nought. Next, that we were so young: I scarce sixteen, she likewise; and youth is noted more for its ardour than endurance. Then, that we were now alone, and poor: for until we left Venice's service, we had not understood how much the regularity of his household was the counterpart of our servitude. And last, our son: that now beat so hard upon his mother's belly, that she could scarce stagger, and I must be housemaid beside breadwinner.

At first, like travellers o'er the Atlantick to the New World, our sails were set fair upon the voyage. We departed from Venice's service with the benisons of all (e'en Amos, glad to see our backs), and gifts of some. With our small plenty of riches, we crossed the Thames, found modest lodging with an honest landlady in the Borough (named Widow Dill, though there had ne'er been a Master of that name), and, while hatching my hope of assailing theatres, like a cautious hen, I found work as fruit vendor on London Bridge (or nearby, when chased off it by the constables).

Let any who spies the bright-eyed, loud-voiced lad that tenders apples, plums or apricocks from his gleaming barrow, and envies his merry lot, desist from jealousy. For he rises ere dawn, pushes his barrow almost into Kent, there haggles with farmers' boys that bring up the fruit (and love naught more than settling a price by assault on London lads), heaves then his barrow up laden to the river, and stands freezing, with the bright eye and cheerful voice aforesaid. Of such enemies and accidents as drunken watchmen, theft by deft children, rotted fruit bought in darkness, or false coin took in light – beside the upset of his whole commerce by the pranks of prentices – I shall forbear to speak, and sigh in recollection only.

As to my assault upon the theatres, this met with naught but disaster. There was not one on Bankside outside whose shut gate I did not long, and in vain, linger; nor no haughty sleeve I plucked at humbly that did not, scarce answering, repel me. Nor was the season fit, for it was winter still; and the theatres, though preparing their conquests, all half voided and in confusion, so that none knew anything, or would allow it. Master Heminges, they told me, was away upon a progress; and as for Will, some said he was in Warwickshire, others, acting before noblemen in country houses, and one, even, that he had renounced the theatre and turned hermit.

Yet I discovered his house, beside the river, with steps leading down to a small platform, with a boat. The windows wore shutters; and when I knocked at the backwards door (on pretext of selling plums), none answered.

One day, ere dawn and my departure, Jenny, sitting up in bed (of which she now took up three-quarters), said, 'Aubrey, if we wed not this month, then shall our son be born bastard.'

'Marry, thou are so close to't?'

'Forget all save "marry"! Neglect thy fruits, I prithee, and hie thee to the priest, else will our fruit be ill-marked when he christens it.'

Then ensued much debate as to who should be our witnesses: I was for few, and Jenny, as is the way of women, many. Yet I would have none from Venice or Genoa, save Peter and Lucy, that were our oldest friends, and in like case (I mean, as to parenthood, if not marriage) as ourselves. And Jenny, sighing for congregations, allowed, if we had fled that world, we should remain apart; so I called upon but priest and Peter.

A church, howbeit small, seems vast when it contain but four, beside the priest and acolyte, and an ancient dame that prayed throughout, beside the door, in some privy devotion that did not concern us. Ere we entered, we must put our names to papers in the vestry; where the priest gazed severely upon Jenny's sweet swollen belly (not to speak of Lucy's), and said he hoped, at least, the child would be brought in for christening. 'Aye,' said Jenny, staring back at him, 'an he that bestow this sacrament be worthy of his office.' This won more holy glares – yet I was in part relieved by this distraction, for I feared his reverence might ask where and when I had been baptised, which was in truth nowhere and never.

Our wedding breakfast was in a pie-house, and of eels, that Peter vowed was fit nourishment for pregnancy; our toasts were in brandy, which Robin had sent from Venice's cellar; and the gifts of our witnesses were a poignard for me, from Spain, and for Jenny, some Valency lace. 'I give you,' said Peter, handing us these, 'our toast of health, wealth and happiness.'

'In that sequence?' said I.

'Marry, yes: for without the first, are the others without value; without the second, wasted, or impossible of attainment; and as to the third, though it proceed from the other two, it casts a glow upon the one, and ensures fruitful usage of the other.'

'Thou art all eloquence today,' quoth Lucy. 'That Aubrey may so acquit himself at our wedding.'

'When it come,' said Peter.

'And this "when" is when?'

'Presently.'

'Thy best "presently" is present me with a ring, as hath Aubrey, Jenny.'

'In good time.'

'It flieth, and the best is presently.'

'Mercy!' cried Jenny. 'To bicker is the privilege of wedlock! Do not usurp it yet, or we shall lack all distinction.'

'Save your marriage lines,' said Lucy.

'Well, Lucy,' said I, 'sure Peter hath given thee better proof than parchment of his devotion.'

'Or of his lust, rather. And what will our child say of this proof?'

'If he had any parchment, he could scarce read it.'

'Mayhap: but he shall soon learn to hate the word "bastard" if his father make him one.'

And in this wise our banquet proceeded: Lucy cross, Jenny tired, Peter greedy of the brandy, and I counting the pence I had lost by neglect of my fruit barrow.

At our lodging, Widow Dill had a surprise for us in shape of wedding gift: that we might quit our attic and, for the same sum, enjoy a room below, whose windows opened not onto the sky, but Borough High Street.

'Aye,' said she, 'now you are wed, it is more meet; moreover, the attic, that can scarce hold two, will never three: and that third eager to crawl abroad, I doubt not.'

'Why, you are kindly, madam,' Jenny said.

'Nay, lonely: and in troth, to have youth lodge by me is a double pleasure. Nor fear not, neither, I am some ancient that fears squawks and pukes of babes. I cannot swear this is music in mine ears: but sure, to my heart, 'tis life.'

'Well, Widow Dill,' said I, 'I doubt our young son will fail you in either screams or vomits.'

'So 'tis to be a son?'

'Aye, marry,' said I. 'For you would not have me servant to three women!'

'What, then, his name?'

But of this we had not thought, nor thought of thinking; for which Gossip Dill scolded us, and said we must bend our brains to chosing one, else would the priest name him for his sexton, if we came to church without any.

When Jenny rested in our attic, I said, 'What thinkest thou to "William" for our son?'

'Well, 'tis a good plain name, that befits or prince or pauper.'

'May he be neither, and twixt each.'

'An thou go not out now with thy barrow, I know which he shall surely be.'

Yet I left it standing in the alley, and walked down beside the river, thinking of wedding days, and of my life; and found I stood before Will's house, where the shutters were now oped, and even a quarter window, for it was not chill. So I knocked, and again, and the glass oped wider, and he said, 'Well, what is this?'

''Tis I, Aubrey.'

'What Aubrey?'

'The Aubrey of the wedding, Will, that today hath had his own.'

'God save us, 'tis the Essex chatterbox! What wilt thou with me?'

'To beg a kindness that will cost thee naught: at least, I mean, in money.'

'Such kindnesses oft cost more! Well, push ope the door, for 'tis unbarred; but stay not, I beg thee, beyond thy question, for I am counterfeiting words.'

When I came in, he stood beside a door that led into a room with books and papers, stacked neat as at a printer's. He lifted some from a chair, poured me wine, and sitting also, said, 'So thou hast made an honest woman out of Jenny.'

'Thou hast not forgot her name?'

'Nay, nor that thou calledst her Juliet.'

'Well, Romeo had not my fortune; he knew friars, but not priests.'

'So thou hast since seen this play?'

'Nay, read it; but seen another, and learned thou hast writ both.'

'Which other?'

'Shylock's tragedy.'

''Twas not Antonio's?'

'I think not.'

'I tremble, Aubrey! For the sweet youth I knew is turned, as so many, surgeon of my intents! And what is this kindness thou wouldst ask me?'

'To stand godfather to my son, that shall bear thy name.'

He looked at me, in a long silence, then said, 'And why I, Aubrey?'

'I know not: because my heart bids me ask thee.'

He smiled and said, 'Or because thy William covets a silver bowl! Is he comely?'

'Marry, I know not; for he is yet in Jenny's womb.'

'Heavens preserve us! And if this he be she?'

'Nay, for Jenny says 'tis a boy she carries.'

'Then must she know; for if not she, who?' He was silent a

furtherwhile, then said, 'Well, Aubrey, I accept this honour that thou dost me, thou and thy wife.'

'That will join her thanks to thee with mine. In a month, God willing, I shall leave word for thee as to what church and hour.'

'Do so; and shouldst thou find me not here, seek me at the *Globe*.'

'That have I already, but in vain.'

'How so?'

'Well, I would speak with thee then, anent another matter.'

He frowned a little, and said, 'And this matter?'

'I would work in the theatre, Will.'

'Alas!'

He said no more, but shook his head at me, heaving his shoulders gently.

'Why this "alas"?'

'Aubrey, I beseech thee! There are twenty lads of thine age I know of, and a hundred I do not, that would be actors!'

'But I would be no actor, Will!'

'Nay? What then?'

'Why, to act I have neither face, nor voice, nor knowledge, nor desire! But I know not a little of commerce, and would serve as apprentice to those that direct thy business.'

'Of what commerce knowest thou this not little?'

'Presently, that of fruit.'

'Fruit?'

'Aye; but ere this, as I have told thee earlier, I was an honest pander: I mean honest to my masters, if not to those they gulled.'

'Marry, Aubrey! Then must I tell my partners, that are grave men albeit they oft act in comedies, that we must take to our bosoms a young merchant of fruit and flesh?'

'Mock me not, sir!' said I, rising. 'For that you will stand godfather to my son, I am in your debt ever, for, by my life, I have learned to honour you! This was all I came here to beg, and you have granted it. As to aught else, I pray you disremember it was spoke.'

'Berate me not, Aubrey!' said he, standing also, and laying a hand upon my shoulder. 'Be seated, prithee, and learn 'twas no mockery, but curiosity. For avow thine is a strange tale, and I would hear more of it.'

'As of what?' said I.

'Why, as of all thou wouldst freely tell me.'

'And these words of thine that must be counterfeit?'

'Now dost thou mock me! Take thine ease, drink, speak, I prithee!'

So I said all: all that is yet set down upon these pages. At first, like a dog sniffing at meat it would devour, I but nibbled at my tale; till spurred on by apt questions, and that joy we all have in speaking of ourselves, I unfolded the great history of Aubrey. Sometimes he laughed, though rarely; at others he asked me to tell some tale that I skipped o'er, more fully; but mostly he sat silent, listening, watching.

Night fell, and we scarce noticed it: not I, surely. When the flask emptied, he called his housekeeper for another; and later for meat. St Mary Overy chimed midnight when I was ended, and I thought of Jenny, and that she might be afrighted.

'Aye, true,' said he. 'And I am a thoughtless knave to deprive her of thee.'

'Well, she hath Widow Dill for company, yet fear I . . .'

'Fear not, and bear her, in my excuse, this gift: nay, ope it not, 'tis for thy wife, not thee.'

'My thanks to thee with hers.'

'Thanks! Well, I have had gifts from thee, too, Aubrey

. . . And tomorrow, thou shouldst seek out John Heminges, at the *Globe*, to whom I shall speak well of thee.'

'He is come back?'

'Aye, our Company was at Windsor till past twelfth night, then resting, or conning lines.'

'For new plays?'

'Even so: we must have three for our new theatre.'

'And they are writ?'

'Two only: one wherein Sir John Falstaff bids farewell to friends that have learned to love him in excess of my comfort. Another, concerning Caesar.'

'That built our city?'

'That did this, and also died; my play is of that last and fatal issue.'

'And the third?'

'We have history, and tragedy, yet we lack a comedy: this also must be writ.'

'On what?'

He smiled, gave me a flask of wine to carry beside the purse, and wished me God speed and adieu.

2

If Jenny live to be four score, or five even, she will ne'er love actors, or the theatre. 'Tis not, need I say, that one who was bawd can scorn their life, which puritans deem lewd as hers was. Nor can she deny, when I have tested her, that actors, in reproof of fable, are sober enough when they have doffed their motley; nor yet that, if not rich as merchants, do but the groundlings love them, and the better persons, they must needs be poor. 'Tis but that to Jenny's mind (or what passes for't), acting is a pursuit of children, and unfit for men.

I had soon learned – as marriage teaches all young husbands – that in disputation with one that calls feeling reason, there can be no victory; and e'en proof positive swayed not Jenny in the least. Yes, she allowed, Master Will had kind heart to send her gifts; was more courteous than any she e'er met at William's christening, and the bowl he gave our son was, beside costly, beautiful, and well chosen. Aye, she averred, Master Heminges was a fair master, and, if the hours of work were long, and much unusual, my wages surpassed by three times what I had earned from fruit. Then what, said I? That acting is for children, answered she.

My task at the *Globe* much resembled that in Genoa's stew: that I was in each chief whipping-boy, minor factotum, and Jack-of-no-trade: to whom, if aught tedious must be done that none would do, came ever the cry of, 'Come hither, Aubrey, do thou . . .' which could be go, come, mend, mar, hoist, lower, speak, hold thy peace, or a thousand like opposites and contradictions. What also, in theatres, resembles stews, is that all is either peace, or frantick flurry: with too few tasks, or an impossible excess.

Master Heminges treated me as men do a pet puppy, that must be or slapped, or fondled; to which I was not contrary, save that – as do doubtless dogs – I ne'er knew why I was in disgrace or favour. For when I toiled long hours, he might cry, 'God's spittle, Aubrey! Art thou born deaf as well as pocked?' Or if I idled, 'Angelic youth, cherub, seraph, wilt thou proceed, I prithee, to the fair harridan that stitches cloth for us, and tell the sweet crone, and in my name, that this garment would disgrace a beggar, and so is ill fitted for a senator?'

One March day, when we alone were on the stage (in which I had been hammering home nails, for in the play some must walk bare-footed), he said, scanning the sky and the increasing sun, 'Aye, fortune willing, we may ope up our eager gates ere April.'

'So soon?'

'Late March can be temperate, e'en if May oft freezes. Well, tell me, Aubrey, for infants have the gift of prophecy (often of dire events, but no matter!). Will they like *Julius Caesar*?'

'As all he writes, and you, Master Heminges, act.'

'I said prophet, not flatterer. What thinkest thou? For thou hast heard us mouth some scenes.'

'Aye, but all in bits and pieces: so that I know not yet what follows which, or otherwise.'

'May our audience have more wit than thou.'

'But sure, Master Heminges, great Caesar doth not die so early in the play as did he when you all stabbed him yestereve in six repetitions of his death and resurrection?'

'Aye, but so doth he! Caesar, though emperor, departs the play all too soon for the satisfaction of the actor that speaks his lines.'

'Then who is the hero? Brutus? Antony? Octavian?'

'Marry, I think there is no hero, unless it be Rome.'

'The groundlings will not like this, for they love heroes – villains e'en more so.'

'Well, they have Cassius and Casca.'

'Nor may the ladies be to their taste, for they are chill and haughty.'

'Well, they are Roman matrons.'

'Aye, but Londoners love shrews to mock, wenches to lust after, and virgins to envy or despise: but not cold pride.'

'Hie thee to my Lord Admiral, and seek his service! For thou art plain traitor here!'

'What of the play anent Sir John?'

'It is all writ, and we are conning it.'

'And the comedy?'

'He is e'en at it.'

'At home.'

'There, possibly; or mayhap in Cripplegate.'

'Why, he hath a house there?'

'Not yet, but he stalks one like a huntsman – a tavern too, so sundry gossips whisper.'

'To live in?'

'Well, not the tavern; but I ween he tires of Bankside, as being too close to theatres; so that he feels like a merchant prisoned above his shop.'

'Yet why Cripplegate?'

'Why not? Thou wouldst not have him return to the tenements of Shoreditch.'

'When came he first there?'

'Eight years since, from Warwickshire; bearing with him little but his genius.'

'And in eight years he hath done all this?'

'Live the next eight, Aubrey! For unless I am mistook, 'tis but now his art bursts into its full flower.'

'And beside his art, his fortune has also prospered?'

'Marry, the Queen should name thee her Lord Treasurer! Aye, of a sort . . . well, he hath London houses, and one bought three years since in his native place.'

'So my Lord Mayor speaks false when he dubs actors rogues and vagabonds.'

'Not were thou actor, Master Impertinence.'

Returned to the Borough, I found all in a flurry. Peter had come, and begged Jenny, by her love for him and Lucy, to run to her instantly, for he swore the midwife was murdering his darling. Good Widow Dill said she would watch William, and we three set out eastward, Peter beseeching us to hasten.

The migration across the river of Venice and Genoa, now

one (at least in face of others), had carried them to a mansion beside the Thames, that had been house of a Cathay merchant, who, deeming himself grown too grand for Rotherhithe, was transplanted to the glory of the Strand: so that the brothers had the house for little. Thus, beside the dwelling, that rambled as doth a pot-house tale, were divers outbuildings and wharves: all fair enough, and convenient to the joint households of the Doges, yet somewhat sorry and declined. Peter told us that great civil wars had raged, after the restoration of their alliance, betwixt the followers of the two monarchs: thus Amos and Beauty battled for office of Lord Chamberlain, and Herman with Breakbone for that of guardian of the gate. As for Cecil, he was in raptures; but Robin not so, as I would soon discover.

I had no wish to enter, being fixed in my determination that all was severed not, sure, with my friends, but from their world; so asked if Robin could come out to me, while Jenny tarried inside with Lucy. This he soon did; and asked would I walk with him beside the river, and visit a tavern there.

For Lucy, he feared greatly; yet blamed her, and Peter also, for carelessness that now brought on her pains. For till the last hour of her confinement, they had lived much as before, and this in spite the warnings of the goodwives of the household: with food and rest too little, and drink and blows too much.

'God be with her,' said I, thinking of Jenny and our William. 'And what of thy father, and thine uncle?'

'Aubrey,' said he, 'I say this to thee that I would to none other: I fear for them, and in especial for my father.'

'Why so? Genoa would still betray him?'

'Nay, for he dare not, or not yet. But I speak of Southwark, that thou knowest now. Gaze on the Thames, I prithee, that flows by us! Who could believe this river, that but cuts a ditch through London, and might seem to serve each shore, in truth divides the city in two cities – two realms and peoples, almost?'

''Tis true they of the south are much other than those northward. For here is little – I mean of the majesty in our city which, from Tower to Abbey, lies extended on yonder shore. And of this, those hereabouts are jealous, remembering the Romans came first here, not there, and that Canterbury was sanctified ere Westminster. So are their hearts eaten out with envy, which they disguise by mockery of their northern neighbour, and would laugh if it should burn.'

'E'en so. And with these must my father and uncle now contend.'

'Yet have they name, gold, and long practice in this business.'

'Aye, but not youth, Aubrey: they are too old for Alexanders, or e'en Caesars.'

'Yet have they sons!'

'Of this would I speak with thee. Cecil hath wit, address and, though he seem womanly, lacks not courage, as thou knowest; yet has he not the brute cunning needed in this affair: beside which his father, prodded by vanity, has taught him to be gentleman, not bawd. As for me, well, I believe I have in me to outshine my father, even; and I speak to thee, Aubrey, with nor modesty nor pride. Yet "in me", say I: aye; in my capacity, but not my heart.'

'And so not in thy will.'

'Aye, there's the rub! I am a son that would serve his father in all ways save that which serves his father's hope.'

'Well, serve him otherwise, and so change his hope.'

'I must. For I am, Aubrey, in the matter of this commerce of my father's, a man of a divided mind. It has made him, and nourished me. Nor, to speak truly, and in such conscience as I have, do I think ill of it: I mean condemn it, or those that live by it. Yet it hath about it, as a church that of incense, or a palace, civet, such a sniff, or stench, a dank odour of sadness and mortality! Men frequent stews for life, pardee! Yet there I see only death!'

'By sometime murder?'

'Nay, nay, death of all youth, health, faith, love, spirit!'

'That were many deaths for one young man.'

'Too many; and so choose I another.'

'Which?'

'I would be soldier, Aubrey.'

'To slay by intent for gold?'

'Aye; and at risk, and openly.'

'Well, God be wi'thee, Robin! Is this advanced?'

'Already. Hearken! Jenny will be two hours at least with Lucy, and I would have thee meet my Captain.'

'She must not be more, for William sucks as twins. Yet she knows this, and her way home; so I shall come with thee.'

We dropped down to Deptford in a boat, Robin musing on the sails, and the gulls arching, when I said, 'Thou art young to be soldier, Robin.'

'Aye, and 'twill not be yet: I must first grow beard, and stouter sinews.'

'And how hast thou met this Captain?'

'Master Wyatt? At sword play; for he is one that came to our old house for practices.'

'And esteemed thy worth?'

'Less than I his: for he hath lost an arm, his right, and learned to play a second time with t'other.'

'And how camest thou to know his house?'

'That he asked me there: to see his store of weapons, and his daughter.'

'Ah, so there is a Mistress Wyatt?'

'Aye, Susan; but he is widower.'

They lived in a small house, cottage almost, behind the

green; with a paved forecourt, in which stood polished canon, and, on the roof top, flew the ensign of St George. He that opened to us, with a clatter to repel cavalry, was short, red and choleric; and if he lacked an arm, his eyes had double glare.

'Ah, Major Robin!' cried he, with mock salute. 'And who is this Colonel that thou bringst to me?'

''Tis my friend Aubrey, sir, of which I spoke.'

'Ah! The hero of Snaresbrook Gap! I hope, young sir, thou wilt not judge our art by those ill daubers.'

'Well, they taught me two lessons, sir: to attack rather than defend, yet flee when e'en valour prevail not against numbers.'

'Both may be done, but the second ne'er said – or privily, that recruits like Robin hear not. Enter.'

Within, all was compact, as in a tent; and upon the walls hung fearsome swords and daggers, dulled and glowing. 'You have fair prizes there,' said I.

'Prizes!' cried he. 'Who speaks of prizes? To win these, a man must be sailor. For 'tis not that we cannot plunder hard as they, but look you! they have ships to bring their trophies in; and we have but horses, or feet only.'

'Yet may you rape as well as they, sir.'

'Aye, and better: for towns captured yield more maidenheads than ships. But hush! here comes my Susan.'

Sue Wyatt was a coy lass, of which I am e'er mistrustful; for it springs from deception, which is bad, or rejection, that is worse. Not bashful, though: for she planted on Robin's down a kiss such maids call chaste.

'And thou hast ne'er thought, Aubrey, to bear arms?' cried Wyatt, for in every soldier, I have perceived, lurks a recruiting officer.

'Why, no sir,' said I, 'for I am peaceable, beside a coward and rebel to all authority.'

'Perfection!' cried he. 'Would that I had thee in my ranks!

For only recruits that love war, fear naught, and curry favour with their officers, are inapt for all save routs, defeats, or else disasters.'

'But sure, Father, a man that bears arms must love them.'

'Aye, but not their use, save in extremity.'

'And be brave also!'

'That can a man ne'er *be*: he or is, or is not.'

'And know obedience.'

'Obedience, quotha! Well, that may hang on who orders him to what. Our blessed Saviour, that loved soldiers (for remember his kindness to the Centurion), spoke of him that said, "Lord, I go," yet went not: of like sort, believe me, Pet, are many gallant comrades I have known.'

'And he that said, "I go not," and yet went?' said I.

'Ah, he broke the prime rule of all discipline: to any order, answer "no" never, be it obeyed or not.'

'And what of him,' said Robin, 'that saith, "I go," and also went?'

'Zounds, I have ne'er met him, in twenty years of service; and that Our Lord spake of his two brethren, and not of him, is proof by Holy Writ that he exists not.'

Susan brought wine and cakes, and the Captain, carrying us to the yard with in his one hand both a glass and a scimitar from Araby, showed (using me as target) how a Moor may slit off a nose, or either ear, without other injury; this being, said he, a sort of mocking insult. He then fell to with English sword and Robin, while I stood beside his daughter.

'You are new wed,' said she.

'Aye; and a father withal.'

'Yet so young; she also?'

'We are of an age,' said I, 'and scarce more than thine.'

'Robin hath many he loves, beside thee?'

'As many as know him, and so love him.'

'Maids also?'

'Thou art the first, Sue, and foremost in his heart.'

'Cozen me not! For all men are liars for their comrades.'

'Well, if thou doubt it, ask him, and not me!'

That Robin might be alone with her, I beseeched the Captain to show me his poignards, lugging him to the front room where, said I, there was a curved dagger, of which I begged him to teach me the thrusts; and held him there so long, attempting parries, that I was near gelded ere they returned – she less coy now, and both russet.

'What thinkest thou?' said Robin, as we were rowed back.

'That thou hast her heart.'

'Yet not her hand.'

'Well, for that thou must duel with Captain Wyatt and thy father, yet she will sure surrender.'

'Thou thinkst her fair?'

'Save Jenny, none more in London.'

But 'twas no fair wife that greeted me in Borough High Street, nor company neither; for Jenny was in a tantrum at my delay, Mistress Dill spoke ill of husbands that neglect their wives, and e'en William bawled rebuke at me.

'An thou misprize thy wife, as did Peter his, then mayest thou also lose thy son!' cried she.

'Say not that he hath, and Lucy!'

'It was still born.'

'Boy?'

'Girl.'

'Jesu! God rest her soul, and comfort them.'

'Had he comforted her, 'twere better.' I said naught. 'Oh, there is this,' quoth Jenny, throwing a letter on the bed.

'From whom?'

'I do not spy on thy affairs, e'en though thou care not for mine own.'

The letter, that was ill writ (or fast) said,

> Aubrey,
> Tomorrow, at the first hour. Home, not theatre. Fail not.
>
> W S.

3

He paced the room, I staying seated, he glancing without across the river to Blackfriars, then, turning, toward the *Globe*, till he sat also, and so looked at me. 'I have writ a play,' said he.

'The comedy?'

'The comedy.'

'Called?'

'*As: You: Like: It;* and these words he mouthed full and slow, as does one that speaks to a deaf man, and peers to see if his words have a clear meaning.

''Tis a sweet name.'

'Aye?'

'That shall give pleasure, and is swift remembered.'

'Why?'

'For that this is what all men wish, and women too, both for themselves and friends.'

He nodded, yet with a doubting frown; then said, 'And thou, Aubrey, hast half writ it.'

'I?'

'Thou. Or its substance, if not its shape.'

'What substance have I . . . Dost thou speak of my tale of the Doges, and Epping, and my friends?'

'Aye, and of thee also.'

'Marry, Will! That was sure meet for comedy! Yet of the

common sort, and thou who hast writ of Lords and ladies . . .'

'And of commoners too, forget not . . .'

'Aye, but in my tale, are they all lowly.'

'So I have changed thy tale.'

'Altered it?'

'In part . . . Hearken! First shall I tell thee how these persons in thy tale have been transmuted in my play. Next, read it to thee, all five acts, with a prayer that thou hold thy peace in patience, and neither cough, relieve nature, nor, indeed, ope thy lips ever. This done, I shall in turn keep silence, whilst thou unburden thy spirit of its load.'

'Proceed, then.'

'First, we have the two Doges, brothers, Venice and Genoa.'

'Aye . . .'

'Peace. They are become Dukes: one, the elder, that was Venice, now called Senior; the other, younger, Frederick.'

'Why Frederick?'

'Peace, peace. For no reason! For any reason! For that "Frederick" is a harsh-sounding name, befitting villainy.'

'So, Dukes Senior and Frederick.'

'Aye. Next their servitors, first those of Senior. Of these, Amos is become Amiens . . .'

'But that is French!'

'Aye, and so is Amiens.'

'But Amos is English!'

'Marry, Aubrey, if thou wilt not let me proceed, nor thou, nor I, nor anyone, shall e'er see *As You Like It* on the stage!'

'Yes, but why French?'

'Because I have carried our whole story into France.'

'Why?'

'Angels and ministers of grace defend me! Aubrey, where met Romeo, Juliet?'

'Why, in Italy.'

'And why there?'

'Because their whole nature, passion, and their fatal issue, were more proper to Italy than here.'

'So find I France more proper to thy tale.'

'Well, what is Sad Jack?'

'Jaques: called Melancholy.'

'Well, he was, pardee!'

'Next, servitors to Frederick. Beauty is become Le Beau. Breakbone Charles, Charles.'

'No alteration?'

'None, save in speech, perhaps, or accent, for French Charles and ours are twin. Gropenut is Touchstone.'

'Marry, well found! Yet why is he not French?'

'He is, and is not! Peace! Now, the two cousins, Robin and Cecil: in the play, are they Rosalind and Celia.'

'But Robin and Cecil are not women!'

'Nor did I think them so. Yet in our theatres, Aubrey, as thou hast mayhap remarked, boys play women's parts. So had I the conceit to make of thy two friends, heroines.'

'Then who are heroes? They are at least men, I trow.'

'Aye, marry: so come we to the sons of Sir Ronald Bowes that, in the play, is called Sir Rowland de Boys.'

'But he is dead!'

'In the play also: I speak of his sons. Of which Bully Noll is become Oliver, Allan, Orlando . . .'

'But is that not, like Romeo, Italian?'

'. . . no matter – and the third son, Jack, is become Jaques.'

'But thou hast already Jaques.'

'Well, this is another: not Melancholy – indeed, almost invisible, for he scarce steps on the stage.'

'And Daniel and old Moses?'

'Dennis and Adam. So come we to the rustics in and about Arden.'

'And what is Arden?'

'As Epping, the forest whither the two Dukes flee in turn.'

'And why so named? Because of Harden?'

'In part this, and because, in France, there is a forest of that name.'

'From which French city, then, do thy Dukes flee as mine did from London? From Paris, perchance?'

'From any French city: 'tis not said.'

'The groundlings may wonder.'

'Let them, for all are soon met in Arden. So now, the rustics. Old Colin the shepherd becomes Corin; Simon, Silvius; and William shall remain so.'

'Well, 'tis a sweet name, though thy namesake merit it not.'

'And last, then, of the male rustics, is thy teacher Martin, that I name Sir Oliver Martext.'

'But that were to mock my step-father!'

'By no means, for mine is no honest scholar, but a knavish cleric.'

'And beside, thou hast now two Olivers; and this, with thy twin Jaques, will spread confusion.'

'I think not: judge better when thou hast heard the play. Now, the peasant women: thy friend Peter becomes Phebe, and thou, Aubrey, Audrey.'

'Then, like Robin and Cecil, are we unsexed and made maids!'

'Not you – only the parts of girls, which I have shaped from your adventures, and that will be played by boys. For we cannot have none but men in a romance.'

'True. And none else?'

'But one: Herman, that becomes Hymen, goddess of wedlock.'

'Ill found! And this is all?'

''Tis not enough?'

'Aye, but what of Jenny? And of Lucy?'

'Aubrey, I cannot stuff every friend or mistress that thou hast into my play! And beside, the maids were not in Epping, or Arden, where it is mostly acted.'

'True, Will. But of all this I may know better when I have heard thy play: to which I shall hearken attentively, and with promise of mouse's silence.'

And so was read to me, from the lips of him who writ it, the comedy of *As You Like It*: which he spoke to me clear and bell-like, and mindful of each person's mood and nature, yet not acting these so much (and he sat still all the while), as being each man and woman in the play. When he had ended, he was long silent, while he passed his hand across his eyes and brow. Then said I, 'I like thy play well, Will.'

'I too . . . shall they?'

'Of a surety. And I am first in the world of this great "they" to hear it?'

He gazed at me, and said, 'The second.'

'Beside thee, is thy meaning?'

'No, there is yet another.'

He rose, and I saw I must not ask who this was. 'Aubrey,' said he, pouring wine, 'before thou suggest to me aught, if thou hast aught to tell, in censure of my play, pray let us eat, and speak a while of other things. Go seek out my housekeeper, I beg thee, and she will know what to serve us.'

While we were eating this, I asked if he remembered Herman, and he said, 'Aye: who, once knowing him, could e'er forget him?'

'And his acting was how?'

'Off stage, excessive; on it, an excess of this excess.'

'He acted ill, then?'

'No, I must allow that if his foliage were pruned, his claws cut, and chords vocal abated somewhat (by bellowing moderation at him e'en louder), then he acted well.'

'Then why didst thou mislike him so?'

'Marry, I did not: but his ranting I did, and that he acted too much his life and not his lines; beside forking out upon his comrades in the theatre, a tongue serpents might envy.'

'He said he had acted much with Marlowe.'

'Then was he blessed.'

'And that Marlowe loved him.'

'This I doubt not: yet was it Herman the boy (as he was then), or Herman the actor that he cherished?'

'Well, he loved Marlowe's plays, and of this I have sure knowledge, for he scarce spake to me of aught else.'

'And well may he love them! For who does not, and who cannot, that hath heart, mind, spirit and speaks our tongue?'

'For him, was Marlowe as a god.'

He was quiet a while, frowned and nodded slightly, then said, 'Hearken, Aubrey: there is no man, and certainly no writer, that hath heard his voice, and is not altered by it. We may remember, also, that he came before many did; so that whatsoe'er the virtue of these come later, they could hear him, and he not them. So stand we all his debtors; or rather, heirs, for he was not a man to lend, but give.'

I had been wiser now to leave him; for beside he was tired, what could I tell him that he did not guess, or be careless of knowing? Yet he had said that when he had read his play to me, I might speak out on't; and little seeing, then, that its lines were so far less about my life than his, I held him cruelly to his bargain.

'So, Will,' said I (with an effrontery that e'en now brings on blushes), 'I speak of the plot, or play of persons, in thy writing. Now, I know these cannot be, or do, inside the play, as they were and did in fact; yet are they oft so mangled and transformed, as to strain credulity.'

At these words of mine, spoke as by a judge to a raw student of the Inns, he looked dark a moment, then smiled wearily, and said, 'How so?'

'Consider myself,' said I, 'or Aubrey, thy Audrey. Now, I would have thee know I was no woman to the goatherd William; no, nor wooed by Gropenut as thy Touchstone wooeth her.'

'Surely. But I have told thee how, and why, I must make women of some boys, else were it a play for monks. Yet in making of Aubrey, Audrey, I have but altered the sex, yet not the nature of this being.'

'How so?'

'First, thou hast told me how that Gropenut, when thou didst serve Genoa, teased thy affections lewdly, as does Touchstone, Audrey's; and as for my Audrey and William, who is more man? I mean hath more of strength and will, in spite of sex?'

'Audrey: for thy William, like mine, is but a loon.'

'Then hast thou answered thyself through thine own mouth. Aubrey, for my play, must be a woman; and yet, as thou didst thy William, does she rule mine, and not he, her.'

'And so it is also with thy Silvius that was Simon, and Phebe which was Peter?'

'Aye, if thou but take these sheets, and read again.'

I did where he pointed, and on divers pages, then said to him, 'Nay, Will, 'tis as I say. For at Harden, Peter was more man, and Simon, that pursued him vainly, womanly. Yet hast thou made of Simon, Silvius, and of Peter, Phebe.'

'True. Yet of my Phebe and my Silvius, which nature hath man's boldness, and which sighs like woman?'

'So Silvius, that is man, is woman, and Phebe, the woman, man?'

He laughed. 'Well, Phebe is woman enough, I trow, and Silvius, though faint-hearted, man. Yet, as before, though I have played with sexes for the play's needs, the human essence of each one stays as in thy story.'

'And so also does thy Phebe, or my Peter, cherish Rosalind, or Ganymede, that was Robin?'

'Well, did he not?'

'And Rosalind Orlando, as did Robin, Allan?'

'That also hast thou said.'

'Aye, I have it now! And yet there remains one affection in thy play where thou hast altered all.'

'Which, then?'

'That Cecil loved Robin, and not Noll.'

'Yet have I so much altered? For consider what thou hast told me, now and before; Cecil loved Robin, thou sayest: and does not my Celia love her Rosalind?'

'Aye, but no more than cousinly.'

'Well, Robin and Cecil are cousins also! And if their affections (or those of Cecil) exceeded what is deemed fit twixt cousins, thou wouldst not have me, when I make them Rosalind and Celia, infuse the inks of incest into the clear waters of a comedy.'

'And what, then, of Celia and Oliver?'

'Well, thou hast said Cecil liked Noll well enough; and for my purpose this enough suffices, for Oliver ne'er claps eyes on Celia (or Aliena) till the play is near ended.'

I pondered on all this, while his intent grew more clear in my muddled mind. 'Well, Will,' said I at last, 'do thou leave London ever, and come bide in Epping, thou couldst win fortune at our fair as juggler, or magician, even.'

'Gramercy! And thanks to thee, Aubrey, for bringing

the fresh meats from which I have cooked this dish.'

'Gladly; though I perceive now thou art more than cook; for thou art chandler also, that brings flesh to the kitchen, beside farmer, that first reared the beasts whence it is cut.'

'Aye, and there are others such beside thou and I.'

'As who?'

'I have called Robin, Rosalind. Yet I must tell thee this comes not of a mere similarity of letters, but that I owe her in part to an earlier namesake, one Rosalynde.'

'And who was she?'

'An invention of one Thomas Lodge, some ten years since, from whose vineyard, beside thine, I have impressed grapes to press my wine.'

'That wrote a play of that name?'

'He did; and from it I have borrowed as, mayhap, others shall from mine hereafter.'

'Then are all writers thieves!'

'All, since Homer; and ere he, doubtless, did we but know.'

'And these thefts are not punished by the ill report they earn?'

'I think not: for all hangs on how the thief uses the fruits of this his plunder. Thus, he may suck them dry and vomit their mangled pulp; or he may plant their seed in his own garden, and nurture it into fresh leaves.'

'Then thy play proceedeth from me, thee, and Master Lodge.'

'As do all plays and, indeed, all that was ever writ. That is, from what the writer reads of writers; hears from his fellow mortals; and learns from his own heart, can he but see into it.'

'And which of these three yields most?'

'His heart, do he but have one, and the wit to know it. For all lives are mysterious and hidden, even our own; yet, however small our knowledge of ourselves, we can know that little a little more than we may know the lives of others.'

I rose now, handed him back the pages (that I was still holding), and said, 'Well, I thank thee, Will, both for hearing this, and thee. May all soon hear each with equal joy, until Rosalind and Orlando (if not Audrey and William) be famed as are thy Romeo and Juliet.'

'Well, these last are liked, 'tis true.'

'May I one question?'

'One! Hast thou asked none other?'

'Many, yet this I would: did that other which read this ere I did, like it as I?'

'So said she.'

'She?'

'Aubrey, I swear that if thou clutter up thy mouth with questions, thou shalt find ears that were open to thee, stopped. True, none learns save by asking; but learn also to digest thy meal of answers ere thou cry hunger, like a fledgling, from a filled belly.'

'So shall I away to digest the rebuke of Master Heminges that I am come late into the *Globe*.'

'Aye, and speak to him anent thy toga.'

'And what is this: a punishment?'

'Nay, a garment. Hearken, Aubrey: in *Julius Caesar*, at which we are labouring now towards perfection, there must be Romans to hear Brutus's speech, and Antony's. Wouldst thou be one? All thou needst do is look wise, sometimes passionate, and ever and anon grunt or applaud. Canst thou do this?'

'But I am no actor, Will!'

'That is no secret. Yet I would have thee learn to be a little, if it lie within thy capacity.'

'Why so?'

He looked at me, as one that doubts his own wisdom, and said, 'Because I would have Aubrey play Audrey, be he willing; and moreover, able.'

'I act a wench?'

'Why not? Dost thou fear laughter of thy comrades? Well, fear not: for to laugh, they will pay gold!'

'But my face, Will!'

'Well, think of Audrey's, prithee. 'Tis sure fair as hers.'

'And my voice! 'Tis a hoarse rasp, all treble vanished!'

'So, I doubt not, was hers also.'

'But if, on the platform, and before the multitudes, I should forget what thou hast writ for me?'

'Well, I have not writ much; and beside, he that plays Touchstone, that will be Master Robert Armin, shall shout a loud whisper in thy waxy ear.'

'Why! Hath Will Kempe, that played clowns for thee, forsaken my Lord Chamberlain?'

'Aye, sadly! He has gone dancing off to Norwich for a wager.'

'Dancing in fact, or fancy?'

'In fact. The highway hath consumed six pairs of his shoes.'

'William, I cannot do it!'

'Then think of William – and of his mother also. For Jenny will surely smile on thee for the greater gold that thou shalt bring her.'

'For acting?'

'Aye, for this. And let me turn prophet, Aubrey, and foretell that thou, so coy now, shalt so bluster and bellow when we first try thee, that our doubt shall be not of thy zeal, but its excess.'

'Will, I shall attempt it!'

'Now valour sits among thy varied virtues! I shall send thee thy lines to learn, and we, the actors, shall be thy first audience.'

'Marry, I would prefer prentices; for they are more

merciful. And to think, Will, 'twas thou that warned me I must ne'er be actor!'

'Trip, Audrey, trip,' said he.

4

In misfortune, friends fly to each other and move closer; and then, it seems, by instinct drift away until, because of this very nearness, they stand further than before. So it was twixt me and Peter. When Lucy lost their child, I saw him much; then less and lesser. Yet still saw him, for though our paths were severing, we were still bound by Essex, and its recollections; and e'en now, in spite our greater knowledge of the city, still met, as we had used, to quiz each other on each fresh mystery it revealed to us.

There was also gossip: for which, whatever they may say, have men warmer passion than the women they reproach for't. Thus Peter betrayed the secrets of the Doges' corridors; and I, what passed behind the trappings of the *Globe*.

'So Cecil has uncovered Robin's Susan!'

'Aye,' said Peter, 'or rather, that Robin would uncover her; and by this is fired to jealousy, and fell revenge.'

'I hope not poison, or a dagger.'

'Nay, though scarce less wondrous. For Cecil, berating Robin, cried, "Think not if thou canst tumble maids, forgetting thy cousin, that I am not capable of each."'

'And this he has attempted?'

'More than that – done; or at least, is in hot pursuit of Anne.'

'As was our Queen's father.'

'Aye, but this one is French, and dark, not russet.'

'And besides these, what is she?'

'Cecil, as thou knowest, eats dinners at the Inns; and reads law there, also, or should so for his father's glory, though I doubt his nose be oft inside a book. Well, this Anne is sister to a student there, called Luc.'

'French also?'

'Aye, as is the lady that Anne serves.'

'Then is she some serving-wench?'

'By no means: of gentle birth, yet poor, as in a fairy tale. Or so says Cecil: though mayhap, being his father's son, by vanity more than truth.'

'And who is this she serves?'

'I know not: some French lady, as I say, that brought her from France, with her brother Luc for her protection.'

'And this Luc would know our laws? Well, he shall not be idle! But what portends this invasion out of France? Are they mayhap Protestants, that love faith more than country?'

'Not so, for they are Romish, and the lady that Anne serves also. Yet there is no mystery in this, nor any invasion. For half London is foreign born; and now we are half at peace with France, these seas betwixt us are shrunk to a mere stream; and indeed, there are more Englishmen in Paris now, than Frenchmen here.'

'And she is fair, this Anne?'

'So says Cecil, for I have not seen her; nor, indeed, has she anything of Genoa's court, nor knows she aught of Cecil save that he is the comeliest youth in England.'

'Yet too young, sure, or too green for courtship.'

'She also: I ween 'tis but a chaste play of children, put on by Cecil to spite Robin, whom it spiteth not. Well, I wish them both joy of their Annes and Susans.'

'Thou rilest much against womankind, Peter, since thy child lived not to make thee love them.'

'Oh, they are all one! We must have mothers, Aubrey, to be born, and wenches to idle with in wasted hours. Save in these, their society is but a penance.'

'So didst thou not speak when thou first knew Lucy.'

'Aye, for I knew her not, nor women!'

'Then what wilt thou do: turn monk?'

'Nay, sailor.'

'Thou? What knowst thou, Peter, of the sea?'

'As much or as little as thou of acting; but we can each learn to master either.'

'Then thou wouldst leave Lucy, Venice, London, and solid earth?'

We were crossing the river now, and Peter, pausing, pointed to the ships. 'They do not beckon thee?' quoth he. 'Those cockles that carry questing men into an alien element he learns to love, not fear? Who, great in our day, has not been sailor? And what would be England, were it not guarded by the sea that also summons it to conquest?'

'Peter, thou hast drunk too deep the pot-house eloquence of broken spars! Thou art bewitched by bubbles, not of salt-spray, but sack!'

'As have been, and are, the bravest of our land, that bring it glory!'

'And to them, scurvy, the lash, chain-shot and a salt grave! Let me walk on earth, for it is solid.'

'Till thou must lie in it.'

'Truly; yet would I not barter gentle worms for the sharp bite of a fish inside my skull!'

I had an errand to run for Master Heminges, which was to his partner, Henry Condell of our Company, that had gone over to Blackfriars, on business at the theatre there. For this, closed ere now by the Council, had oped its doors again to the boy actors, Children of the Chapel; and Master Condell must dispute with them, anent the use of plays belonging to my Lord Chamberlain.

Observation has taught me that a man's trade may oft be divined, e'en when he be not about it: I mean, as soldiers out of uniform, lawyers bereft of wigs, and actors whose hour of glory on the stage is cast aside. For that which men are, they soon become, and women, also; and I ween none would mistake a bawd for a nun, e'en naked on judgement day.

But from this rule (if it be one), Master Condell was quite exempt; and when he was first shown to me, by young actors at the *Globe*, I mistook this man of such vast experience in the theatre for some grave functionary, that came into the *Globe* on a matter of law, or of finance. Truth to tell, though the general of actors ne'er o'erawed me (for beside aught else, they are an amiable sort of person), I dwelt in terror of Master Condell's grave eye and solemn tongue. Nor was I alone in this; for e'en those that knew him longer, trembled no less. Only Master Heminges was at ease; and only he, the intimate of Henry Condell.

I left Peter at the door, lest Master Condell, that hated youth (though he was marvellous in scenes of courting damsels), should launch his fires upon him; and tendered him the message Master Heminges had given me. To this he said naught, but rather, 'Thou wouldst be actor!'

'I would attempt it, sir.'

'Why?'

'Why? That I am so bidden, and willing to essay it.'

'To be puffed up with conceit?'

'Well, I hope not, sir.'

'That the lewd of each sex may ogle thee, and offer guineas for thy ill favours?'

'Marry, an they do, sir, and I not deny them, I shall not be the first actor so requited.'

He gave me a slap, and hard. I half drew my dagger. 'That you must not, sir, be you ever so powerful, and I nothing!'

'Thou art less than nothing! Away!'

'I was bidden by Master Heminges to tarry for your answer.'

'Then tell him 'tis that he send me a fit messenger.'

'This message I shall fitly bear to him, who I know will thank me for my service, he being a gentleman.'

He raised his hand again, and I my knife. 'Marry,' said he sourly, 'thou shouldst play Brutus, not one of the sweaty multitude of Romans.'

'I shall play what I am bid, sir; and seek to mend mine ignorance of your art by hearkening any who will flavour his counsel with some courtesy.'

'Aye! Thou art a very Brutus! For beside thy dagger, thou art all morality!'

'Then be not proud emperor to me, for he was slain.'

This won me a thin smile, warm as an icicle. 'Boy, come with me,' said he.

In a small room, that was in much disorder, he took up a bag and from it printed sheets that he counted, and then handed to me. 'Thou knowest Paternoster Row?' said he.

'Hard by St Paul's.'

'And thou canst read?'

'Fair English, can I.'

'On these is writ the printer's name. Bear them to him, and say I charge him repair the multitudinous errors he has made.'

'E'en as you have corrected them,' said I.

'E'en as I tell thee, and no more.'

'Aught else?'

'Nay, unless he have fresh sheets for me that thou canst carry over to the *Globe*, for thither I am returning.'

'*Ave, Caesar!*' said I, and scaped the kick he levelled at mine arse.

Passing with Peter through Blackfriars, I found I was skirting Noll and Allan's house, wishing no more of them, not e'en by proximity. Peter said he had seen naught of either, but Beauty had told him Noll was much cast down and, save in matters of his faith, passing under Allan's chaste dominion. Such, thought I, are the powers of the forgiver o'er the forgiven!

The printer was at board, but one of his prentices, that took Master Condell's sheets, cried out, when he saw them, in dismay, and vowed that were Henry Condell as ardent a pursuer of wenches as of commas in a text, why then! he would have a hundred bastards.

'But what are these sheets that so engage his ardours?' I asked the lad.

'Why, 'tis that Master Condell, and his friend Heminges, have a madness to snatch texts from writers' hands, and bring these to us; and this ere their ink be dry, or the actors have yet conned their lines.'

'If so, why so, prithee?'

'For that writers of plays, unlike poets, remit the day of printing, fearing theft of their lines by others that might read them. Poets press on our presses in such numbers that our Row is as a nest of nightingales. But writers for theatres hide their lights, be these bright or dim, neath privy bushels.'

'But so hiding, their lines may be lost; and the immortality thy art confers on them, delayed or e'en denied.'

'So say Condell and Heminges, and would betray the writer's present prosperity by their firm faith in his futurity.'

Farewells bidden to this prentice, Peter remarked how quickly these lads took on the tincture of their trade: thus, printers' pedantic, butchers' bloodthirsty, brewers' besotted, and goldsmiths' greedy. 'And actors, arrogant,' said he.

'Nay, amiable. And what of panders? Are they not pestilent?'

'Pitiable,' quoth he.

'Yet are sailors stalwart.'

'Aye, and lawyers lecherous. So being now nearby Cecil's Inn, wouldst thou not cross the Fleet, and hear from his own lips of the assault on Anne?'

'Well, he will give us wine, an he be there.'

I had ne'er yet seen Cecil in his full panoply of gentleman; for though, when he came among us in the East, he was e'er courtly and sweet-spoken (save when in a rage), he was not surrounded, as now inside his Inn, with all the accoutrements of gentility that his father had foisted on him. And such were the dignity and address of this lad nurtured in the stews, that he had all the nobility of those earls of our realm whose ancestors were likewise bawds and robbers.

'So now art thou in love,' said I to him, when Cecil admitted us two ruffians to his chamber.

'*Mais oui, et follement*,' quoth he, kissing his fingers from his lips, and raising his eyes as if to paradise.

'And Cupid hath taught thee Anne's speech, in despite of ours?'

'Nay, not he, but her brother Luc, so that I may converse with Anne in the tongue of troubadours.'

'Well, I would learn some from him, for my thoughts are much in France presently, at least, its forests.'

'Naught easier; for his chamber is on the same stair and, be he there, he shall eftsoons be here.'

Luc was a grave and stately lad, yet one whose fair address could scarce disguise from us that, being a Frenchman, he must ever, if outside his country, suffer the company of barbarians. 'And why, sir,' said he, 'do you honour us Frenchmen with the favour of your attention?'

'Because, *Monsieur* Luc, I must act in a play of France.'

'Of Paris?'

'Nay, of a forest called Arden, that hath lions in it, beside divers amorous animals of the human sort.'

'Well, I know not of lions in the Ardennes, but as to the others, you will find them anywhere in France.'

'Or in England, *Monsieur*, when they come to steal hearts of poor swooning swains like my friend Cecil.'

'My sister Anne, as I need scarce tell you, delights in the acquaintance of one of Cecil's distinction. But she is too young for swooning, or to cause it; and has, beside, her duties to her mistress to engage her.'

'And who, sir, is this lady that is her mistress?'

'Sir – a lady. One that hath lived in your country some fourteen years, ere she came here from France; at the same age as comes my sister, which is fourteen also.'

'And came hither why, *Monsieur*?'

'As comes my sister to her, sir, to serve, so came *Madame* Marie-Claire, at the time of my sister's birth, to serve a lady.'

'A lady also French?'

'Sir, you are curious.'

'Aubrey,' quoth Cecil, 'that is oft close as a miser with what lies close to his bosom, supposes the treasures of all others should be laid ope to his prying eyes.'

'In our times,' said Luc, 'there are secrets that, beside being of no purport to him, are dangerous to pryers.'

'Why, now sparkles the jewel whereof we speak!' cried Cecil, that was standing by the window. And before Luc could rise to fetch his sister, Cecil darted to the court and brought her up to us.

Mistress Anne was grave as her brother, though with less severity, mayhap because younger than he was. Yet though sedate, her eyes bore a wanton look, that mocked, and made me think – if such creatures be – of a saucy nun. She watched much, yet said little; making pretence she knew scant English, though by her listening hard, I knew she did.

'Anne,' quoth Cecil, 'thou must walk with me about the Inns, and there learn, by sight of our dread justices, the solemnities we would nourish in thy brother.'

'*Monsieur*,' said she, 'I must on an errand for my mistress.'

'Of gallantry?' quoth Cecil.

'*Mon ami*,' said Luc, with a frown, '*Madame* Marie-Claire is a devout lady; nor does the oppression of her faith by your countrymen encourage frivolity, did she feel inclined thereto.'

'Your master shares your mistress's faith?' said I to Anne.

'Sir, I have no master, since my mistress is a widow; though her husband, God rest his soul, was, like her, a true believer.'

'And like her, French?'

'No, sir; he was a Scots gentleman.'

'*Mon cher* Cecil,' said Luc, 'thou wilt excuse my sister and me now, for I have family matters to relate to her.'

'And my French lesson from dear Anne?'

'Later, perhaps, when you are less occupied (here a frown at Peter and me) with your friends.'

I feared a rebuke from Cecil for my questions, but he spoke of naught but Anne, and of her graces. So Peter and I, well schooled by Jenny and Lucy to extol the virtues of anyone's lover when he, or she, proclaims them, said we had ne'er seen one so radiant as his. Yet walking together down to the river after, we followed another law of those that speak of their friends' lovers, which is, their backs scarce turned, to be more open, if less kindly.

'The brother is vain, the sister shrew,' quoth Peter.

'Nay, turn not thy coat so arsy-varsy, and sneer where thou

hast sung! Sure, he is proud; but then all Frenchmen are; and she demure, yet skittish, as are their girls.'

'I vow they are both spies.'

'Then must thou be one, so swift to read their minds! For we scarce spoke with them the time twixt two quarter bells.'

'And who can this mistress be, this French Scotch Papist widow?'

'Marry, an thou wouldst know, go ask! For there walks French Anne beside the river!'

She was alone, and turning towards the wharves. We saw her step into a wherry, and the watermen carry her across. Where she landed was not sure, for we could not see through the masts, though I thought 'twas on Bankside, not far from Will's.

'Mayhap,' said Peter, ''tis she that is gallant, not her mistress, as said Cecil.'

'Besides being spy? Thou wouldst give an ill name to these French exiles, Peter.'

I left him by London Bridge, for he would look at ships before he returned to mope at Rotherhithe; and I continued to the *Globe*, where I reported to Master Heminges the discharge of my office to his friend Condell, anent the texts. But to this he listened not, and said, 'We have garnered in some numbskulls and rapscallions from among those that were once actors, but preferred drink, Bedlam, or the Fleet, and fell away. Do thou take thy place fitly among them, for we would read o'er the scenes where Brutus, and Antony, address the Roman rabble.'

Though true, there were none to see us in the theatre, save some few actors besides carpenters and the like, this was, as his first musket drill to a young soldier, my baptism into the life theatrical. First Master Heminges explained what was toward, for none of the fellows gathered on the stage knew aught of *Julius Caesar*: I mean, what Will had made of him. Heminges said further he would be both Brutus, then Antony (for the purpose of the practice, the true actors of these parts being about other business), and that we all must, by manner and gesture, express first horror, then admiration, at moments which were apt to what each said.

This may sound simple, yet 'tis not. Let an actor have lines writ for him, and he may say them, be it well or ill; but if all speech be left to his own invention, he may fall into two errors, or mayhap both: to say naught and gawp, as some did, or to say more than is needful for the purpose. Into this last fault I tumbled. For when Master Heminges cried out, 'Friends, Romans, countrymen, lend me your ears!' I gave answer as loud, 'Aye, marry, Marc, and that right readily!' for which I was roundly scolded by Master Heminges. Though his fiercer fury fell on an old actor (come straight, I trow, from much bibbing in a tavern) that, when Heminges cried, 'I come to bury Caesar, not to praise him,' gave answer, 'Do thou praise him too, John, an it be writ down for thee.'

Another basic of the actor's art that commands much trial, and which is as hard in performance as easy in appearance, is but to move; and when moving swift, not to fly off the stage. For when we were ordered to run this way or that, in a howling mass, some vanished from sight to east or west, and others o'ershot the stage and, togas billowing, fell into the cockpit. At length Master Heminges, who shouted louder than did Marc Antony to his followers, established some rule among us; though swearing that, had the Romans been as addlepated and disorderly as we, they would ne'er have conquered Britain.

I got fruits by the Bridge from the lad that had bought my barrow, who would ne'er take payment from me for, beside selling him this, I had told him all the secrets I had learned.

He had kept for me early strawberries for, though 'twas but late spring, some had come up from the south, where 'tis more balmy.

But if I thought to win smiles from Jenny by my gift, I was mistook; for I could see that, by the thunders on her brow, and her scolding of William to show that his father, not he, was in disgrace, an ill evening portended.

'So!' quoth Jenny, putting aside William (and the strawberries), and facing me akimbo. 'So! And hast thou then doffed thy skirts?'

'I wore no skirts today, Jenny, but a toga.'

'And what is that, prithee?'

'Why, 'tis a sort of gown, worn by the Romans.'

'A gown!' quoth she. 'And what is a gown if not a skirt?'

'Well, I must not wear woman's clothes till I play Audrey in our comedy.'

'Comedy, forsooth! Aye, 'twill be a comedy indeed when our honest neighbours see my husband decked out as a harlot.'

'Audrey is no harlot, light of my life!'

'And is a lewd wench not a harlot?'

'Not in the country, beautiful. For there may maids be lewd yet honest.'

'But not in Surrey! I know not how it be in Essex, but in Surrey are wenches or lewd, or honest, one or t'other!'

'And hadst thou not, my heart, a lewd intent when thou camest from Surrey up to London?'

'Oh! So thus stands it! That my husband dubs his son's mother a whore!'

'I said "was", angel, not "is"; yet this I shall tell thee: that there is none more puritanical than a reformed bawd.'

'"Bawd", forsooth! Then let thy bawd wife tell thee this! That howe'er deep her depravity, she ne'er disgraced her sex by pretending to another!'

'But Jenny, my sweetest, 'tis but pretence! All acting is, in a sense, but that! Why! Thinkest thou that when I win gold for thee by acting Audrey, I shall not still tumble thee by acting Aubrey?'

'Well, thou shouldst not come to me in skirts!'

'Aye, marry, no!'

I have oft thought that, if women were but soldiers, they would win all battles; for they understand that, if one cannonade snatch not victory, they must e'er be ready with another.

'Mark Robin!' quoth she.

'How, mark him?'

'And Cecil also!'

'Well, I have marked them.'

'Nay, that hast thou not! For though each comes from the stews, they now seek honest service, as soldier or as lawyer; they do not, like thee, seek to better themselves by going from ill to worse.'

'And Peter would now be sailor.'

'Then from thine own lips art thou condemned! Of four youths, but one witless, and him I must call husband!'

'Then wert thou witless to love him thou callest so.'

'Frown not, Aubrey!' cried she, turning douce in an instant, like an April day. 'Indeed I love thee! But not that thou shouldst be mocked, and I shamed, and William grow to blush for his father's trade.'

'Then what wouldst thou have me be?'

She took my hands winningly, and I perceived once more her military art, which was to feint bombardments on either flank before mounting her main assault. 'Thou shouldst be innkeeper,' said she.

'Innkeeper? Jenny, of years I have scarce sixteen, guineas spared mayhap four, and knowledge of inns, none.'

'All can be remedied by time, patience and resource.'

'Aye, time, sure; but what resource?'

'After me, and William, who lovest thou most in this world?'

'Why, Martin, that taught and succoured me.'

'And what is he? Is he not innkeeper?'

'Aye, marry, but . . . Jenny, Martin is old and wise, hath money, and his inn . . . beside, 'tis not as in London, but a mess of thatched huts and privies built of wattles.'

'Yet hath he beds, ale, and his own address; and this is to be an innkeeper.'

'Aye, and to have gold wherewith to build an inn.'

'Hearken, Aubrey! As to thine age and inexperience, these can be remedied by time and application; as for the money, when thou art more advanced, thou shalt speak with Robin.'

'That he should lend me this? But he is dependent upon Venice.'

'And Robin is Venice's only son, beside being the apple of his serpent's eye.'

'Truly, I know not, Jenny.'

'Yet do I! Quit the theatre, Aubrey, it is not for thee! For beside aught else, as thou waxest more man, canst thou play wenches ever? Or if to play men, hast thou the skill for aught save wearing a toga in an ill-rewarded crowd?'

'Yet this Audrey must I act, an thou like it or no; for I have promised Will, and he hath been my friend, and stood godfather to our child.'

'Do this, then,' said she, 'and then no more.'

'Ah,' said I, rising, 'yet how shall the *Globe* spin without me?'

'Smoother,' said she, 'come to bed.'

5

One dawn soon after, when fallen to heavy slumber after a night of imploring William to rail less against the world, I was woken again by Widow Dill, that said one stood without, that was distracted by his eagerness to see me. And this was Cecil, that would not come in, for he said none must hear his business but I; which did not displease me, for Jenny, though she still cherished Robin, had quite turned against his cousin.

In the Borough, the ale-houses ope early for the markets, and the travellers to the south; so we chose one that was less cluttered than the most, and called for wine and some chicken, for I was a-hungered. Then, 'Luc is taken, and in the Clink,' said Cecil.

'On what ground?'

'Suspect of treason.'

''Sblood! And his sister?'

'Safe yet, yet fearful.'

'"Treason"! Yet can a Frenchman be treasonable to an English Queen?'

'Well, spying, plotting, I know not what: in commerce with treasonable Englishmen.'

I looked about. 'And this is so?' said I.

'I know not.'

'Come, Cecil!'

'It could be . . .'

'Then beware for thyself, lest Mistress Anne and her brother have thee too inside the Clink, or on the gallows!'

'But I would help her, Aubrey!'

'Then do so, and I beseech thee, tell me naught of't.'

'But 'tis this I would tell thee!'

I looked around once more, then seized his arm and said, 'Hearken, Cecil, and hearken well! I know the Clink, by helping Noll in such a business! And I am wed now, and have a son, and want none of it.'

'Then what shall I do?'

'Go to thy father! Genoa hath many friends among the justices!'

'Did have, aye, but now he rebuilds his fortune with mine uncle, he must walk wary.'

'And must not I? And hast thou not gold?'

'Aye . . .'

'Then seek out thy French friend thyself, by bribery.'

'I?'

'Mary have mercy, thou! Who else? 'Tis thy Anne, and her brother, and neither mine.'

'I have spoke of thy love for me to Anne.'

'Speak to her of my love of farting, an thou wilt, yet will I none of this!'

'And she has spoke to her mistress, that would speak with thee.'

'In French, I doubt not!'

'And give thee gold.'

'What gold?'

'Much.'

'Aye – much; to buy treason and the rope!'

'Nay: only to carry a message in to Luc.'

'Cecil, good-morrow!'

But he grasped my hand as I rose to go, and cried, 'Aubrey, I conjure thee by our friendship that thou do this for me!'

'As Jenny would conjure me, by our sacred vows, to say thee nay.'

'By my love for thee, Aubrey!'

I looked at him, then said, 'Well, I shall speak with this *Madame*, but promise naught till I have heard her.'

'God save thee!'

'Amen. Where doth she live?'

'In Mary-le-bourne, hard by Tyburn.'

'Zounds! 'Tis an ill omen! Well, I shall go to her.'

This took me across the fields to the north, and past villages I had not yet seen. The house I sought stood by itself in a small orchard, and I wandered about it at a distance, to see if any watched, but saw none. So I walked up among the fading blossoms and pulled at the bell.

The door was oped by Anne, that said naught to me but, '*Bon jour, Monsieur Aubré*,' and led me to a room, where I was left alone. None came, and suspecting treachery, I moved towards the window. In the garden outside, all was still, though not my heart inside my breast. Lowering my eyes to a shelf, I saw on it a double locket, each side shaped as a cross, and fastened with a gold hook. I prized it open, and a voice behind me said, '*Bon jour, Monsieur*.'

I spun round like a top. '*Madame Marie-Claire?*' said I.

'Aye. Be seated, pray, my friend.'

A boy of sixteen thinks all older women matrons, yet I could guess that, though past her first youth, she would still see some summers before her thirtieth. She was small, dark, and I thought her eye evil; yet when she moved or spoke, bore a commanding grace.

'You have come to help me,' said she.

'Aye, *Madame*, an I can.'

'You can.'

She took from her dress a purse, and gave it to me. 'Go to Luc,' said she, 'whom you know. Say to him only this: that they come from Ireland will release him; tell him, he must not speak.'

'He will know which "they", Madam?'

'He will now. And now you may go.'

'An if I cannot see him?' said I, looking at the purse.

'You will; and the purse is yours.'

She said no more, so I rose, bowed to her, and moved towards the door. From behind me, she said, 'You looked inside my locket?'

'Aye, Madam,' said I, turning, and gazing down.

'You know whose those two faces are?'

I looked at her eyes now. 'I saw them first,' said I, 'the first day I saw you.'

'And where have you seen me?'

'At my Lord Southampton's wedding, when you came to speak an instant with Master Will.'

'Ah . . . You were the serving-boy?'

'Aye, madam.'

She stood up, looked through the window, then at me. 'You have seen either since?' said she.

'Not my Lord; for the other, I work now in his theatre.'

'Art thou the country lad that gave him matter for his comedy?'

'Aye, and I am to act in it.'

'So,' said she; then after a pause, 'Thou wouldst not betray Will's friend?'

'An you are this friend, Madam, no; nor would I have done, had I not known you were his friend.'

''Tis well,' she said, '*merci et adieu.*'

Anne waited outside, and showed me to the door. 'Before I go,' said I, 'pray teach me some words of your French speech.'

'Which words?'

'"They that are come from Ireland will release you."'

She told me, and I fixed it in my mind by repetition.

Then thanking her I went out and stood a while, watching. I turned off the path into the trees, and when these hid me both from house and lane, took out the purse and stuffed it twixt two branches. Then I walked outside the gate, whistling. If any stopped me, my tale was that I had come seeking to buy fruit cheap, yet with no fortune. But though I circled for a while, I saw no one; so climbed back through the hedge into the orchard, and secured my purse. It held the same sum as my worldly wealth, four guineas.

I thought to consult Gropenut, or even Sad Jack or Amos, as how best to approach my old acquaintance, the Chief Gaoler of the Clink; but turned against this, both by my wish to have no more of them, as that a shared secret doubles danger. How Jenny had worked her way inside to offer bribes, I in part knew, yet could not ask her now; yet guessed it was by sweet smiles, which would not serve me so well. Then could I ask Will? No, for I sensed that whate'er his friend had asked of me, he would not wish my prying in his affairs.

Well, if I did not know what to do, I must discover this by doing something. First, I went home, and hid in the roof, from all eyes, e'en Jenny's, two of my guineas in the purse. Of the remainder two, I changed one in a tavern for smaller coin, and put the other in my pocket. Then I walked to the Clink and, breathing a prayer, asked the watchman if I might speak with the Chief Gaoler. 'Thou wouldst speak with him, or lodge with him?' said he.

'Speak only, friend.'

'Anent what?'

'My lass,' said I.

'This is no woman's prison, fellow, 'tis elsewhere.'

'Aye, but her brother is not, whom she begs me to visit for her.'

'And who is this brother?'

'A Frenchman, Luc.'

'Ah!' He stared at me. 'And what wouldst thou with this traitor?'

'Naught of treachery, but matter of the heart.'

'"Heart"!' He laughed. 'We do not count hearts here, but heads.'

'Count these, then,' said I, handing him small coin.

'Well, tarry here, but I can promise naught to thee.'

After an hour, while I sat in a sweat, I was summoned up. The Chief Gaoler greeted me with silence, gazing at me, then came round his table and seized me by the throat. 'Tell all!' he said, shaking me.

'Sir, an you not release me, I can tell naught.'

'Speak, then!' he cried, throwing me on the floor.

'You do me ill, sir,' said I, 'to suspect me. For you must know that were I guilty of aught, I should ne'er come here.'

'Then why comest thou, Master Innocence?'

'Sir, my mistress Anne, this is sister to the prisoner Luc, beseeched me to bring him her love and faith in him.'

'Dost thou suppose,' said he, 'I am Master Innocence also?'

'Sir,' said I, 'I beg you but bring Luc here, and let me say this to him in your presence!' Now I stooped, and rising said, 'And saving your presence further, sir, methinks this was dropped when you struggled with me ere little.'

'Aye,' said he, taking the gold and looking at it. 'Methinks it was. Turnkey!' he cried, putting the coin away. 'Fetch up French Luke!' I stood silent while he observed me. 'These are troubled times, Aubrey,' quoth he.

'You remember my name, sir?'

'And thy face, that none could forget! With such a countenance must a man live honest, whatsoever his desire.'

'Aye, and I do, sir.'

'At thieving, pandering, or spying?'

'At none of these: I am an actor.'

'Thou?'

'Aye, sir. I shall act in the new play at the *Globe*.'

'I know not,' said he, 'if thou be actor in a theatre, but sure thou art one outside it.'

'Not I, sir!'

'Then art thou other than a thousand rogues that have stood before me! Tell me, Aubrey. Thou wouldst not, for more gold than thou hast seen today, reveal the plot of thy French friends to me?'

'Sir, believe me, I know of no plot, nor of what *Monsieur* Luc stands accused.'

'That he is French accuses him enough! What make they here, if not to disturb our peace? And all other Papists and traitors that come swarming to our shores?'

'Which, sir?'

'Which? Thou knowest not that my Lord Essex and his friends are come back from Ireland?'

'Why, no, sir. Yet sure, the Earl of Essex is no traitor, nor a Papist.'

'My Lord of Southampton is both; and both have conspired in Ireland.'

'Then why are they not, sir, in the Tower?'

'That will come! They would to the Low Countries now, to render further service to Her Majesty, quotha! To betray her further, rather.'

And now came in Luc; and into my mind also the horrid illumination that they which were 'come from Ireland', whereof the French lady had told me, were doubtless these same noblemen the Chief Gaoler had denounced to me.

Luc bowed to me slightly, and said, '*Bon jour, Monsieur*.'

'English!' cried the Chief Gaoler. 'Naught but honest speech twixt honest men!'

'*Monsieur Luc*,' said I, 'I bring greetings to you from your sister Anne. Who commands me tell you that *ceux qui sont venus d'Irlande vous délivreront*.'

'Rogue!' cried the Chief Gaoler, seizing and buffeting me. 'What hast thou told him?'

'Naught, sir, prithee, prithee!'

'Naught! And was not one word "Ireland"?'

'Hear me, I beseech you, sir!'

'Speak, varlet!'

'Sir,' said I, 'his sister is, alas! made pregnant by some scoundrel, and of this I sought to tell him privily that he be not shamed of it in your presence.'

'And this seducing scoundrel, sirrah, is from Ireland?'

'Nay, nay, you have mistook the French word of "pregnant" for that of Ireland.'

'Liar!'

'Sir, you trust none! Believe me! 'Tis as I tell you!'

'To the cells with Master France!' he bellowed at the turnkey.

When we were alone, he said, 'Aubrey, be warned. An I find thou knowest aught of this, beside thou art put to torture, I shall ensure thou art turned out of any theatre.'

'Sir, I hide naught from you, having naught to hide.'

'Hide thyself, then! Begone!'

In the theatre, 'tis as if a cook must prepare one meal, in the same time as he serves another. For now the banquet of *Julius Caesar* was ready to set before the spectators, *As You Like It* must be swift brought forward too. And here arose an obstacle – the first, indeed, of many – which I discovered on my return from the Clink into the *Globe*.

The Company of my Lord Chamberlain had four lads that

played women's parts (beside others, on occasion); and these, though ruled severely by the actors, were, in truth, as sons are to their fathers, as much anxiety as treasure. For no play could be put on without them, yet were their young lives fraught with special dangers. Their voices could crack into a man's, rendering them useless, and all the labours wasted on them. My Lord Admiral, or other Companies, might try to steal them away by offer of gold or greater glory. The Church, my Lord Mayor, or e'en their fathers that profited by their wages, might rebel against their corruption by the theatre, and denounce it. Or some ardent lord or lady might covet their persons, and seek to deny the display of these to others.

The lives of these lads were therefore ruled as much by fortune as any wise prediction; and at this moment, the goddess that governs theatres, showed herself fickle. For of the chief boy actors, one, overnight, was no more boy, but barked in a horrid basso; another lay wasted by a sudden access of the plague; a third, that must take his First Communion, was warned by the priest that he must choose between church or theatre and, impelled by his family, had renounced the stage; while a last, that had played with the Company at Windsor in the winter, had stayed there with a tender lordling, and would not come back.

Yet others had been found and schooled for *Julius Caesar*, and for this sufficed. For this is a play of men; indeed, I think there is none that has seen it who does not wish, when the Roman matrons declaim their lofty lines, that they would have done, so that the battles of the men, which are the play's chief substance, may continue. Beside, any play wherein Master Richard Burbage is chief actor, is worthy to be seen, e'en if there be naught much else to it.

But in *As You Like It*, there was no part for Master

Burbage: none, I mean, that suited his great gifts, though he could have played any, had he wished to – even Audrey! And beside this lack of a part for Burbage, there was an even graver: which was, who should play Rosalind?

For of all the plays Will writ, I think there is none other wherein the chief personage of all, is a woman. On Rosalind hangs the play, and be she ill acted, it is nothing: or worse than this, a fair thing fouled by want of art. Any lad of wit and some skill could learn to be Celia, Phebe, Audrey, or Hymen; to play Rosalind, a boy must be as rare as she.

For days now, one youth after t'other had read her lines, while Will sighed, Master Condell glowered, and John Heminges tore at his locks. Even the boys for Celia and Phebe were not apt, though more so, I doubt not, than I as Audrey. It seemed now that naught could be done but put forward the play till later, when lads of more talent could be unearthed, or borrowed from other Companies.

'Twas then that Aubrey had the great inspiration of his life. If I could play Audrey, why not Herman, Hymen; Peter, Phebe; Cecil, Celia; and Robin, Rosalind?

I would never, today, have the effrontery to make such a proposal to any anent anything: I mean, go to the chief actors in the realm, and say to them that three lads of which they knew naught, and one (Herman) they knew all too well (or ill), should come out of nowhere, knowing nothing, and act beside them. But I was then sixteen, and beside, believed in my heart this thing was possible; and I wonder if that Aubrey who felt this (and rightly, in the final issue), was not, however rash and forward, one braver and wiser than the Aubrey I have become.

This plot I unfolded, trembling as with an ague, to Master Heminges. 'Sir,' said I, 'I think you are not pleased with the young actors.'

'They are, in troth, less fit for anything than thou, if that were possible.'

'Then, Master Heminges, should you not seek others?'

'And have we not? I have listened, these past weeks, to a score or more nurtured in Bedlam.'

'Aye, John, but there are better.'

'What, in the Marshalsea?'

'Nay, here in London: of wit, grace, and no small knowledge.'

He was hearkening to me now, but with more of a frown than an attentive ear. 'And who are these others of such no small knowledge?'

'Four friends, John, that are named . . .'

'Go to, Aubrey, go to! An thou wilt summon up every rat of thine acquaintance out of the sewers of Shoreditch, to win from us a pint of ale and a pie for their assault upon our ears, thou thinkest me more patient with thy jesting than I have inclination.'

'No jest, John, I swear it; and they are well schooled by Herman.'

'Herman! Jesu, Maria, and all the Saints! Is it the Company of my Lord Herman that thou wouldst foist upon us?'

'I swear I know the lad that can play Rosalind!'

'And who is he?'

'Robin, my friend.'

'"Robin thy friend"! And thou hast friends for Celia, and Phebe, I doubt not.'

'And Herman for Hymen.'

'Aye, well . . . that, at least, would not be ill matched; for the goddess of wedlock in the form of an ancient catamite would sure please the lewder of the groundlings.'

'John, wilt thou at least not speak of this with Will?'

'Go thy ways, Aubrey! We have cares enough without thy

conceit of helping to mar that whereof thou knowest less than naught!'

I think if Master Heminges had said, 'Aye, thanks lad, yet 'twill not do,' or any such courteous dismissal, I should have thought no more of it. But now he had roused in me both pride and mulishness; and if I am not o'erburdened by the first, the second is half my nature. Yet if I should persist in the plot of making my friends actors, there came to me, too, the thought that I had best ask them if they wished it; else, like Sir John Falstaff, would I be offering soldiers that loved not battles.

At Rotherhithe, they were all about, and I contrived to gather them into Herman's pantry; no easy task, for to assemble four young men one must be sheep-dog. There I told them, in brief, all; and there was at first a silence.

'Thou hast then thought fit,' quoth Cecil, breaking this, 'to barter the secrets of thy friends, for mockery in a theatre? To tell our privy tale to strangers?'

'And what a theatre!' quoth Herman, dilating his nostril like a countess that sniffs a turd. 'And what actors, too – I know them well, and their thin gift in ranting of raw verse!'

'Marry, I never!' cried Peter. 'I told thee I would be sailor, yet not player.'

Now felt I like one that tenders a banquet to men suffering from gout, colic or the stone. 'And thou, Robin?' said I.

'Well, I like thy conceit,' said he.

'I may say thou wilt essay it?'

'Marry, that will I, and why not so? True, I would be a soldier: but until I may bear arms, why should I not seek to learn this other art?'

'And thou wouldst wear skirts?' quoth Peter.

'An Aubrey will, why not I?'

'And if I be Celia, Aubrey, the man that plays Oliver would buss me?'

'Aye, Cecil, an thine Anne forbid it not!'

'But petticoats!' quoth Peter.

'Hearken!' quoth Cecil. 'Priests wear 'em, and they may marry now! Moors also, that are renowned for lust! Why, e'en sailors do, for I have seen mariners that wear tunics like thy Lucy's.'

Herman raised a hand, closed his eyes till fell silence, and then spoke. 'Before you say aye or nay to this strange proposal of Master Aubrey's, remember that he, like all fresh new convertites, is more proselytiser than the Pope. Remember also that the actor's life, that seems soft and alluring, is beyond description hard. Further remember, that though I have instructed you some little, you are all unripe things, and hence more ripe for mockery than adulation.

'Yet youth must be served, and this e'en in its follies. Therefore, Aubrey, perpend: go to thy masters, tell them we shall consider this and, should we like the play, and mislike not our fellow actors, and enough gold be tendered us, we may, perchance, accept.'

'I must say all this to Master Heminges?'

'Use thine own words, lad, provided he understand their essence.'

Robin took me afterwards apart, and said, frowning yet with a smile, 'Thou thinkest I can do this?'

'Robin! I have seen six or more of thine age read our Rosalind's lines, and not one had thy wit or grace to play her.'

'And there is no shame in acting women?'

'Well, in half of the play, Rosalind is Ganymede, in hose and doublet.'

'I should speak on't with my father . . .'

I laid a hand upon his arm. 'Do as thou wilt,' said I, 'yet consider this. Should thou ask Venice this, he may spurn it, and say thee nay; yet when he sees thee applauded by hundreds in the *Globe*, his heart will swell with pride, and he shall tell all he urged thee to it.'

'Mayhap . . . well, I must think on this.'

'Think well: and conjure Cecil, if thou canst, to some hopeful discretion.'

Yet though I said this of him, Cecil was discreet enough when I went, and he followed me out into the street. 'I have seen Anne,' said he, 'and must thank thee for serving her mistress as thou didst promise me.'

'Well, I was paid for't.'

'She would herself thank thee.'

'Who?'

'*Madame* Marie-Claire.'

'Let her keep her thanks, and I my gold.'

'Nay, but, Aubrey, she would know if thou hast seen Luc, and what passed.'

'Do thou tell thy Anne she may say to her mistress this: I saw him, and said what I was bid.'

'Her mistress would hear it from thy lips.'

'This was not in the bargain.'

'She knows this; yet awaits thee if thou choose to come to her.'

6

Jenny had turned kinder to me after my promise to leave the theatre: as, indeed, wives do after victory. I could not hide from her that I had lured my comrades along the same ill path, for I knew she would discover this. But to my surprise, she said only that her husband would be thought less fool if he had like company.

Nor did I tell her of how I got the gold hid in the attic; yet knowing how well she loved this metal, and esteemed me if I could pluck it from the air (if this be with hands untainted by excessive villainy), I could not forbear to bring my two guineas to her, saying they were a gift from my Lord Chamberlain for that I had found four fresh actors, when he stood in such dire need. I fancy she disbelieved me, for my words earned a sharp look; but the gold she eyed tenderly.

Yet in spite this scene of matrimonial accord, and domestic bliss, with Jenny boasting of William's prowesses to Widow Dill, that had called in upon us, I was restless as a badger in a trap. Why is it that, when man has peace, he spurns it? Knows secrets are not his, and dangerous, but must uncover them? Why is it also that loving one he knows with all his heart, he may yet tremble at the thought of another he knows little, and then only to mistrust?

'Jenny,' said I, ''tis hot, I would abroad a space.'

'Thou hast not eat yet.'

'Nor would so.'

'Nor conned thy precious lines.'

This was spoke sarcastical, for I had begged Jenny to read the scenes with me wherein Audrey appears, and be Touchstone, William, or some other; that I might perfect my lines, and e'en more, actions: which she executed with all the joy of a fop in a byre.

'I shall murmur them as I take the air.'

'Well, take it not too far nor long; for I did not marry thee to see only thine arse exiting each eve.'

I crossed the Bridge, and though 'twas late, we were nearing midsummer, and there were stars with the last sun's light. I set off across the city, north and west, climbing from the river. When I reached Mary-le-bourne, it struck eleven.

I circled the house, that was lit dim, and paused to listen each forty paces. I crept into the orchard, and froze still by a tree when the door opened, and one came out, muffled.

This figure left the path, and walked across the orchard, pausing as I had. When he had passed on, I waited still, and then moved forward. A sword pricked my neck, and a hand gripped my dagger arm. 'Die, dog!' a man's voice whispered.

'Sir, I came but for some apples!' said I, trembling.

'Green ones? They are like to pain thy belly e'en more than this!' He still held my arm, and I could feel the sword cut my cloth and prick chill upon my kidney.

'Sir,' said I, 'do you but speak to the lady of the house, and you will learn I am bidden here.'

'To steal apples? How art thou named?'

'Aubrey.'

'I know not this name: what knowest thou of this lady?'

My mind flew, for a wrong answer would slay me. If he were friend of hers, to say I had served her might serve me; if foe, I would serve his sword for pin-cushion.

'She has summoned me here, sir: I know not yet why.'

'And how is she called?'

'*Madame* Marie-Claire.'

He said naught, though breathed hard. At length the sword pricked in, and he pushed my shoulder forward, so that I stumbled onto the path, and so up to the door, which he kicked lightly with his boot.

It opened a few inches, and he said over my shoulder, 'Thou knowest this fellow?'

'Aye, he is the lad I sent to Luc.'

'Thou hast bid him here?'

'To tell what passed. Do not harm him, Henry.'

'Well, take him in, I must not linger. Nay, seek not to see

me, fellow! Go in!' And he pushed me through the door and banged it fast.

'Good even, Madam,' said I, panting like a hare.

'Come within, child.'

I came into that same room where I had spoke with her this morning, and she told me to sit, and poured me wine. 'Thou art not hurt?' said she.

'Frighted, only.'

'He is a dangerous man.'

'Aye, marry!' said I, drinking.

She watched me a while, then said, 'And Luc?'

'I saw, and spoke with him; briefly, but enough.'

'He was not harmed?'

'I think not; but in prisons . . .'

'Aye, prisons! Who has not known them in our age?'

'Even our Queen, when she was younger . . .'

She looked hard at me. '*Thy* Queen!' she said.

'Madam, I know that you are French, and so . . .'

'Not for that reason, for my husband was a Scot. Yet were he not, I would not name Elizabeth queen.'

'Who, then?'

'She who was, and, if not murdered, would be yet.'

'Mary of Scotland?'

'And of England! For she was no bastard, but true born to both these crowns.'

'Madam!' said I, glancing at the curtained windows, then the door, 'I prithee, prudence!'

'Prudence!' said she. 'Aye, 'tis an English virtue.'

'I speak not of virtue, but of danger. For in these times, there are spies beneath each bush.'

'So poor Luc has discovered.'

'Aye, but Madam! Is he not also one, perchance?'

'If to serve his faith and cause be spy, he is.'

'I seek not his secrets, nay, nor anyone's. But if *Monsieur* Luc, or any other, serve Rome presently in England, 'tis at their peril.'

'Thou art Protestant, boy?'

'Madam, I am nothing! Yet am I one that would live out his span.'

'And then?'

'And then, Madam?'

'Thy span of prudence ended, wilt thou knock on the gates of paradise with this single virtue?'

'Well, I hope I have others, also.'

''Tis true thou art brave, and I think faithful . . .'

'Praise not these, unless you blame also avarice; for you gave me gold.'

'Thou didst this for gold?'

'For my wife and child, rather.'

'Then that is not avarice, but love.'

'I hope so, madam. Would you aught else of me, or may I go?'

'Thou fearest my company, thou that I have called brave?'

'Madam, not you, but what you have half told me.'

'And what is this?'

'That Luc spied for Rome; and that he will be rescued by those from Ireland.'

'And have I half told you who they are?'

'Nay, but my wits have; which tell me also one of these held a sword naked to my neck.'

She stared at me in silence. Then said, 'And who was he?'

'My Lord of Southampton.'

'His face was not masked?'

'Cloaked, Madam, yet I saw it. Beside, you called him "Henry".'

She nodded, then said, 'Boy, thou hast knowledge wherefor the Council would give thee more gold than can I.'

'Did they hear me, aye.'

'And that also, wherefor my friends might seek to slay thee.'

'An I gave them cause to.'

'Yet must we trust thee with our safety?'

'Had you not done so, you would ne'er have bid me serve you; and why you did so, I can half guess.'

'Guess, then.'

'You know I am true friend to Master Will.'

'Boy, we scarce spake of thee! Save of some country lad that had served him in his play.'

'Mayhap. Yet Luc, and Anne also, have spoke with my friend Cecil, and so know, and have told you, that I am that country lad that serves him.'

She looked at me with a faint smile. 'And now,' said she, 'art thou tumbled in a scene that has naught in't of comedy.'

I nodded to her, and waited. She was as one proud yet frighted, aloof yet forward, sure yet unsure. 'I think, Madam,' said I, 'that you have conned o'er this play of Will's.'

'Yes, I have read it.'

'And liked it, or no?'

'It is a pretty thing; yet I think he has writ better, and shall more.'

'You have read many lines that he has writ?'

'Aye, marry, many lines!'

She rose now, and I also, and kissed the hand that she held out to me. 'What is thy child?' she said. 'A boy?'

'Aye – William.'

'Then give him this,' and from a drawer she took out a thin chain of silver, with a cross. 'My mistress gave it to me when I was thine age, or less.'

'I shall teach him to thank you, Madam.'

'Teach him rather to love his mother, as I did my mistress, that was as mother to me, beside true monarch.'

I took the chain and, looking in her eyes, said, 'Was this Mary of Scotland?'

'Go now!' said she.

7

There are those that malign merchants, saying if one have goods, and another need them, then what service can the merchant render save to rob each? Aye, yet they forget that without Master Merchant, they that would sell, and buy, may wander forever seeking each other, like lost souls in eternity. For the merchant is trade's Cupid; and earns his wage by finding two ripe hearts for his gilt arrows.

This I discovered when I sought to market my friends as actors to Master Heminges, and Master Heminges to my friends, as prompter of their fortunes. Ne'er did bustling blind Cupid find such coyness, yet such desire! For the theatre was now desperate for boy actors; my friends had grown dazzled by the stage; yet Master Heminges would not listen to me, and my friends said, aye, they would, mayhap, an they be summoned, but they could not knock unbidden on the *Globe* gate.

In this fix, I did what Cupid doubtless oft must, which is, having launched his shafts, bring the fond unknown lovers face to face. This I engineered by telling my friends Master Heminges awaited them, which he did not; and by o'er-hearing him say to Master Condell, that they must meet that eve to examine costumes in the theatre.

When we arrived, all five and Robin bringing his Susan,

either to give him courage, or to calm any denial from her, the theatre was empty, so we stood about the cockpit, waiting. But not Herman: for he, like an old charger that sniffs a battlefield, climbed up upon the stage and declaimed in thunderous tones some noble lines writ by Master Marlowe. At this moment, entered Master Heminges.

He gazed upon this scene in some amaze, then cried, 'Enough, thou worn out ghost of yesteryear! Begone!'

'Good Master Heminges!' quoth Herman, hand raised to shade his eye. 'Can it be thee that mine eyes dimly see?'

'What are these, Aubrey?' cried Heminges, staring at my friends so fierce that they fell back a pace.

'Why, they are my friends the actors.'

'Actors!' cried Heminges, pouncing upon Peter. 'Act, then, boy – act!'

'Good sir, I know not how!'

'And thou! What art thou – Sheba's Queen?'

'Nay, sir, I am called Cecil.'

'And this, that cowers behind a wench! What wouldst thou play, fellow?'

'Rosalind.'

'Thou? Rosalind?'

'Aye, sir. And this that you call wench, and beside whom I stand, not cower behind, is my lass Susan.'

'Good even, sir,' said she.

'Aye, well, enough of this – away!' said Heminges.

'Good friend,' said Herman, who had stepped down off the stage and now come up. 'Whate'er thou mayest think of me, imports not; but of my worship of our art, and true devotion to it, thou canst not doubt. So in the name of these, I beg thee: hear this youth speak for Rosalind.'

Heminges looked at him, then at Robin, and said, 'Come hither lad. Give ear attentively:

Alas the day! What shall I do with my doublet and hose? What did he when thou saw'st him? What said he? How looked he? Wherein went he? What makes he here? Did he ask for me? Where remains he? How parted he with thee? And when shalt thou see him again? Answer me in one word.

Canst thou say this?'

'Once more, sir, then I may.'

Heminges spoke the lines again, then pointed to the stage. 'Declaim them there,' said he, 'remembering who thou art, both part and actor.'

We stood silent as Robin clambered on the stage, for it was of those instants that, among men, give birth to all or nothing. He walked to the centre, stood a while gazing down, then raised his head and, not looking at us, but up and outward in the theatre, spoke.

There was another pause: broken by Herman saying, 'Some six words faulted, though not ill spoke; yet were it I . . .'

'Silence, fool!' cried Heminges; then raising his voice, 'Once more, lad: not louder, yet a slight more slow; and speak not to us, but to thy cousin, Celia, that in imagination stands beside thee.'

I have seen many actors since, and a score at least finer than Robin could e'er be, did he give his whole life to this hard calling. Yet what he had, have few; and this was, beside grace and a sweet clear voice, a siren's art to invade all ears and instantly compel all spirits. I can but say this: off stage, his voice and presence were agreeable; yet once on it, these were so multiplied that, when he spoke, not to listen was not possible.

'Stay, John!' cried a voice; and down from the gallery came Will with Henry Condell, that had gone up there, and been listening. They beckoned Heminges over, while we, and Robin that had come down to us, stood watching, saying little. After a time that seemed an age, Master Heminges returned to us, and said, 'Approach – give ear.'

We crowded round about him.

'Naught is decided,' said he, 'nor can be, till we know more. But this we would ask: can you all read?'

'Aye,' we said.

'Then listen. I shall give you some lines: not to learn yet, but to study. Tomorrow, at eight bells struck in St Mary Overy – which is not nine, nor ten, nor one minute e'en after the appointed hour – you may, should you still wish it, come hither, and we shall hear each of you.'

'Save me, I trust, if this be some trial of novices,' quoth Herman.

'Come, or come not!' said Heminges. 'Yet an thou be not, Master Herman, then thou art not. As for thee, Aubrey, Will would speak with thee. For the remainder part of you, the gate lies thither, that summons you to go, and shall ope to welcome you on the morrow. Mark well, as you leave, St Mary Overy's!'

The three partners of the *Globe* stood speaking further, while I waited apart, till Will summoned me, saying, 'Come, Master Pander, and tell me how thou art turned bawd for theatres.' Yet he spoke not until we reached his house, where he led me in, and we first ate, speaking of nothings. Then he summoned me to his room beside the river.

'Aubrey,' said he, 'first, must I thank thee.'

'For what?'

'Thy chief thought in this was mayhap to help thy friends; yet thou hast sought also to help me, and the Company which thou servest.'

'I hope I have: what sayest thou, prithee, of Robin?'

'Nothing, for that I know nothing, save this: that he is no nothing, though what sort of something, we shall know better tomorrow.'

'And the rest?'

'Of them we know less, even, than nothing; and only the morrow can instruct us. Yet one, must we banish absolutely; and that is Herman!'

'Yet is he the only actor in our number!'

'The only wan lily, also, in a bunch of primroses! Beside, he is a pestilent fellow, and my actors will have none of him.'

'But Hymen is not a large part, and he has a sweet falsetto.'

'And a sour temper.'

'He taught us all, Will! He laboured hours to sew where thou may reap!'

'Aubrey, I would tell thee a hard truth: in a theatre, can there be nor kindness, pity, gratitude nor aught save striving to perfection. For we are as soldiers, that must reward not past repute, but present valour.'

'Then let him be pensioner, as are older soldiers.'

'Aye, but in hospitals, not on battlefields.'

'Will, I have asked so much, yet ask but this, then silence: canst thou but hear him tomorrow, so he be judged not in his absence.'

'Well, he may come, but I promise nothing. As to the others, and even young Robin, there is this that troubles us: they come late to the stage. Thy voice, Aubrey, has already tumbled, which matters not for Audrey; thy friend Peter, might barely pass for Phebe; and e'en Robin and Cecil, whose voices still pipe so prettily, sprout down I like not, howe'er it may delight their maids.'

'Mayhap, Will; yet what of all those thou hast already tried, and liked not any?'

'Aye; there is a strange lack of larks in London presently.'

'And the hawks? Are the men's parts happily bestowed?'

'We think so; and thank thee, Aubrey, for thy solicitude.'

'And what wilt thou play, if anything?'

'Old Adam.'

'Then now know I why thou, that in thy youth never did apply hot and rebellious liquors in thy blood, dost offer me none neither!'

'Go fetch them; and may they bring thee the means of weakness and debility!'

He was watching the boats when I came back, and said, without turning. 'Hast thou e'er sailed in ships?'

'No, never.'

'Nor I, unless Dover harbour be my Atlantick, where I sailed like Columbo in a fishing smack . . . And yet I would write about the sea!'

'In comedy?'

'In one more, mayhap, in but one more . . .'

'I have been in boats here in the habour. Seest thou Wapping, yonder? There met I a blackamoor upon a ship.'

'A Moor?'

'Aye; called Lucifer.'

'How didst thou meet this demon Moor?'

'Marry, I carried to him a whore.'

'Not black also?'

'Nay, Doll Pretty, that was more red than white, and yet he liked her well enough.'

'And she him?'

'Well, she was afrighted by him, but he won her heart.'

'Her heart?'

'What such women call this organ – aye, I think so . . .'

'And what was he on the ship, this blackamoor?'

'Mate at least, Captain mayhap, I know not! Yet sure he was a man that could command.'

'E'en a bawd's heart! Well, 'tis possible . . . For what is not, twixt one creature and another?' He turned to me now, 'Thou hast,' he said, 'seen a French lady that is known to me.'

'Aye, Will: she that entered the room the day that I first met thee.'

'Why didst thou not tell me this?'

'How could I tell thee what I knew not? 'Twas not till I visited this lady that I discovered she knew aught of thee.'

'Aught! She knows more than aught . . . Aubrey, think not I blame thee in any sort for this; but my counsel is, and my command even, see no more of her!'

'Because of danger from the justices?'

'Because of many dangers; and not least, that if thou wouldst act in my play, this plot should suffice thee; leave any others, I prithee, to those that understand or, at least, hope to profit by them.'

''Tis some affair of Papists, and of a rebellion, I have heard tell.'

''Tis a matter of many things, most dark, all desperate; and one wherein many I know, and some I love, are perilously intermingled. Yet forget not this, Aubrey. The theatre has many foes; yet the Queen, love her or love her not, protects us.'

'Why, thou dost not love her, Will?'

'I said naught of that: I said the Queen loves plays, and therefore guards us. So have we double cause to fear rebellion.'

'Then shall I not see *Madame* Marie-Claire, though I would wish to.'

'Why wish to?'

'Mock me not, Will, but she has half bewitched me. I

know I am less than naught to her; yet has she an art to make that nothing, precious.'

'Aubrey, I mock thee not nor, God knows, can I, or any that know her well.'

'Thou knewest her long, beside also well?'

'When first I knew the theatre, first knew I her.'

'I think she once served the Scottish queen.'

'She told thee this?'

'She did not deny it when I taxed her.'

'Thou hast been at thy quizzing; hast thou now met thy match?'

'Aye, marry! She wears a frown that commands silence. Then true, she served Mary of Scotland?'

'One short sad year. She came from France, a girl, to Scotland; there married one of the Queen's lords of the few that followed her to English exile. When the Queen was cut off, she came to London, exiled still.'

'Because she was Papist?'

'Aye, and her lord also; and loved for't e'en less in Scotland than in England.'

'Yet is she widow now.'

'Aye, her lord died.'

'Ere thou met her?'

'After.' He put his hand to my shoulder, and steered me to the door. 'Aubrey,' said he, 'enough of this, now and always. I beg thee we speak of it no more, and that thou wilt remember what I have enjoined on thee of prudence.'

'Sure,' said I; ''tis a sound virtue, that I shall try to strengthen in me.'

8

The *Globe* was ruled, as Rome was oftentimes, by a triumvirate; in which Master Heminges was all passion, Master Condell ire, and Will patience and sagacity. Thus, when a play was being tried, first blew the whirlwind Heminges, blasting upon the actors; then flashed the thunderbolts of Condell, that struck some near dead, and resurrected others; when all this confusion had subsided, Will's sun shone through clouds and zephyrs, fructifying seeds creative that were cast about by such a turbulence.

So we began with Master Heminges: singly, then in groups, he reading in a loud monotone all the necessary male parts. He took Herman first; and it soon appeared that Heminges' purpose was both to humble Herman's boundless pride, and then by mockery, to show how we must not do, when our turn came. And it struck us half dumb with amaze to see Herman, our erstwhile tyrant of Epping, himself brought under the fierce lash of the *Globe*.

'Too much, too much!' cried Master Heminges. 'Thou art goddess of wedlock, not high harlot of a whorehouse! Leer less, look loftier, I prithee! And when thou sayest

> Good Duke, receive thy daughter;
> Hymen from Heaven brought her,

mince not nor roll thine eyes as if proposing incest to His Grace!'

At this Herman stamped his foot and cried, 'But great Edward Alleyn oft hath told me . . .'

'Enough! 'Tis Hymen we would hear, not Master Alleyn!'

To Peter, that came next, he was more kind, and had great need to be; for after we hoisted him on the stage, and he stood on it trembling as an autumn leaf, whispering in a shrill pipe,

I would not be thy executioner . . .

Master Heminges cried out, 'Marry, lad. 'Tis not thee that must be chopped, but Silvius! Courage, therefore! For doth not Rosalind say of thee that thou art proud and pitiless? Speak out then with pride, lad, no pity for our ears!'

Yet if he need spur on Peter, with Cecil he must tug upon the curb, for our friend tripped dancing round the stage, his lines gushing faster than a fountain. 'Nay, nay, nay!' cried Master Heminges. 'Remember, Cecil, that those paying for a play, would hear it. A theatre is not a church, where all know their Book of Common Prayer, however fast the rector gabble it! Here all is new to them; so that each word, and its proper sense, must be clear e'en to the meanest witted.'

With Robin he was more kind, yet more severe: as is a father that, loving more, requires more. Yet though he spent more hours with Robin than any other, he held the rein gently, using a rare spur or whip. And I think his reason was that with this part of Rosalind, by which all would stand or fall, he must break the foal firm, yet gently.

'Sweetly, sweetly,' he said, beckoning Robin down from the stage among us. ''Tis a fair beginning, if 'tis but that: well grounded, if not yet rising where it shall do. Thy concept is sound, Robin, and well studied; what it lacks yet is variety: of pace and tone, emotion and expression. Bethink thee, I prithee, that Rosalind is no actor, but a woman: proud yet fearful; loving yet spurning; borne up by her wit, beset by languor. She is a various creature, and so would I have thee make her. Have no fear, presently, of excess; for by this thou canst probe the limits of a passion which, if it become too strident, may be curbed later. Hold firmly to thy vision of her with thy mind, yet yield freely to thy feeling for the woman thou wouldst portray to us.'

After a rest, and some watered wine, we were drilled by Master Condell; who would not have us act at all, nor e'en go up upon the stage, but say our lines only, over and again. He had also a notion that if Rosalind spoke with Celia, then she should study Celia's lines beside her own: not learn them by rote, but try to enter fully into their meaning, so that Rosalind's replies to Celia should not be soliloquy, but apt rejoinder. He was patient with us, save at a fault repeated; at which he would not shout like Master Heminges, but groan, look gloomy, and gaze at us as if we were bereft of sense.

And now came to us Will, that had been watching from the gallery throughout the day: sometimes looking down on us and listening, at others writing on papers that he held there. He thanked us for our labours, and hoped we were not tired (which, pardee, we were). Then said he to us,

'A play is like a maze. You know it hath within it a heart, a centre, that can be uncovered; for the maze is devised for this, as is a play to disclose, at last, its meaning. Yet once entered, this maze seems, for many weary days, a meaningless confusion: of paths that lead in false directions, or else nowhere. But knowing these, while seeking to find your way, you may learn what is not, so that what is, may also be revealed. Therefore be not cast down at the inception, which is beating in the dark towards a light yet dim; for by doing so, you will come upon the secret suddenly: so swift, indeed, when you at last perceive it, that you will wonder the maze e'er seemed other than a straight swift path to your desire.'

'Aye, marry, indeed!' quoth Herman. 'For intricacy may be but itself, or serve to mask simplicity; so that this maze,

Master Will, whereof you speak – using a metaphor which I find apt – shall, to the amazement of these callow youths, unfold itself, as 'twere, to be no maze at all, but a straight string: as does, as an instance, carded wool that, being unravelled, seemeth no more the woolly maze it was, but straight as a Roman road. And thereby, in this word "Roman", hangs a pleasurable duty that I owe, Will, to you, which is to say your *Julius Caesar* is a fair writ thing. Aye, indeed, 'tis not ill, no, whatever any may declare; for none, I ween, has e'er denied you are endowed with more than ordinary aptitudes.'

'I am beholden to thee, Herman, for thy words, and rich embroidery on my simpler theme.'

The days that followed this were as a dream: sometimes a nightmare; for I swear we toiled as galley slaves towards a perfection that eluded us. Two, indeed, sought to desert ship: Peter by fear, and Robin pride. For Peter felt all this was beyond his grasp; while Robin, once he understood what should be done, fell to lamenting he was unworthy of what now stood revealed to him: I mean the rare beauty of Rosalind, and of the play. We others quelled these mutinies, and did not report them to our galley masters.

Nor was it easier when we came at last to practise with the other actors. A lad of sixteen does not comfortably confront a man twice his age in any business; but in this, where they knew all, and we nothing, imagine our confusion! And how they sighed and groaned at all our faults, mocking our clumsy endeavours without pity! And how impossible, to us, seemed their perfection when we watched, rapt, scenes where there were no women! And yet we progressed, ant-like, toward something almost seemly; gaining some dominion on ourselves, and better understanding of our lines; and even winning some small coin of praise from the older actors. But when we heard the play would come on in August, and had been entered already in the Register, our hard-won rapture vanished instantly; for we were now at the beginning of July.

Jenny, whose wit was sharper than she would show, had noticed my anxious looks, now but four weeks remained till I must face the groundlings. Yet though Jenny was not a kind girl, she was fond and true; and seeing my ill ease, had quelled her bantering, and sought (though mocking still) to give me courage.

'So thou hast not yet practised in thy skirts,' said she.

'This week must we try them; but in truth, I have seen mine, and they are less gowns than mud-caked rags.'

'But Robin shall be more rich attired?'

'Aye, both as man and woman, being Ganymede beside Rosalind. Cecil, also, shall be neat bedecked; and this pleases him much.'

'And what says his Mistress Anne, that he should so unsex himself?'

'Anne is not, like thee, a raw country girl, lacking discernment; nor Robin's Susan neither. They know plays are fine things, that e'en monarchs admire.'

Our talk was broke up by William that, not for the first time had half swallowed his silver chain. As to who gave this to our son, I had told not my wife the truth, saying it was a further gift from Will; and this Jenny had accepted, as she had the chain in her son's name.

I was by the window while Jenny was beating on William's back, and saw, across the High Street, a small carriage stopped, and a man in livery that was come down from it, speaking with idlers, that pointed towards our house. I told Jenny I would fetch some ale, and before she could deny me, ran down the stairs and came out in the street, where I stood by our door, waiting.

The flunkey approached, and asked, as if of right, where Master Aubrey might be found.

'He stands,' said I, 'before your honour.'

'So, fellow, thou art he!' I did not reply, and he continued, waving at the carriage, 'Thou art to come with me to see my master.' I still said naught, and he took my sleeve.

'Have a care, varlet,' said I.

'Thou knowest to whom thy pert words are spoke?'

'Aye, to some lord's lackey.'

'And which lord?'

'One that has not taught his servants courtesy.'

He let go my arm, bared his teeth at me and, half bowing, said, 'Would your worship deign to grant audience to my Lord of Southampton?'

I looked about me, then back at him. 'And how know I,' said I, 'that he has sent you? For I see no arms upon this carriage.'

'My Lord,' said he, 'sends no such carriage to fetch such a one as thee.'

'Then my Lord should send a carriage, and a messenger, that wins some trust.'

He frowned now. 'Master Aubrey,' said he, 'if he you be. I am, as you say, a servant: I have orders, to seek and fetch you. Be not so proud with me, and come instantly to my Lord.'

He was, in truth, as I must soon learn, exact in his rebuke of pride. For in a short space, so many changes had befallen as to make me believe fondly I was some statesman of the stamp of Cecils. Had I better preserved my rustic wits, or remembered my promise to Will no more to intermeddle with matters far beyond my scope, I should have turned my back on this fellow instantly. But no! My Lord of Southampton would converse with Aubrey! What more natural? And how could I, the great Southwark manipulator, deny this service to my Lord?

The carriage, being ill kempt within, and carried on square wheels, gave me a jolting ride over the river and the Fleet, then along the Strand toward Westminster. I had thought we would stop soon, for this was where lords lived; but no, we continued into Whitehall and, by a nether alley there, entered a covered court. The lackey pulled ope the door and said, 'If your worship would pray descend.'

Inside the house, two further fellows, that said naught, beckoned me, walking on either side, towards a door; there knocked, listened, and signed me to go in, closing it behind me and not entering.

It was not my Lord who greeted me, but one that gazed on me in silence for four long minutes. He was small, crook-backed and of middle years, and dressed dark, that made his face seem whiter; his eyes were near white too, and did not blink.

'Why,' said he at length, 'didst thou suppose this nobleman would speak with thee?'

'Who are you, sir?'

'Answer, not ask: why?'

'Because the coachman said he wished it.'

'I shall repeat my question. Answer it, and not some other. Why didst thou suppose my Lord of Southampton would speak with such as thee?'

'Because of my trade, sir; my calling.'

'Which of thy callings?'

'I am an actor, sir. And those high born that frequent the theatre may sometimes speak with players.'

'An actor. Aye. Now, hearken, I ask thee a third time, and a last: why didst thou think this nobleman would see thee?'

I stood faltering, and he rang a tinkling bell. The two

again entered, took my arms, and led me out and into a rear room, hung about with curtains, where stood another.

'Boy,' said he, glancing at me sideways, 'we are swift and simple here, unlike the Tower.'

'But who are you? Where am I?' I cried out.

'Thou art guest to the Council. Hold him fast!' and he plucked out of his gown a thumbscrew.

'Nay, an you use that, I will speak!' I cried.

'After!' said he, clamping the screw on against my struggles.

As I write this, I look at my mangled thumb, yet can recall only my horror, not the pain, for memory cannot contain aught so terrible. I screamed like a gelded calf, then swooned in blood.

I was woken by shaking, and a splash of water, and then agony. They heaved me up, and half lifted me along to the front room, and pushed me in, once more alone with the pale crookback. This time, I would have told him all the little I knew of any lord.

But he did not ask me, and said, 'Thou knewest the French student of the law, called Luc?'

'Aye, sir,' said I. 'And . . .'

'Answer only what I ask. And went to the Clink to speak with him?'

'Aye, I did.'

'And told him how he should escape?'

'No, sir, not I! Is he then scaped from thence?'

'What, then, didst thou tell him?'

'That he would be rescued, but not how: for this I knew not.'

He frowned and rung the bell. I started forward, crying, 'No!' – but the men were not summoned to drag me out. For the crookback, pointing to the floor, said, 'Wipe the blood and fetch a dish.' This was done, and he dismissed them, telling me to hold the bowl with my sound hand, under my oozing thumb.

He watched to make sure none spattered on his carpet, then said, 'Where is the French spy now hid?'

But while all this of the dripping blood was being put right, a fire had come into my spirit. For pain, that may double fear, can make it hatred, if anguish have not yet broken the will; and with this care for carpet, not my thumb, hot pride surged too, and shrieked revenge.

'I know not, sir,' said I humbly.

'I ask again: where is he hid?'

I fell now on my knees, my left hand clasping my right about the wrist, and gulping hot tears that were not fully feigned. He rose from behind the table, picking up the bell, and said, 'Where, then, is he hid?'

Rage killing agony, I seized up the carpet and flung it over him, hurled him to the floor, wrenched ope the casement window, and leapt eight feet into the yard. Fellows seated saw me, but I was out the porch e'en as they rose and cried. I dived down alleys, praying in pants none would lead or to a wall, or into the river. And so, with feet behind now pounding, and shouts of 'Hold! Hold!' I ran up into the Strand.

Citizens turned, surprised, as I pushed through; then seeing it was Authority that pursued me, after a startled pause they fell on me, and held me fast.

'Prentice! Prentice!' I cried, till one clapped a fist across my mouth.

The Council guards had me now, but not long; for out the shops, came first few, then more, all, when they saw the fight, shouting their rally cry. I was torn from the guards by four stout fellows, that dragged me into a lane, and through a gate into a carter's yard.

They left me, set seated on a wheel, and went back to the gate, watching and clasping staves. But none came; and, still holding their clubs, they gathered round me.

'Prentice to what guild?' said one.

'I am an actor.'

'Thou? In what theatre?'

'The new *Globe*.'

A fellow laughed. 'Then art thou prentice by false pretence,' said he, 'for that is no guild.'

'What is with thy hand, lad?' said another, taking it up and showing it to the others, whereat they whistled.

'I was tortured by the thumbscrew.'

'Aye, marry, that see we! Constables?'

'The Council.'

'Thou art well scaped! Clarence, fetch water, and make ox's eyes at our miser Mistress for some spirits.'

'What would they wring from thee?'

'Names.'

'Of traitors?'

'I know not if they be traitors.'

'But their names thou knewest.'

'Some.'

'And told?'

'Almost, ere I scaped.'

'Persons of consequence?'

'Nay, vex not the lad, for he is sick, and enough questioned! Drink this, and let me bind thy hand.'

When this was done, they conferred together, and he that had sent for wine and water, turned to me and said, 'Well, lad, we must spirit thee away. For our Master may not be twisted, and our faces are well known to constables.'

'I would not reward thy kindness with my peril.'

'Clarence, go with him to the river, some way off, and find

watermen of trust that can carry him swift over to Bankside.'

We walked, all innocence, down to the Watergate, and onto the flats beneath the palaces; where Clarence found a wherry, and said, with a smile, he would pay the watermen, if I would pass him privily inside the *Globe*. This I promised, and said he should bring his comrades also, that had rescued me.

The watermen, advised by Clarence, set off at once for the far shore, to coast along it rather than on the north bank where I had been in danger. But half-way across we must pause, for a huge barge came down from Westminster, oarsmen in livery, and with banners; and the men shipped oars to watch it pass.

'Essex men,' said one. 'He comes from Court.'

'Their master will be else king, or in the Tower.'

'Aye, and his followers! Look, there stands Southampton!'

'A profligate, beside a Papist.'

'And near in disgrace now, with the Queen.'

We watched the barge pull in to the pier that led up to Essex House; and of a suddden I thought, 'Well, if vanity gulled me into believing my Lord of Southampton would speak with me, why should not greed make me think he might do so now? For sure, my thumb and silence have both served him.' So I asked the watermen to pull in after the barge, and with some demur (for Clarence had said I must in haste to Bankside), they shrugged agreement, for this was less work for the same pay.

At the wharf, I said I would speak with my Lord of Southampton's steward; and when they would heave me in the river for my presumption, I flourished my thumb beneath their noses, and said I had won this in my Lord's service. None believed me, and all thought I was some beggar; but blood has on all men curious effects, either of making them wish to shed more, or of arousing a kind of fearfulness; so they called in the Captain of the Guard.

He was stern yet civil, and said if I would see the Steward, I must tell him why. I answered I could not do this; but if he would tell the Steward I came because of my Lord's French friends, I doubted not he would receive me. He gave me a sharp look, told the guards to let me neither enter the grounds nor go, and stalked away.

This brought out, after a long pause (and crueller throbbing of my wound), the Steward who, eyeing me, said, 'Thou art some spy, that would lose another thumb.'

'And if I near lost one, 'twas to serve my Lord.'

'Thou? My Lord? What knowest such a one as thou of such as he?'

'That the Council questions those that know who he knows.'

'Come apart, fellow, and tell me who are those whos.'

'I need not come apart to tell you I shall speak only to my Lord.'

'Who shall not speak with thee.'

'Who has done, in the orchard of *Madame* Marie-Claire.'

'Silence!' The Steward looked about him, then said, 'Come!' and led me up some steps, and then into a room above a small inner court. 'Wait here,' said he.

From the window I soon saw, walking across the court alone, unlaced at ease, mine auburn Lord, his locks swaying on his sleeve, and one hand resting on my familiar, his sword. He vanished and, in an instant, walked quiet inside the room, and looked at me, who bowed.

''Tis as I thought,' said he. 'The eater of green apples.'

'Aye, my Lord, and sucker of sore thumbs.'

''Tis an ill wound. Who did this, and why?'

'Those of the Council.'

'Where?'

'In a house twixt Whitehall and the river, I know not which place . . .'

'Aye, 'tis the Council. That asked thee what?'

'My Lord, the lady of the orchard hath a serving-woman, Anne, that hath a brother, Luc, that hath escaped the Clink.'

'Truly?' He smiled cold, and then, 'And 'twas anent these "haths" they questioned thee?'

'Aye.'

'Naught else?'

'Sir, they would, I think, have asked more of others, had I not scaped them.'

'Few scape the Council. How didst thou?' I told him, and he smiled again at my examiner wrapped in his carpet; then turning grave, said to me, 'Some saying they scaped the Council, serve it yet.'

'My Lord! Do such first suffer torture to deceive those the Council would deceive?'

'Mayhap not.' He sat on a table, both hands on his sword, and looking at me still. 'And what wouldst thou with me, then?' said he.

'My Lord,' said I, 'I cannot say I kept silence, though suffering torture, about any others, for they had not time to wring this from me. Yet have I come here, in duty to my Lord, to tell him.'

'Aye, but of what? And why?'

'As to what, that the man they asked me of, Luc, knows she that knows my Lord. As to why, in hope of your Lordship's bounty.'

He looked angered, and a pout came to his pretty face. 'So!' cried he. 'Thou, one of hundreds of low meddlers, tell me a tale of torture, and beg a spy's fee! My Steward should have had thee whipped!'

'Then why did he not, my Lord? And why have you come?'

He stood now, hand on sword, flushing and frowning; and then, as a babe's wet rage turns swift to a sweet smile, he sighed, and said, 'Well, thou hast suffered, lad, be it for me or for another. My Steward shall see thee paid ere thou depart . . .' I kept silence, while he softly paced the room, and then he turned to me, and said, 'It is a great trick of the Council to sniff plots where there are none, and put on false witnesses among the lesser, lacking courage to assail the great! Yet shall they learn to rue it! For some that sit now with the Council may fall sooner than those they would o'erthrow!'

'But what, sir, if they pursue me more? For I do not believe I can suffer again in silence.'

'They will not come: for if they have struck fright, it can be struck in them, and shall be. For thee, best safety lies in staying a while hid.'

'Yet how can I, my Lord? For in but a few weeks, hundreds will see me in the *Globe*.'

'In the new comedy?'

'Aye, sir: I am to be a country wench.'

'With a thumb bit by a swine.'

'No, sir: by a goatherd. Has my Lord read the play? For I know my master Will lays first his treasures at my Lord's feet.'

He smiled again now, with that double look of he who smells flattery, yet spurns it not. 'Not read yet,' said he, 'but I shall see it, and mayhap thee.'

'I dare think my Lord will like this of Master Will's, even as he has others writ by him.'

'I doubt it not.' He paused, brooding, then said, 'Speak not, prithee, to Will of what has passed.'

'No, sir, an you wish it; though he sure has cognizance of such matters . . . I mean of plots, secrets, spies . . .'

'Plots, surely, and secrets too, but in the theatre, which is his kingdom; whence I have ne'er sought to entice him into realms beyond his scope.'

'Yet others have so sought, my Lord.'

'Which others?'

'The French lady of Mary-le-bourne, methinks.'

'Aye, she!' He was silent a long while. 'Women,' he said, 'are the real and only traitors! But swear to serve them with your heart, and they will require service to their wills; and this e'en when their own heart is withered. For some men, that have but little heart to pledge, there is no danger in't; for others, peril. So do not speak of this to Will.'

'Not I, sir.'

'So, boy, farewell; act well in this, as in the *Globe*.'

He bestowed on me a smile of great dazzle and small warmth, and left me waiting for the Steward who, after a short while, came, handed me a purse, and said, 'Go down to the wharf; a small boat will carry thee across.'

The watermen were not fellows of my Lord's, and knew naught of my business save that they must put me down beside the Bridge. And this was prudent of Master Southampton; for if any, seeking me, seized upon me, the watermen could deny all knowledge (as could my Lord).

But there was naught untoward; and when at last I came into Widow Dill's, there were great shrieks from Jenny, and greater when she saw my thumb, and frantick weepings.

'Aye, Jenny,' said I, 'but 'tis I that am wounded, not thee, and I have a fever and so must to bed.'

'What hast thou done!' cried she, in a torment. 'I know it! I know! This is some further folly of the theatre!'

'Boil water, woman, and wash my hand and arm.'

'I covet not this purse! I would not be rich, Aubrey, by thy death!'

'Then give the purse to the poor; and as for my death, an you help me not to bed, and heal me, thou shalt sure wear weeds darker than Mistress Dill's.' With which shaft of wit I swooned.

9

The weeks passed as days, days hours, and now 'twas The Day: the unfolding of *As You Like It* to the world.

All this time, I had been sore beset. My mangled thumb, swollen to twice its size, must thrice be lanced by the Borough barber. Kindness from the actors I had little, save for jests anent Audrey poking her finger where no maid ought. I walked the streets trembling, for fear of justices, and suffered by ill dreams. Worst of all, my wife, that should be a comfort to her man's distress, was shrewish and scolding, making endless parley with our William (that understood naught of it) as to the follies of his father. So I walked daily from a home where was no welcome, to a theatre where all was confusion and dispute.

The afternoon before, we had performed for ourselves, and for a small audience of actors not in the play (that lolled about the chief seats of the galleries, gazing on us with an amazed disdain), the last, ultimate practice of our work; and all this, bewigged and costumed. Naught proceeded as it should: lines were forgot, or spoke in the wrong place; those that should enter, entered not, or when they ought not; quarrels broke out, fiercer than those of Orlando and the wrestler Charles; and as for us boys, Cecil proved a true Celia by bursting into tears, and Peter had the sulks, saying Robin played sweeter to Cecil than to him. Master Heminges roared, Master Condell groaned, and Will stayed hid; the only one even in temper was Robert Armin, that played Touchstone and who, when not on stage speaking, sat on a chair smoking, or else asleep.

At dusk (for this play that should last two hours, exceeded four) we all gathered, like soldiers after a skirmish and before a battle, to be addressed by our commander, Will:

'Rest well tonight,' said he 'and think not of our play until, at noontide tomorrow, we shall assemble. Then, fear not at all: for from the pains and trials of today, shall spring perfection. For we are like those, pardee, that wracked in long torment on the rack, shall step onto the scaffold with serenity!' The old actors laughed, and Will turned then to us. 'As for our ladies, let them conduct themselves like men: I mean, with a man's valour, if in women's weeds. And let them, as men, remember this. Actors are loved by few, and, e'en by that few, oft scorned. Yet I tell you this. There is naught more arduous, for any that loves fair speech and apt conceit in verse, than to put forth his understanding of both these, by the gift of his very person. The poet writes – aye, and painfully to wring order out of chaos! Yet need he not, the poet, do what you must: create not by his mind alone in solitude, but by his whole self before a multitude. To dare this, and achieve it nobly, is the highest courage any artist hath, and the bravest service rendered unto poesy.'

The Day was brilliant, and I was woken late by the sun, and by Jenny coming in from out the street; and when I asked where she had been, she said to church (where she went never) to pray for me: at which I would send William to Widow Dill, and pull her back into the bed; but she said, Fie! and Nay! and I must preserve my forces for the afternoon.

Nearing the theatre, I saw many gathered without, though the gate was closed, and would not ope till two hours hence.

Some were idlers, that gather whenever aught fresh is toward; some of Gropenut's fraternity, pacing the field of battle in preparation for their coney-catching; there were already some hopeful harlots; and what vexed me much, fellows set on by other theatres, and by the Bear Pit, to cry ill on our play, and vow livelier entertainment could be had within their doors.

'How now, Master run-away!' cried a voice, and I started like a hind, until I saw these were no constables, but the prentices that had helped me scape the Council. 'See, gentle Mistress, we have brought thee a ribbon for thy hair!' And with much ribaldry, they bound it in my locks, swearing they would all lie with me when the play was done.

'I know not of that,' said I, 'but drink with you, I surely shall. See yonder! There is the tavern, also called the *Globe*, that is the ordinary of the actors; and there, when I doff my petticoats, I prithee await me.'

As I came round to the actors' door, the lad that would later hoist the flag was making practice, and he showed me the sun shining full on Hercules' bum, which he said was a fair omen. Within, all the roister of yestereve had calmed; and though all went swift about their business, they moved stately; and few spoke, save those that muttered lines unto themselves, and I e'en heard Will, now Adam (that, having writ his own first line, should know it), whispering, 'Yonder comes my master, your brother.' Though I guessed 'twas not remembering this that troubled him, but that he must, when the play started, hearken in long silence to Orlando's narration of his misfortunes, before he could ope his lips to make reply.

Of we lads, donning our wigs and dresses, I was more cheerful than I felt, Herman spoke without cease and listening to none, Cecil fluttered like a trapped bird, Peter grunted and sighed, and only Robin said naught save 'Aye' or 'Nay', as if he were bewitched into a dream. Master Heminges came for a last fuss, and Master Condell, for a last scolding. Will looked in once and said, 'We actors are, without you, nothing; and all, Robin, are nothing without thee.'

Then, like sound growing as a traveller comes near a river, there arose, from without in the theatre, first a murmur, then a rumble, then soon a roar: as if all London were foregathered there, and half the world! Strange, but we were less affrighted than filled with an elation so that, looking at each other, each saw shining eyes. 'They have come to see *us*!' cried Cecil, clutching his false breast.

We could scarce believe our ears when, of a sudden, as the din a bit abated, we heard,

> As I remember, Adam, it was upon this fashion bequeathed me by will . . .

and for a moment thought this was yet one more practice of our lines: but no! we had begun.

Those that know Will's plays will know also he has a trick, or necessary device, which is that the whole ever begins with a matter of minor weight, such as music, flourish of trumpets, or some speech which, if it be lost to the auditors, all is not; and this is needful to give time for the groundlings to subside, like rattling pebbles, into a sort of silence. Also that some violence is soon promised, to whip up their appetites; as here, the promise of Charles to Oliver that he will break all Orlando's bones. When the public and players are then thus engaged, as in a tourney twixt indolence and attention, the real matter of the play can be begun; which in the present case, may start when Rosalind and her cousin first come on.

He who has lain with one he cherishes will know that, in these combats, there comes, after the first fumblings, a moment when both lover and beloved are sure this is no wanton trifling (as it may oft be), but an entry into the very lists of love. And so it is when the two cousins first come on: for if the audience love Rosalind and Celia, and love them swift, then they will love the play; if not, they will start shuffling and soon yawn.

So now, when Oliver had dismissed Charles to prepare his treachery on Orlando, we all waited scarce daring to breathe. For beside this instant was so critical, nor Robin nor Cecil were yet known to frequenters of the theatre, and had thus no claim upon their favourable disposition. Each of our actors now looked upon them with a kind of awe; as must an army on two champions that can win victory, or bestow death on all. And what we all saw now, to our rapt amaze, was that as they both stepped on the stage, Robin was become Rosalind, and Cecil, no less, Celia.

And if there were any doubt of this among some few, the moment Master Armin bounced on as Touchstone (winning laughter ere he oped his mouth, for he was much beloved), the battle was well won. And lest fortune should, in any sort, try to reverse our victory, each fresh actor came in among us like another warrior to affirm our power. Nor did the wrestling twixt Charles and Orlando lack anything of cracked skulls and sweaty groans to please the less discerning of the multitude.

So when we all came to Arden, we carried the hundreds thither with us, where they were soon bound by all the spells of Will: speech broke by song, loftiest conceits by bawdry, love of all species rich displayed to view. As to these, and of the baser sort, I near wet my petticoats waiting till the play was half-way through, before I could prance on with Master Armin; and, after standing sucking my thumb like an idiot while Touchstone spake, pronounce my first great line! And this with a bellow in broad Essex, that was not my intent, nor what I had been drilled into, but burst out of me like the fart of a yeasty bottle, new uncorked.

And if I trembled, as I did, to see that ocean of faces gazing on me, this was transformed by the wobble of my legs (and not any intent of hectic wit) into a sort of country jig, that won roars from the groundlings (and privy frowns from Master Armin). And indeed, I could not but dance about, and bleat and ogle like a new-weaned calf, for in much of the time wherein Audrey must be on stage, she hath not a word put down for her to speak!

As for poor Peter, who came on with his Silvius e'en later than I must, the frowns gathered by his waiting well befitted the haughty tones he gave to Phebe. And in truth, there was about Peter (I mean even when not acting) a sort of earnestness, coupled with a fierce disdain, that made his Phebe as scornful as Rosalind charged her with being; and because of his fondness for .Robin, he spoke true to Silvius the lines wherein Phebe avows her conquest by the greater pride of Ganymede.

And Herman! What words may express his vexation at waiting out the whole play ere he appeared, and the extreme fervour with which, his brief moment come at last, he paced stately on the stage, borne thither by still music! What majesty in his voice (that cracked a little, but slight), in his gesture, what nobility! Duke, courtiers, lovers, seemed as naught beside his radiance! And indeed, he made this clear to all on stage and, raising his head and sweeping his eyes about the theatre, to each that heard him. For he cried out loud,

> Peace ho! I bar confusion:
> 'Tis I [*pause*] must make conclusion . . .

What sweeter gift could Will have given to any lad, if he

play Rosalind fittingly, that when all is ended, and the remainder actors gone, he stands alone before so many well contented, and speaks his darling Epilogue. For it was as if, as they listened, all gratitude for their pleasures from the play and actors, must be given, in a cry of rapture like a thunder, to this one boy!

Beneath the stage, after, was a tumult indescribable. The actors embraced us, kissing hands and slapping rumps, according to our natures. Master Heminges swore Robin o'ertopped young Goffe, e'en Master Condell smiled, and Will gave each of us a little pin that held a jewel (mine was sardonyx, for that 'twas August). A whole host of persons, that privilege or effrontery admitted, came in among us, and Herman was swift surrounded by a twittering of every catamite in London. As for the lordlings, that strolled about as if we must admire their presence more than they our performance, many said fair words to Will, among them, with a brief smile and whisper in his ear, my Lord of Southampton; while others spoke courteously to the actors, the more forward sort jesting with us lads. Robin, indeed, was much besieged, and told me after that four promises for his advancement had been proffered; and a popinjay in brocade silver, swore he would see me breeched ere he departed, for if Audrey was lusty, he believed Aubrey was e'en more.

From all this, feeling fatigued and wishing to meet my friends without, I went, when fresh dressed, out towards the actors' gate; but passing behind the stage, stept up on it once more, as does a lover, alone, to an old trysting place. The theatre was not yet emptied, though almost so, and longer shadows fell from the galleries athwart the pit; and a sadness came over me, I knew not why, like the sight of a known bed without its beloved. Mayhap my feeling was that the life of that afternoon, when my spirit soared so high, would make other days seem drab; or mayhap that, because of my waxing age and Jenny, I must leave it all. As I brooded thus, some seemed to stir in a far gallery where my eyes roved dreaming, and I blinked to see what I thought a shade of *Madame* Marie-Claire; and, like a ghost beside her, the crookback of the Council. I looked intent, stepping forward on the stage; but if there, they were gone.

Outside the gate, I was enfolded by my wife Jenny, that had refused to come, yet had; and she laughed and wept, and said I was an artful rogue to act women so well, and that she must take care, lest I steal every secret of her sex; and I told her never fear, there was one that was hers only, which men ne'er tire trying to uncover. Then came up Widow Dill, bearing William, who said she knew me for Aubrey well enough, but swore she would ne'er believe Robin was a boy. Well, said I, let us to the tavern, and you may nuzzle the down on his cheek, an he permit it.

Inside and out was a vast concourse from the audience, come to praise or blame the play, and compare it to a hundred others. No actor need pay his ale or wine, for our tables were soon loaded with their offerings; and their praises too, that far outdid their strictures, which we knew should belong in truth to Will, but any modesty of ours was silenced by their blandishments.

One that feigned discontent was Lucy, for though 'twas plain she rejoiced Peter's glory shone upon her, yet she said the play was a poor thing, with words out of books that no man e'er spoke, and too much chatter without action. 'Lord have mercy!' cried she, sniffing. 'An those that come to lie with me prattled such long hours, I should ne'er earn a guinea in a twelvemonth.'

Peter said naught to this, having long learned dispute with Lucy was wasted words; but Cecil rounded on her shrilly, saying a slut like her knew naught of love, beside being clumsy in mere fornication. At this Peter grew vexed, and Anne, that was with Cecil blushed (saying *O, la la*), whereat Cecil grew enraged also, saying it was Lucy's fault, that had first spoke of love so lewdly.

So I drew Anne aside, in part to try to calm this dispute, but more to see if she would tell me what was with her brother, Luc.

'He is now in France,' she whispered.

'Rescued, then, from prison?'

'He is safe in France.'

'And you, Mistress Anne, are not pursued, as he?'

'No. Why should I be?'

'Nor the lady that you serve?'

'She? Never! She is protected.'

'By whom?'

'She is protected.'

'Methought I saw her an instant in the theatre.'

'She does not go to theatres.'

'Yet she knows Master Will.'

'I may know the priest, and yet not go to his church.'

I left them then, and went with Jenny to another table, so that she should meet with Susan, Robin's maid, and her warrior father, Captain Wyatt.

'Well spoke, lad!' cried the Captain, seeing me. 'Thou broughtst to mind a Frisian slut I knew once in a village we had battered down, wherein all men were slain, and all women violated, save she.'

'Then was her virtue more than ordinary, or her sluttishness?'

'Neither, lad, I must tell thee. For what saved her from violation by our troops was that e'en a regiment could not encompass it.'

'How so, sir?' said Robin.

'Why, boy! Thou canst not speak of violation when a lass, being possessed by all, and some repeatedly, cries out for more, putting our gallant lads to shame!'

'Fie, father!' cried Miss Susan. 'Thou givest to Robin, that would bear arms, an ill portrait of thy profession.'

'By no means!' cried the Captain. 'For are not the Romans our preceptors in all military arts? And did they not ravish, to the glory of Rome, the Sabine women?'

'Who speaks of ravishment?' cried Herman that, like a queen bee with its hive, approached amid a throng of mincing foppery. 'Believe me, sir, there is no such thing, unless poppy be used as opiate. Else 'tis but feigned reluctance or, as oft, that the lass ravishes the lad. For do not, sir, forget, that if Lucretia declared Tarquin had his will of her (as she must do, to deceive her husband), 'twas not chaste Adonis that sought to violate the lusts of Venus.'

'Go thy ways, Herman, go thy ways!' cried the attendant foppery.

'Aye, marry, shall I!' said he.

At a table outside, sitting somewhat apart (as best they might in the press), I could see the two Doges, and their followers; who, though united now, were still divided, for the factions of Venice and Genoa were at each end of a long table. Perceiving I saw him, Venice raised a gloved finger that summoned me to his presence.

'Sir,' said I, 'I hope you are well pleased with the praises bestowed by all on your son Robin.'

He lowered his hooded eyes, and said, 'That praise came better in another play.'

'How so, sir?' said I.

'How so?' cried Genoa. 'That my son Cecil should, by my hard-won consent, posture before these people' (stabbing a finger at them), 'I may allow, since the theatre is also a resort of gentlemen. But that his father and uncle be so mocked, I may not suffer!'

'Mocked, sir? How mocked?'

'Come, boy!' said Venice. 'The matter of this play bears nearly on events that are not unknown to us – nor to thee, that first sucked our sons into this enterprise.'

'Sir, you are grievously mistook!' cried I. 'For Master Shakespeare, that writ it, has taken the whole plot out of an old play *Rosalynde*, by one Thomas Lodge.'

'Then were Master Lodge prophet,' quoth Venice. 'And I must read his play.'

'No sir, I beseech you! For does not each man see, when at a play, himself, when it is not himself? Are we not all, in our conceit, when at a theatre, or Falstaff, or Romeo, or Caesar?'

'Or a Duke,' said Venice, eyeing me.

'Or one that is falsely dubbed usurper!' cried Genoa, looking dark.

'Good sirs, be content, I pray you, that this play has served to glorify your sons, and so, your illustrious houses.'

While I delivered this bombast, made of part fear, deceit and excess of spirits, I saw the followers of both Doges put hands to weapons and look fierce; for there now approached sundry other villains, that I knew to be of the South London nobility of crime. And like packs of hounds, that circle each other snapping, yet avoid any fatal issue, there groups glared at each other, making loud talk of what scurvy rogues there were about the inn this day, and how there were those that should look to themselves, did they wish for long life. I backed prudently away, to hide myself behind Jenny's skirts; and looking back, saw that the two Doges and their henchmen had risen, and were stalking slowly off; which I took as an ill omen of their establishing any supremacy upon Bankside.

Through the press came Master Heminges, that called me away and, taking my arm, said, 'Will entertains the actors in his house tonight, and thou art bidden, if thou wilt, to serve us wine there; but say naught to the other lads, for this is a meeting of the senate of our craft, and our venerable ears must not be blasted by an infant din.'

'First must I take Jenny home, and bed my son.'

'Her, too, an thou wilt; yet creep out, prithee, from thy sweaty couch ere cock crow.'

10

Yet 'twas not late when I left the Borough, for Jenny was fatigued, and revealed to me her fancy that mayhap William would soon have a sister; which led to yet another sermon on the need for honest labour, to all of which I agreed so soothingly, she fell asleep.

The summer was now in its decline, yet though the moon was up, there was still a pale lemon glimmer to the west. Bankside had fallen still, save for some shouts from taverns; and the *Globe*, beside the Thames, was become a great dark hulk. I came down the path to Will's, along the river, which was silver, with soft lappings. The house was part lit, and I heard voices from the road: loud, but not riotous. I knocked on the nether door and, after a while, Master Heminges oped and let me in.

'Madam Housekeeper is abed,' quoth he. 'Eat thy fill in the kitchen, quaff what thou wilt, then come to us when we call; for grave matters are being spoke presently, beyond the small range of thy unformed wit.'

So I eat, and drank, and when none called me, walked into the small room behind the larger where the actors were all gathered; for there I might find a couch whereon to rest. This I did, and lit the lamp, and took down some books among the profusion upon the walls, and looked at them idly.

In their margins, there were scribbles writ by Will, and sometimes he had altered another's line, as if to better it; till I came to one volume, wherein the leaves were loose, and all was all set down in his own hand, and these seemed sonnets; though whether by him, or copied from another as an exercise (as of translation), I knew not yet.

Nor knew for sure, the more I read in them, for there were past an hundred; and by the figures put beside them, were begun some eight years since, continuing four more. From those I plucked, turning the leaves over to read some, their tale was of one, a man, that loved another, younger; chiding him that he should marry, and have issue. Then came a woman, that first the one loved, then lost to the other; to both she had been mistress, and all three were adulterers. The first friend fears this woman shall, to the second, bring naught else but woe; at length this second tires of his stolen mistress, that returns to the first friend, but with loss of love to all.

I fell asleep on this into a long dream.

I was waked by the book snatched from my knees, and Will was stood holding it, gazing at me with scorn and hate. 'Dog!' said he, low beyond rage. 'Spy! Traitor!'

'Will, Will, I . . .'

'Out to thy kennel whence thou camest!'

I gazed at him amazed, and he plucked me up by my doublet, and flung me to the door, crying, 'Away!'

I hastened out into the street, trembling. Then standing, back to the river, looking at the house, I, father of one and soon of yet another, began weeping like a boy. The door oped, and he stood there in its light. 'Aubrey!' he said. 'Come back within.'

I came up cautiously, fearing a blow, and said, 'Where are thy friends? The house is all silent now.'

'They vanished whilst thou hast slumbered. Come, drink what they have left for us.'

He poured, I took the glass, but could not drink. After a silence, I said, 'Will, what have I done?'

He looked at me, and said, 'Naught, Aubrey: 'tis what I have done, not thou . . .'

'I should not have seen thy poems: but, Will! I did it idly!'

'No, thou shouldst not see them, for none may see so much of another's life.'

'Had I thought to offend thee thus, I would cut off my right hand, rather.'

'That thou hast near lost a thumb sufficeth.' He smiled like a thin ray in winter. 'Drink, lad, thou art forgiven.'

I drank, spilling wine, and cursing my curiosity and thoughtlessness.

'This long, long day tired me, and so angered,' said he. 'I tell thee, Aubrey: I have seen near twenty plays given birth; and like a mother that has as many children, I swear, after the first day of a new play, that it shall be the last. For each of these births is like a death to part of mine own life.'

'Thou wilt feel otherwise, for thou hast already with the others; and beside, those that love what thou hast writ will ne'er allow thee rest.'

'One day,' said he. 'One day . . .'

He poured a glass also, but held it looking at the wine, and did not drink it.

'Yet wert thou not pleased,' said I, 'at how much all those that hear it were?'

'Who could not be? Aye, sure, some plays hereafter may be disputed, but this one will be e'er loved; for in it is a farewell to joy, the shadows have not yet fallen upon Arden, though they approach it.'

'Bethink thee, Will,' said I, 'that Rosalind and Orlando are well matched? My meaning: once out of Arden, what will they become?'

He looked at me and smiled. 'Let us not think on't,' said he. 'For he, alas, fat, honest, worthy; and she, e'en sadder, somewhat of a shrew.'

'So fades all first love, then?'

'Why! Consider our grandames! And all grandfathers!'

'Yet cannot passion sometimes wax with age?'

'Aye, yet not into peace, but conflict. For an old man with a young heart loses both vigour and serenity, and is sustained by neither.'

'Then should we learn to live with age.'

'Learn to! Aye! Yet how can a man learn to be that which he shall be never! I tell thee, Aubrey! There is naught sadder in this world, nor more lost and mockable, than a lover past his prime.'

'Or hers.'

'Aye, hers also; yet can a woman preserve passion into age with less absurdity . . . Consider our Queen!'

'Is that not rather lust than passion?'

'Well, they are cousins; sisters, almost.'

Out of my mouth came words I should not have said, yet could not stop. 'Will,' said I, 'thou still lovest this lady.'

'Aye.'

'And she thee?'

He heaved a great sigh. To that question, lad,' said he, 'she would answer, yes.'

'Yet she loves also my Lord?'

He frowned at this, then said slow, 'She loved me a little, then him more, always herself most.'

'And now he loves her not?'

'Loves her?' He paused. 'My Lord, that I love, loves victories; perchance memories; tomorrow most of all.'

'So she returns from him to thee.'

'Would do; but she who returns is not she who went; nor is he to whom she would return, him she left.'

'So what shall she do?'

'What? What shall she, or shall not! I have read deep into hearts, Aubrey, or thought to; yet is all this but divination! For no heart is a book full writ till it cease beating.'

'Yet shall she seek still, methinks, to serve my Lord.'

He gazed at me frowning, and said, 'What is this sage thou art become, that whispers wizard's words as if to fright me?'

I told him then of what had passed with my Lord (that I had promised not to tell); and also the truth about my thumb, which I had said to the players had been mangled in a fight twixt constable and prentices. He heard all this, as if not surprised, then said, as to himself,

'Poor frighted, perilous, loving fool! Aye, she would spurn my Lord for spurning her, yet forward his mad plots with Essex! Or fly to me, that she has spurned, and cry an I receive her not, she shall betray him! Who, indeed, will she not sacrifice to a passion that, in the end, is one but for passion itself? Aye, she would serve him or betray him; me also either; most dangerously, herself.'

He paced the room now, rubbing his bald dome and pulling at his locks; then threw out his hands, shrugged, sighed again, and said, 'Aubrey, I shall be old as the Adam of our play, an I sleep not now; and thou a drowsy Audrey.'

'Farewell, then, Will; and of this I have heard, or read, I have heard nothing.'

'Aye, aye! Thou art a worthy guardian of secrets, as thou hast well proven!'

'Of thine, Will, aye, I am.'

'Be so, then.' He put a hand upon my shoulder, and said, 'Thou hast not, surely, betrayed me in thy work today; for thou wert a profitable Audrey.'

'I shall hope to be her better.'

'Nay, nay, I prithee! For there is, in thine unripe conceit of an actor's art, a danger: that of being not Audrey, but Aubrey being Audrey.'

'Instruct me further.'

'He that would learn to act, must learn also not to o'er-act. Leave Audrey, then, as she is; do not embellish her, prithee, nor seek to out-rival Rosalind in the general favour.'

'In truth, Will, I am no actor, and know it well; and take this occasion to beg thee that, when this play is done, I may tear myself forever from the blandishments of my admirers.'

'Thou art weary already of thy labour? Spurning fame ere it descend upon thee? But I could find thee small parts if thou wouldst continue, as a man, in our strange calling . . .'

'E'en if I wished it, Will, my wife would leave me, an I did.'

'I thought her no Puritan, Aubrey.'

'Nor is she: but wishes to make me innkeeper.'

He stood considering, then said, 'Perchance has she read her husband well: stout, blotch-eyed, drinking more ale than serving, full of old taproom tales and hearkening patiently to older . . . But for all this, there lack two things: an inn, and knowledge of them.'

'An I persist, wax wiser, and find help, I may be this blotch-eyed babbler.'

'Aye.' He thought, then said, 'Aubrey, in Cripplegate I have a house; and conjoined to it, a tavern. Now, though I doubt not thy capacity to rule all England, wouldst thou not deign to be assistant to the innkeeper, and so learn his trade? For to be this with success, the first necessity is to master all tricks and wiles of those that serve him.'

'Aye, gladly; and later, mayhap, my friend Robin, or his father, will furnish me, an I can pay back their loan, without losing a pound of my fair flesh . . .'

'Well, Jenny must be thy Portia. Go to her now, and kiss thy son for me.'

II

Our play ran alternate to *Julius Caesar*, and sometimes *The Merry Wives*, though this was ne'er loved as much by groundling as by lordling; for the first preferred Sir John in misfortune, and among the lewd. Thus we were not always in the theatre; nor Will neither, for he did not always act, and was said to be working at new plays: of which we knew naught, save that one dealt with seafarers, wrecked into a foreign court, and was a kind of comedy; and the other was said to be a tragic tale of Danes.

The city stayed uneasy, though in different from yester-year. Then, when rebellion loomed, the shock was sudden, and the fear; but now, though there was still as much talk of treachery, the nervous state of doubt had waxed habitual. My Lord Essex was still feared, though by many still admired; yet 'twas felt chance had passed him by and, should he revolt before embarking for the Low Countries, or e'en after, it would be too late for his purpose. The whole truth was, that prayers for the Queen, so long feared and revered, were mostly for her death. People craved certainty, e'en were it brought to them by snivelling Jimmy out of Scotland. Of one thing all felt certain: that whoever reigned, or triumphed, there would be Cecils at their table, e'en if they must eat whey among the lackeys.

My wife, like the nation, remained ill-tempered; though this I put more to the vomitings of her pregnancy, than to her ill-content with me; for I had told her of my dreams of inns, that were taking on now some faint reality; and she knew I would stay faithful to my promise of acting parts no more. She said hourly I must speak with Robin about money; for women have no shame to spur men on to ask gold from their friends, which shames them most.

Besides this, of all our old friends that still won Jenny's favour, in her deft portrayal of the reformed whore become prim, there was only Robin; and because of him (and I think too that she liked her), she was fond of Susan, Robin's wife to be. So at a time wherein our play was put aside for a whole week (some of our actors being lent out to other Companies), Jenny said we should hire a cart, and load in it food and drink beside ourselves, and drive out into the fields to eat there, before the summer ended.

The which, leaving William in fond care of Widow Dill, we did; and set out for the hills above the City, to the north: whence, like a map, it lies out all displayed, seeming a toy town, the river winding through it like a thread of wire.

Jenny and Susan entered swift into that communion of women which, unlike those of churches, runs not by invocation and response, but partakes of a dialogue in which each speaks at once, yet hears the other. Unworthy of any part of this, and quite neglected, Robin and I went strolling, while the carter unhitched his mare and prepared the feast.

His first news was of those I had half forgot, the Brothers Bowes. 'Death and misfortune have struck there,' said he.

'How near and to whom?'

'First died old Moses, sudden, of the plague; nursed

tenderly by Allan who, for his cares, caught it, and was carried off as well.'

'Poor Puritan! May his heaven be kinder than he believed it. Who told thee this?'

'Their servant, Daniel, that I encountered. He, and his master Noll, fled the house for fear of this infection: but Noll caught worse, or nearly; for disracted by his brother's death, and by remorse, and general fear of persecution for his faith, he has quite lost his wits, and now is tended by his brother.'

'Which?'

'The third, that was in Ireland, Jack.'

'Rosalind,' said I, 'thou hast soon lost thy Orlando.'

'Aye, marry! I ne'er loved those brothers much, yet Allan was a kindly sort of fool, and all deaths of those we know are partly ours.'

'For my sake, then, live long! And ponder thine intent of being soldier.'

Robin looked over toward Susan (still prattling with Jenny), and said, 'No, it is now decided.'

'Because she wills it, or her father?'

'Because I choose it, Aubrey! Thinkest thou I have pledged my will beside my love?'

'No, sure, and be it thy wish, so be it. Yet what is, then, decided?'

He glanced around cautiously, and said, 'I am to the Low Countries in the Earl's army.'

'Thou? How is this possible?'

'Sue's father, that served a Colonel of his regiments, has begged that he will take me as a Cornet, though I know naught of soldiering.'

'With officers, or file?'

'With both; for like a half-cooked thing, I must serve in the ranks, and dine with those that order them.'

'And this shall be when?'

'Soon: when our play ends; mayhap before.'

'The actors will not be pleased shouldst thou desert them.'

'Nor I to do so; but in truth, Aubrey, I have no choice. Soldiers are made by wars, and here is one; but beside, I must tell thee I love not the stage.'

'Of which thou art our fairest ornament.'

'Aye, and who would be that? An ornament! When I stand on that stage, I am as if cleft in twain: part puffed with pride, the other sunk in shame.'

'Well, is it so shameful?'

'For a man, yes, that acts women. Frown not – I do not speak of jesting, such as thine own as Audrey. But to feel manhood waxing, and lisp like a frail maid . . .'

'Aye . . . they should have women to act women. But ere that come, the heavens will fall about the puritanic heads of England! What saith thy Susan to all this?'

'She is soldier's daughter that would be soldier's wife.'

'And thy father?'

Robin smiled. 'He liked not kissing farewell to the gold he must give the Colonel.'

'His fortunes are fair now, Robin?'

'Are and are not. What my father possesses, none knows save he, not even Sad Jack or Amos. Yet by the calm upon his brow, I know he has salvaged some out of the wreckage in St Helen's.'

'And won more on Bankside?'

Robin looked dark. 'He tells me nothing: yet am I sure this project of incursion into Southwark comes to naught, for it comes too late. His rivals are too firm entrenched, and dangerous; my uncle, smile as he will, is still a villain; and most, my father is too old now for this enterprise.'

'What will then ensue?'

'Aubrey, I fear for him, and have dared beg him to withdraw from London, which he likes not, for he is proud. As for mine uncle, I must give thee warning also, of which thou shouldst speak with Heminges, or with Will. Genoa plans some ill against our play.'

'What can he against what all London grows to love?'

'His vanity is mocked, and he is sour; and in our play, he sees a taunt at all the ill chances of his Southwark enterprise.'

'Well, I shall speak with Will, though he will but smile.'

'Let him put on more guards, not smiles.'

I took his arm. 'Robin,' quoth I, 'thou knowest I, too, shall leave the theatre, and study to become innkeeper. Good Will shall help me, and Jenny too, to learn this trade in a tavern that he hath. Bethink that, in due time, thy father would lend me money in such a venture? And lend me honestly: I mean by contract with notary, and with no privy pledge that I would build a bawdy-house for him: for of this Jenny will have naught, nor I.'

'Aubrey, thou must ask him, though I shall be thine ambassador. For he is a very oracle: answering none save those that pray before his temple, from which issue or rich gifts, a dark curse, or a silence.'

The girls called us from afar, as though to say, how could we chatter thus and so neglect them? 'And what of Cecil?' I said to Robin. 'Shall he return among his quills and instances?'

'My cousin was born weathercock. Today, he is enraptured with the stage. Tomorrow, it may be the law again, or whatever else.'

'And his Anne?'

'Well, I like not his Anne! For I fear she will lure him into these Romish rebel plots of which we know a little, and would know naught. For already, she is beckoning him to Rome.'

'Cecil?'

'Aye: he consorts with priests. And I have heard him say he would to France with her, and turn Gaul as well as Papist.'

'Well, may he find his Arden there. And Peter will to sea in quest of El Dorado.'

'Aye, he has signed articles, to which he begged my father to be witness.'

'Already?'

'He shall sail late in September, for the Americas.'

'Leaving Lucy forlorn.'

'Oh, that is ended; and Lucy will not languish long. Those that condemn my father, Aubrey, and his trade, believe girls are gulled into harlotry, and ruined. Some, certes; but others none could ruin, for they are as devout for stews as nuns for convents.'

After we had eat, and the carter snoring, Robin and Susan walked away holding hands; and Jenny and I, looking after them, sighed sudden like two ancients gazing at the follies of young love; then laughed and she, kissing me, said, 'Well, we are not yet so old!'

'Nay, but it passes quick; not three years since I left Epping, yet an age.'

'And for me, Surrey seems a dream now scarce remembered.'

We looked out on the flocks and fields and gardens, that enclosed the city as a sea; and I said to my wife, 'Dost thou hanker for the country, ever?'

'Aye, yet were I there, I know I would for London. Thou?'

'Well, I know not; both are cruel, certes, yet do the country evils seem mostly those of nature; here of man.'

We slept also, and awoke to the nudgings of the carter, that said he was not hired to drive into the town by dark; so we clambered in, and set off, gently downwards, in the shrinking even.

The carter must take another way returning, and when I asked him why (since it was further), he said, his master had bid him fetch some fruit in, which could be had cheap in the orchards, and was now waxing mellow. I sought to persuade him from this, but he was obstinated as his nag. And so we came down, as I half feared into Mary-le-bourne, where at an orchard the carter stopped, parleyed with the farmer, and asked us all to help him gather in the fruit.

I wandered away from the rest, thinking, well, if fate has brought me here, let me discover why; and stepping through the hedges, came up among the trees towards the house of *Madame* Marie-Claire; where, on a lawn beside the terrace, she was seated, with Anne, in the evening light.

Seeing me, she dismissed the French girl, and, as I walked up, half rose, bade me be seated, and offered me some cyder that she said the farmers made. 'As do we in Normandy,' said she, 'and also a fierce spirit from the apples.'

There was calm in the garden, and the far sound of London, and faint cries from the orchards. 'I think, Madam,' said I, 'you saw our play.'

'In part,' said she. 'For he has e'er let me read them, and listened to what I said. Yet to see a play only read, is to learn new meanings.'

'And what, by seeing, did you learn of this?'

'That the chief character, as always, is himself.'

'But the chief of all is Rosalind.'

'She is his dream, of a world that he would wish. But when he speaks true, 'tis through Jaques that rejects this sylvan world, knowing it is not real.'

'For which he is rebuked by the Duke Senior.'

'Aye, but who is this Duke? A politic, comfortable man, a trimmer, such as himself despises.'

'Madam, I believe you wrong in this, saving your pardon. For if Will indeed were Jaques, that must not mean he believes such as he should rule a realm: but rather one that, like Duke Senior, is politic.'

'Or your Queen!'

'Aye, Madam, our Queen! For this may be said of her: that those who have plotted her downfall, fall, while she, and her people, wax in strength.'

'And in docility! In abasement! For what is become of these proud English that can be ruled by one that is nor Christian, legitimate, Queen, nor even Virgin?'

'And what, Madam, has become, and may, of those that plot against her? Nay, be not vexed with me, for I have learned this by pain. Consider this hand, prithee! Then what of the necks of those on whom suspicion falls more grounded?'

'They may be proud to die, as thou to suffer!'

'Well, let them live on pride that brings them death! Not I, Madam; for I am no martyr, no, to none nor nothing.'

'Save to the vanity of this world.'

''Tis the only I have seen, or am like to cherish.'

She sighed, and looked at me without anger, as at a child lacking discernment. 'Well,' said she, 'my Lord told me thou wert brave.'

'My only courage, Madam, was to flee, and my only wisdom.'

'Aye . . . thou art a wise coward of the common sort.'

'And you, Madam? What, then, are you?'

She was not enraged at this, and speaking low, said, 'One that should be born a man.'

'Well, women teach men: for did not Eve, Adam?'

'She did, and was henceforth cursed for it! Yet this is also true: that when Our Lord suffered for us, all were faithless save for women.'

'Are all men faithless then?'

'Wise like thee . . . politic like that tedious Duke. . .'

'Even my Lord?'

'My Lord will hasten to help victory, or where he sniffs it; but not to serve a cause, come fair wind or foul.'

'You mean hasten to my Lord Essex?'

'He is already with him.'

'In Flanders?'

'Aye, he is now gone.' She laid a hand upon my knee and said, 'I tell thee, Aubrey, thou that believest nothing: there is not one man in England with the spirit of the martyred Queen!'

'But, Madam, they live to have no spirit; and she no more.'

'They to endure in shame, and she in glory!'

'Well,' said I, 'one that will endure with no shame for prudence, is, of a surety, Will.'

'That is true. Yet endure for what he writes, not what he is.'

'Which are the same. For he is not, like my Lord, a nobleman, but noble.'

'And is, like my Lord, faithful only to his star: and to naught else, and least a woman!'

'Could he learn faith to a woman from yours to men?'

Her hand flew from knee to cheek in a great slap. 'Madam,' said I rising (and, in troth, near to trading blows), 'my wife expects me.'

'Thy wife! Thou! Thou nothing! What is all this to thee save words, ill understood?'

'Lavish no more upon me, then!' said I.

At this, from woman's armoury that Jenny had taught me to know well, she brought forth a gush of sobs, and clung to me. 'He has left me!' she cried. 'Dismissed me, that would do all for him, and be all.'

'Who – my Lord?'

'Aye, cast aside who alone can teach him how to rise to his desire! Who only can see his hour that, once lost, all is! Who, though denied wedlock, still would serve him! Who else would stand silent at his nuptials, yet consecrate a broke heart to his service, and to hers, and to his house? And how am I rewarded that asked nothing save his love? And how does your Will, aye, this enduring prudent Will, reward me also, when I turn to him, that loved me, and does yet, for consolation? By a politic silence: one flies to war, the other to his quills! Aye, aye: a hero and a poet, what to them is any woman?'

'Calm yourself, Madam. Seek consolation rather in your faith.'

'My faith! Yes, thou also! Thou, a child, a boy, a less than no one, darest turn my words upon me, darest to assail me with a sanctity thou shalt ne'er understand! Yet, have a care, thou nothing, and those greater that are nothing, tremble also! For I can be spurned on by traitors to betrayal, by those faithless to my faith to faithlessness! Aye, elf!' she cried, gripping my wrists and staring at me, and holding up my ravaged hand. 'It is not only thou that should fear the Council!'

These words she spat out and, wrenching from me, ran within. I wiped my face, rubbed on the throbbing of my hand, and walked out through the orchard. Ere long I found the rest, that rebuked me for gathering no fruit, and I made excuse the pies we eat had been ill baked, and I had vomited.

'Faith,' quoth Jenny, 'we are become a family of pukers; yet have William and I better cause for't than thee.'

'Mayhap some excess of wine,' said Robin.

'Or pears,' quoth Susan. 'For I swear he has eat all, and gathered none.'

And so, cross and forlorn (save for the carter, that had half buried us in fruit), we went on into the City where, crossing the Bridge, I said I would walk a while, for the cart rocked like a boat, and my feet would steady me; and after admonitions to shun taverns, I was let off.

But not to visit any inn: 'twas rather that I must warn Will, in case the lady's talk of betrayal had some ground beyond spoiled pride. But advise him I could not; for when I knocked, his housekeeper said he had gone down to Stratford.

12

As summer waned, and there came that kind of death into the year, e'en when at its fairest, our performance of the play grew raw and spiritless; and the audience that came, more feckless and slow to please. All plays, whate'er their theme, require persistence of the actors to be what they are upon the stage, whate'er, off it, they have, by lassitude, become. Yet I vow in no play is this more difficult than *As You Like It*: for it must bestow a radiance, emit a kind of glow, that is hard of achievement when these are not felt by any actor.

Also we noticed, among the groundlings (and how could we not, so vociferous were they?), a kind of hatred of us, and of themselves; of us for that, mayhap, we had too long tarried; for one another, in an increase of noisy, pushing people that seemed to be come not to see us, but others like them. Thus, sometimes our play was rivalled by another, in the cockpit, of drawn swords; or, when we spoke, got laughter where there should be silence, and silence at our jests. Nor were the lesser sort impelled to good conduct by the better: for those best had already seen us, and they in the gallery now, were but forgeries of their betters. And so we ourselves grew fatigued, and yearned for Rosalind's last Epilogue.

One morning, when I woke late weary, came Widow Dill to tell me an old fellow stood without, that said he knew me. I bade her tell him to return when I was rested, but he would not go; so I must rise, and vexed, go to him: and it was my step-father, Martin.

'Heaven forgive me!' cried I, embracing him. 'Did I know 'twas thee, I had flown out the window in thine arms!'

'No haste, no haste, Aubrey!' cried he. 'For I have wasted time happily, renewing acquaintance with the town.'

'Well, come within, and meet Jenny and thy grandson. And eat with us, unfolding to me all raw Epping gossip.'

Jenny, as all wives, liked not her husband should have any family beside that she provided; nor did she, in general, love the aged. Yet Martin, she knew, had given us gold, and might (thought she) give more; and besides, she knew my fondness for him, and that she must respect it at peril of my beating her (which I did but rarely, for the salvation of her soul). So she dropped a curtsey to old Martin, and brought to him William, and a cup of wine.

And indeed, he looked older: which we notice the more in those long parted from us and, in especial, with all ancients: for these, that seem so many years wrinkled yet ripe, may shrivel suddenly, as now had he.

'And who guards the inn?' said I, 'and all thy flagons?'

'The pot-boy, with a dog and cudgel, and, I doubt not, some forest hind that keeps him forbidden company. But he shall not be usurper long; for I am come up but one night to feast my eyes on the prodigy that spurs the envy of every Alleyn and Burbage in the theatre.'

'Alas, thou shalt sit at a tired banquet of broke crusts and emptied flasks; for we are not so fresh as when we first sat down to feast.'

'No matter! I shall help thee earn thy wage this very afternoon.'

'And what of my friends in Harden? Doth William still grunt, and Simon ever sigh?'

'Aye, but old Colin is no more.'

'Of what did he die?'

'Of death; he was twelve years past his span.'

There was a silence, till Jenny said, 'Master Martin, I must not blush an I feed our greedy William?'

'No sweeter sight, lass, than a cream dug in a pink gum. Fall to, William! For if we drink, why not he?'

I deemed it politic to leave Martin, a while, alone with my wife, so she might freely subject him to her tyranny; and saying I would meet with him after the play, went off to make ready for my transformation of a gloomy self, into a bouncing Audrey.

I found 'twas not only I that felt in no mood for Arden. For e'en Herman that would, I swear, delight playing chief part at a funeral, was wan and reluctant. The men also, that treated us now, inside the theatre, not as mere lads, but actors, were barking at us as we were boys crept in without a payment.

'Watch well today,' said Robin to me, apart. 'Genoa means mischief, in spite my father, and others mean mischief more to both.'

'Why must they use this for their battlefield?'

'A theatre gives pretext for assembly with a masked intent. If all is peace, why! they come but to see a play; if not, not so, and out knives. Beside, packed confusion is most apt to scape the constables.'

I have told how, at our dawning in this play, magic descended on us when Rosalind came on with Celia. Today, they were surly at this scene, so that, rather than rising up, we swift declined into a sort of chaos: made wilder by a chance that had ne'er happed before, which was that Celia's voice, when she must say, 'Indeed, there is Fortune too hard for Nature . . .' sudden became Cecil's, I mean his descended to a man's: which, after a shocked silence, won unkind laughter. 'Twas usual that, when Orlando flings down Charles, they shouted for the victor: but this afternoon, they cried out, 'Up, Charles, and buffet the Italian!' The first song of Amiens won e'er applause. But now, when Jaques spake after it, calling 'fools into a circle,' one cried, 'As we in this cockpit, that have paid for a nought also!' And Jaques had scarce said, 'I'll go sleep, if I can,' when a multitude began to chorus, 'We too, we too, and As for all this, We Like It not!'

Then erupted, swift drowning our voices, small battles, and waxing into great: and yells, surgings, clashes, and turning of backs upon us. The turmoil grew so wild that, abandoning the play, we came all out upon the stage: we now the audience, ours become the actors. Most fought for fighting; but others had an intent, and I could see, as they pushed up nearer, those of Venice and Genoa that seemed both battling with each other, and with three larger groups, well armed. Some constables ran up, beating heads, and were themselves beat down and trodden. Cries of pain arose, and rage; and Robin and Cecil leaped down into the mess, skirted, yet clutching planks. 'Stay!' shouted Heminges, holding we three remainder back, but Herman cried, 'Friends!' and jumped in, where he was stabbed instantly.

'Come, Peter,' cried I, and we tumbled over, heaving Herman back, that bled now like a pierced pig. 'Bear him through the actors' door!' I cried.

And now some shouted, 'Fire!' and there was indeed smoke rising from the turbulence: at sight of which, all flung towards the gate, trampling on others, while some, clambering up on the galleries, reached to the thatch, and sprung off. We dragged Herman to the door, and laid him outside, both panting; when from the uproar came sudden Gropenut: that I was ne'er better pleased to see in all his life or mine.

'Help us bear him away!' cried I. 'For he is sore wounded.'

'Whither? To thy house?'

'Too far: let us carry him to Will's, and there seek succour. Peter, I prithee, seek quick an apothecary.'

But Gropenut, that had peered close to him, said, 'A priest, rather.'

I leant over him, and said, 'How now, Herman?'

'Aubrey,' said he soft, 'I leave the theatre: do thou likewise, for as it serves me now, so serves it all:

> A kind of twilight break . . . this false morn
> Brought forth the day before the day was born.'

Then came coughing, gush of blood, heaving groans, feet pounding on the ground.

We stood still, aghast, with the din roaring afar off. Gropenut (that alone crossed himself) said, 'Alas, 'tis not only he.'

'Who else?'

'All of Genoa: he, Beauty, Charles, and of followers I know not how many. A very massacre: six swords to one, twelve daggers to each wounded.'

'And Cecil?'

'Seized by the constables ere he could reach them: ne'er thought I, I would live to bless them.'

'And Robin, and they of Venice?'

'I know not: lost to view in the press.'

'Come!'

We left Herman lying, and ran searching: and what

frighted me most was in troth not thought of Robin, but old Martin: weak and buffeted in this storm. The crowd was now splitting into groups, running this way and that: for after thunderclaps, that great disperser of wild throngs, the rain, came splashing on us. We looked, called, asked strangers, finding none; till the torrent so drained us, we ran into the inn before the *Globe*, now filled with those drenched, murmuring, panicked, half ashamed.

'Thither!' cried Gropenut.

At a table, there sat Venice, Sad Jack, and Robin, whose breast they had bared, to staunch a flow. Propped still beside them, motionless, was Amos.

'God's wounds!' cried Gropenut. ''Tis a corse.'

'What?'

'Amos! See!'

Venice, as we approached, looked up, and voice calm (yet his whole frame a-tremble) said, 'We need linen, heated water.'

'In the tavern here?'

He looked away, shrugging, at the clamour and confusion by the kitchen. 'Let us carry him to a house nearby,' said I.

'Safe?' said Sad Jack.

'Aye: one of the theatre.'

Venice shook his head, as if numbed.

'Let me go, father,' said Robin. 'I know the house, and I can lie there. Do thou save thyself, and Jack, from further peril.'

'Take refuge in the *Swan*,' said I. 'They will not think to assail another theatre, and we have friends there. Peter, go with them thither; and Gropenut, help me bear Robin into Will's.'

'Come, sir!' said Peter. 'We are safer separately.'

Venice rose up like a ghost and, with a last look at Amos

(whose eyes still stared), we walked toward the door: catching more stares, in spite the fears of each man for himself, for three among us were still clothed as women, though we had hitched up our skirts about our middles. Outside, without further word, we went severally.

'And Cecil?' said Robin, looking about him as we walked.

'Fear not!' said Gropenut. 'He is where he is best, inside the Clink, whence we shall buy him out tomorrow. Think rather of thyself: how is this wound?'

'Not deep: the knife jarred on a rib, and fell upon the ground. And what of Herman?'

'We know not,' said I, for this was no time to speak of deaths. 'Bear up, we shall be soon within.'

'Well, Robin,' said Gropenut, ''tis a sad triumph for Venice o'er Genoa.'

'Triumph! We are both conquered! Hast thou not seen those southern hordes marshalled against us? The whole of Southwark! All Bankside! Now, hear me well! From this day, I am my father's father: he shall quit all this, and I so shall order him, else loses he his son!'

At the kitchen door, Will's housekeeper let us in, and she, God's mercy, a woman of that firm and placid sort who has seen all, and whom naught surprises. We laid Robin on the table, cut away his dress, and as she bathed and bound the wound, she said to us, 'Bed, gruel, and sleep for this young coxcomb, and no sight of damsels for a fortnight.'

'Then, Madam,' quoth Gropenut, 'you do not help him. For he sees one now, and of the fairest.'

'Go thy ways, take up yon flask, and stop thy mouth with wine,' said she.

Gropenut soon left, to find a cart to carry Robin into Rotherhithe; and when he had gone, and Robin settled upon pillows, the housekeeper turned to me and said, 'The theatre, at least, still stands?'

'Aye, Madam: there seemed a fire, but was not; yet many alas, are murdered in the riot.'

''Tis not the first: I remember me well the bloodshed of *Titus Andronicus*.'

'Upon the stage?'

'And in the theatre: for the gore of the actors was contagious, and the mob, of a sudden, would outdo them.'

'Pray heaven, after today's business, the sheriffs seek not to prevent the *Globe*.'

'Would that they do! And that eftsoons!'

'How so, prithee?'

'I have oft told Master Will, but he hearkens never (though agreeing ever), that plays at Court, or in the closed theatres of Blackfriars, are well enough, and seemly; but here in this stew of Southwark, the mob merits naught better than Bear Pits! Ah, how I sigh for Cripplegate!'

'You shall move over soon?'

'Hopefully; and I can tell thee this: I shall nag at Master Will until we do, for this malodorous marsh is no fit place for gentle folk.'

'Truly, Madam! I myself hope to leave it, and my wife.'

'Ah, thou art married, then?'

'Indeed, and beside husband, father.'

'Then art thou fortunate and wise; and I have oft said to Master Will, he should not leave his poor good lady in the wilderness of Warwickshire. A man, young sir, needs a wife: and what least he needs, for 'tis most ill, is a painted French whore like that!'

'Like which, Madam?'

'She loitering in there!'

Mine eyes followed her finger, pointed like a dagger at the wall. 'Is *Madame* Marie-Claire within?'

'Aye! I could not prevent her, for she hath a key; and besides, my master, I know not why, has bidden me treat the vixen civilly.'

'Let me go speak with her.'

'Have a care she not stab, nor poison thee.'

She was seated in the river room, reading, and looked up sharp when I came in. 'How now, Madam?' said I.

'How now? Ill. He is in dire danger.'

'Who?'

'Both: my Lord and Will.'

'What danger?'

'The Council now know all: it has been revealed to them.'

'As for my Lord, I know not: but of Will, what could any reveal that might disturb the Council?'

'He has stood close to my Lord, forget not. And so came I here, to see if there are papers that must be destroyed.'

'I doubt Madam shall find any. For beside I suspect that there were none, had there been any, he should have carried them to Stratford.'

'Ah, but I have found these poems; and well know that read close, they tell too much.'

'They tell much, indeed; yet naught of treachery to the State.'

'He has not shown them to thee?'

'I have seen some, and these must never be destroyed.'

'I say they shall! For these are secrets that the world must never know!'

'Give them to me, Madam.'

'To thee? These? For whom were they writ, prithee?'

'By Will, for Will: come, give!'

She snatched them against her breast, and made fast

towards the door. I tripped her, and she staggered, letting fall the book, that I quick seized.

'Restore them!' she cried.

I said naught, and she drew a poignard from her bosom. I plucked my own from Audrey's tattered gown.

'You had best go,' said I.

She stood still, clutching the knife, and staring. I looked back at her. 'And who, Madam,' said I, 'gave information to the Council?'

She glared, her breast heaving, then lowered the knife, saying, 'All this is beyond thine understanding: it goes too deep.'

'Treachery is ever deep.'

'Never mine to Will: have I not come here to see there are no papers that may harm him?'

'Aye: yet how could he be harmed if none had spoken?'

She put back the knife, and held out both her hands. 'Give to me, friend, what he gave,' she said.

'To him,' said I. 'Who may then give, or not give, to whosoe'er he will.'

She shrugged slight, shook her dark locks, smiled soft, and hastened from the room. From the window, I watched her walking to the river.

In the kitchen, Robin had risen, and Gropenut was helping him to the door. I thanked the housekeeper, and gave the book into her hands, making her swear she would guard it carefully for her master.

We climbed in the cart, and were silent till London Bridge. I got off there and, pressing Robin's hand, said, 'Live long, Cornet.'

'Farewell, God go with thee.'

'Amen, and thee. Adieu, coney-catcher.'

'Mummer, God speed.'

Martin was upstairs in our room, bruised only, and fussed

and pampered by my wife. I embraced him, then turning to Jenny, said 'Wife, pack all, pay Widow Dill, and gather thyself and William for a journey.'

'Husband! What rash folly is this that thou . . .'

'Silence, be still! Tomorrow we leave this hateful city, and go with my father Martin into Epping.'

13

And so I became innkeeper: though if earlier than I thought, of a hostelry less splendid. Jenny, at first sight of the *Forest Hart*, threw up her hands and wept: was this what we were sunk to? she lamented. But 'twas in most part woe at the discomforts of our journey which, with the early autumn rains, the cart's joltings, and all William's mischief, was a worse torture than our ride last year.

''Twill never do,' said she, gazing bleak at the gilding leaves, when we sat outside in the pale September sun.

'Then must it,' said I, 'and shall do.'

'But what can we make of this?' cried she, pointing at Martin's tumbled huts.

'Why, marry, what we will! For we have strength, wit, and if not much money, some. Martin is ready to make over to us and, indeed, begs us to care both for his inn, and him. William will love the forest, and wax, I vow, into a fat carlot; and our daughter shall be born, thank God, a country maid, like thee.'

So Jenny sighed, and Jenny groaned, and Jenny lamented, and became, within a month, bustling tyrant of the inn: kindly ever to Martin (after several sharp warnings, and one drubbing with an ash plant), the terror of the pot-boy, and step-mother herself to a girl, near child, that we discovered in the wood, abandoned; while to the customers, she was the very soul of affability and condescension. As for me, I brought over Simon and William, and others from Harden, where the approaching winter gave less work, to make new buildings, from wood we felled privily from the Queen's forest; and soon the *Forest Hart* looked something of an inn.

But as winter dragged on, there came fewer, so that all our hopes were for the spring. Though one day we saw an old coach rattling up through snow and bog, and out of it, shivering and blue-nosed, stepped Venice and Sad Jack.

We hustled them in to thaw, without at an elm fire, within by hot spiced wine, and Venice tumbled early into bed. The rest soon followed after, Jenny bidding me, as was e'er her wont, not to bide up too long.

'Well,' quoth Sad Jack, speaking low, 'in Venice, thou seest a man but a shadow of the self we knew. For save life, he has lost most all.'

'His fortune?'

'Worse: Robin.'

'How?'

'In Flanders: he died a young soldier that had ne'er seen battle. Their landing was disputed, and shot rent the ship ere they set foot on conquered soil.'

'This is beyond doubt?'

'His Colonel writ to Captain Wyatt, who carried these tidings, weeping, to his father; that wept not, he, by an excess of woe.'

'Ah me. Sweet Robin!'

'Aye, and sad Venice, more truly than I, Sad Jack! Aubrey, he is come here to die. Fear not – he shall be no charge upon thee, for not all he had is lost. But as he moped out the days, scarce breathing there in London, I spoke to him of Epping, and he said we might come hither.'

'We shall all seek to serve him. Cecil knows of this?'

'Of Robin? Well, I know not: for Cecil is gone over into France.'

'With what intent?'

'None knows. After his father's death, he vanished quite.'

'With Anne?'

'Aubrey, I say I know not. His only message was he must to France.'

I poured more wine, and said, 'Aye, thou art well named Sad Jack, to bear these tidings.'

'Blame me not, Aubrey, for I know none loves a messenger of the fates. Yet I must tell thee the cup is not yet filled.'

'Well, speak: who now?'

'You have mind of the autumn storms? Into them sailed Peter's barque forever.'

'Lost?'

'It was seen sinking.'

'So Peter also!'

'Aye.'

I rose and said, 'Jack, sleep well, but I can no more, and must now leave thee.'

'Aye, Aubrey. Believe that I share thy sorrow, and if mine seem the less, 'tis that I live with it the longer.'

That was a wracked night, whereto e'en my wife brought me no comfort. I was up at first light, for sleep had abandoned me with any joy, and walked out into the wood to where my mother lay; but this brought me no ease either.

Martin, who rose ever betimes, was out in the yard when I came there to chop timber. He greeted me, and handed me a package.

'Thy friend,' said he, 'Master Jack, durst not give thee this last night, and woke me to beg I do so.'

'Why, is this more ill news?'

'Aubrey, I know not. Take it and see; or mayhap put it by a while.'

He went in, and I looked at the package, sighed, and tore it open, finding a letter and a book. First, the letter of Master Heminges:

Aubrey,

Greetings to thee, from those that were thine, and still lament thee. Yet is thy name enshrined in the tablets of our Company (as in our fond memories), for that thou wert, beside first Audrey, till next year at least, the last. For after the strange happenings of which thou wert also witness, we have removed this play awhile from a public so unworthy of it; and beside, as thou knowest, we must find the play new ladies.

We work now at *Henry V* (will there be no end to these Henrys?), a piece of broad bombast (saving Will's fair repute) that I like not, though it hath comic soldiers (ever the joy of groundlings), fine rumbustious rantings for him that plays monarch, and some scenes in a sort of French, with a princess of those people (that Will likes more than I do). For the year coming, we are promised two rare gems; one diamond bright, one ruby red: to wit, *Twelfth Night*, a comedy with tempests (both of nature and of human passion), with a part in it to delight Master Armin, of a steward like a *hidalgo*; and *Hamlet, Prince of Denmark*, of which I know little yet, save that the mistress of the Prince, one Ophelia, dies by drowning in a river.

Soft now, for this I breathe only in thine ear. Thou must surely know, as did we all, that Will wasted his heart (and too much of his talent) on a French lady, that was once with him oft, though latterly, less so. Yet on the evening of this riot, and when Will was away in Stratford, she came, seemingly, to his house in Bankside; when leaving it, and for none knows what reason, she stepped into the Thames without summoning a waterman; and if crediting miracles, was deceived, for she, like Ophelia, drowned.

Will was much cast down by this, and none must speak of it. And we of the Company are cast down also; for we doubt not we must ever forswear comedy (that is, after *Twelfth Night*), and henceforth give all our lives to tragick themes.

All wish thee good fortune – e'en thy familiar Master Condell. As for Will, he bade me, hearing I was writing to thee in answer to thy kind Christmastide remembrances, to send thee this volume which, on his order, I have had copied out for thee by our printer's prentice.

The book was the play of *As You Like It*, with Audrey's scant lines put into gold, the remainder part in customary black. On the first leaf was writ, in a hand as ill as the prentice's was clear,

For thee I watch, whilst thou dost wake elsewhere,
From me far off, with others all too near.